SINCE YOU
WENT AWAY

CHILDREN OF THE PROMISE

Volume 1: *RUMORS OF WAR*
Volume 2: *SINCE YOU WENT AWAY*

· CHILDREN OF THE PROMISE ·

VOL. 2

SINCE YOU
WENT AWAY

· DEAN HUGHES ·

DESERET BOOK COMPANY · SALT LAKE CITY, UTAH

FOR GENE JACOBSEN

Library of Congress Cataloging-in-Publication Data

Hughes, Dean, 1943–
   Since you went away / by Dean Hughes.
     p.   cm. — (Children of the promise ; vol. 2)
   ISBN 1-57345-285-8
   1. World War, 1939–1945—Fiction. 2. Mormons—History—Fiction.
I. Title. II. Series: Hughes, Dean, 1943–   Children of the promise
; vol. 2.
PS3558.U36S5   1997
813'.54—dc21   97-36179
                                           CIP

Printed in the United States of America   18961

10 9 8 7 6 5 4 3 2

I

Wally Thomas didn't know how many days and nights he had been marching up the coast of the Bataan Peninsula. He was almost too numb to think, too full of pain. He tried to keep a steady pace, but the Japanese guards pressured the prisoners to keep moving, forced them close together, and in their exhaustion the men stumbled and knocked each other off stride. When that happened, the extra effort was almost overwhelming; there were times when Wally thought he would go down—and not get up—the way so many other prisoners had already done.

Each day the men started their march in the dark and continued until the sweltering heat sapped their strength. Then, early in the afternoon, they were herded off the road, crowded into tight groups and made to sit almost on top of each other. They tried to sleep in this congested condition, but Wally never felt rested. Along the way, he had sneaked a few drinks of water from the flowing wells near the road, and now and then he had been able to snatch a stalk of sugar cane to chew on. This had been his only nourishment, and he thought it had been six days now since he had eaten—but it might have been longer. He simply couldn't keep track of time anymore.

When the march had started on this particular morning, Wally's friend Barney had not been able to get to his feet.

Wally had lifted him, but Barney had sunk to his knees again. "I can't do it," he said. "Just leave me here."

"The guards will kill you," Wally told him.

"I don't care."

Wally knew what Barney meant. The fatigue hardly felt worth fighting. Besides, the guards seemed intent on pushing the men until all of them died. More were dropping all the time. Ahead of the Americans were the Filipino troops, and Wally had seen their bodies by the road, bloating in the sun. One day he had been at the front of the Americans and had watched what was happening to the Filipinos. When a man would lag behind or collapse, the guards would run him through with a bayonet or shoot him in the head. Wally tried to stay in the middle of his own group now—so he wouldn't have to see what was happening ahead and so he wouldn't be in danger of falling behind. He was marching with a large group of men—maybe a couple of hundred—and he liked the idea of having plenty of them around him.

"Hang on for another day, Barney," Wally pled. "They'll have to feed us, sooner or later."

"No. They're starving us to death on purpose." Barney had already shed a lot of weight. He had tightened his belt until his trousers were gathered into pleats around his middle, and his face was so drawn, his beard so long, that it was hard for Wally to think of him as the same man he had known since their days together at Clark Field. He was still holding Barney by the arm, but the big man was folding, and Wally didn't have the strength to hold him much longer.

"Help me," Wally said to the men around him. "We have to keep him on his feet."

The men had become increasingly silent as the march had continued. At first the guards had enforced the silence, but gradually words had become an unwanted exertion. Jack

Norland and Warren Hicks, who always stayed close to Wally, stepped up to Barney, and the three pulled him upright. "You can do it," Jack said. "Just hold out today and see what happens."

Barney didn't answer, but he stayed on his feet. When the guards shouted and began to push, the prisoners shuffled ahead until they were able to spread out a little and take longer strides. Barney trudged along with them, but he was breathing heavily already. That was not a good sign.

Wally heard someone say, "Miller didn't get up."

Miller was one of the men who had become sick. Dysentery had begun to take its toll. Puddles of water lay along the way, and some of the men, too thirsty to resist, had been scooping it up in their hands and drinking it. Others warned them to wait for a chance to get water at wells or streams, but the temptation had been too much, and those who had drunk the stagnant water were beginning to pay for it.

Part of the problem was that all the men had been weak when the march had begun. They had lived on short rations for several weeks. The Japanese had attacked the Philippines on the same day they had bombed Pearl Harbor. Under the direction of General MacArthur, the American and Filipino troops had withdrawn into the Bataan Peninsula and tried to hold out until help could arrive. Without proper food and weapons, however—and with the numbers against them—it had been only a matter of time until they had been overrun by the Japanese. In April of 1942, over seventy-five thousand men in the Peninsula had been taken captive, about twelve thousand of them Americans, and now the Japanese were marching all the prisoners to a destination known only to the guards. There was no telling how much longer the torture would continue.

No one said another word about Corporal Miller. Deaths were happening so often now that it was impossible to muster much emotion. Besides, each man had enough to do to concentrate on his own survival.

"I need water," Barney said, his voice a hoarse gasp.

"I know. We all do. But wait until light. And wait until we find a well."

The guards seemed to think only of moving the men ahead, and so they never allowed anyone to step off the road. If a man were caught going after water or sugar cane, he was beaten to death or stabbed with a bayonet. And yet, strangely, if those same guards saw men chewing sugar cane as they marched, they seemed not to care; so the danger was in being caught off the road. The vast numbers of prisoners could not all be watched, but Japanese soldiers were scattered all along the route, and no one knew where they might be.

The first light was beginning to break when the men finally came to a flowing well. The water spilled into a little pond and then dribbled across the road. Wally heard someone say, "Water ahead," and he looked to see that a couple of men had stepped off the road and were filling their cups or canteens.

"I'll try to get us some," Wally said to Barney. Wally still had his mess kit cup, which he carried in a little mosquito net. He got the cup out and edged his way to the left side of the road. He looked up and down the line, but he could see no guards. Many of the men were stepping to the water and then moving quickly back into the lines. In the half light, Wally could see that some were taking big chances—staying at the water, taking a drink and then refilling—or trying to fill a whole canteen. One man had dropped onto his knees and was scooping handfuls of water into his mouth.

Wally waited. The men were moving slowly now, crowding toward the water and waiting for a chance. This was dangerous. A guard could spot the slowdown and hurry to the area. Wally felt his own panic. He wanted to get water for Barney, but he was also desperate for a drink himself.

As the men crushed forward, Wally finally got his turn. He stepped more quickly than he thought himself capable, and he plunged his cup into the water. He drank the whole cupful in two long gulps and then filled the cup again. Just then he heard someone whisper, "Guard!"

Wally jumped back to the road, and as he did, most of the water spilled. He handed the cup to Barney, who grabbed it, threw his head back, and tried to get all that was left. "That's not enough," he gasped. He bolted toward the water.

Wally grabbed Barney, pulled the cup from his hands, and tried to muscle him back into the middle of the crowd. But Barney twisted his shoulders and slipped past Wally, who had no strength to hold the big man. Barney strode to the water, dropped to his knees, and plunged his hands into the water. Wally slipped to the edge of the line of men but stayed on the road, and then he looked both ways. He was about to go after Barney when he saw guards hurrying up the side of the road.

Barney had gotten a drink and was after another. "Barney!" Wally whispered.

But it was too late. The guard raced forward and slammed the butt of his rifle into the back of Barney's head. Barney grunted and fell on his chest, his face in the little pond. Then the guard spun the rifle and plunged the bayonet into Barney's back. Wally heard a cracking sound as a rib must have broken, and he heard a quick, sharp cry of pain as Barney's head jerked upward, out of the water. But someone was pulling Wally back into the line of men and then shoving him toward the middle of the group.

And that was that. Barney was gone now, and Wally was still alive. The Japanese soldier was shouting violently, warning the men in words they didn't understand but in tones that were not difficult to decipher.

Wally tried to think about Barney—about the days they had spent together in Manila when Wally had first arrived in the Philippines in 1940. Wally had been away from his Mormon parents for the first time and had tried his wings a little; he hadn't considered it a great sin to indulge himself in a few beers with his new friends from his Army Air Corps squadron. Wally tried to draw on those memories now. He wanted to feel some grief, but the buzzing continued in his head, the ache in his stomach, the overwhelming exhaustion. "Bless him, Father," Wally prayed, and in his own mind, it was a kind of funeral. He knew of nothing else he could do.

Wally waited for a time, and then as the full light of day came on, he spotted Warren and Jack ahead of him. He worked his way past a few men to get to them.

"Did you guys get some water?" Wally asked them.

"No."

"How are you doing?"

"Okay," Warren said. "We'll get some next time."

But Jack said, "I've got to get something soon."

He meant more than water; he needed food. Wally knew that Jack was more on the edge than Warren or Wally and that they had to do something to keep him going.

The dust was deep on the road, and the shuffling men kicked it up until it filled the air like smoke, which only added to the choking heat and the grimy discomfort. The wooded area to the left—the thick jungle and the rising hills—were lush with spreading banyan trees, palms, and the dense growth of ferns in the shadows, but the closer the jungle was to the road, the thicker was the humidity. The screech of monkeys in the trees, the cries of birds, were mere background sounds that Wally rarely noticed. Out to the right, the east, lay the waters of Manila Bay, sometimes visible to the men. The water looked tantalizing, inviting, but it was not worth thinking about—just a blue-green patch in the unreachable distance.

Several times along the way the prisoners marched past severed heads hoisted on poles or hanging from trees. At one point a disemboweled Filipino soldier had been draped, backward, over a barbed-wire fence. These depredations were clearly intended as warnings to those who left the road, but they hardly made a difference anymore. A severed head was no more gruesome than a swelling body, baking in the sun.

Wally almost never looked at anyone. The hollowness of the men's eyes, the wasted, dirty faces, were all an ugly reflection of himself. It was better to stay within himself and not see the death in others' eyes.

"Father in Heaven, help me," Wally kept saying. "Please help all of us. Let there be some food today."

He had been praying since that first night of the march, when he had realized that the Japanese had no apparent plans to feed the prisoners. When he was younger, he would have concluded that the Lord was not listening, that his prayers had not been answered. But that was not what he felt now. He was still alive. He was putting one foot in front of the other. He would make it through this day. His strength was coming from somewhere—whether he was worthy to get help or not. All Wally's life he had been too quick to give up. His father had called him a quitter once, and that statement had hurt him as few things had in his life—partly because he suspected it was true. But he was not quitting now, and so he felt grateful he had made it this far.

He also tried to concentrate on another source of strength: his family. Wally's father was a stake president in Sugar House, on the south end of the Salt Lake Valley, in Utah. Wally knew his family would certainly be praying for him, and he knew they would all suffer if he were to die. He thought how he would feel if something happened to one of his brothers or sisters, and he told himself he couldn't let them down.

Wally tried to let his mind focus on his parents, and then his siblings, one after another. He tried to hold them each next to him for a moment. He had sometimes resented Alex, his older brother, but he felt none of that now. And he longed to see Bobbi, his older sister, who was in nursing school in Salt Lake. He had always been able to talk to her more openly than anyone else in the family. Gene and LaRue and Beverly were younger than he was. He wondered what they were like now, how much they might have changed since he had left home almost two years earlier. He promised himself that somehow he would see them again.

What he was experiencing seemed unreal; his home was his reality: his parents, his brothers and sisters—and now, even the Church. He thought of Sunday evening Sacrament meetings in the summer, everyone fanning themselves in the heat, and a speaker going on and on. It was almost funny now to take joy in the idea of being there again, to experience all that. He had hated long meetings more than anything, and now they would be such a pleasure to him.

Wally told himself he could, and he would, possess all that again; he would not give up. He would keep walking, and he would trust that food would come, sooner or later, and he would survive on whatever he got for however long he had to. But he would make it, and then he would be part of everything he had once been so willing to throw aside.

Wally also thought of Lorraine Gardner. She had been his girlfriend, but she had broken up with him out of disappointment over his directionless life. He didn't expect a chance to marry her, but he still pictured her—her prettiness, her loveliness—and she symbolized the other thing he wanted: a family of his own someday.

And so, all morning, Wally forced his mind away from the pain and the weariness, and he kept finding the energy to focus on the reasons he wanted to live. And he prayed. He no longer asked the Lord to relieve his pain, to take away all this agony; he asked only for strength to hold up under whatever else might lie ahead. And he asked continually.

"I'm in trouble," Jack said.

"Don't say that," Wally told him.

Warren, on the other side of Jack, said, "We'll get some sugar cane as soon as we can."

The men had been walking past plenty of cane, but the guards had stayed close since the incident at the well that morning. Normally, these guards disappeared at times. Wally believed they left the road to eat, not wanting the prisoners to see them. He was certain another chance would come if he and his friends were patient. He just hoped Jack could hold out.

Then something unexpected happened. The prisoners were approaching a *baibai*—a thatched house, on stilts. An elderly Filipino farmer came out from a shed behind the house, looked both ways, and then hurried to the men. He was carrying a basket. The men nearby suddenly rushed toward him, and the farmer began to hand something out—vegetables, Wally thought. Wally instinctively hurried ahead, but the surge of men was all around him, and he felt a sudden panic that the farmer's basket couldn't possibly hold enough for all of them. Something in him said that he had to beat the others to that basket—and something else said that if the men started fighting each other for the food, all was lost for them.

And so he didn't push forward, and then he heard the screams of a guard. The prisoners fell quickly back into their four-abreast lines, and the farmer hurried away, but the guard ran up the road, stopped, aimed his rifle, and fired. The poor old man had scurried past his house, but a bullet struck him in the back. He dropped on his face and didn't move.

The guard turned and began to shout at the prisoners, pointing his rifle. But the men had eaten what they had—or had hidden it—and he didn't shoot at anyone.

"What's wrong with these stinking Japs?" Jack said. But the effort to say that much had cost him. He began to cry.

"Don't think about it, Jack," Wally said. "We're going to get through the day. Let's just think about that."

But the day kept dragging on, and the guards stayed close. The men passed a couple of streams, but there was no chance to get to them. That was hard enough for Wally to take, and he had had one drink that day, but Jack was suffering, turning inward, breathing hard. Wally knew the signs. Almost always the men who went down started by voicing their discouragement, letting their emotions take over.

Wally's feet hurt, his body ached. Early in the march he had thrown away his heavy steel helmet, which had served only to bake his brains, it seemed, but now he wished for some protection against the searing sun.

"We're going to get home, Jack," Wally said. "We're not going to let these Japs beat us."

Wally knew it wasn't Christian to feel such hatred, but the anger helped him. At times he told himself he shouldn't pray just for himself and his buddies but also for these misguided guards. But he couldn't get himself to do it.

Jack didn't respond. In fact, a moment later he stumbled, and if Wally and Warren hadn't grabbed him, he might have gone down. After that, they kept hold of his arms and the three plodded on together.

When the sun was high in the sky, past midday, finally the guards ordered the prisoners into a plowed field, crowded them close together in a standing position, and then signaled for them to sit down. It was so cruel to pack the men in so close. Wally supposed it was to keep a tight perimeter for the guards to cover, but it was just one more act of ruthlessness that was hard to accept. A few times Wally had thought of his friend Mat Nakashima, back in Sugar House, and he had tried to remember the things Mat had said about the Japanese. But all that had nothing to do with these men—whatever nationality they were. They were simply vicious, for whatever reason, and Wally could think of no reason to forgive them.

The prisoners dropped to the ground, relieved to be off their feet, but they were on a plot of dirt with no protection from the sun. Wally glanced about and saw the despair in the men's eyes. He knew that many of them would not get up in the morning. He saw that the guards were allowing some to walk to the edge of the field, drop their trousers, and squat. He knew these men had dysentery, and they had no chance of living much longer.

And then he watched as across the field several guards

walked into the crowd and hoisted four men to their feet. The men were marched to the top of the field, not far from the circle of prisoners. There, the guards handed them shovels and demanded that they dig. Wally assumed that the Japanese had decided to prepare a place to bury the prisoners who would die that night, but he wasn't sure why they were bothering to do that—so many had already been left along the road.

All afternoon the men continued to dig. Wally watched them from time to time. They were struggling just to stand, and when they tossed the dirt, it threw them off balance. Wally knew this was a death sentence. The extra work would be the end of these four—chosen for no reason that Wally could guess. But in time the prisoners were hip deep in the hole, and that seemed to satisfy the guards. They shouted commands, in Japanese, and took the shovels away. Then one of the guards shouted loudly toward the rest of the prisoners. Many were curled up, lying on their sides, asleep, and at first they didn't respond. But one guard kept shouting until everyone was roused and looking. No one had any idea what he was saying. A few of the guards spoke a little English, but the man who was shouting trusted only in the harsh sound of his voice to communicate his anger.

Once all the prisoners were looking his way, he turned back toward the men in the hole, and he said something to them—something they would never understand. And then the guard gave a command, and the other Japanese all raised their rifles. Wally realized only a second ahead of time what was going to happen. He shut his eyes and heard the report of the rifles, and then he opened his eyes to see the four men gone, fallen into the hole, one of them hanging over the edge. A guard pushed that man with his foot, and then he turned and waved for some nearby prisoners to come forward and backfill the grave.

Wally had not known any of the men who had been shot. They were all army soldiers, not air corps. But he remembered that look on their faces, the wide-eyed realization just before the gunfire. And now they were just four more who were gone.

"Why?" Jack asked.

"Maybe they took some of that food from the farmer," Warren said, but it was such a terrible reason—if it was a reason at all.

Wally saw in Jack's eyes that he was losing control, his anger spilling over.

"It's okay," Wally said. "We won't let them lick us. Some of us have to make it."

Jack took three or four long breaths and stared straight ahead. Wally knew he was trying to make a decision.

"Think of your family," Wally said.

For a moment Jack focused directly on Wally, his eyes full of questions, but he said nothing, and he sat still for quite some time before he said, "I'm starving to death."

"I know. We'll get something tomorrow."

Again Jack looked at him, and he could have said, "That's what you said this morning," but he didn't.

An hour passed. Wally and Warren tried to create a little room for Jack, and they told him to lie down and sleep. He rolled onto his side, his legs stretched out between his friends, and he was soon breathing steadily. Wally just hoped he would wake up when the Japanese pushed them ahead again.

Wally was in something of a stupor, half asleep himself, when he sensed that something was going on. He watched as he saw, and then heard, some rumor spreading through the men. He heard the word "turnip."

"Someone dug up a turnip," a man was saying.

And by now, all across the field, everyone was in motion, digging at the ground, using cups or mess kits or anything they had. Some distance away, Wally heard another man say, "I got one." Wally and Warren began to dig with their hands. Jack roused as he felt the motion around him. "Turnips," Wally said to him, and Jack sat up.

Wally looked toward the guards. They had seen what was happening, but they didn't seem to care, and so Wally grabbed for his mess kit cup, ducked his head, and dug hard again. He drove it into the dirt that had been plowed but had hardened under the scorching sun. He felt a terrible sort of anxiety, the fear that there were only so many turnips and he might not get one of them. He almost hated the men near him who whispered that they had found one.

It was Warren who finally dug one up—and a good-sized one. He clawed at it and then used Wally's cup to dig around it and pry it out of the ground. Wally watched and waited, and so did Jack as Warren scraped the dirt off. "Take a bite and pass it around," Warren said to Jack, and the three of them understood. The turnip was theirs to share.

Jack took a bite. He let his eyes go shut as he savored the taste in his mouth, sucked at the juice. He handed it to Wally, nodding, saying nothing. Wally took a bite and was almost shocked by the intensity of the flavor. The turnip was fairly dry, not full of the juices he wanted, but he chewed very slowly, getting all the taste and moisture he could from it. He handed it on to Warren.

No one had taken a big bite—out of respect for the others—but Wally also knew he wanted more than one helping, more than one moment of pleasure. He had the notion that strength was already pumping into him from the little bit of nourishment.

The turnip went around three times and could have gone again, but the guys next to Warren had found nothing. He looked at Jack and Wally, said nothing, but both nodded, and so Warren turned and offered the remains of the turnip to the two men behind him.

Wally felt something in his throat that was like crying. He was glad to have had the pleasure of this bit of food, glad to see Jack looking a little better, but he was even more touched by the men who had found nothing and had almost despaired until Warren had offered them what was left. And all around the field, Wally could see the same thing happening. Almost everyone was getting at least one bite. And when new turnips showed up, they were sometimes being passed through the hands of starving men to the hands of others who had, as yet, had no chance to share in the joy.

"You'll make it now," Wally told Jack. "Maybe we're only going as far as San Fernando. That can't be too much farther."

"That's what you said about Balanga."

"I know. But we have to stop somewhere."

"We'll get some sugar cane tomorrow," Warren said. "And some water. We just had bad luck today."

Jack nodded, and he did seem a little encouraged.

As the sun sank low over the hills, Wally tried to curl up and sleep. As usual, his sleep was fitful and unsatisfying, but it was still the best time of day, when the ache disappeared for a time. Deep in the night, however, he awoke suddenly with a stabbing cramp in his stomach. He realized that he needed to get to the side of the field quickly or he would fill his pants. He also knew, instantly, that this could be the beginning of the end for him. If he had dysentery, he would have little hope of surviving.

He pulled himself to his feet, and in the dark he tried to work his way over the bodies. Men moaned and complained as he stumbled over them, and from behind him, Warren whispered, "Wally, what's wrong?"

"Sick," was all he said, and then he continued to struggle over the men until he reached the edge of the packed-in bodies. A guard grunted a challenge, and Wally said, "Benjo," the Japanese word for latrine.

He relieved himself and then walked back to the men. He wanted desperately to find his way to his friends, but he knew he shouldn't do that now. He still felt sick, and he knew he might have to go again. He couldn't bother all these men to cross over them time and again.

And so he lay down on the edge of the group. At least there he could stretch out a little. But the uproar in his insides was not abating. Dysentery could dehydrate him quickly and sap away his remaining strength. It didn't take long until men who got the disease were passing blood. Without water to drink, and something to eat, he would be gone in a day or two.

All Wally's confidence was suddenly gone. He prayed, but he wondered whether he would have the strength to keep pushing. He remembered the day on the East High School track when he had wanted to push to the end of the race. His body had given up to the pain in spite of his resolve. He told himself he couldn't let that happen again. This time his life was on the line. But he wondered whether he would have any choice, whether the strength was in him.

2

Wally was still sick when the guards shouted for the prisoners to rise and start their day's march. But he'd only had to relieve himself that one time. Maybe he didn't have dysentery. Maybe his stomach had merely reacted to the turnip—something so strong coming into his system after getting no food for so long. But when Wally stood, he felt dizzy. All sorts of diseases were rampant among the men. Most everyone had contracted malaria during those last months of battle when medicine had been in short supply. At least Wally had some quinine tablets that a doctor had given him. He kept them hidden in a little tin in the top of his boot. He thought of taking a tablet now, but he decided to wait until he had a better idea what was wrong with him.

He waited for the men to move out, and then he worked his way into the crowd and said, "Warren. Jack."

This brought an immediate shout from a guard, who didn't want any talking. But in a moment he heard, "Over here," and Wally worked his way toward the voice.

When he got to his friends, Warren asked, "How are you doing?"

"I'm still sick," Wally said. "But not real bad. Maybe it's not dysentery."

"I'm sure it isn't," Jack said. "Guys with dysentery know it. It comes on fast."

Wally could tell that Jack was trying to be the strong one today. That was good.

Some things went better that day. Virtually all of the men were able to get a good drink of water in the morning, and then again later in the day. And Warren made a dash to a field of sugar cane, where he brought back stocks for Jack and Wally and himself to chew on. The sugar sent a shock of power through Wally's body, which was wonderful, but soon after, he felt the dizziness again. He also knew not to chew on the cane too long, since the fibers had a way of wearing his mouth raw.

Up until noon or so, Wally held up pretty well. He felt the weakness, the pain in his stomach, but he kept trudging along—and at least he didn't feel any urgency in his bowels. But the final hour or two of the march were agonizing for him. Every step was a tremendous effort. His friends gave him support, but they were worn out too, and the three stumbled over each other at times, almost bringing each other down.

Wally knew this was his test, and the worst part of it was to have no finish line—not to know how much longer he had to hold out. He kept telling himself he could keep going a little longer and then he would be allowed to rest, even if it was out in the hot sun. But gradually, the sickness was coming on stronger, his stomach cramping and his head pounding.

He was moving along in a haze of dust and lethargy, leaning on his friends more than he wanted to but still pushing his feet forward, when suddenly he realized that he was falling forward. Jack and Warren were clinging to him, but he was slipping from their grasps, and then he was in the dirt, on his chest.

A strange peace came over him. "At least it's over," he thought, and he let the dark begin to take him.

But someone was pulling at his shoulder and shouting in his ear. "Remember what you told me? Think about your family."

Wally fought to understand the words. He wanted the pain to end, but he knew the words had meant something yesterday, when he had spoken them himself, and he struggled to grab onto them. His friends were pulling him up, and he worked to get his feet under himself. Then he pushed with all his strength. He couldn't see, couldn't even tell whether his legs were working right, but he began to make the motion again—stepping, stepping.

The next thing he knew he was in a field somewhere, and he knew he had been asleep for hours. Dark was coming on. He looked up at his friends, who were sitting near him, staring down at him. "You guys got me here," he said.

"No. You did it yourself," Warren said. "You kept walking, but you were out on your feet. You didn't answer us when we spoke to you."

Wally knew the truth immediately. "I didn't do it myself," he said, and he felt almost overpowered with thankfulness.

"How are you feeling now?" Jack asked.

Wally tried to think. "I don't know. I don't feel sick. I'm just tired."

"Sleep some more."

And so Wally did sleep. And when the guards woke the men in the middle of the night, he felt more strength this time. He didn't have dysentery; he was sure of it now. He certainly wasn't well, but he thought he could make it through another day.

"Maybe this will be the last day," Jack said. "We've got to be close to San Fernando by now."

"How many days have we been walking?" Warren asked.

"I don't know. I've lost track."

"I think it's been five days, or maybe six," Wally said. "But we didn't eat for three days before that."

"We can do another day," Warren said.

Wally wanted to give some strength back. He knew what

his buddies had done for him the day before. He tried to smile. "Nothing like a nice walk," he said.

And so they walked all day again, and all along the road Wally saw dead men. Most of them were Filipinos from the group ahead, but men in his own group were also going down. Late in the morning, Len Granfield, a staff sergeant from Wally's squadron, seemed to die in his tracks. He had been wheezing hard all morning, but he had been keeping up with the others, and then, without warning, he simply slumped to the ground. Another friend of Wally's, Don Cluff, tried to pull Granfield to his feet, but Len was clearly gone, and so Cluff dragged him to the side of the road. A guard ran up and forced the lieutenant back into the lines. Then he gave Len a kick, got no response, and walked away.

Wally said another prayer, asked God to take Len home, asked for comfort for his family. But he didn't glance back. He kept tramping ahead.

Again that day Wally and his friends managed to get a little water and a bit of sugar cane, but Wally hardly had the energy to slap at the mosquitoes that landed on him, and he wondered how long it would be until he came down with more diseases. If the march didn't stop soon, and the men didn't get some food, they would all die.

As the sun reached its zenith and continued on by, the men were forced to walk longer than usual. And now they faced a new challenge. This part of the road had been paved at one time, but the asphalt had been torn up by all the heavy military traffic, and clumps were lying about. Wally had a better pair of boots than most of the men, but even so, stepping on the lumps of asphalt burned his feet. And not stepping on them required too much effort. Wally watched and avoided the stuff when he could, but his feet seemed on fire, and some of the men were suffering much worse, actually crying out when they took a wrong step.

Jack finally said, "It's long past the time we usually stop. What's going on?"

But someone behind them said, "Look up there."

Wally looked and saw that they were coming to a town. And then he saw the church tower he had seen on Christmas Eve, where the bells had been ringing at midnight. It was San Fernando. Maybe this was their destination. Maybe the guards were giving one last push to reach the end of the ordeal. Wally felt some strength come back. "I'll bet we're stopping here," he said to Jack, and he reached over and patted him on the back. "We can make it that far."

The men continued into the town and then were guided to a dilapidated old building, where they were herded inside. The building seemed to be a little dance hall that had long since fallen into disrepair. For the moment, it seemed good to be out of the sun, but the place was little more than a shack, and it would be very crowded. Wally walked all the way to the end of the room. He sat down and leaned his back against the wall. That comfort—the rest for his back—was almost too pleasant to believe, and within minutes he was sound asleep.

Late in the day he awoke, remembered where he was, and then tried to sleep again. But the shack was like a steam room by now, and sweat was running off him. He wondered how many more would die if they were kept in this place very long. For quite some time he was restless in the heat, but late that evening the temperature improved, and finally he slept once again.

Early in the morning Wally felt a nudge, and he opened his eyes. "Food," Jack said. "They have rice for us. We have to get in line."

Wally was afraid to believe it, and yet he could smell the rice. He had to get up, and his body ached with the effort, but the thought of eating was so exciting that he could feel his hands begin to shake. He took his mess kit and cup, and he lined up with the other men. When he eventually got to the front of the line, just inside the door of the building, he saw the rice for the first time, cooked with something green in it, maybe a vegetable, and he couldn't help himself. He began to cry.

He glanced at Jack, ahead of him, who was holding out his helmet, since he had no mess kit. The guard slapped a cup of rice into the helmet, and Wally saw the tears in Jack's eyes, too. Wally reached out his mess kit and received his own portion. Another guard was pouring water from a bucket into any container the men had. Wally got his cup filled and took a sip, but he saved his rice until he could sit down. When he got to his place, he scooped some of the rice up with two fingers, stuck his fingers into his mouth, and sucked the grains in. The taste was nothing special—just bland rice, pasty and maybe even burnt a little—but it seemed the best food Wally had ever eaten.

Wally wanted to take his time, but he couldn't force himself to do it. He shoveled it in quickly, every last grain, and then he finished his water. He looked at Warren, who had taken a little more time, and he was jealous that his friend still had something left.

But that was it. The food was gone, and Wally's hunger had only been reawakened. He wondered immediately whether there was any chance for more. But each man received his ration, and then the guards left. Still, Wally thought he felt some strength, and he hoped that this would be the pattern now—maybe three meals a day.

The men were kept in the stifling shack all that day and another night, but no more rice came. A little water was offered, but nothing more, and after that first taste of food, the need for more only seemed greater.

Wally could see that some of the men were breaking. More died that second day in the building, and they were dragged from the room. Wally watched, hardly feeling anything, and he found it hard not to think about the added comfort as the room became less crowded. He knew that something deeply instinctive in him was taking over, and he understood that to remain human, decent, he had to fight the impulse to think only of himself, but almost constantly his obsession was the thought of getting more food.

On the following morning the men were left sitting in the little room again, and the tediousness, the weariness, was almost impossible to endure. But around noon the guards roused the men and marched them outside. The air felt good for a few minutes until the sun began to burn into them as they stood and waited. No one knew what would happen next, and Wally feared that it would be another full day of walking. He was almost sure he couldn't do that. But the guards marched the men through the town to a little train station, then directed them into metal boxcars. At first the prospect of riding was relieving, but far too many were forced into each boxcar—a hundred or more in a car that was only about thirty feet long. There was no room to do anything but stand, and the men were pressed together tightly, their stinking bodies forced against each other. Then the doors were slammed shut so that no air could pass through.

"They can't keep us in this thing very long," Wally told Jack and Warren. "We'll die from the heat." But Wally was sorry immediately that he had said it. He saw that Jack was losing his resolve again.

"We'll get by," Warren said. "This must be the last leg of the trip. Maybe it's a short run." Wally was impressed with Warren, who seemed never to lose his inner strength.

As the train chugged along all afternoon, swaying and bumping, Wally began to believe this was the worst ordeal yet. There was no room to move, to do much shifting or adjusting of weight, and the heat was overwhelming. In time, men began to urinate where they stood, with no other option available to them. And some of the sick men, with diarrhea, had no choice either. One man vomited blood all over himself, as well as on the man in front of him. Not long after, Wally heard someone say, "This guy is dead." But there was not even a way to let the man's body slump to the floor.

All day the train continued. At times Wally hallucinated, his brain shooting strange, quick little images through his consciousness. He was on the edge of passing out, and he was not sure that didn't mean he was on the edge of dying. Every inch of his body ached, and gradually he became almost desperate for air, raising his head and sucking deeply, trying to get more into his lungs. He was taller than most of the men, but that put his head only about a foot away from the top of the car, where the heat was like a furnace.

Wally was almost finished when the train finally stopped. Everyone else was too. No one said a word. When the door opened, they merely staggered out. Wally was one of the last, and he saw half a dozen men who had died along the way and had finally been released to drop to the floor. He limped out onto the loading dock and saw that the guards were forming the men into a line, two abreast, and marching them away. He welcomed the movement, the air, no matter how exhausted he was.

"We can do this," he told Jack. "We must be almost there." "Okay," Jack said, but there was very little left in him. Wally could see it in his eyes.

A guard slammed Wally in the back with the stock of his rifle. Wally stumbled ahead, hardly giving a second thought to the added pain in his back. He took Jack's arm and pulled him along, and together the two began to hike up the dusty road.

A couple of hours went by, and Wally and Jack continued to shuffle up the road. Warren was right behind them. On both sides of the road were vast fields of rich, deep *cogon* grass, but no water, no food, and Wally saw no destination ahead. He felt like a machine, taking small but steady steps, and continuing on in spite of his depletion. Finally, however, the end did come into sight. Some sort of camp, ringed with a barbed-wire fence, lay ahead. The men marched in through the gate, under watch-towers on high stilts. This place, whatever it was, had the look of a prison camp, and so it seemed likely that the men really had reached the end of their trek.

Inside, the men saw a row of neglected bamboo buildings with *Nipo* grass roofs. There were even a few wooden buildings that appeared to be the headquarters of a former military camp. The place was run-down compared to Clark Field, and there wasn't a tree in sight, but Wally thought only of finding a place big enough to stretch out. He wanted to sleep for as long as possible and then wake up to a meal. But the men were marched to the center of the camp and lined up. More prison-ers continued to arrive while those inside had to stand and wait, not even allowed to sit down. Eventually the entire train-load, hundreds of men, reached the area. Around the outside of the crowd were dozens of guards, and in time a Japanese officer stepped onto a box, with a guard next to him, on the ground.

The stocky officer, dressed in a short-sleeved shirt and a baggy pair of shorts, shouted at the men. For some time he continued his apparent diatribe before he allowed the inter-preter a chance to speak. A small man with wire-rim glasses translated, "I am Captain Tsuneyoshi Yoshio. I am camp com-mandant. You are prisoners of the Imperial Japanese Government! You are cowards! Japanese soldiers would kill themselves before surrendering. We can only treat you with contempt and dishonor. Only my honor—the spirit of *Bushido*—keeps me from putting you to death, as you deserve."

Wally felt the anger swell in him, and he liked it. Anger made him feel alive again.

What followed was a long list of instructions: The prison-ers would take turns serving as guards, and if anyone escaped, every guard on duty at the time would be shot. The men would be fed, but they would have to work, serving on water and wood details. An area would be set aside for Filipinos on one side of the camp, and the various services—army, air corps, navy, and marines—would be segregated and then governed by their own officers. These officers would see to it that no one escaped—or they would die themselves. Prisoners would be required to salute all Japanese guards, regardless of rank.

Finally, Yoshio raised his voice to a shout again, and the translator, in very correct English, told the men, "Asia is for Asians! You had no right to come here, to intrude upon our people. You have killed many noble men of the imperial army, and for this you must pay! You have your president to blame for this. He is the one who has made this war necessary. Japan is prepared to fight America for a hundred years, if it takes that long, and in the end, America will be ours."

The men stood in silence, but Wally knew the resentment everyone felt. He thought of a dozen things he wanted to shout back at the man, but of course he said nothing. And he was happy when the prisoners were marched off to their sections of the camp.

The air corps people were taken to the far end of the compound. On the opposite side of a high, barbed-wire fence, Wally could see Filipino prisoners. Wally was already thinking about survival in this place. He grabbed Jack and Warren and said, "Let's stake out a place under one of these buildings. We'll be sheltered from rain down there, but some air will get through."

Jack and Warren agreed, and they looked around until they found a good spot. Then they climbed under to establish their place and to get out of the sun. All three were asleep in just a few minutes. But by evening Wally awoke, thinking of food. He climbed out from under the building and tried to find out what was happening. What he learned was that this place was called Camp O'Donnell. It had served at one time as a training camp for Filipino soldiers but hadn't been used for some years. The rumor was that food would be served that night, but no one knew when.

Wally went back to his friends, and the three continued to wait. He said very little because the anticipation of food pre-occupied him almost entirely, but it was late in the evening before the food finally came. The men lined up and limped to the front of the line, and this time the portion of rice was greater than it had been in San Fernando, even more than they had often gotten in Bataan before the surrender. Wally walked away with enough rice to look like a meal, and it was laced with a good deal of eggplant. The flavor was bad, but the food filled his stomach for the first time in weeks, maybe months, and Wally felt almost human as the nourishment found its way into his body.

What he saw around him, however, was almost too painful to watch. Some of the men, so worn out and sick, couldn't get the food down, or vomited soon after they ate. He knew that many more were going to die, and he was thankful that he still felt his hunger, still had some strength left. The illness that had struck him, whatever it had been, was almost gone.

Wally sat in the shade of the rickety building, and he and his friends savored their food. Wally saw Jack come back to life before his eyes. Once they each had enough food down them to take away the agony of their hunger, they ate more slowly, trying to make the rice last as long as possible.

"We're okay now," Wally told Jack and Warren. "We've made it through the worst. If they'll feed us like this every day, we'll be okay."

Warren grinned. "If I can get this much rice in me for a few days, I'll start to notice how bad it tastes."

"I notice already," Jack said. "And I still like it."

"We did this together," Wally said. "Now we've got to keep each other alive. If one of us gets sick, the others have to take care of him. We have to figure this place out, find out if there's any way to get some extra food, some meat or vegetables, any-thing that will build us up."

"How can we do that?"

"I'm not sure. But that Jap officer said there would be work details. If we get outside, the Filipinos will help us get food. Back in San Fernando, I saw the local people on the streets flashing the "V for victory" sign when they thought no Japs were watching."

"I know. I saw that too," Warren said.

Wally laughed. "You guys look pretty bad," he said.

"You look awful yourself," Jack said, and he laughed too. "Worse than that."

Warren had light, thin hair, and it was a tangled mess. His face was caked with dirt, his eyes red. His blue coveralls were also covered with dirt and torn at the elbows and one knee, and his hands were grimy and scaly, like alligator skin. Jack looked no better with his stringy dark hair and his stubble of black beard.

"We need to clean up. I found out there's a water pipe down by the army section. It's the only water at this end of the camp, but it runs all the time—or I guess it just dribbles. If we wait in line we can get us a good drink and wash up a little."

"Let's do it." Jack got up.

"But let's make a vow. We keep each other alive. Okay?"

Jack and Warren both agreed.

"Do you guys want to have a prayer?" Wally asked.

"Sure," Jack said, and he nodded. He was not a Mormon, as Warren and Wally were, but he had become a lot more religious in recent months.

"You say it," Wally told Warren. "You've kept in better touch with the Lord than anyone."

Warren shrugged. "I don't know about that," he said, but he bowed his head, and then, as though he were talking to a friend, he merely said, "Lord, we made it this far, and we thank thee. Please give us strength now—all of us—to keep going."

Wally was suddenly crying. He had almost given up hope the night he had been sick, so this seemed a second chance. But he knew a great trial lay ahead. He hugged Warren and then Jack, and then the three went off to stand in line at the water spigot.

Wally, along with Jack and Warren, learned fast. They were some of the healthier men, so they drew a lot of work assignments. Some days they carried water in five-gallon drums from a nearby pond, two men hoisting the drum on a long pole. This was tiring and uninteresting work, but other days they left the compound to haul loads of wood or rice from the nearby village of Capas. There the men came in contact with local people, and they were sometimes able to get food. All life for the prisoners came to revolve around scrounging extra food. Normal rations were a watery rice cereal, called *lugao*, for breakfast, and a decent serving of rice with eggplant or *camote*, a sweet potato, at night. Extra food meant crucial vitamins, but the extra flavor, extra satisfaction of any food other than rice was the only thing to look forward to—and the only way to get food was to get outside.

One day a Filipino woman gave Wally a bottle of ketchup, and Wally managed to smuggle it back into camp by slipping it inside his coveralls, under his arm. The guards who took the men into the village didn't seem to care whether the prisoners got hold of food or cigarettes while outside, but the guards at the gate took delight in confiscating the booty and then beating the men who were caught with the stuff. What Wally learned was that he had to watch his chances at the gate. When he could see that he would be searched, he would sneak to the fence and sell his take to Filipino prisoners. The Filipinos had plenty of money, smuggled to them by locals. The money was easy to hide, and it could be used to purchase food on the next work assignment. Wally would split his take of money with his friends, and between the three of them, they would watch for new opportunities to buy chocolate or anything else available. On one occasion Warren managed to get hold of several bottles of ketchup and some canned meat—and he got them past the guards. By then he had designed a little bag that he draped under his arm and kept inside his coveralls. For days after, Jack and Warren and Wally ate rice with meat, flavored with the ketchup, and they felt like kings.

All this, however, was taking a great chance. Anyone caught was beaten unmercifully. Sometimes the guards would break a man's arm, on purpose, which was a death sentence. Without means to heal such an injury, and with inadequate nourishment, a broken bone would soon take a man's life.

The worst duty was the burial detail. Once men became seriously ill they were taken to a so-called hospital. It was actually a filthy, foul-smelling, fly-infested building where men were merely allowed to die. There were no mops to clean up the blood-filled vomit and feces, no way to disinfect the floors the men lay on. The men called it "St. Peter's Ward." No medicine, no care was given. Men simply dwindled and died on the wooden floor with no sort of comfort for their final hours. The guards saw no reason to waste food on dying men, and so those with any hope of surviving died of starvation. Every morning the bodies had to be carried out by men who feared to touch the diseased bodies. The corpses were usually covered with sores and ulcers, sometimes with maggots and blowflies clinging to the decay. The men carried the bodies in blankets outside the compound to graves that had been dug the day before. If the graves were not adequate, the bodies were left on the ground. New graves were begun each day. Hundreds of men died in the first few weeks at O'Donnell—one of every six.

Wally tried to keep clean, but the trickle of water was not adequate to allow for much of a bath. He'd managed to buy a "shelter-half"—half of a pup tent—and he used that to protect him and his friends from rain blowing in under the building where they slept, but the rainy season was coming on, and he knew conditions would not be good. His coveralls were holding together so far, and his boots were not too bad, but his socks had worn out. He managed to buy a tattered khaki-colored hat that protected his head from the sun. He also had his cup, half of a mess kit, and a spoon. And he had his quinine pills, which he was likely to need.

Gradually, as weeks went by, the guards began to provide less rice each day, and the eggplant almost disappeared. That made scrounging even more important, and men began to take bigger chances. One morning Wally was assigned to guard duty. It wasn't a bad assignment since no one really tried to escape, but just as Wally was about to leave his sleeping area to take up his duty, an officer came by and said, "Hicks, Norland, you two have the rice detail today."

Wally spun around. "Could I go too?" he asked. "I have guard duty, but anyone can do that—even the sick guys."

"No. We've got the detail filled. I just need these two."

Wally didn't know why this bothered him so much. Part of it was that he liked to have the chance to scrounge, but he also felt strange when he was separated from Jack and Warren. Still, he knew it was silly to care whether they were separated for a day. As the officer walked away, Wally told his friends, "Come back with something good, okay? We need a good meal."

Jack laughed. "I'll try to buy a side of beef. There's room for it in my coveralls."

It was almost true. Jack—all the men—had lost a tremendous amount of weight. Wally could see all his ribs when he took off his coveralls. When he looked down at his legs, he was reminded of a flamingo. "I'd settle for a can of fish," Wally said.

"We'll see what we can do," Warren said, and the two walked away.

At about noon an officer walked up to Wally. "Son," he said, "there's a long-term work detail, and the Japs are asking for everyone who can do hard work. Go to the gate and report. They'll haul you out of here in trucks."

"What do you mean 'long-term'?" Wally asked.

"I don't know. You know how they are. They won't tell us anything. We told them that all the healthy guys are out working, but they want three hundred men, and they want them now. A lot of sick guys are going to have to go, and I hate to think what will happen to them."

"Hey, listen, isn't there some way out of this? My two buddies are out on detail, and I'm—"

"Hey, I know how you feel, but there's not one thing I can do. We've been trying for an hour to talk them out of this."

"I know, but—"

"Son, go to the gate. Right now. I'm sorry."

Wally nodded. All the military stuff, saluting and the like, had gotten lost along the way, but this was still an order by an officer, and Wally knew he didn't have any choice. He could say no to the American, but he wouldn't be able to say no to the guards. And so he walked to the gate, but he felt as though he were walking off a cliff. Who knew how long he would be gone? Maybe he wouldn't be brought back here. Maybe . . .

Wally had to fight back the tears. He knew that was stupid, but he didn't have much to hang onto in this place, and now the one thing he did have was being taken away from him. He wouldn't even have a chance to tell his friends goodbye.

3

Bobbi Thomas, with the rest of her family, sat at the dinner table and listened to Alex's end of a telephone conversation. When Alex hung up the receiver and walked to the table, President Thomas said, "So what was that fellow telling you?"

For the past year Alex Thomas had been working for his father. He was running a company that produced parts for defense companies, mostly for airplanes, and he had gained lots of contacts in the business. For weeks now, Alex had been trying to use these connections to find out whether his brother Wally was still alive. The man he had just been talking to was with the Boeing Company in Seattle.

"He finally got through to the people who should know something," Alex said. "But even the big boys in Washington say they have no information—no list of prisoners, no casualty list. The Japanese won't give them a thing."

"So we're right back where we started," Dad said.

"Pretty much. But he did say one thing that sounded hopeful. The air corps people he talked to said that Wally's pursuit squadron was down at the tip of the peninsula, away from all the serious fighting. He said chances were almost certain that Wally was taken prisoner."

"That sounds good," Sister Thomas said. She was sitting at

one end of the long dinner table, her husband at the other. Alex sat down between his two younger sisters, LaRue and Beverly. Gene and Bobbi were sitting on the opposite side.

"It does sound good," Alex said. "I think you can be almost certain that he was alive when the troops surrendered."

"I always have been sure of that," she said.

Alex nodded. He sounded careful, however, when he added, "The only thing is . . ." He hesitated and looked at his mother. "There have been some reports from Filipinos that the prisoners haven't been treated all that well."

"What do you mean?"

"I'm not exactly sure. I'll try to find out more."

No one said a word. Bobbi was disturbed, even a little sick at the thought that Wally might be suffering.

"I don't think our troops will get back to the Philippines right away," Alex said, "but at least the tide is already turning in the Pacific. Knocking out those Japanese carriers at Midway went a long way toward evening things up." He leaned forward and patted his mother's hand, and his necktie draped onto his empty plate.

"We need to knock out the Japs fast and then go kick Hitler's pants," Gene said.

"It's not going to go that way," Alex told him. "Churchill has Roosevelt convinced that we have to devote most of our attention to Germany for now. Some people say we're going to land in Europe this year, but from what I see, I don't think so. We brag about our war production, but right now—while we're getting things going—things are really a mess. And Hitler has better weapons, especially tanks. I talk to military men who think the war in Europe could go on for four or five years."

"Oh, no. I doubt that," Dad said. "Hitler made a mistake when he invaded Russia. He may have the Russians on the run so far, but I think he's stretched himself too thin."

"Maybe," Alex said. Then he added, quietly, "But don't look for us to get Wally free for a while—not this year at least."

This was not a new conversation in the Thomas household, and Bobbi didn't like to hear it. She didn't want to think that Wally could be held for a long time. "Have you tried to write to Wally yet?" she asked her mother.

"I've sent two letters now," Sister Thomas said. "I finally got an address I could use—but I have no idea whether the mail is going through. So far, no letters have been coming out of the prison camps."

It was June, 1942, and Wally had been a prisoner of war since early April. The agony of waiting and wondering had been terrible, and today Bobbi could detect the stress in her mother's voice. Maybe she sensed, as Bobbi did, that Alex was holding back. He seemed to know more than he was saying.

"We've talked enough about this," Mom said. "Let's say the blessing, and let's eat. We need to enjoy each other tonight. We won't have another chance like this for a long time."

The grandparents—both the Thomases and the Snows—as well as many of the uncles and aunts and cousins, had come over to say good-bye the night before, but this dinner was for the immediate family. In the morning, Bobbi was leaving. She had graduated from nursing school late in May, and now she had taken a commission in the navy. In another week Alex would also be on his way, heading to Georgia for his army basic training.

Dad said the blessing on the food. As always, he prayed for Wally, but he also thanked the Lord for his children and prayed for Alex and Bobbi's safety.

"Thanks, Dad," Bobbi said. She was moved by her dad's obvious concern for her. He could be stern at times, and too controlling, but she could hear the tightness in his voice now, and she knew he was struggling with the reality that two more of his children were about to leave.

Bobbi would be serving at a navy hospital in Pearl Harbor. Her mom and dad were worried that the Japanese might attack again, but Bobbi didn't think the hospital would be in any danger. Apparently a lot of nurses were not so sure of that. The navy had been working hard to find enough women who were willing to go there.

Alex had decided to join an airborne unit. The army was seeking top-rated volunteers to begin a new basic training experiment: the recruits would receive jump training along with their boot camp. To Bobbi, Alex hardly seemed the type to get involved with a "crack" outfit, but the recruiter had been especially interested in Alex because he had served a recent mission in Germany. The promise was that Alex could very well end up in an intelligence unit, where he would translate German documents or radio transmissions. Alex saw that as a way to help the cause without shooting anyone. He hated the idea of returning to fight the people he had learned to love during his mission.

Gene scooped some mashed potatoes onto his plate and then passed the bowl to Bobbi. "Did I smell a cake baking?" he asked.

"Well, yes," Mom said, "but it's just a small one."

"How did you get enough sugar?"

Bobbi laughed. Gene was a growing boy and a big eater. He really missed the sweets—all the cookies and cinnamon rolls and cupcakes—that Mom had now stopped baking. Sugar was the only commodity the new Office of Price Administration had restricted so far, but according to the newspapers, many other items would soon be rationed. As of the end of May the production of almost all durable goods had stopped. Any factory that had made sewing machines, kitchen appliances, washers, and the like, was being converted for the building of armaments. And no one was producing automobiles. If Dad hadn't begun making parts for military use, he would be in big trouble now, with only a few used cars available to sell at his Hudson/Nash dealership.

"I used every bit of sugar I had in the house—and borrowed a little from Grandma," Mom said. "Don't expect any on your oatmeal mush the rest of the week."

"Oh, great!" Gene said. "I'll take scrambled eggs, please—unless the OPA passes a law against chickens laying their eggs."

"Quit complaining," LaRue said with an exaggerated shake of her head. "We all have to *sacrifice* to win the war."

Gene rolled his eyes. "You sound like these *posters* they're putting up all over the place."

"Well, the posters are right. Don't you think Wally would like to have some mush right now—even without sugar?"

Gene, of course, didn't answer that, and Bobbi was a little surprised at LaRue. She had never been particularly idealistic, but she was obviously taking all the new slogans seriously. That was fine, of course, but Bobbi felt sorry for Gene. No one missed Wally more than Gene did, and right now he was caught in the middle. He was still in high school, too young to fight the war but old enough to feel the pinch of all the things that were being taken away from him. The schools were cutting back on activities—mostly because of gasoline and rubber shortages. Fuel and tires were needed for military vehicles, and the Japanese were now in control of Malaya and the Dutch East Indies, the former source of most American rubber. Gasoline rationing had started on the East Coast and hadn't been established in Utah so far, but tire sales had come under very tight regulation. People who owned unmounted tires were being required to sell them to the government, and everyone would soon have to have their tires inspected four times a year to prove they hadn't bought any on the black market. Joy riding was a thing of the past. Tires were going to have to last a long time—perhaps even for the duration.

"For the duration." It was a phrase that had started popping up even before Pearl Harbor, when everyone first realized that America would have to sacrifice to help England. But now, with the United States in the war, almost every aspect of normal life was on hold until the war came to an end.

"Mom, when are you going to add two more stars to the window?" LaRue asked.

"You obviously haven't looked. I put them up this morning."

Bobbi turned and looked at the living room window. The sun was well to the west now, but still, the glow through the south window made the blue stars and the red trim show up against the little white flags they were sewn to. All around Salt Lake City, and across the nation, the banners were showing up now. Each star represented a member of the household who was serving in the military. And already, a few gold stars—for those who had died in action—were beginning to replace some of the blue ones.

The image touched Bobbi. The three blue stars represented the commitment of a whole family, but they also signified three lives that were being separated from the eight they had always been tied to. Bobbi had been fairly excited about getting away and seeing a new part of the world, but here in this afternoon glow of light, she felt as though the sun were going down on everything she had always known.

"You'll have to add another one next year," Gene said. "I'm signing up as soon as I graduate."

"Don't get so anxious, Gene," President Thomas said. "It's nothing to wish upon yourself."

"I'm going, either way. I might as well sign up and get into the branch of the service I want. Besides, I want to go. I want to kick the Japs out of the Philippines."

Bobbi knew that Gene was telling LaRue she could talk all she wanted about pulling together for the country, but in another year he would be putting his life on the line. She had no right to question his patriotism—even if he missed his sugar.

The food continued to move around the table—fried chicken, potatoes and gravy, tossed salad, garden peas, and home-baked rolls. Bobbi looked over at Beverly, who was still just ten. She had always been a serene little girl who loved to play with dolls and live in her own imagination, but she had grown quieter than ever, and Bobbi wondered what kind of worries she was storing up inside.

Beverly had been very attached to Wally before he had left. Now, Alex was heading into that same war, and children were learning quickly that big brothers didn't necessarily return. Bobbi had always been one to chat with her little sisters, to spend time with them, and she knew they were struggling with the idea of her leaving, too. It didn't help to hear Dad and Mom fretting about the dangers of Pearl Harbor. Beverly had cried one night and told Bobbi she was afraid everyone in their family was going to get hurt. She hadn't said "get killed," probably hadn't dared to say the words, but Bobbi knew it was what she meant.

"You'll be safe here," Bobbi had told Beverly, but Bev had looked up with tears in her round eyes and said, "Maybe bombs will fall on us. At school we have to practice getting under our desks—in case the Japs come."

This was not a good time—not for anyone. But right now Bobbi felt more concern for Beverly than anyone else in the family.

When the food was finally distributed and everyone had settled into eating, Dad said, "I do want to say a few things to you today." He grinned. "But I won't talk very long."

Bobbi knew what he meant. He had become aware of his reputation for preaching too much.

"First of all," he said, "I want Bobbi to know how proud we are of her. I'm happy that she wants to serve her country—now that I've gotten used to the idea."

Everyone laughed. They all knew how hard Dad had resisted the idea of Bobbi's going into the navy.

"I'm also proud of Alex—even though he's fool enough to think he wants to jump out of airplanes."

"Alex," Gene said, "be sure to use a parachute."

"I'll flap my wings," Alex said.

LaRue giggled. "He's an angel," she said. "Didn't you know that, Gene?"

Dad cleared his throat with exaggerated volume. "Now come on; I'm serious," he said. He waited, took a bite of his chicken, chewed for a moment, and let everyone get ready. Then he set the chicken down, wiped his hands on his napkin, and said, "There are different kinds of missions in life, and I hope before too many years Gene will have the chance to serve a proselyting mission, just as Alex did. But for now, we have a mission to stop what's happening in the world. Elder Widtsoe, at this last general conference, told us that the Lord allows Satan to go only so far in creating human misery—and then he puts a stop to it. But God can only work through good people. We, the members of the Church, have to help lead the world back to purity."

General conference had been strange this year. To cut back on travel, only leaders had been invited. The conference talks, however, had appeared in the Church section of the *Deseret News*, and Bobbi had read the one by Elder Widtsoe. It had given her some hope that evil would not win out—even though it seemed to be prospering so well at the moment.

"Your mother and I are doing our part by running the plant," Dad said, "and Bobbi is going to care for the wounded. Alex will probably see action in battle. But we're all, in different ways, going to do our share."

"Me and Bev are collecting scrap metal again this Saturday," LaRue said.

"That's right." Dad dabbed at his potatoes but didn't actually eat any. When he looked up, Bobbi saw the emotion that had come into his eyes. "What I want, no matter where we are, or what happens—is for all of us to keep the faith. I know what war does to people. We have to keep close to each other in whatever way we can, and we have to rely on the Lord."

Everyone had stopped eating. Bobbi found herself wondering what heartaches might be coming to the family.

"I want to say something to you that may be obvious, but I want all of you to think back on it when you need to. I *know* the gospel is true. And I know God will not abandon us, no matter what. If at some time you find yourself doubting, will you remember that I *know?*" He looked to the other end of the table. "Your mother knows too. Just as surely as I do."

"I do," Mom said, and she took the chance to make eye contact with each of her children.

Bobbi was seeing something new in her mother these days. She was stepping forward, taking her place alongside her husband.

She seemed to be offering her testimony with a new sort of authority, and even though Dad may have called on her as an afterthought, he at least had called on her. He hadn't always done that.

"Dad," Bobbi said, "will you give us a father's blessing before we go?"

"You know I will." He looked at her steadily for a time. "Are you a little scared?"

"Not for my life. It's just . . . a big change."

"I'm scared," Alex said. "Not exactly for my life either—but you know—I feel like I have a lot to lose."

Everyone knew what he meant. Alex had baptized a family named Stoltz in Germany, and he had fallen in love with the daughter, Anna. He hadn't told her that while he was there, but he had written to her since then, and the two had promised to wait out the war and marry each other. He obviously didn't want to lose the chance to do that.

"I wish I could make guarantees," President Thomas said. "I do feel that in the end we'll hold strong, but I can't say that nothing bad is going to happen to any of us. I read just the other day that Elder Hugh Brown's boy—a pilot—was shot down. He's missing in action, maybe dead. If it can happen to the Browns, it can happen to us."

"If something bad happens to any of us, it happens to all of us," Bobbi said. "Like with Wally."

"That's right." Dad nodded. "And excuse me for bringing up our heritage just one more time, but remember that the Thomases and the Snows are a noble, good people. When hardship visited them in the early days of the Church, they got stronger, not weaker, and they passed their strength on to the next generation. I hope you'll never forget who you are: like the hymn says, you are children of the promise."

It certainly was Dad's old tune, but it had a new ring to it now. For the first time the family understood something about the "refiner's fire" Dad always talked of. Their pioneer fore-fathers had gotten through some tough times in Missouri and Illinois—and on the trek west—but maybe this war was going to be as hard as any of that.

"We just have to—" Dad stopped. "Well, let's eat. You know what I have to say. I've said it a thousand times. I know how tiresome I can get."

Wally had always teased his dad about his endless preach-ing, but Bobbi had never minded so much, and she didn't mind now. She suspected Wally might not either. But they ate, and Bobbi was sure everyone was thinking about the change that was about to come, and about the possible dangers.

"Have you seen Lorraine Gardner lately?" Alex asked. Lorraine was the girl Wally had dated before he left for the air corps. The two had broken up before he left, but Bobbi knew that Wally had never really gotten over her.

Mom said, "She calls me every few days. She's as anxious to hear about Wally as we are."

"I wish Wally could know that," Bobbi said.

"I know," Mom said. "I told him in the letters I sent, but I have no idea whether they will get to him."

"If he had something to hope for it might help him."

"That's true. But I didn't feel I could make that kind of promise."

Bobbi felt the sadness of it. Lorraine had had plenty of good reasons for breaking up with Wally—and who could tell?—this experience in the war might make him a worse person, not a better one. It put Lorraine in a bad position.

"She wants to write to him herself," Mom said. "I think that's the best thing."

Dad said, "We offered her a job this summer, at the plant. She turned us down at first, but when she called the other day, she told Bea she might take us up on the offer after all. I guess she's tired of the place where she's been working."

Bobbi wasn't sure how good that would be, but she was happy to know that Lorraine was going to write to Wally. If he were to get the letter, it would surely be a help to him. Lorraine had always been a good influence in his life.

"A Jap came to our house yesterday," Bev said.

There was an awkward silence for a moment, and then Mom said, "Honey, that was our friend Mat Nakashima. He's lived here all his life."

"I know. But he's a Jap. LaRue said he was."

"His family came from Japan a long time ago," Bobbi said. "We don't have anything against Japanese people—just the ones who . . ." But Bobbi couldn't think how to finish her sentence.

Mom said, "Mat is a wonderful man. He has a nice family." But she sounded unnatural, and no one else seemed to know what to say.

It was Alex who changed the subject just a little. "What's happened to Mat's brother?" he asked. "Have you been able to do anything for him?"

"No," Dad said. "Everyone just tells me that he was in the wrong place at the wrong time. All the Japanese on the coast are being held, and the government is moving them to inland relocation camps. One of them is going to be down in central Utah, west of Delta. The fact that Ike is from here doesn't seem to matter to anyone."

"Can't they figure out which ones are really spies and just put them in jail?" Gene asked.

Alex said, "I don't think they have proof that *any* of them are spies."

"That may be true, Alex," Dad said. "But how can they know? And if you leave a lot of Japanese in the same neighborhood with white people, I'm not sure what might happen. I'm afraid people will take out their anger on them. They'll be better off in these camps."

"The last I heard, they were Americans. Maybe it's the people who bother them who ought to be put away—and not the other way around."

"Well, I'll tell you something, Alex. There are very few people who feel that way. After talking to Mat, I have a lot of sympathy for him and his people. But I still think this might be the best answer for now. I just don't know why they won't let Ike come home. A few Utah Japanese were arrested, but only those with connections to the old country. Ike doesn't have that."

Alex let it go. He glanced at Bobbi and seemed to seek some agreement. Bobbi looked away. She liked Mat Nakashima, but she didn't really think of him as Japanese. Japs were the people holding her brother in a prison camp, the ones causing this war and killing young American boys. That's what she had wanted to tell Beverly.

"Is this lettuce from the garden?" Bobbi asked. And now she was the one changing the subject, on purpose.

"Yes. From our new, expanded 'Victory garden,'" Gene said. "Can't you tell how sour the stuff is?"

"We all have to produce more of our own food," Mom said.

"I know, I know," Gene said, and he laughed. "But that doesn't make the lettuce taste any better."

"Those peas are wonderful," Mom said. "Lettuce is just a little trickier. We're going to get better. We haven't done enough with our garden the past couple of years, but there's nothing better than fresh vegetables."

"Now tell me how much Wally would like to have some right now." But like the Wally everyone remembered, Gene had gone a little too far, and the silence made that obvious. "I'm sorry," he said. "I was just kidding."

But even the apology reminded Bobbi of Wally, and she suddenly ached to see the boy—just to know how he was doing.

When everyone had finished, Mom brought out the little cake. It had no icing, but mom brought a big pitcher of milk with it. At least dairy products weren't in short supply.

Everyone was in the middle of dessert when a knock came on the front door. "That's my gang," Gene said, and he got up from the table. "We're going swimming out at Wasatch Springs."

"What's this?" Dad said. "I thought we were all going to be together tonight."

"Al, I think I told you about this. Gene made plans before we decided to get everyone together."

"Can't you—"

Gene got up and walked toward the front door. "I won't be gone too long, Dad," he called back. "Bobbi and I can stay up late and talk about how much she loves me and all that stuff."

Bobbi smiled at him. "It'll take me *hours* to stop missing you. Or at least minutes."

"Tell the truth. You—"

But Dad obviously didn't like this. "How are you getting there?" he asked.

"Don't worry. No cars involved. We're taking the trolley."

Gene opened the door. "Come on in for a minute," he shouted. "You can all watch me finish my cake. None for you, though. Sorry."

Sister Thomas glanced at Bobbi and shook her head. Then she stood up and turned to look at the kids who were filing in through the front door: three girls and three boys. They were all kids from Sugar House, some of them from their ward. Bobbi was sort of glad to see that the count would be uneven when Gene joined them. That meant the little excursion wasn't exactly divided up into couples. Somehow Bobbi hated to think her little brother was old enough to get attached to any one girl.

"Kids, I'm sorry," Mom said. "I baked a little cake, but we've eaten almost all of it."

One of the girls, Millie Ellertson, walked forward and touched Sister Thomas's arm. "Don't worry. Gene was just smarting off, as usual." But then she did something surprising. She took hold of Gene's arm and looked up at him, into his eyes. Gene claimed to be the tallest in the family—by half an inch—and he looked it right now.

Millie was a girl from the ward. Bobbi had known her forever. She was wearing a straight skirt with saddle shoes—the outfit all the girls in high school were wearing these days—but she seemed to be wearing a touch of lipstick, and she had, suddenly it seemed, taken on the shape of a woman. She had also taken a very firm grip on little brother Gene.

Bobbi glanced at her father, and she saw that he had noticed too. He stood up, slowly. "How are you kids doing?" he asked, but he was staring at Millie.

"Hello, President," Millie said, and so did the others. He was stake president to all of them.

"You're going swimming, I understand."

"Yes, but I'm a terrible swimmer," Millie said. "Your sport-star son might have to save my life."

"I don't see how I can," Alex said. "I'm not going."

Gene laughed. "Don't even start with that," he said. "This year I'm going to break all your records."

"Hope springs eternal," Alex said, and he grinned at his little brother.

Gene had already pulled loose from Millie, and he walked

to the table, where he swallowed the rest of his cake and gulped down his milk. Then he walked back through the living room into the parlor and toward the stairs. "Just let me get my stuff," he told his friends.

A red-haired boy named Ralph Nielson took up the kidding with Alex. "East will have its best football team ever this fall," he said.

Alex argued that the team he had played on could come back and whoop them, even now, but Bobbi was again surprised when Millie, whom Bobbi remembered as being rather quiet, said, "I doubt that, Alex. Gene could probably handle you guys by himself."

"Oh, really? I didn't know my little brother was Superman."

"Well, he is. Unless you know where you can get some kryptonite, you'd better not try to duke it out with him." She doubled up her fists as though ready to fight.

Just then Gene charged down the stairs, two steps at a time, and he herded everyone out the door. As the door shut, Sister Thomas sat down and said, "Well, a person doesn't have to have x-ray vision to know what that girl has on her mind."

Everyone laughed, and LaRue said, "You and Dad are always the last to know about everything. Millie's had a crush on Gene since junior high."

"And what about Gene?" Dad said. "What does he think about her?"

"Oh, you know Gene," LaRue said. "He doesn't care that much about girls."

"That's the best news I've heard today," Dad said.

Suddenly the door flew open and Gene charged back in and hurried to the table. "Sis," he said, "you'll be up packing tonight, won't you? And staying up late?"

"Yeah. I'm sure I will."

"Okay. I do want to talk to you, or . . . you know . . . have some time to say good-bye."

"Aren't you going with us to the train in the morning?"

"Sure. But, I want to have a little time with you. Okay?"

"Okay."

"I'm going to miss you, Bobbi. I was just joking about that."

"I know."

He tried to say, "Alex is the one I won't miss," but the words failed him halfway through, and tears came into his eyes. "See you later," he said, softly, and he hurried away.

No one spoke for quite some time after he was gone. Beverly had begun to cry.

But Dad said, "Now might be a good time to do those father's blessings—before anyone else leaves."

So the family moved into the living room, and Dad brought a chair from the table. He blessed Bobbi first. He rested his big hands on her head, the warmth pressing through her hair, and he told her how much he—and the Lord—loved her. He blessed her that she would be kept safe. He also said something that struck Bobbi as rather ominous. "May you learn the things you are supposed to learn," he said. "May you use the trials that will come to you as means to further growth."

When Alex took the chair, President Thomas placed his hands on his son's head, but he didn't speak for a long time. His words seemed carefully considered. Bobbi knew that her father feared he would lose this firstborn son. She heard the concern in his voice, which was much softer than usual, even tremulous at times. At one point he said, "I bless you that you might remember Moroni's rent coat, the Title of Liberty for which he fought. Defend your God, your religion, your freedom and peace, and your family, but like Moroni and Helaman and the stripling warriors, never give way to hatred. Keep a spirit of peace, of love, of goodness, in your heart. Be a noble warrior, a fierce fighter if need be, but keep the spirit of Christ with you all along the way."

And then, finally, President Thomas said, "Helaman called the stripling warriors his little sons. And Alex, you are still my little son. I hold all the images of your wonderful childhood close to my heart." His voice broke, and he began to shake. "I would rather keep you here, as you know, rather cling to you selfishly, but these times demand that our fine young sons defend us as the armies of Helaman once defended their parents. I give you therefore to the Lord, and to our country, and I ask only that you honor both, no matter where you are called to serve."

Later, after dinner had been cleared away, Bobbi went upstairs to pack. When she walked downstairs after a while, she heard her dad and her brother talking. "Can I kill and still have the Spirit with me?" Alex asked.

She didn't hear the answer, but she remembered the question, and it haunted her long after.

4

The Stoltzes were sitting on their mattresses in the cellar. Each had taken a turn exercising, and now they were reading. President Hoch had brought home a copy of Goethe's *Faust* from a bombed house, and Anna was reading it once again. She and her father spent hours discussing Faust's decision, and Anna liked the way those discussions filled her attention and made time pass. It was June now, and the family had spent almost a year in hiding. Sometimes Anna wondered how much longer she could stand the tedium.

The Stoltzes were from Frankfurt, but when a Gestapo agent had tried to rape Anna, she had lashed back, cut his face with a kitchen knife, and the family had been forced to go on the run. They had made their way to Berlin, where they had found the branch president of the Mormon Church, and he and his wife had let them hide in their cellar. Every week Brother Stoltz vowed that they had to move, find some other place to wait out the war, but there seemed no options, and so their lives had become a monotonous daily attempt to stay healthy and sane. Brother Stoltz was decidedly anti-Nazi, and so he hoped for Hitler's fall, but he loved Germany, and he hated to think what it would take for the Allies to bring Hitler down. Berlin had been under attack for a long time, and from listening to British radio, he knew that many of the cities of Germany were being bombed repeatedly in nighttime Royal Air Force raids. Lately, huge armadas, with a thousand airplanes or more, had pounded Cologne, Essen, and Bremen.

But this day had been uneventful, and it seemed certain to remain so. Then the cellar door flew open and President Hoch hurried down the steps. "Everyone upstairs, immediately!" he insisted.

Peter bolted to his feet and then helped his father. Sister Stoltz was asking, "What's wrong? What's happened?"

"A man will come to the door in a minute or two. He's a block warden for the Gestapo. One of his informants has seen us carry more food into the house than seemed necessary, and he reported us. I told the block warden that you were bombed out of a house in the city, that I merely brought you here until you could find a place to live. But he wants to talk to you; I don't think he believes me."

Brother Hoch turned and hurried back up the stairs, but from upstairs he called back, "You'll have to give him names, and—"

"We have names ready," Brother Stoltz said. "We'll tell him our papers were lost in the fire—after the bombing."

Brother Stoltz struggled to climb the steps. He always had a hard time walking when he first got up. Herr Kellerman, the Gestapo agent who had tried to rape Anna, had beaten Brother Stoltz unmercifully, had broken his kneecap and his shoulder blade. Brother Stoltz had probably recovered as much as he was going to.

"Ursula Hofmann," Anna whispered out loud, reminding herself of the name she had chosen for a time like this.

"I'm Karl," Peter said.

Someone was already knocking on the door. Brother Hoch pushed the rug back over the entrance to the cellar, and then he walked to the door and opened it. "Herr Biedemann," he said, "please come in."

The man stepped in, a short man in a rumpled suit and a tie that was angling crookedly under his double-breasted coat. He looked around the room for a moment, his eyes darting quickly back and forth, and then he finally focused on Brother Stoltz. "Your name?" he asked.

"Hofmann. Norbert Hofmann. This is my wife, Maria." He gestured to Sister Stoltz, and she nodded to Herr Biedemann.

Biedemann wrote the names in a little notebook and then looked at Peter. "And you?"

"Karl," Peter said.

Anna heard his nervousness. She waited and then tried to sound natural as she said, "Ursula."

Biedemann took a look at her. Anna knew that men considered her pretty, but this little man leered at her, and she wished she could turn away from him. Instead, she smiled just a little and tried to seem friendly. He looked around at the others again, and then he stepped closer to Peter. "Tell me, young man, how did you and your family get here?"

"Our apartment was destroyed," Brother Stoltz said. "We were struck in a bombing raid, but fortunately we had all—"

Biedemann turned to Brother Stoltz. "I didn't ask you," he said with force. "I want to hear it from the boy."

Peter nodded as Biedemann turned back to him. Everyone was standing stiff, the Stoltzes all in a line, with Peter on the end. Anna glanced at Sister Hoch, who was white with fear.

"It was as my father said," Peter began. "We were in a bombing raid, but we had gone to the basement. The building was blown apart, and we lost everything. At least we were not hurt."

Peter had done well. He might have seemed a little tight, but that was only natural, with this man staring at him. He was fifteen now but still small for his age. His voice had changed, but under pressure, it could still become tight and squeaky.

"And I suppose you have no papers."

"No. Everything was lost."

"I thought you would say so. How long ago was this?"

Peter looked at his father. "Let's see," he said, hesitating.

Brother Hoch was quick to say, "Almost two weeks ago."

"I don't want any of you answering for the boy," Biedemann said. "I won't put up with it again."

"I'm sorry."

"Yes, it was almost two weeks ago," Peter said. "I know. Because it was on a Tuesday."

"I don't remember a raid at that time," Biedemann said. "Are you certain?"

"Yes. I am."

"Are you a Jewish boy?"

"No."

"What religion are you, Karl?"

"*Evangelisch.*"

Anna wondered why he wanted to know. She couldn't think where all this was going. She could hear the big clock ticking, like a drumbeat. The very air around her seemed to have turned solid. Brother Hoch was standing too rigid, his wife too wide-eyed. Biedemann had to know something wasn't right.

"Tell me this, Karl. What was your old address?"

"Thirty-one Gerhardtstrasse."

"Gerhardtstrasse? I don't know that street. Where is it?"

"Near the *Tiergarten.* Just north of there."

"I know of no Gerhardtstrasse in that area."

"I don't know what to tell you. It's there. Go look. I lived there all my life—until now."

Peter was warming to this, doing better all the time. But Gerhardtstrasse was in Frankfurt, the street they had lived on there. Anna hoped Peter hadn't accidentally given something away—something the Gestapo could end up tracing. She also knew that once Biedemann checked, the Stoltzes would be in trouble. They would be on the run again. After all the dreadful time in the cellar, suddenly Anna wished she could go back to it and stay.

"Tell me this, then," Biedemann was saying. "What kind of work does your father do?"

"He's a teacher."

Anna saw Peter hunch a little as though he regretted the words already. But he had had to answer quickly, and he had done the best he could.

"Teacher. What kind of teacher?"

"At a grammar school."

"What school?"

"I'm at the Holzheimer school," Herr Stoltz said. "It's on the—"

"I told you not to answer," Biedemann shouted. And he rushed at Brother Stoltz. "Why are you covering for this boy? Why are you lying?"

"I'm not lying."

"If I call the school, will they verify that you work there?"

"Of course they will. Call them immediately."

"Is there a telephone here?"

"No. I'm sorry," Brother Hoch said. "We have none."

"I thought you wouldn't." Biedemann ran his hand along his cheek. He had not shaved very evenly, the stubble of a beard visible on one side of his chin and not the other. He appeared anything but intelligent, and Anna hoped he didn't have the sense to keep pursuing the questions. She began to pray, silently, for some sort of miracle.

"Herr Biedemann, I don't understand this," Brother Stoltz finally said. "We are a good German family, hard-working people, and we've lost our home to these stinking British bombers. I have no idea what you suspect us of. Please, just call my school. You'll find that all is in order."

"I will call," Biedemann said. "And I will be back very soon with Gestapo agents. They will talk this over with you in more detail."

"What is it you think? That we're Jewish? I would hope you could look at us and see that we're not that."

"One never knows. You may be Jewish. You may not. But something is not right here. I know of no Gerhardtstrasse. Not in that area, in any case."

"Please check. You'll find that it's there."

Biedemann walked to the door. "Do not leave this house. I will be back *very* soon. Herr Hoch, if they are gone when I come back, I will hold you responsible. So will the Gestapo— and you don't want that."

"They have no reason to leave. Certainly, they will be here." But the instant the door shut, Brother Hoch turned to the Stoltzes. "You must go. This moment."

"How can we do that?" Brother Stoltz said. "The Gestapo will take it out on you."

"I'll tell them you must have been lying to me all along, that I took you in out of pity, and I believed your story. I'll tear my shirt, tell them I tried to hold on to you, and you fought your way loose."

Brother Stoltz nodded. "I pray you'll be all right."

"Let's all pray, together. Quickly."

Everyone knelt—except Brother Stoltz, who bowed his head—and Brother Hoch said, "Father, I call on you to bless this good family. Guide them and protect them. Take them to a safe place. I ask this in the name of Jesus Christ, amen."

Everyone said amen and then got up.

"Listen. I just thought of something," Brother Hoch said. "I worked on a row of bombed-out houses last week. There was little warning, and many people lost their lives there, but it might be a place where you can hide if you can get in without being seen. Go straight into the city, to the Kreuzberg area. Near Mehring Platz, on Lindenstrasse, you will see all the damage. There is a large, gray building—or the remains of one. It's the biggest in the row. Go to the back. You can crawl through the back window and get into the basement. It's not so bad down there. There is an apartment with some of the furniture left inside. It's a place to hide for a time. I'll try to contact you there if I can find a way to help you."

"All right. We need to go."

"Yes. Hurry." President Hoch grabbed his hand, then pressed some money into his palm.

Anna was already pulling back the rug and lifting the cellar door. She wasn't leaving without Alex's picture. She ran down and got it, and then she looked for the laundry bag they had used the year before. "Gather up our other clothes," her father whispered, but that's what Anna was already doing. She also grabbed her picture of Alex and the little Delft plate her mother had saved from their apartment in Frankfurt. Then she hurried up the steps. She stopped only long enough to hug the Hochs and to wish them God's protection, and then she followed her family out the back door.

The Stoltzes hurried down an alley, crossed a street to another back lane, and got through the block. They turned then and walked in the opposite direction they wanted to go but toward the bus they needed to catch. When they saw the bus in the distance, they waited at a stop and anxiously watched to see whether they had been followed. But no one appeared, and so they stepped onto the bus and were soon heading into the center of Berlin.

This much had been easy, but Anna couldn't think what her family would do after tonight, and she wondered what might be happening to the Hochs. Brother Stoltz reached forward and touched Anna's shoulder and then Peter's. "We'll manage somehow, just as we did before. Stay calm." And then he added, "Peter, you did a good job. I was proud of you."

"I said too much."

"No. You thought fast. You did the best you could."

"Will the Hochs be all right?" Anna asked.

"I don't know. I hope so. It was a noble thing they did. Now the Lord needs to help them."

"He didn't pray for them—only for us," Sister Stoltz said.

"I know. But we've all been praying for them, haven't we?"

And it was true. Anna had prayed for them almost as soon as she had left the house.

The Stoltzes had to change buses once, but when they got off at Mehring Platz, they had no trouble finding the destroyed buildings. When they walked down a back street, however, they realized they wouldn't be able to get to the apartment house without being seen. It was a busy area, and the buildings had been turned into piles of rubble. The Stoltzes would have to climb over the heaps of debris to get to the window Brother Hoch had told them about.

"We'll have to wait until dark," Brother Stoltz said. "Keep walking, and we'll find a place to wait."

In all the hurry and fear, Anna had not taken any joy in being outside. She began now, however, to notice the sounds of the city, even birds, and the movement of her hair in the breeze. She wanted to enjoy all that, but she felt vulnerable out here, and she wondered about every person she passed. Was she being watched? Followed?

"We'll need some food," Sister Stoltz said. "We can't be going in and out of that basement very often."

"Yes. That's right," Brother Stoltz said. "I have enough money for now, but . . ."

For the first time, the true enormity of their situation struck Anna. They had run from immediate trouble, but there was nothing ahead. A place to hide for the moment really solved no problems at all. They had to eat, and if they couldn't find another family to help them, they would need to work. But they could never do that without identification papers. The other fear was that the Gestapo might put all this together and realize who the so-called Hofmann family really was.

But the Stoltzes kept doing what they had to do. They bought bread and cheese and a few other things, and they waited in a park for the long June evening to pass. Anna lay on the grass and let the angling sun warm her face, but with every sound her eyes popped open. Sister Stoltz kept asking what they would do next, how long they would stay in the basement, but her husband only repeated, time and again, "I don't know right now, Frieda. I'm trying to think everything through."

Anna looked at her parents and seemed to see them clearly for the first time in a long time—here in the sun, in this setting. They had aged so much lately. Her father was a broken man. He was not yet fifty, but the lines in his face were deep, and his thin hair had grayed a great deal in the last year. He still had those powerful shoulders, the bulk in his chest, but his face looked delicate, sad, not forceful at all. Even the intensity of his blue eyes—that were so much like Anna's—seemed to have diminished. And Mother, who had such a lovely, sculptured face, looked pale and thin. The skin around her eyes had tightened, it seemed, and her mouth was drawn at the corners. She was hardly the same person Anna had known all her life.

By the time the sun finally set, Anna was eager to get to the hiding place. What she hoped was that they could all find a decent place to sleep. She wanted to escape all her worries for a time before she had to deal with the next day.

The Stoltzes walked back to the building. Twice they approached and then kept going when they saw people passing by. Finally, they climbed over the rubble from the back and found the open window to the basement. It was only a small window and awkward, especially for Brother Stoltz. Everyone helped him, but twisting his body was agonizing. Still, he made it, and once inside, it seemed unlikely that anyone would find them, at least for the night.

The problem was, they had no light, and it was difficult to find their way about. Peter went exploring, and after a minute or so, he called out, "There's a bed in here but no bedding."

"It's all right. It's not cold," Brother Stoltz called back.

"It's covered with dust or dirt—or something."

"Yes. That's only to be expected. We can turn the mattress over. Check the other rooms. Are there other beds?"

Anna heard Peter moving about again. "This is the kitchen," he called. "I think there's only one bedroom."

"We must be in a living room," Brother Stoltz said. "There must be some furniture—a couch perhaps."

"Let me find what's here," Anna said, and she stepped carefully forward, reaching out. In a moment, her legs bumped something low and hard—a coffee table. She felt around it and then found the couch. She followed it along and found a rather stiff chair at the end. "There's a couch and chair," she finally said. "They're not very soft. And they're covered with filth."

"It doesn't matter," Brother Stoltz said.

But Anna could hear how strained his voice was. And Sister Stoltz was silent. Anna knew she was disheartened. All the same, Anna tried to wipe away the dust from the chair, and then she came for her father and led him there. "It's not a good chair for sleeping," she told him.

"I'll manage. Your mother can sleep here on the couch. You and Peter lie down on the bed. Check the closets. Maybe there is something we can put over us."

And so everyone made the best of things. But when Anna lay down without a pillow and pulled an old coat over her, she felt as though she were hiding in some dismal cave. She had no idea what was around her, or whether the building was safe. She remained stiff and scared and wide awake. Out in the living room she could hear her father shifting in his chair and breathing with strain—not the peaceful sounds of a man sleeping.

All the same, when morning came and light filtered into the basement from three little windows, the place didn't seem quite so bad. Anna got up early and explored a little—found that the apartment had been cleared for the most part. Only the larger pieces of furniture remained. At least the toilet worked all right, and an old broom in a closet would help.

Brother Stoltz also got up early. He began searching through the rooms. He went to a door and found that it opened into the hallway. "Anna, come with me," he whispered.

Anna followed him into the hall and then up the stairs. "I want to get into the apartments above us."

"They're destroyed, aren't they?"

"Not entirely. Some of the walls are still standing on the first floor."

"But what—"

"Let's just see whether we can find anything that might help us."

The entrances to the building, both front and back, were blocked by rubble, but inside, the stairs were clear, and Anna and her father could get through to the two apartments on the next level. Anna assumed that her father was looking for bedding, kitchen utensils, and such things, and that did make sense, but she wondered how dangerous it might be to enter the rooms. What they found at the first level was that the doors to both apartments were jammed.

"This one is open a little, but it's all twisted," she said. "I can't move it. Things might fall if we force it open."

"Is there anything we could pry with?" Brother Stoltz asked as he looked around.

"Would that be safe?"

"I don't know. But we have to chance it."

Anna couldn't imagine that anything in the apartment could be worth that much, but she told her father, "There's a broom downstairs. I'll go get that."

Anna hurried downstairs and brought the broom back, and Brother Stoltz was able to budge the door a little with it, but not enough to get inside. "Stand back a moment," he said. "Let me try something."

He raised his foot and slammed it into the door, and it moved a little more. But Brother Stoltz had to stand and breathe for a time—overcome by the pain—before he could try again. "Oh, Papa, don't," Anna said. But he repeated the kick several times and then finally was able to squeeze his way in.

Anna followed him. She saw immediately that the apartment was in worse shape than she had expected. Most of the place had collapsed. Only the living-room walls were still standing. Brother Stoltz glanced around, and then he walked to a little desk in the corner. "Anna," he said, "see whether that closet door will open. Check to see what's inside. But be careful."

Anna had already noticed two little pillows on the couch that would be helpful. The couch was better than the one downstairs, too, but there was no way to get it out, and she wasn't about to suggest that anyone sleep up here. She tried the door on the closet and found that it opened. Inside, she saw boxes and old shoes, even some clothes. She could sort through those things later, but they weren't of any immediate help.

"Anna, come here," Brother Stoltz said from across the room. "I've found something."

She walked to her father. He was standing by the desk. He held up a little booklet, and suddenly Anna realized it was a set of identification papers. And now she saw that her father's eyes were full of tears. "In the night," he said, "I fell asleep for a time. And I had a dream. I was looking in a drawer, like this one." He pointed to the desk. "I found a man's papers. And now, here they are. God is still helping us."

Anna took the papers from her father. She looked at the picture of the man, read his name. "Horst Niemeyer. But he doesn't look like you, Papa."

"I know. I'll have to figure out what to do. But it's something. And God led me to it, so it must have a purpose."

"Won't Herr Niemeyer have applied for new papers by now?"

"If he was back there, in one of the bedrooms, he might not

have made it. His whole family must have been lost. President Hoch said that many died in this building."

Anna felt a chill go through her. "Let's go," she said.

"Yes." But he touched her forearm. "Anna, I don't know why things happen the way they do. But I had the dream, and the papers were here. I'm not going to ask the other questions. I'm merely going to trust in the Lord—even though it's not my usual way of doing things. You do the same."

Anna nodded, and then the two walked back to the basement apartment.

CHAPTER

5

Bobbi arrived in San Francisco on a train that was jammed with troops. She got in three hours late, at two in the morning. She had tried with little success to sleep sitting up, and she had put up with a lot of soldiers, most of them younger than she was, who were away from home for the first time and trying to act like big-time lady's men. Flirting was one thing, but some of these fellows were obnoxious, and once they got drunk, they became vulgar. Bobbi was worn out by the time she managed to get a cab and then check in at the St. Francis Hotel, with the night almost gone.

But she had another full day before her ship departed, and so she slept until almost ten and was only then awakened by the phone ringing. Bobbi picked up the receiver and heard a girlish voice say, "Excuse me. Is this Barbara Thomas?"

"Yes."

"My name is Afton Story. I'm one of the nurses going to Hawaii—like you."

"Oh. Thanks for calling. Are you here in the St. Francis?"

"Yes. We all are. Twelve of us. Or at least we all will be, once everyone gets in. I noticed on the list that you're from Utah. Does that mean you're LDS?"

"Yes, I am."

"Oh, golly, that's good. I am too. I'm so glad to know another Mormon girl will be in the hospital with me over there."

Afton sounded awfully young, and maybe she would turn out to be too dependent, but right now Bobbi was very pleased. "Oh, that's good," she said. "Do you want to have lunch—and then maybe look around town a little?"

"That's just exactly what I was going to ask you. Gosh, you don't know how relieved I am."

And so the two young women agreed to meet. Bobbi took a hot bath and then did what she could with her hair. She had fine hair—sort of blond, a little red, and always rather difficult. She never looked in a mirror without thinking that she was not very glamorous. She had a smattering of freckles across her nose, and round, gray-blue eyes. This morning, when she looked at herself she could think only that she was the same Bobbi but that *everything* else had changed. She had cried when she told her family good-bye, but she had also been excited. Now, alone in this hotel and knowing that she might not see her family for at least two years, she was suddenly homesick. The grand adventure of getting away from Salt Lake—which she had longed for—suddenly seemed far less appealing than she had expected.

And so she hurried—and tried not to think. She put on a civilian dress, not the white, Class-A navy officer's uniform she had traveled in, and she found her comfortable loafers in her suitcase. Then she headed down to the coffee shop, fifteen minutes early. As it turned out, Afton was a little early herself. She was a nice-looking girl, with dark, rather short hair and an especially engaging, wide smile. The two walked to a table and sat down, only to notice soon after that everyone else was waiting to be seated. The girls were embarrassed, and they laughed at themselves, but immediately, Afton said, "Oh, Barbara, I'm having a hard time. I got in yesterday, and you're the first person I've said a word to. I've never been away from home." She giggled—but she was clearly trying not to cry. "Gee whiz. I can't believe I'm such a boob."

"I know what you mean," Bobbi said. "I was doing okay until it hit me I wouldn't see my family for *years*."

"Oh, don't say that. That's what I've been thinking." Afton was definitely crying now, but she was still trying gamely to smile. "You can't die of homesickness, can you?"

About then a waitress in a white dress showed up at the table. She had a glass coffee urn in her hand. "Coffee?" she said, and she reached for Afton's cup.

"No!" Afton said, sounding almost alarmed.

The waitress jerked her hand back. "Excuse me," she said.

"Oh, I'm sorry. I just meant I didn't want any."

The waitress, a woman of fifty or so with severe, thin lips, took a long look at Afton as if to say, "What is wrong with you, girl?" But she only said, "Then what would you like?"

"Oh . . . uh . . . do you have root beer?"

"No, ma'am. We have coffee, tea, milk, or Coca-Cola."

"What about lemonade?"

"No, ma'am. Coffee, tea, milk, or Coca-Cola." The woman let her eyes drift away, as if to say, "Why do I have to put up with this?"

"Oh, let's see. Could I just have some ice water then?"

"Of course." The waitress looked at Bobbi.

"The same for me."

Without a word the woman turned and walked away, and Bobbi and Afton looked at each other and laughed. "Oh, Barbara, I'm such a hick," Afton said.

"Call me Bobbi, okay?"

"Oh. I'm sorry."

"You don't need to apologize," Bobbi said. "You didn't know."

"I'm sorry." And then her face brightened. "Golly, do I do that too much?"

Both were laughing again. And they were already friends.

Bobbi sensed without putting the thought into words that Afton was a godsend, someone to get her through this experience.

And so the two ate club sandwiches—with ice water—and they talked about their backgrounds. Afton was from Mesa, Arizona, the sixth of nine children. Her father was a dairy farmer—and a bishop. Two of Afton's older brothers had recently joined the army and were still in training. Bobbi got the impression that the Storys were prosperous enough but that the depression had been a strain on them, as it had been on almost everyone.

"My mom sold eggs and even worked part-time at a cannery in the fall each year," Afton said, "just to help me get through nursing school. After all that, she about croaked when I told her I was joining the navy. But I felt like I was going to end up staying home my whole life—and everyone I knew was leaving."

"What about boyfriends?"

"Oh, Bobbi, I'm so stupid. I'm in love with this dumb boy who treats me like I'm a fence post or a tree stump or something. And now he just got drafted. I don't think I'm ever going to get married."

Bobbi didn't think Afton was exactly over the hill, but she understood her worry. So many young men were going off to war, and so many girls were being left behind. A lot of them probably wouldn't find anyone; Bobbi had already accepted that, and she feared the worst. But she didn't want to think about it. "What are we going to see today?" she asked.

"I guess we sail under the new bridge—the Golden Gate—in the morning, and that's the one thing I wanted to see for sure while I was here. I've never seen the ocean either, but I think we'll see lots of water in the next few days."

"Well, let's just start walking, and we'll see what there is to see."

And so the girls finished their sandwiches, and Bobbi added

a second dime to her tip when she saw that Afton hadn't remembered to leave anything. Then they strolled outside into the cool June day. They wandered through downtown San Francisco, in and out of stores and into China Town. Later, they caught a trolley to Fisherman's Wharf. Afton complained about the smell of the place, but they ate fried shrimp at a little outdoor cafe, and finally, both being very cold, decided to go to a show.

They saw "My Gal Sal," a musical, starring Rita Hayworth and Victor Mature. Bobbi found it rather silly, but it was in Technicolor, which was exciting, and it was enough fun to take Bobbi's mind off her homesickness. They had come in too late to catch the first part of the movie, so they stayed to see what they had missed. Before the feature started again, however, the Fox Movietone News came on, with films of the Battle of Midway. The crowd cheered at the pictures of smoking, sinking Japanese carriers. Four big flattops had been destroyed, but the *Yorktown*, an American carrier, had also been sunk. Lowell Thomas, in his penetrating voice, explained that the advantage the Japanese had established over the American navy at Pearl Harbor had now been reversed. Bobbi did feel good about that, she supposed, but the destruction was so ugly. Afton leaned toward Bobbi when she saw scenes of wounded men being transferred off the *Yorktown*—before it could roll over and go down. "I wonder if some of those boys will end up at our hospital," she said.

That made it all real to Bobbi. This was not just a "great victory," with little pictures of burning ships on the front page of the *Deseret News*. Thousands of actual men had died, both American and Japanese.

The next news segment was about the prisoners of war in the Philippines. Bobbi felt her breath catch; she was almost sure she didn't want to see this. There were no actual films— except a few of the battle before the surrender of the American and Filipino forces—but on a map, the march of the prisoners was shown with a moving black line up the east coast of the peninsula, and Lowell Thomas described rumors of the "hellish" treatment the prisoners had received. "Hundreds, perhaps thousands," he said, were reported by Filipino contacts to be "dead from starvation and disease." He called it the "Bataan death march."

Bobbi put her hand to her forehead. She suddenly felt sick to her stomach. Alex had hinted at some of this, but he had played it down. Thomas made it sound much worse. All Bobbi could think was that Wally wasn't the sort to hold up under that kind of deprivation.

Bobbi had already told Afton about Wally, so she wasn't surprised when Afton took hold of her hand. "Are you okay?" she whispered.

"I guess so," Bobbi said. But she hardly noticed what was happening when the feature came on.

After only a few minutes, Afton said, "Jeemaneze, Bobbi, let's just go. You don't want to watch this now, do you?"

"It's all right," Bobbi said, but mostly she wanted to sit there a little longer and not have to talk.

After a few more minutes Afton said, "This is where we came in. Should we go?"

Bobbi got up, and the two walked outside. Out on the street, Afton put her arm around Bobbi's back. "How are you doing?" she asked.

"I'm okay," Bobbi said. "It's just hard to think of my brother being *starved*, of all things."

"I hate the Japs so much!" Afton said. "They don't have to treat people like that."

It was exactly what Bobbi had been thinking, but not what she wanted to feel. Just minutes ago she had experienced a real sense of compassion for the Japanese sailors who had gone to the bottom of the sea. She didn't want to hate anyone, but she had been fighting with the impulse to hate the Japanese since the day Wally had been taken prisoner. "Wally would never hurt anyone," she finally managed to say. "He only went into the air corps to do something exciting. I don't think he thought at all about going to war."

"I hate this war," Afton said. "I just lost a cousin who was only nineteen. He was on the *Lexington,* in that battle in the Coral Sea—just a few weeks ago. A lot of the sailors got off, but my uncle thinks my cousin was killed in one of the explosions. He was kind of a rebellious boy, and he had gotten away from the Church. But that only makes it worse. My aunt and uncle felt like he was starting to straighten things out in his life—and now he's gone."

San Francisco was under a blackout; all outside lighting had been turned off, and the streets were dark. With so few cars moving about, the city was also quiet. Bobbi could hear the echo of hers and Afton's footsteps. She wasn't frightened, but she felt the gloom of the darkness. She wanted to get back to the hotel and go to sleep. Or just go home.

"Wally's healthy," Bobbi finally said, "but he isn't tough. He doesn't stick with things very well. If the Japs are brutal with him, he might not be able to take it."

"Maybe he'll find his strength when he has to."

"Maybe. But he's not very religious either, and I don't know whether he'll get stronger or be destroyed." Bobbi thought about that for a moment and then added, "But why would the Japs not feed them? I don't understand that."

"They're not human, that's why. They'll commit suicide rather than be taken prisoner. And they do awful things to . . ." She stopped. "I'm sorry. I shouldn't be talking about that."

Bobbi didn't have to hear the rest. She knew the stories of Japanese torture and depredation. Again she felt the hatred well up in her, the anger. It was so easy to talk about loving your enemy in a Sunday School class, but these people were hurting her little brother.

On the following morning Bobbi and Afton met the other nurses on board the ship. About half of them had already been serving in the nurse's corp, and they were merely transferring to Pearl Harbor. The others, like Bobbi, were new to the navy and not very clear about military protocol. They had each received a little orientation but nothing more. What they were told was that they were nurses first and navy officers second, and they would receive most of their training on the job.

Some of the women were in their thirties, and they had the aura of having "been around." Bobbi sensed even a kind of hardness about them. A couple of them smoked, and most of them seemed to lace their talk with more swearing than Bobbi had ever heard from women.

The younger girls, however, seemed more like Afton and Bobbi. A girl from Iowa named Dolores Matthews seemed especially nice, and maybe even a little more frightened of being away from home than Afton was. She had made friends already with a girl from South Carolina named Iris Smithton, however, and Iris seemed much more confident. She was a beautiful girl, with lively eyes and an open, easy way of dealing with people. Bobbi liked a number of the girls, but she knew she would always feel more kinship with Afton.

The ship got under way just after nine. It was pulled slowly into the channel by a pair of tugboats, and then it sailed under the Golden Gate and out to sea. Clouds were hanging over the top of the bridge, which blocked some of the view, but the massive structure looked ethereal, seeming to hang from the clouds. It was fun to pass under it and then to look back toward the city. Bobbi took a few snapshots with her Kodak, and then she turned around and looked at the ocean, which seemed to stretch out forever.

"Gosh, it's so amazing!" Afton kept saying. "Sort of like the desert, only gray."

By then Bobbi had discovered the reality of traveling on a large luxury liner with a couple of thousand soldiers on board—and a couple of *dozen* women. To Bobbi, it was not the paradise that some of the other nurses seemed to think it was.

She and Afton couldn't walk ten steps on deck without hearing catcalls. Just as Bobbi had experienced on the train, most of the men seemed to have lost all sense of propriety. They came on strong—suggestive if not outright insulting. The draft, so far, had only extended to the age of twenty, but many younger boys were signing up, and many of these guys seemed awfully young. Bobbi had planned to do some sunning and swimming, but she and Afton decided quickly that they didn't dare put on their swimming suits—to be stared at by thousands of eyes. They did go out to the pool in their uniforms, where they took their jackets off and sat on lounge chairs.

Almost immediately, a pair of soldiers, neither one seeming to be out of his teens, walked over to them. "Hey," one of them said, "how ya'll doin'?"

"We're all fine," Afton said.

"Oh, now wait a minute," the boy said. "Are you making fun of me just because I'm from the South?" He was a tightly built, rather short boy, with a natural, nice smile. Bobbi noticed immediately, however, that his teeth were stained from smoking.

Afton sounded entirely too flirtatious when she said, "Would we do that? We have nothing against the South."

"Well, where you from? Pittsburgh, or somewhere like 'at?"

"Nowhere like *at*. I'm from Arizona."

"Is that in the U-nited States, or is that a foreign country?"

"Now you're making fun of yourself," Afton said, and she giggled.

The other fellow was taller, thinner, and his uniform looked newer, the crease still in his trousers. Until now he had seemed to be the quiet one, but a subtle, rather dangerous smile appeared, and he said, "Where are you from?" to Bobbi.

"Salt Lake City," she said.

"Really?" He sounded surprised.

"Yes. Why?"

"I just never knew anyone from there." His speech was giving him away now. He wasn't quite so refined as he had appeared. Bobbi guessed him to be a small-town boy, but not from the South. "I thought only Mormons lived out there."

"No. Other people live there too."

"Yeah. I can see that."

"Well, actually, you can't. I *am* a Mormon. We both are."

Bobbi saw the surprise in both boys' faces. But it was the shorter one who said, "I don't believe that."

"Why not?" Afton asked.

"Mormons don't join the service, from what I've heard. And they wear black clothes all the time."

"We do not," Afton said, and she laughed again.

Both of the soldiers seemed awkward now, apparently beginning to believe Afton, but not sure what to say. The taller one finally said, "I thought Mormons drove around in buggies. And can't have radios or dance or anything like that."

"You're probably thinking of Mennonites," Bobbi said. "Mormons have modern conveniences—as opposed to you backwoods boys. And we do dance. But not with a couple of young enlisted men who only just recently left their mother's apron strings."

The soldiers smiled. The shorter one said, "I think we'd better salute and move on. What do you say, Mike?" The tall one snapped to attention and saluted, and the two walked away laughing.

"Bobbi, why did you scare them off?" Afton said. "That short one was kind of cute."

"For a little boy."

"Well, we had a chance to do some missionary work. We could have told them what we believe."

"Oh, yes. I'm sure they were interested." But more soldiers were walking over, three of them this time. "Let's get out of here," Bobbi said.

So Bobbi and Afton escaped to their cabin, where they thought they might sleep a little, since neither had slept very well the night before. But in the cabin they lay on their beds and talked. "Do you have a boyfriend back home?" Afton asked Bobbi. "Or in the service?"

"No. I was engaged once, but I called it off. And then I got interested in another man, but that didn't work out either."

"Oh, wow. Golly! Two already. I want to hear all about this."

Bobbi didn't go into a lot of detail, but she told about Phil, the tall, dark, handsome—and a little-too-good-to-be-true—fiancé she had broken up with, and then she told about her non-Mormon professor friend, David Stinson, whom she had fallen for completely only to find that the Church was too much of an obstacle between them. He had agreed to join at one point, but not with any real conviction.

"Oh, Bobbi, I can't believe all the stuff you've done. How old are you?"

"I'll be twenty-three in September."

"Well, you're two years older than me, so I guess you've had a little more time. But the only guy I ever cared about doesn't give two hoots for me. Lowell Staley is his name, and he's a swell guy—so good looking he makes my knees go weak—but I've made up my mind to forget all about him."

"Actually, we're lucky, Afton." Bobbi was lying on her back with her head propped up on a pillow. She was looking toward a porthole, and for the first time she was beginning to feel the motion of the ship. She was already thinking that her stomach was less than happy with the experience—even though the ocean was quite smooth. "We're young, and we're heading out on a great adventure. Just think—Hawaii!"

"Gosh, I know. That's what I've been telling myself for about six months now. But I wish I could find a guy to marry. And I don't think we're going to meet a lot of Mormons in Honolulu. I could bring me home a Hawaiian, I guess, but I don't think my parents would be too excited about that."

Bobbi's father had had a chat with her on that very subject

before she had left. "I'm sure there are some fine young men over there—islanders, who have the priesthood and all," Dad had said. "But it does cause problems when people from different races intermarry. I just don't think it's good."

Bobbi hadn't argued the point. This was one time she thought her father was probably right. "Let's forget about boys for now, Afton," Bobbi said. "Let's just enjoy ourselves. We can be married all our lives—raising kids and cleaning house—but this is our one chance to do something most girls never even think of."

"Bobbi, that's right. Goll-darn it, I just have to start thinking that way."

But Afton didn't sound very convinced, nor was Bobbi entirely sure that she believed her own words. She still thought a great deal about David, and she wondered whether she would ever meet a man who was that exciting—and LDS. David had been impulsive and full of fire, almost scary at times, but he had loved to talk to her, genuinely loved to be with her. And when he had kissed her, she had experienced a passion she hadn't thought herself capable of. But she wasn't sorry about the way things had worked out. She wanted to meet someone who would marry her in the temple.

The voyage lasted five days and was actually rather disappointing. A little storm came up, and while Bobbi didn't get deathly ill, she never felt much like eating, either. Upon the nurses' arrival in Honolulu, a bus was waiting to pick them up. Lieutenant Kallas, the woman who greeted them, seemed rather hard, and she was certainly all business. She directed the girls onto the bus and then said almost nothing on the way to the base.

Bobbi twisted her neck in all directions, and what she saw was even better than she had expected—all the exotic flowers, the feel of the air. But the bus pulled onto the base at Pearl Harbor and then stopped in front of a long, white, two-story building that looked like a barracks. Lieutenant Kallas stood up and announced in a barking voice, "I've kept the same room-mate assignments you had on the ship. That's just simpler for right now, so don't request any changes. We'll be meeting at 1500, and we'll have plenty to talk about, but just let me say this for now: You're in a war, not on a vacation. You will work long hours. If you think you're going to have a nice holiday here, think again. When you get off shift, you'll be ready for bed. Trust me on that."

She stepped off the bus, and then the new arrivals followed. As they climbed down, they told the lieutenant their names, and she handed out keys. Inside the building, what Bobbi and Afton found were very simple quarters: two beds, two little closets, two chests of drawers, and a shower room down the hall. Bobbi felt the austerity of the little cube of a room the minute she stepped into it, and she could see that Afton was having even a harder time. "Gee, do you think they'd let me buy a pink bedspread?" she asked, and she tried to laugh.

But the girls unpacked, and then they did have some time to walk outside and look around. In the distance they could see the docks where the famous bombing raid had taken place, but they could see little sign of the damage now. What they did see were bougainvilleas, ginger plants, and hibiscus shrubs. Even the white cinder-block buildings, as uninteresting as those on any military base, seemed exotic in this setting, with ferns and palm trees around them and set off against the deep blue water of the harbor in the distance.

"Do you think it's going to be as bad as that Kallas lady made it sound?" Afton asked.

"I think we'd better learn to call her 'lieutenant' and not 'lady.'"

"I know. I have to remember that. But do you think we'll just work and sleep and nothing else?"

"I don't know. She was probably exaggerating a little—just to get us thinking straight."

"Maybe. But right now I sort of wish I hadn't come here at all."

Bobbi was thinking the same thing.

6

Brother Stoltz took a breath, hesitated, and told himself to relax. Then he opened the door and stepped into the office. A man behind the counter didn't bother to look up for a time, so Brother Stoltz merely stood in front of him and waited. He could see that the man's left arm was gone, and that his coat was pinned beneath the stump. There were so many amputees in Germany these days: men, home from the war, who were perhaps lucky to be alive, but not looking as though they felt very lucky. After most of a minute, the man raised his head. "*Ja, bitte,*" he said.

"My name is Horst Niemeyer. Last winter—about six months ago—my house was bombed. I was badly injured. I'm only just now recovering. I found my identification papers in a desk, but as you see, they were partly burned in the fire. I'm ready to work again now, but I need papers before I can find a job."

Brother Stoltz handed the remnant of the identification papers to the man. Brother Stoltz had carefully burned away most of the picture, leaving only a bit of the chin and the side of the face, and then he had burned off the other edges without destroying the name and personal information. It all looked a little too convenient, and Brother Stoltz fully expected to be challenged, but the clerk didn't seem to care. He glanced only briefly at the pass, and then he got up and walked to a shelf where he chose a *Leitz Ordner*—a two-ring loose-leaf notebook—and brought it back to his desk. The notebook held a thick collection of filed papers, and the man thumbed through it until he found what he was looking for. Then he studied the sheet for a long time before he looked up and said, "According to this, Herr Niemeyer, you are dead." He smiled, ever so little.

"No wonder I feel so terrible," Brother Stoltz said, and he forced himself to smile.

The clerk looked tired, his eyes apathetic, his whole manner ponderous. He was a bulky man, with a heavy jaw, but his voice was soft and flat. "It says that your family died in the bombing raid with you."

"My family did die," Brother Stoltz said softly, "and I was hospitalized for many months. My shoulder was badly broken, and my right knee cap. I still have trouble getting around."

"It's much easier to die than it is to be made alive again," the clerk said. "You will have to talk to my supervisor, and then you will have many forms to fill out."

Brother Stoltz had certainly guessed that. He had gone through the wreckage of the Niemeyer apartment, searching out every bit of information he could find, and he had talked to a man who had known the Niemeyers. He knew the names of the wife and children, had memorized their birth dates, and he knew a smattering of information about Horst, but his knowledge was sketchy at best, and he had no idea what might be required of him. He hoped to take the papers home so he could consider his answers carefully, even search out government documents, if that became necessary.

The clerk removed a sheet of paper from the notebook, and then he walked to the back of the room and opened a door. Brother Stoltz heard a muffled conversation, and then the clerk returned and ushered him behind the counter. "Just sit here," the clerk told Brother Stoltz, and he pointed to a wooden chair by the back office door. "Herr Lindermann will speak to you as soon as he can."

The wait was actually not long—ten minutes at most—but it seemed more like an hour. Brother Stoltz knew that any mistake on his part could lead to a telephone call to the Gestapo.

The man who finally stepped from the office was a little, neat man, and he spoke politely. "Herr Niemeyer, please come in," he said. He turned and stepped back into his office. As he sat down at his desk, he looked up at Brother Stoltz. "I understand that a mistake has been made. Please, sit down."

"Yes, Herr Lindermann. I hope we can correct it. I want to go back to work now."

"You understand, we must be careful in these cases. For all I know, you could be someone trying to create a new identity— perhaps a spy."

"Of course. I understand that. I'm willing to do whatever is necessary. And I certainly understand how a mistake could be made. My wife and children, God rest their souls, were all lost, and I was buried in the wreckage. It was many hours before I was found—unconscious—and taken to a hospital. All was confusion in the neighborhood with so many houses struck. We had no warning that night. No one had gone to the shelters."

"The British have no shame," Herr Lindermann said, with sudden, surprising volume. "They are swine. Bombing civilians, coming at night like thieves."

"I curse them every day of my life."

"Yes, yes. I'm sure you do."

And yet, somehow this all didn't seem quite real. Lindermann was saying the right things, but Brother Stoltz thought he saw a game of cat and mouse coming.

"Tell me, Herr Niemeyer, where are you living now?"

"With friends. I'm very eager to get back to work now so I

can afford a place of my own. And I know the Führer needs workers. I want to do my part."

"You are certainly right that we need workers. So many are gone off to the war. And so many men have lost their lives. But it would help us if you had other papers—birth certificate, or perhaps a notice of your baptism. Have you any of these?"

"I've gone back to my apartment, but all was rubble. I was lucky to find my pass in a demolished desk. But everything else either burned or was buried. I thought of requesting copies of other certificates, but I'm caught in a trap: without my papers, I doubt I can get them. That's why I came here first."

"You are exactly right, Herr Niemeyer. This *is* the problem. Tell me this much. Where were you born?"

"Dresden."

"Are you an educated man, Herr Niemeyer?"

"Not extensively." Brother Stoltz had to be careful. He didn't know exactly what education Horst Niemeyer had received, and Lindermann might have some way of finding out—if he cared. "I wish I had attended a university, but I was never able to."

"What sort of work did you do—before your injury?"

"I worked in an office. I kept books at a small factory—one that made hardware. Door locks, hinges, fancy brass fittings, those sorts of things. It's out of business now."

All this was true. One day Brother and Sister Stoltz had gone out from the basement to buy a few groceries. On the way back, they had met a man who was standing out front, gazing at the damage. The Stoltzes hadn't dared to make their way into the building, and so they had stood and chatted with the man, who said he had once lived in the house. Brother Stoltz had taken the chance to say, "I believe Horst Niemeyer lived here, didn't he?" Then he had managed to ask enough questions to get a general sense of Niemeyer's background.

"I see," Herr Lindermann was saying. And he seemed to be thinking things over. "Can you give me your parents' names, and their parents' names?" he finally asked. "That's the surest way for me to track down your paperwork."

"Yes. Of course. Do you want me to take the paperwork and record all those things. That might be—"

"Yes. That will have to be done. But for the moment, simply give me the names."

This was a test, and Brother Stoltz was pretty sure he had lost the game. He knew Niemeyer's father's name but nothing more. What occurred to him now was that he had to handle this as best he could, tell what lies were necessary, and then get out with his life. Getting papers this way had probably been a silly thing to hope for. But he looked Lindermann in the eye, and he recited names, choosing the first names of some of his own uncles and aunts, merely so he would not forget what he had said.

Lindermann wrote the names down, but when he had done so, he pushed the papers aside, and he took a long look at Brother Stoltz. Finally, he said, "Herr Niemeyer, I'm going to trust you. You may be someone else. You may be a Jew. I don't know. But all is in chaos in this city, and I have only one assistant out front, as you see. I could send him out to track all this down, but it would take him at least a full day, and I can't spare him that long."

"I assure you that—"

"It's all right. I don't mean to insult you. And I must admit, I have something in mind that might help both of us." He waited, and considered again, while Brother Stoltz tried to breathe as normally as he could with so much anxiety raging inside. "You said something important a few minutes ago. You said the Führer needs workers. And more to the point, I need help. If I see to it that your forms are processed quickly, and you get your papers, would you come to work for me? I have approval to hire someone; I simply haven't been able to find a person to do the work."

Brother Stoltz nodded and hesitated. He was trying to

think this all through. Would he be in future danger? Would this be a good place for him? He wasn't sure, but he hardly dared to turn the man down, given the offer. Brother Stoltz nodded a second time and said, "Yes. That might work out. This doesn't strike me as a job I might dream about, but it's office work—with no heavy lifting—and that's what I need. Yes, Herr Lindermann, I would be willing to work here."

"Good. Fill out the papers. If you can't get everything, it will be all right. Don't be running off to Dresden to track down birth certificates. Fill out what you can and I'll take care of the rest."

"Thank you, Herr Lindermann. That's a big help to me."

"I'll tell you, Horst, if I may call you that."

"Yes. Of course."

"Right now, I don't care much if your real name is Churchill or Roosevelt. Every day there are new displaced people in this city, and there is simply no keeping track of everyone. The paperwork piles up deeper all the time, and I can't do much about it. If you can move some things along for us here, you will lift a great burden from my shoulders."

"I'm sure I can do that. I'm happy to do it."

Lindermann stood up. "It's Thursday. Yes?"

"Yes."

"Bring the papers back tomorrow. I'll put you to work on Monday. Can you do that?"

"Yes. Of course."

Lindermann, for the first time, was actually smiling, showing a row of crowded, crooked teeth. "Oh . . . and don't misunderstand. I was only joking about hiring a spy. You understand that, don't you?"

"Yes. Certainly." Brother Stoltz laughed.

"You're not Jewish. I can see that. And I can't think what else could be wrong with you. A case like yours is really quite common. I'm forced to trust people sometimes. I don't know what else to do. You won't repeat anything I've said here, now will you?"

"Of course not. We are under attack by a vicious enemy. And we need to concentrate on that—not turn on each other."

"Exactly. Very well put, Horst. That is precisely the way I feel."

It was all a code. Many Germans were weary of the war—and even seemed to recognize how it would turn out, in the end, and yet they knew what they had to say. "Let's make the best of this," Herr Lindermann seemed to be saying. "Let's help each other out here, and let's both survive."

"I assure you, I am not a spy," Brother Stoltz said. "And surely not a Jew."

"Certainly. I'll see you tomorrow then." He reached out and shook Brother Stoltz's hand.

On the bus, on the way back to the bombed-out apartment house where his family was waiting, Brother Stoltz began to realize the full measure of his blessing. He had seen, while talking to Herr Lindermann, that God was opening another door, but now it occurred to him that he might—once he had worked a while in the office—be able to make papers for his wife and children. If he could create a Niemeyer family, all with proper identification, his wife and Anna could get work. He could rent an apartment, and his family could live like other people.

Brother Stoltz got off the bus and walked down the back alley toward the destroyed building where he and his family had been hiding for over a week. He watched for a chance and then hurried through the pile of debris, where the Stoltzes had cleared a little pathway. Then he climbed a pile of bricks onto the first-floor landing, which Peter had worked hard to open, and he made his way down the stairs and into the basement. "Frieda," he called as he stepped into the dark apartment. "It's me. I have good news."

His wife and children were in the living room, where they

received a little light from a window. They all stood up as he entered the room, and he could see more anxiousness than happiness in their faces. It was hard to trust in good news these days. The last week had been tedious in this dreary, dusty basement, with too little light and nothing to read, nothing to do—and every day the fear that bulldozers might show up to push all the debris aside. One day President Hoch had called down through the window and visited them for a few minutes. He had brought some money and offered some encouragement, but he had little idea what to advise them to do. He had even been skeptical about Brother Stoltz's plan to attempt to get identification papers. It seemed a dangerous move.

Brother Stoltz, of course, had considered all that, but every other approach seemed unfeasible. Going on the run again—without papers—would keep them in constant danger, and trying to get out of Germany was very dangerous.

The best news from President Hoch had simply been that he was all right. He had told Herr Biedemann that he had made a mistake to take the "Hofmanns" in. They had claimed to be misplaced people, and he had pitied them, but he had no idea they had any reason to be on the run.

The Gestapo agents who returned with Biedemann had made no accusations, didn't try to harm President Hoch, even seemed to accept his story about being knocked down, his shirt torn, but one of the agents had asked, "Did you ever hear these people use any other names?" And then, "Did they ever mention anything about Frankfurt?"

President Hoch had given nothing away, and the agents had mentioned nothing about the Mormon church. Perhaps they knew nothing about that. What they knew, of course, was that a family of four, with a son and daughter, was on the run for some reason. Perhaps by now Herr Kellerman had received that much information.

"This should be our last night here," Brother Stoltz

announced to his family. "We can start to live like normal people."

"Heinrich, how can we ever do that?" his wife asked, sounding skeptical.

"I'm getting papers. Tomorrow. And a job. I'll begin work on Monday. We have enough money to stay in some sort of guest house for a week or two until I get my first paycheck. And then we can rent an apartment, if we can find one."

Brother Stoltz could see that it was all too much to believe. Anna was so much like himself; she was running all this through her mind, considering the dangers and possibilities before she embraced the idea with full enthusiasm.

"Tell us what happened," Peter said. He was clearly the one most eager to escape from the boring existence they had lived for so long.

Brother Stoltz sat down on the old couch where his wife had been sleeping for the past week, and he rehearsed the story in complete detail. When he was finished, Sister Stoltz was crying. "The Lord has done this for us," she said. "He keeps looking out for us."

"Yes. I believe it's so," Brother Stoltz said. "And think of the possibilities. Once I've been in the office for a time, perhaps I can make up papers for all of us. Then we could wait out the war without much fear. Peter could go back to school. The rest of us could work."

"What if Kellerman is looking for us?" Anna said, and he saw the fear that was lingering in her eyes, even though she clearly wanted to be happy about this news.

"I doubt he could find a way to track us now."

"But if he knows we're in Berlin, he would have a way to focus his search. He might have pictures of us circulated, or he might come here himself. If we come out of hiding, perhaps we'll be noticed."

"It's possible, Anna. I don't know. But things have changed in the past year. With cities being bombed all across Germany, there is so much confusion. I don't think the Gestapo would place us very high on their list of priorities."

Anna sat down next to her father. "Maybe," she said quietly, "but I've thought about this so often. I can't imagine that Kellerman will ever give up searching for us. I cut him so badly. Every time he looks in the mirror, he will think of me—and he'll keep trying to find us."

Brother Stoltz didn't want that kind of talk. This was a day when things had finally taken a better turn. "Dear Anna," he said, and he put his arm around her shoulders. She seemed far too thin these days, even though he was sometimes stunned to realize all over again how beautiful she was—and how much she looked like the woman he had married so long ago. "This is difficult for all of us. But we should have been dead a long time ago, and we have survived. I was once a skeptic about such things, as you know, but I agree with your mother. The Lord is looking out for us."

"I know. It seems so. But if Kellerman comes to Berlin, would he come to the office where you're going to work? Wouldn't that be a place he might check, to see whether anyone like us had been trying to get papers?"

"It's possible."

"What if you were sitting there at the desk and he walked in? What would you do?"

"Maybe I can disguise myself. Wear a mask." He laughed.

"I'm serious. What would you do?"

"I don't know, Anna. But I don't think it's very likely."

Still, the joy was gone from the room, as everyone recognized that Anna had a point, that the office had its advantages but also, clearly, its dangers.

"Papa, can't we get out of Germany somehow?" Anna asked. "If we get papers, isn't there a way to do that?"

"I don't know. It's something worth looking into. But if we were caught at the border, we would be considered traitors. We could all be put to death."

"I know. But if we got out, we could live again."

"Yes. And you could go to America and marry your Elder Thomas."

Anna nodded. "Yes. You know that's what I want to do. But we don't even know where he is. He may be fighting in the war by now. It's even possible that something has happened to him."

Brother Stoltz had thought of all these things. He nodded and said, "I know, Anna. But I think things are going to work out all right somehow. For now, let's be thankful we're getting out of this basement."

Peter laughed. "I'm happy enough for all of us," he said. Anna took a long look at Peter. It suddenly struck her that all the confinement was a greater loss to Peter than to any of them. These were his years to explore and discover who he was, and he was spending them hidden away with his family.

7

Alex was sitting on his bunk. He was leaning forward, his elbows on his knees, and he knew that he would soon reach down and unlace his boots. For the moment, however, he didn't have the energy. It was seven o'clock in the evening, miserably hot and humid in the barracks on this July evening, and he and the men in his company—E Company, 506th Regiment—had been going strong since four that morning. Camp Toccoa was miserable, and the combination boot camp/jump school was a sadistic idea. Airborne men were supposed to come out of their training ten times tougher than anyone else, and that meant the training had to be ten times harder—or at least that's what Sergeant Willard, the drill sergeant, claimed.

When Alex had stepped off the bus the first day, he had looked at Mount Currahee, which loomed over the camp. He had heard one of the other recruits refer to it as a mountain, and Alex had joked about it being nothing more than a hill, but Curtis Bentley, a fellow from Georgia whom Alex had met on the bus, had told him, "My guess is, they won't let it go to waste—no matter what you call it. We'll probably have to run to the top of that dang thing to graduate."

That had sounded like a reasonable guess, but the next

morning—at four—the climb up the mountain was used for *initiation*, not graduation. The men double-timed to the top on the first morning—or at least most of them did. Some passed out and had to be hauled back in ambulances. Others dropped out, and that meant they were dismissed from the paratroopers on just their second day.

Since then, in three weeks of training, Alex's company had made the run every other day or so, but today's climb had been cruel beyond belief. That morning the "sarge" had told them they got a day off—no running. Everyone was overjoyed, and they ate a huge lunch of all the spaghetti and meatballs they could eat. Then Sergeant Willard calmly announced, "Our orders have changed. We're running after all."

Needless to say, the men vomited spaghetti all the way to the top of Mount Currahee. Several didn't make it—and were dropped from the company. Alex knew what Captain Morehead—the Company Commander who had given the order—was up to. He wanted to break all the men who *could* be broken. E company was going to stay together as a battle unit, and every mission they undertook would be murderous. The men had to be ready for anything.

After his dirty trick, Morehead stood before the men and gave a speech about Currahee. He said it was an Indian name that meant "we stand alone." He explained in lofty language that airborne soldiers had to stand alone—together. It was all very pretty, but Alex wondered whether the biggest challenge wouldn't be to stand against a weasel like Morehead.

Alex had felt sick from the run, had continued to feel that way during the afternoon training. It was while he was eating dinner that the exhaustion had really hit him. Now, sitting in this ugly, bare-wood building, with naked light bulbs for lighting, he found himself wondering why he was here. He could have avoided the draft; he had had the perfect excuse.

"Hey, what's the matter, old man?" someone was yelling.

Alex looked up, and then he smiled. He was staring at the

belt buckle of a kid from Rhode Island—Alberto Rizzardi. "Congratulations, Al," Alex said. "You just spoke an entire sentence without swearing."

So Al let out a blue streak—a whole string of profane epithets—and then said, "How does that sound to a missionary? Hear any words you recognized?"

Alex didn't respond. He finally did reach down and untie his laces. It wasn't dark yet, but Alex wanted to stretch out and go to sleep as soon as possible.

"Leave that man alone," one of the southern boys yelled. "He's missing all those wives he left behind in Utah."

Again, Alex didn't honor the remark with a response, didn't look around, but he reached down and pulled his boots off.

"Ain't that right, Thomas? Ain't you used to beddin' down with some of them wives every night?"

Alex knew that the guy who was doing the talking was a moose of a fellow named Duncan. Everyone in airborne training had to pass an intelligence exam as well as a rigorous physical, but Alex couldn't imagine how this guy had passed either one.

"Duncan," Rizzardi said, "that's not a nice way to talk to a missionary. And a college boy. Be a little more respectful."

Alex wished he had never admitted so much about himself. The first day, on the bus to Toccoa, the new recruits had been asking each other about their backgrounds. Alex had simply told some of them what he had been doing the past few years. He hadn't thought it would create such a problem.

"Hey, I do respect him," Duncan roared. "I've gotta respect a bull who can take care of a whole herd of cows. I just wish I could change places with him."

Alex stood and turned around. "Duncan, that's enough," he said, and he surprised himself with the power in his voice.

Duncan walked toward him, grinning. He was a huge kid, with shoulders like bags of grain. If he lost another twenty pounds, as he surely would at this pace, he was going to look like the picture of Goliath in Alex's children's Bible. But Alex was no small-fry himself.

"Golly gee, Thomas, can't you take a little guff from one of your good buddies?" Duncan walked too close, clearly trying to intimidate Alex with his size.

"That stuff isn't funny, Duncan. My great-grandfather was a polygamist, and I'm not ashamed of that. He was a fine man."

This got a surprisingly different reaction from what Alex expected. Most of the men laughed.

Duncan continued to grin, with teeth that were deeply stained from tobacco chewing. "So your grandpa had all the fun, and all you get is the guff? Is that how it is, Thomas?"

"Just lay off, okay?" Already the anger was gone and embarrassment was setting in. How could these guys ever understand plural marriage? It was useless to respond to such stupid talk. Alex stepped back to his bunk and sat down.

Duncan walked away. "I ought to paste ol' Thomas in the kisser," he said, "just for talking to me like that. But I wouldn't want to ruin his pretty face."

Alex pulled off his fatigues. The back of his shirt was already soaked through with sweat, even though he had showered an hour before. He lay back on his bunk, and for at least the tenth time, he thought seriously of dropping out of airborne. On that first afternoon in this barracks, Sergeant Willard had walked in with Lieutenant Summers, the platoon leader. All the new recruits had jumped to attention, and Summers had walked by all of them—looking them over, sizing them up. Then he had barked, "At ease," and Alex had had his first chance to get a good look at the guy. He was tall and lean and deeply tanned, no older than Alex, and he was wearing starched khakis with silver airborne wings over his left pocket. "Men," he had shouted, although he was practically on top of them, "you have made a *big* mistake. You have come to the wrong place. No one in his right mind wants to be a paratrooper."

He walked along, looking into each man's face. "We are the shock troops of the army. We get the *worst*, most *dangerous* duty. We get dropped behind enemy lines and then fight our way out. The odds are, you're going to die in this war if you stick with us, and I invite you, right now, to drop out and go back to a straight-leg unit. If you have any brains, raise your hand right now, and I'll send you away—no dishonor at all."

Airborne troops wore jump boots, not shoes, and they tucked their pants inside those boots and then bloused them out. Everyone recognized a paratrooper, and every paratrooper looked down on regular infantry soldiers. That was clear enough, and Alex knew that Summers was actually selling an image. But the recruiter had told Alex he would be safer to fight with a crack company, and now the lieutenant was saying the opposite. Alex wondered which was true. All the talk that Alex's German background would earn him an intelligence assignment had been forgotten, never so much as mentioned since Alex had arrived.

"All right, no hands up so far," Summers said, and he lowered his voice a little. "In the next three days Sergeant Willard is going to put you through the wringer. You're going to hope to die and get it over with rather than wait for some Kraut to shoot you. You'll double-time everywhere you go, and you'll keep going until you think you can't go any more, and that will be your warm-up. If you think I'm blowing smoke, just wait until tomorrow morning."

He paused and looked around. "When things get bad, just remember that you do have a way out. Just quit. Any time of the day or night—for three days—just say, 'I've had enough,' and you're on the next bus out of here. No problem. We'll be glad to see you go. But I have one piece of very important advice."

He paused, and then he walked all the way back along the row of men, who were standing at the foot of their bunks, by their wooden footlockers. He stopped at the end of the long building, and he whispered, "Here's the secret. Quit now. Or quit tomorrow. Quit in these first three days. I beg you to do that. But don't come to me for a quit slip after that. If you do, you become . . . listen to me carefully . . . you become a *dog*." Suddenly he shouted again. "Did you hear that? We put you in the dog unit. We'll dress you in blue denim fatigues, and you'll do KP all day every day. You'll serve food to the men, but you won't be allowed to look them in the eye."

He paced to the middle of the room. "Okay. Let's see the hands of all those who want out."

Not a hand went up. But Alex was thinking. All this was insane. He might go in and quit tomorrow—not in front of all these guys, but quietly, when he could catch a bus to some other boot camp. He didn't need all this gung-ho stuff.

True to the lieutenant's promise, the next day was the worst of Alex's life. Twenty-six men from the company either failed to make it through the first run up Currahee or decided to quit afterward rather than face the climb again. Quite a few more dropped out before the three-day deadline, and each day after that others had either been removed or had decided they would rather be dogs than go on with the training. The numbers were down to just over half of those who had begun, and four of the original twelve were gone from Alex's squad, but something kept Alex in, and part of it was Duncan and a few of the other guys who had started in on him early. They told him over and over that he would never make it, that he was too old, too soft. Alex simply couldn't stand to let them be right.

It was a stupid reason to stay, but every time he thought of walking to Summers's office to ask for a quit slip, he thought of Duncan's pleasure, and he couldn't do it. The truth was, he had held up better than Duncan—as well as anyone, in fact—and he told himself he could make it through if anyone could.

But now, lying on his bunk and wishing he could sleep—but feeling too tired ever to be truly rested again—he knew he had stayed for all the wrong reasons. He would survive the physical challenges, no matter how bad they were, and he wouldn't become one of the degraded "dogs" he saw every day in the mess hall, but he hated the attitudes of the other soldiers. He was sick of their harassment. He had pictured an elite unit, with everyone pulling together, but these men resented him, disliked him, and he saw nothing to admire in them.

Alex did drift off to sleep before the lights were out. And then, suddenly, it was morning—if four o'clock could be called morning. The day started with calisthenics and a long run before breakfast. The men were already in much better condition than they had been the week before, and the run was not so bad. At least there seemed to be no Currahee climb today. But by the time they had showered and shaved and sat down to breakfast, they were already tired.

Combining basic training with jump training meant that airborne techniques—and the mandatory five jumps to receive paratrooper wings—had to be compressed into the same time that a normal boot camp would take. All the regular close-order drill, weapons instructions, and combat training were done quickly, and the sergeant had to assume that the men were sharp enough to pick things up fast. Never a minute, all day, was lost. Even during break times the sergeant would call out questions and expect immediate, accurate answers. Any mistake, even a hesitation, always brought the same punishment. "Hit it for twenty-five," Sergeant Willard would shout, and the soldier would drop to the ground, on the spot, and begin doing push-ups.

Sometimes Willard went out of his way to think of excuses to punish people. When Dale Huff, a soldier in Alex's squad, listed the parts of the M-1 rifle correctly one day, he smiled with satisfaction. Willard howled, "Huff, there's not one thing funny about your M-1 rifle!" and told him to hit it. Tom McCoy, a buddy of Huff's from Ohio, smiled in response. So he got twenty-five of his own.

The first or second set of twenty-five wasn't so bad, but as the day continued and bodies became weary, the men dreaded any mistake that would force them to drop for another go at it. And sometimes, for no reason at all, just when everyone was almost dead, Willard would shout, "Leaning rest position. Move!" That meant the whole squad dropped to their chests immediately, and then, with the command, "Ready—exercise!" another twenty-five would begin.

One other little game Willard played was to require an automatic response to the word *jab* whenever it was spoken. Every soldier had to strike his left breast with his right fist— quickly and in unison with the others. If anyone failed, or didn't move quickly enough, everyone did push-ups again.

After breakfast, when the men thought they had their run in for the day, Willard told them to prepare for a march. That meant full gear—forty-pound packs, steel helmets, rifle, gas mask, canteen, and all the rest. They set off on a forced march, not at double-time but steady hiking for fifteen miles across the dusty countryside.

For ten minutes, at the end of each hour, Sergeant Willard let the men take a break, but during the breaks, he grilled them on the subjects they had been studying in afternoon classes. It was during one of those breaks that Willard said, "All right, Thomas. I want you to try to kill me. Show me what you've learned about hand-to-hand combat."

Sergeant Willard was not as tall as Alex, and he was slight of build. He looked more like a schoolteacher than a fighter, with his solemn, straight-line of a mouth and wire-rim glasses. But there was also an intensity about him, a focus in his dark eyes and a fervor in his raspy voice.

The last thing Alex wanted to do was fight this guy, especially with everyone watching. But Sergeant Willard pointed his rifle at Alex's chest, and he dared him to take it away. So Alex moved suddenly, slammed the rifle aside, as he had been taught to do, and grabbed . . . but he was on his back before he knew what had happened. And all the men were laughing.

"Leaning rest position . . . move!"

Alex jumped up and then dropped again, and he did his push-ups with the others.

When the men were finished, Willard shouted, "All right, Thomas, act like you mean it this time."

Alex leaped at the sergeant this time, tried hard to get to him, but he ended up on his chest in the dirt—with Willard kneeling on his back.

When Alex climbed to his feet, Willard stood nose to nose with him and yelled, "You can't come at me like I'm your trainer. You have to kill me—or I'll kill you. Do you understand that?"

"Yes, Sergeant."

"Then get me this time."

Alex stood up and stepped back. He was not going to be made a fool of again. He rushed Willard, got past the rifle, but when he grabbed the man's shoulders to thrust him over his hip, the sergeant drove his forearm into the side of Alex's neck, and Alex went down hard. Everything spun for a moment, and Alex felt a searing pain in his neck and head.

"You don't hate me enough," Willard screamed. "You don't care about your own life, either. Do you think some Kraut or Jap is going to give you a break?"

Alex pulled himself up. He glanced around and saw that the men in his squad were grinning, fully enjoying this. "Do you want to live or do you want to die?" Willard was shouting. "Both the Germans and the Japs are fanatics. They kill without a second thought. Do you understand that, Thomas?"

Alex decided not to answer. He didn't want to get into all that.

"*Do you understand that?*"

Alex glanced away, tried to think what to say.

"I asked you a question, soldier."

"Sergeant Willard," Alex finally said, "I don't know about the Japanese, but most Germans are just like you and me.

They'll kill because they don't want to be killed. But they aren't killers by nature."

Alex expected a loud response, but what he got was shock—silence—not just from Willard but from the men in the squad.

Alex felt a need to explain, but he wasn't sure how to go about it. "Look, I'm opposed to everything Hitler stands for," he said. He glanced around at the other men, tried to appeal to them for understanding. "But you have to understand, I lived in Germany. Some Germans are devoted to the Nazi cause— but many of them are just—"

"Hit it, Thomas. Give me *fifty.*"

Alex dropped to the ground in the dusty road, and he pumped out the first forty push-ups fairly easily. The last ten got hard, and it was during those final ten that Alex realized how stupid he had been to say anything other than what was expected of him. But he hated the things he kept hearing about Germans. It made him sick, and he didn't want to be any part of it.

Alex made it to fifty and then jumped to his feet. He stood at attention in front of Sergeant Willard. "Thomas, don't talk to me about Germans being this way or that." He cursed and then spat in the dirt. They'll shoot a prisoner if it's not conve- nient to take him along. They *hate* Americans, and the only way you're going to stay alive is to hate them more."

Alex nodded, knowing that he had to comply, at least out- wardly. But he was not going to change his mind about the German people. Willard knew nothing at all about them.

"It's time for your quit slip, Thomas. You're not one of us. You show that every day. You need an office job somewhere, away from the action."

Alex stood his ground, said nothing.

"Do you want a ride back to the barracks right now?"

"No, sir."

"We'll see about that. Come to my quarters tonight, right after dinner."

The march began again, and Sergeant Willard said nothing more to Alex all day. But Duncan, when he got a chance, told some of the men, "This thing with Thomas ain't so funny to me no more. What he said about the Krauts made me sick to my stomach. What do the rest of you boys say about that?"

Most of the men mumbled one thing or another, but a guy named Lester Cox, a young kid from Texas who had become Duncan's buddy, said, "I'm not going into battle with a *Kraut lover*. I'll kill him myself before I fight next to him." Then he added a string of obscene oaths to his vow.

Alex said nothing. He spoke to no one the rest of the day. The only thing he was sure of was that he wasn't signing a quit slip. He wouldn't give these guys that satisfaction. If the brass wanted to kick him out, that was another matter.

That night, after supper, Alex knocked at the sergeant's door. Sergeant Willard appeared in a moment, but then he said, "Follow me. We're going to see Captain Morehead." When they reached the captain's office, Alex stepped up to Morehead's desk, saluted, and stood at attention until Morehead told him to stand at ease.

"Sergeant Willard tells me that you're not cut out for the airborne," Morehead said. "How do you feel about that?"

Morehead was a polished man, with an eastern, Ivy League background. Alex stared into his eyes. "*Sir*. I think I'm doing just fine, sir," he said.

"Sergeant Willard says you handle the training all right, but he says you have the wrong attitude for a combat soldier."

"*Sir*, I lived in Germany. I don't believe all the propaganda about Germans. But I hate what Hitler has done to Germany, and I'm willing to fight against that, sir."

Morehead smiled. He leaned back in his chair. "So you want to fight the Nazis—fight Hitler—and not fight the soldiers who'll be trying to kill you?"

"*No, sir!* I didn't say that. I'll do what I have to do, sir."

"That's not good enough, Thomas. A soldier doesn't go into battle ready to kill if necessary. He goes there expecting to kill, and what's more, *eager* to kill. That's the only way we're going to turn the tide of this war."

Alex didn't say anything.

"Thomas, you're a nice young man. You've got some education—some good background—but we don't want you. I want you to sign a quit slip."

"No, *sir.* I'm not a dog, sir." He looked intently into Morehead's eyes, and he said, in a measured cadence, "Sir. When the chips are down, you're going to wish you had more men like me. It's some of those loud-mouthed braggers back at the barracks you should worry about." Alex took a breath, and then he added, "You can kick me out of the airborne if you want, but I'll never quit, sir."

Morehead smiled again. "Well, now, that's the first sign of some mettle I've seen in you." He stood up. "All right. You go back to your unit. But I'm going to ask Sergeant Willard to make your life miserable. I want to see whether you're all talk. You can start by getting your rifle and pack, and then by double-timing around the compound until Sergeant Willard thinks it's time for you to stop."

"Sir. Yes, sir."

Alex was already dead tired, and the thought of double-timing now was devastating, but he preferred it to spending the time with the men. So he walked to his barracks and, without saying a word, grabbed his equipment and headed outside. He heard some laughter and some mumbled comments, but he left too quickly to catch any more than that.

For a solid hour he double-timed without stopping. Early in the morning that wouldn't have been so bad, but at this time of day, it was agony. His conditioning was good enough that he handled the breathing all right, but gradually his legs were

giving out, and the humidity was sapping his energy. He had
no idea how long Sergeant Willard would keep him going.

The men in his squad had soon discovered what he was
doing, and most of them had come outside to watch. Each time
he passed, they worked him over. What they didn't know was
that they were keeping him going. Alex found new energy
every time he came near those guys.

Finally Sergeant Willard walked into the compound, and
he watched as Alex approached. Alex lifted his knees a little
higher, held his rifle up firmly in front of him. He wasn't going
to let the man see how tired he was.

"Halt," Willard called out. "Thomas, how do you feel about
Krauts about now?" he asked.

Alex hardly knew what to say. All this wasn't really about
Germans; it was about the army. It was about Morehead and
Willard and the airborne.

"I asked you a question, soldier."

"Sergeant, some of the finest people I've ever known are
Germans," he said.

Willard stared at Alex. He called him a filthy name, and
then he said, "You're not going to survive this camp. I'll guar-
antee you that. You haul your butt off to bed now, but don't
look forward to morning. You're looking at the longest day of
your life."

"I'll do what you ask of me, Sergeant, but I won't quit," Alex
said, and he knew the truth. Willard was letting him off the
hook tonight because he wanted to get to bed himself. And
that was the clue that this guy didn't have as much will as Alex
did. Willard was not going to beat him.

When Alex walked into his barracks, the men were getting
ready to go to bed. Some were already stretched out, asleep
with the lights on. It was Duncan, of course, who said, "Hey,
Thomas, did you have a nice little run?"

Alex put his helmet and rifle away. Then he sat down to
take his boots off. He didn't want this tonight. But Duncan was

walking over to him, and so was Lester Cox. Cox was half the size of Duncan, but he liked to strut about in his undershirt and show that he had some muscles.

Alex looked up at them. "What do you want?" he asked.

"We don't want to go into battle with you," Duncan said. "Maybe you can understand that."

Alex stood up. "Okay. What do you want to do about it?"

"Oooh, ooh, the missionary boy sounds a little angry. Maybe he doesn't like you, Duncan." This was from a guy named Austin Campbell, a boy from Minnesota and a nice-enough guy most of the time.

"No, no. Don't say that," Duncan said. "Thomas is a religious boy. He even loves his enemies. So I know he loves a sweet little fellow like me. Ain't that right, Thomas?"

"Duncan, I'm tired. I want to get a shower and go to bed. Just leave me alone."

But Duncan took another step closer. "Thomas, we want you out of our squad—out of the paratroops. A pansy like you won't just get himself killed; he's going to get other guys killed too."

Alex stood up. "I'll tell you what, Duncan. I think the real worry for our squad is that we have a big blowhard like you in it. You're the one who'll put us in danger."

Duncan came at Alex, reached for him, and suddenly the new training kicked in. Alex knocked Duncan's arm aside, and he drove the heal of his hand straight at Duncan's face. He caught the big guy flush on the nose. Duncan staggered backward, and Alex was on him again. He drove a fist into his sternum and then hammered a forehand blow into the side of his head.

Duncan went down. He lay on his side, holding his face. Blood was oozing between his fingers. Alex was standing over him, waiting, but Duncan didn't get up. The room was silent, and Alex was already humiliated.

Alex looked around. Everyone was standing up, staring at

him. "I'm sorry," he said. "I didn't mean to lose my temper like that." But the words were incongruous. Everyone was still looking astounded, and Alex saw in them a new kind of respect that was exactly the kind he didn't want.

"Duncan, I'm sorry. Are you all right?"

Duncan got up—slowly. He didn't answer, but he also showed no interest in continuing the battle.

So Alex walked to his bunk, pulled off his sweaty fatigues, grabbed a towel, and headed for the shower. And when he came back, with a towel wrapped around him, the room fell quiet again. Alex sat down, pulled on some clean underwear, and then lay down on his bunk. When he glanced toward Duncan's bunk, he saw that the bed was empty.

It was then that Curtis Bentley, who bunked next to Alex, rolled over on his side. "Are you all right?" he asked.

"I don't know," Alex said. "I wish I hadn't done that."

"I'm a Christian too," Curtis said. "A Baptist. I understand what you're saying. I don't like to hurt people either."

"Where did Duncan go?"

"To the infirmary. He thinks you broke his nose."

"Really?"

"Look, Thomas," Bentley whispered, "I don't know what's right. Duncan had it coming if you ask me—even if that's not what the Bible teaches. The Bible also says not to kill, and here we are going off to war. If we don't kill, I hate to think what kind of world we're going to have."

"I think we can hate evil without hating people."

"How can a guy do that?"

"I don't know. I sure didn't do it tonight."

Bentley chuckled. "Well, I don't think anyone around here is worried anymore about fighting next to you."

Alex rather liked that, whether he should have or not. But it wasn't what his father had asked of him; wasn't what he had asked of himself.

8

Wally was in the middle of a jungle in Tayabas Province. He didn't know exactly where that was, but he knew he and the men on his work detail were supposed to be cutting a road through the jungle and out to the ocean. In the beginning, the Japanese guards had promised that the detail would last a month and food would be plentiful. But he had been in this jungle six weeks now. The canned meat and other foodstuffs were gone. The prisoners were now living on a diet of nothing but rice. They cooked it themselves each night, boiling it in a wheelbarrow over a fire. The rice on the bottom burned, that in the middle turned pasty, and that on the top remained virtually raw. But that was the best they could do, and the prisoners, most of whom had come to this place already sick, were dying fast from starvation and from the new diseases they were catching. Half of the three hundred men were already dead.

It was early August and still the rainy season. It rained every day in the jungle, off and on, but the heat never let up. Wally and his friend George Robbins—an airman from his former squadron—had teamed up just as Wally and Warren and Jack had done before. They had rigged up Wally's shelter-half to keep a little rain off, but they were never dry, day or night. And the truth was, George was going downhill fast. Back at

O'Donnell he had survived dysentery, but only barely, and he had come to Tayabas still weak. He had done his best to work, and to eat, but the dysentery had returned, and he was being decimated by the diarrhea and lost nutrition.

George could no longer work, and the Japanese had given up on forcing him—as they had had to do with many of the men. That meant those who could stay on their feet—less than a hundred now—were receiving great pressure to keep the road project progressing. But the truth was, the road was going nowhere. The soft, moist dirt of the jungle was easy enough to shovel, but roots snaked through all the soil. Some of the roots were hard as stone, and the men had nothing more than little handsaws to cut with. Each day they worked as diligently as their strength and tools would allow, while the guards increased the abuse and pressure to push ahead, but significant progress was impossible. Some of the guards knew enough English to insult the men, to tell them they were weaklings, unable to hold up as Japanese soldiers would do, but each night the guards returned to their own camps, where they ate much better meals, and they rarely came near the prisoners' camp—probably because they feared the diseases there.

When the men returned from their road work each day, another job was usually waiting. Often, a man had died that day and had to be buried. The sick were too weak to dig graves, and so those who could work in the day had to work in the evening. Again, the dirt was not hard to move, but the roots and vines made digging in the jungle a terrible chore. Most of the graves didn't get very deep, and everyone knew that roaming dogs or wild animals often dug into the graves and devoured the bodies.

One morning when Wally heard the guards shouting for the men to get up, he pulled himself up from where he had been sleeping on the wet ground under the shelter-half. For Wally, getting up in the morning was a daily battle with pain and exhaustion, but today he saw that George was almost gone. Lately George had been able to get very little rice down, and yet he continued to vomit and suffer with diarrhea. Wally had seen the blood in his body fluids, the pus, and that was always the sign that the end was near.

Wally helped George from the little shelter and sat him down, leaning him against a tree. Then he brought him some water. "Are you comfortable like that?" he asked.

George stared at him for a time, as if he hadn't understood, but then he said, "Wally, I'm not going to make it."

"Of course you are. You're going to beat this thing. You need to keep eating, and you'll come through it again, like you did before."

But Wally didn't believe a word of that, and he knew George didn't. "I need to talk to you about a few things," George said.

The guards usually roused the men—from a distance—and then gave them time to cook their morning rice. Wally always helped with the cooking, but this morning he stepped over to one of the soldiers from his work crew, Alan West. "Alan," he said, "can you help with the rice? I've got to help George."

"Sure," Alan said. He was one of the strongest men on the detail and, like Wally, had been able to keep working.

Wally knelt next to George again. The birds were making a racket in the trees, and it was actually a pretty morning, the rain having stopped for the moment, and the sunlight filtering down through the dense forest. But the humidity was so heavy that a person would never have felt dry even if the rain hadn't pelted down so much of the time. The mosquitoes were bad in the morning, too, and the men knew how dangerous they were, but there was no way to fight them off all the time.

George was leaning back with his eyes closed, and Wally could hear his labored, sputtering breath. George had been a big man at one time, thick but solid—and handsome. He had had a shy, country-boy smile with bright white teeth. But now his face was gray, and his dirty beard and hair were tangled and matted. Wally saw nothing that reminded him of the man he had known. One of his sleeves was torn away, and the arm that was showing was nothing but bones. His face was all bones too, and his eyes were as dull as his skin.

"Wally, I know you're a Mormon," George said. His voice was weak and gravelly. He didn't open his eyes. "My parents are Mormons. They joined your church quite a few years ago. My dad is a branch president up in Montana now. Or at least he was when I left."

"I didn't realize that."

"I didn't want you to know. I feel bad about some of the things I done during my life." He stopped and took a breath. His eyes came open, and then he let them go shut again. Wally wanted to wipe the moisture off George's forehead and clean up his face a little, but there was nothing dry to do it with. "My dad always wanted me to learn more about the Mormons. He thought I maybe ought to join. But I didn't ever listen to him much. I just made fun of him."

"I wasn't so different. And I was a member. We do those things when we're young."

"I know. But I'm not going to get another chance. I don't know what I might have done—if all this hadn't happened—but I've seen what kind of guy you are, and I think maybe I would have joined now, if I coulda made it home."

"Come on, George. You're going to be all right."

"Don't, Wally. Just don't."

Wally nodded, knowing full well what he meant.

George lay there and breathed for a while. Wally knew he was reaching for some strength. "I need you to do a couple of things for me, if you don't mind," he finally said.

"Hey, I'll do anything. You know that."

"Yeah, I guess I do." He opened his eyes and looked intently at Wally. "When you get back to the States, will you look up my parents? Tell them that I'm sorry I wasn't a better son to them. And tell them that I love them. I don't think I told 'em that since I was just a little kid."

"Sure," he said.

"My dad's name is George, same as mine. They live just outside of Butte in a little town called Walkerville."

"Okay."

George took some time to breathe again. "Here's the other thing, Wally. I don't want dogs to eat me. Will you make sure I get buried deep enough so they can't get to me?"

"Sure. Of course." But this was a little too much for Wally. He had seen so much that he thought he was beyond emotion, but now he felt a shakiness in his chest, his hands.

"Okay." George let his eyes go shut again, and Wally was afraid he would die at any moment now that he had said what he had to say.

"Look, George, you've got a canteen right here." Wally put his hand on it. "Try to eat a little rice when it's ready."

"No. I can't."

Wally let his breath seep out. "Okay. I understand." He remained there on his knees for a time. "Listen, George, there's something Mormons believe that you ought to know. We believe a person goes to a waiting place when he dies. It's not heaven; it's where people wait until the judgment comes. But you'll be able to accept the gospel there, and someone can perform your baptism for you, back on earth. We do it in the temples. If you don't make it home, your parents can do that for you. I'm sure they will."

"Okay. That's good. That'll mean a lot to Mom and Dad."

"I'll tell them what you said—that you were thinking you might like to join the Church."

"Yes. Tell them that. That'll help them too. But Wally, don't tell them how bad it was here. Just tell them you buried me, and it was a pretty spot, or something like that. I don't want them to have any of this in their heads."

"Yeah. I understand. I'll just tell them you got sick."

"Okay."

Wally stood up. "I'd better check on the rice," he said. "Those guys burn it if I'm not there."

"Sure. Go ahead." Wally turned and took a couple of steps away. But George said, "Wally."

Wally turned back.

"I hope you make it. I think you will."

"Yeah, I think so. But . . . you know. All it takes is—"

"No. You're going to make it. I feel sure about that. And then you can talk to my folks."

"Thanks, George. I'm sorry things turned out this way." Wally was surprised to feel tears on his face.

"Yeah, well, that place you talked about—that waiting place—sounds pretty good right now."

"It is, George. I really believe that. And I believe we'll see each other again—you know, on the other side—no matter what happens to us here."

"Good. That makes it a little easier." But George was exhausted now, his voice hardly audible.

"I'll check back with you before I leave."

So Wally helped with the rice, and then he tried to eat enough of the disgusting stuff to sustain him through the day. When he checked on George, he got very little response. Wally was sure the end couldn't be far off.

So Wally marched out to the road with the six men in his work group, and he faced another day like all the others. But this day seemed more than he could take. His energy was gone already after what he had just experienced with his friend. Wally had developed a way of letting a certain numbness fill him, as though he were existing outside his weary body, but today George had forced reality on him. He admitted to himself that all the men in this detail might die. The Japanese were not backing off; in fact, they were adding pressure as the numbers diminished.

Wally wondered how much longer he could keep his

strength. He felt sick all the time now, but at least he had been able to continue to work, and he felt sure that was best. He knew that when men finally lay down, they didn't last much longer. Wally could feel the fever in his body at times, the chilling, and he felt the diminished power in his muscles. His ankles and legs were swollen so badly he could hardly stand the pain at night, and that probably meant pellagra, which could break men down if it got bad enough. Still, he was eating, and he was holding his food down. And he got up each morning and kept moving. He couldn't let himself think about the end of the work detail, the length of the war, or anything else of that kind. He simply had to get himself through another day and then deal with the one after that when it came.

In the middle of the morning Wally was cutting away at a big root when his arms got so tired that he stopped to take a rest. He always had a sense of about how long he could do that before the guard would yell at him, but he pushed the time this morning, decided to hear the Japanese curses before he began to saw again. When the yelling finally started, it came with force. Without warning, the guard's boot flashed at him, struck him in the ribs and knocked him over.

"Work! Work!" the guard was shouting. "I kick."

Wally pulled himself up to his knees, took one long breath, and then began to saw. He could hardly breathe, but he knew better than to hold off any longer. He had seen far too many men beaten to death right before his eyes.

Wally was angry for only a moment. He hadn't the mental energy even to cling to his wrath this morning. What he knew was that the guards were playing a game that seemed prescribed for them. The guard who had kicked him was a thin guy with a narrow face. The men called him "hatchet" behind his back. He wasn't as brutal as some, but he was moody, and no one ever knew what to expect from him. The fact was, and Wally knew it, this detail was no party for the guards either, even if they ate better than the prisoners. They still had to live in this miserable jungle, and they must have been receiving pressure from their officers to finish the job.

Hatchet had calmed a little now. "Work. No kick," he said, and strangely, Wally thought he heard a kind of apology in the tone. It was so hard to know what was in the minds of the guards. Wally wondered what kind of perverse ideas could have been battered so deeply into their brains that they could treat other humans this way.

But Wally didn't expect answers. He simply kept working, and he hoped his ribs weren't hurt too badly. One more pain actually didn't make that much difference, but he didn't want broken bones or internal injuries. No matter what else Wally felt, he wanted to live, and he believed he was going to do it.

So Wally used his favorite defense, almost his only one. He imagined himself at home. Sometimes he walked around his neighborhood, looked at every house, thought of the people who lived in each, remembered the kids he had grown up with. Sometimes he took himself up to Parley's Ravine, near the mouth of the canyon, and splashed in the cold water of the creek, or he chased after horned toads. He even played at war—the running, shouting, "I got you" kind of war, where everyone went home at the end of the day.

Today he took refuge in his favorite thought. He pictured Lorraine, tried to remember her on certain special occasions— the night at Lagoon when they had danced in the parking lot to "I Get Along Without You Very Well." He let some of the music filter through his mind, but he knew better than to think about the words. He thought of the time the two of them had sneaked onto the Country Club golf course and he had waded into the pond to steal golf balls. Sometimes, without warning, he would hear that husky way that she laughed. But as always, he came back to the last time he had talked to her, when she was standing on the porch in a pretty blue polka-dot dress. She had told him that their relationship would never work. But Wally didn't choose to hear those words. He saw her: her slim waist and the A-line shape of her skirt, her beautiful legs; and he saw her pretty hair, illuminated by the last of that day's sun. He heard her say, "Wally." Then, when he had turned around, she had whispered, "I love you, too."

Lorraine was the most precious memory of his life, and in his mind she represented everything he had lost here in this jungle—the softness and goodness and rightness of people who didn't hate, didn't kill. Lorraine had become a symbol of Salt Lake, of the Church, of home and neighborhood, of love and warmth. He remembered the times when he had kissed her—moments almost too exquisite to recall.

He let his mind drift to his family. He pictured Gene, probably tall now, and about to start playing his senior year of football. Or did all of that still go on back home? What had changed because of the war? He hoped there were still football games, and cheerleaders. He needed to believe that those things were still happening. Someday he would sit in a stadium again and cheer for some team he cared about. He wanted to go back and find everything waiting for him, absolutely unchanged.

The day passed, slowly and tediously, as always, and at the end Wally felt some extra pain in his ribs, but not enough to worry about. Hatchet kept the crew going until everyone was exhausted beyond the point that they were producing any real work, and then he commanded them, "Go!" This was the word he always used to announce the end of a day's work, but Wally thought he heard more frustration in it than usual. He knew as well as anyone that the men had accomplished so little that day that another year at the same pace would not get them beyond this jungle. And these men didn't have another year.

As Wally walked back, he hated to think what he would find, but from a distance he spotted George still sitting against the tree. Wally allowed himself to hope, for a moment, that maybe he had gotten through the day all right. But as he came nearer, the truth was obvious. George's eyes were open, but nothing was there.

Wally took a breath, but he didn't react a great deal. He had lost George that morning. This was only the inevitable being carried out. And so Wally found Alan and said, "George is gone. He asked me if I would bury him deep—so he won't get dug up by the dogs. Could you help me?"

"Sure. But we need to eat first."

"I know." And there was no question about that. Wally hardly had the strength to walk right now, let alone dig. And so he helped build the fire, and helped cook the polluted rice, which was full of insects and rocks. Then he ate a good deal of the stuff. The irony was that as men died the ration of rice didn't change, and those who could eat got plenty. The problem was, and everyone knew it, they were getting nothing else—no vegetables or meat, nothing to provide them the vitamins they needed. They could eat every day and still die of malnutrition if they didn't get some other kinds of food from time to time.

Still, Wally ate his fill, and then he took a shovel and a pick and the little saw he used during the day, and he found a clearing among the tall trees of the jungle. The ground was covered with grass and vines and ferns, but the growth pulled away easily from the moist earth. The digging also went easily until Wally began to hit roots, which he worked to saw away.

After a short time Alan arrived to help. He was an infantry sergeant, a man who had spent ten years in the army before the war broke out. He was originally from Oklahoma, but his wife and two kids lived in California. Wally had seen pictures of them: two little boys with dark, neatly combed hair and big eyes. Alan had told Wally once that he was going to get home no matter what it took. He would *not* let his wife down, and not those two boys.

Alan didn't say anything now. He simply knelt down and began to saw at one of the roots that Wally had uncovered.

And they worked that way for some time. The men had all acquired the habit of staying within themselves when they worked, saying very little, and perhaps finding, as Wally did, that other images—memories—were more sustaining than shared feelings about the present. But eventually Alan said, "Where was George from?"

"Montana. Up by Butte."

"I've never been up there," Alan said. "It's supposed to be nice."

"Yeah. It's pretty. I went on a trip to Alberta, Canada, one time. We drove through that country."

"That'd be something," Alan said. "You know. Take a trip. Drive a car. Things like that."

"I was thinking today I'd like to go to a football game. Remember how that used to be, sitting at a game on a fall afternoon?"

"Yeah." Alan said nothing more for a time, but the thought must have stayed in his mind. "What about George?" he finally asked. "What did he do back home?"

"He grew up on a little farm. He worked hard, I guess, from what he said. He didn't finish high school. What he talked about lately was having a farm of his own."

"What about you, Wally? What are you going to do after this is all over?"

"I don't know. The only thing I'm sure about is that I want to go back to college—and make a better go of it this time."

"And go to those football games—with a date. Right?"

"That's right."

"I want out of the service," Alan said. "I want to stay home with my wife and my boys—see them every day."

There was a long pause, and then Wally said, "I wish George had gotten a chance to see his home one more time. He used to talk a lot about Montana. He missed the mountains."

But that was more sentiment than either one wanted to

deal with. They continued to dig, and eventually they got the grave down four feet or so. That was as deep as they were going to get it, but it was deep enough. And so the two walked back to the camp and picked up George's body. It weighed very little, less than a bag of rice. They placed him in the grave, and then Wally went back for a jacket George had brought with him to the jungle. At least it was something to cover up his face before they threw dirt back over him.

The backfill didn't take long, and they tamped the dirt down as best they could. Then they stepped back together. The sun was going down, and in the half-light Wally was touched by the beauty of the place. "Well, at least it's green here—even if it doesn't look much like Montana," Alan said.

"Maybe we ought to say something—or have a prayer," Wally said.

"You go ahead. I'm something of a churchgoer, but I'm not much at praying out loud."

So Wally bowed his head and folded his arms. "Father in Heaven," he said, "we have laid to rest here our friend George Robbins. He was a good man. We bless this spot of land, far from his home, that it might be a resting place for George's earthly body until he is called forth in the resurrection. We pray that thou wilt accept his spirit home with thee. Grant him his wish that he might hear the gospel preached, and that he might take it to his heart. And bless his parents that they might be comforted until the time when they will be joined with him once again. We ask these things in the name of Jesus Christ, amen."

By the time Wally finished, he had begun to shake—maybe as much from the exhaustion as the emotion. Alan put his hand on Wally's shoulder, and the two stood quietly for a time. And then Wally said, "Alan, I've got that shelter-half. It keeps a guy a little bit drier at night. Would you like to sleep in there with me?"

"Yeah. I sure would."

"All right."

"Are you a preacher or something?" Alan asked. "I never heard any regular fellow say a prayer like that."

"I grew up with prayer. My dad was a leader in our church. I just tried to say what he would have said."

"Do you pray a lot, on your own?"

"Every day. Almost every minute."

"Yeah. Me too. But I'm not very good at it. Could you maybe say a prayer for us?"

"Sure. I'd like to do that." And so this time the two men knelt by the grave, and Wally prayed for the two of them, for all the men in the detail, and for all the prisoners on Luzon.

Wally felt good about Alan. He was a strong man, likely to stay alive. The two of them could help each other. But when they lay down that night and tried to get some sleep, Wally thought of Warren and Jack. He still missed them all the time. Even those days in O'Donnell seemed pretty nice now, back when they had managed to get a bottle of ketchup or a can of meat once in a while. If he couldn't go home for a long time, he hoped he would at least get back to his friends. And maybe Alan could join their little group.

9

Bobbi had been at the hospital almost two months now, and she was fairly comfortable with the procedures. What she had trouble handling were the demands. Nurses worked twelve-hour shifts, and they were supposed to be on duty only four days a week, but she had never seen a week that easy. Men were being brought in from the Pacific Islands or off ships, and the hospital was crammed full at all times. Sometimes, after twelve hours, she had to stay on to help as a new load of wounded sailors or Marines was admitted, and she usually worked six days a week.

Most of the men were decent, many of them just kids, but they had been at war and had taken on the bravado of soldiers. She heard such a barrage of foul language that it soon became part of the noise of the place, something she hardly thought about, but the constant overtures and off-colored suggestions were still difficult for her to tolerate.

One morning in August she walked into a burn ward, where ten men were crowded into a room for six. These were patients who were well on their way to recovery. Some of them could now get up and shower on their own, but others were still confined to their beds and needed to be bathed. "Who wants to be first?" she asked, and she laughed.

Some of the men were shy about bed baths and dreaded them, but most of them didn't mind. "Do you use the same water for all of us?" one of the boys asked. He was a seaman named Zobell, a guy who never seemed to stop talking—or shouting.

"Yes. Of course I do," she said. "If one of you has a skin disease, we want you to share it with everyone."

"I believe that," Zobell said, and he swore. "You're trying to kill us off." But he was laughing, and then he added, "You can scrub me right now—while the water is still hot."

So Bobbi stepped to his bed and set the basin on a little stand nearby.

"You sure look nice in white, Bobbi. You ought to wear it every day." He grinned at her. He was older than most of the boys, and he often joked about his dissipated life—lots of drinking, lots of women. He looked hard, too, with a filminess in his eyes, and premature wrinkles in the skin of his neck.

"That's Ensign Thomas to you, sailor."

One of the men yelled from across the room, "You'd better salute that girl, Zobell."

Zobell sat up a little straighter and tossed his bandaged right hand toward his eye, purposefully clunking himself in the forehead. He had been caught in an explosion aboard his ship, and he had burns over most of his body. He was healing pretty well now, but he still had a lot of skin grafts—and pain—ahead of him.

Bobbi did feel sorry for him when she considered what he had gone through. "That's enough," she said. She pulled his sheet down to his waist.

Zobell was laughing. "Bobbi, don't you know I'm in love with you? When are you going to let me take you out?"

Bobbi didn't answer. She was helping him pull his pajamas over his bandaged hand.

"Maybe we could spend a quiet night at home—here in my bed."

Sometimes Bobbi let all this slide off her, but she was tired of it. She preferred to work with patients more recently wounded—men who needed her more. "Zobell, you say one more thing like that to me," she said, "and I'll report you."

"What? That I love you? I can't help it. I can't resist those cute little freckles on your nose."

An older Marine at the far end of the ward began to sing, in a roaring voice, "She's got freckles on her *but* . . . I love her."

All the men were laughing. "Don't confuse love with lust, Zobell," someone yelled. "Bobbi's got a shape like Mae West."

This got another huge laugh, and it stung Bobbi more than she wanted to show. She knew he was making fun of her, that she wasn't "curvy," and that was fine with her, but she was humiliated to have men commenting on her body. They had no right to do that.

"I'm serious," Bobbi said, still looking at Zobell. "I'm not going to put up with any more of this."

"Hey, I'm serious, too. My heart *bleeds* for you. I can't think of anything else all day. What can I do?"

"You can wash yourself," Bobbi said. She left the basin and began to walk away.

But as she walked past the bed toward the door, Zobell called out, "But Bobbi, that's what drives me crazy—that cute little walk of yours."

Bobbi kept going, and she walked directly to Lieutenant Kallas's office. She knocked on the door and after a moment heard, "Yes. Come in."

Bobbi was shaking, but she didn't want her boss to see that. By the time she had stepped into the lieutenant's office, however, she was having trouble keeping control. "I want to put a sailor on report," she said.

Lieutenant Kallas was looking down at some papers on her desk. She had a pencil in her hand. "What's the trouble?" she said, without looking up.

"He made lewd remarks to me."

"How bad?" Something in her voice seemed to say, "So what else is new?"

"He asked me to get in bed with him. He talked about my body, said . . . a lot of things." Bobbi's voice was shaking.

Kallas finally looked up. "Did he grab at you, pull at your clothes—anything like that?"

"No. But he never lets up. Every time I'm in that ward, he starts in on me."

"That's only because he gets a reaction from you." Kallas looked down again, as though she were finished. She was not really a big woman, but to Bobbi she seemed huge, with her snarling voice and her strong shoulders.

"What gives him the right to—"

"Thomas, if I try to discipline every boy in this place who makes a pass at a nurse, I'd have them all in the brig. If you act like a shrinking violet and get all flustered, these guys love it. Or they think *you* like it." She cursed, and then she added, "Just ignore all that bunk and go about your business."

"I can't go back to that ward now. I told him I was putting him on report."

"Do you even know what that means, Thomas?

"Not exactly. I just—"

"I'm sick of this. They send you kids to me right out of nursing school, and I have to throw you into a situation you can't handle."

"Well, I'm sick of being treated that way by those men." Bobbi's voice had finally taken on some sharpness.

Kallas pushed her chair back and stood up. "Maybe you're the one going on report. Don't take that tone with me again. Do you hear me?"

"Yes, ma'am."

"You go back and show those men you're a professional. If you want respect, earn it. If a man starts pawing at you, we can deal with that. But some sailor making a few jokes, that's nothing I want to hear about."

"Yes, ma'am."

"You Mormons grow up too sheltered. You don't know the first thing about life. If you'd hang out in a bar for a few hours, you'd see how men act when they're *really* on the prowl. After that, a little kidding in a hospital wouldn't bother you."

Bobbi didn't reply to that, but she was beginning to lose control. Tears were running down her cheeks.

"And Thomas, don't *ever* let me see you cry again. We aren't a group of *little girls* here. We're pros. You get yourself together—take five minutes—and then go back to work."

"Yes, ma'am." Bobbi thought she was probably supposed to salute, but she was never clear about that. She saluted anyway, and Kallas shot back a casual little flip of her hand that looked more like a dismissal. Bobbi was as embarrassed as she was angry. More than anything, right now, she wanted to go home—where no one had ever spoken to her the way Zobell had, or the way Lieutenant Kallas had either.

But she walked to the nurse's rest room, and she washed her face. And then she strode down the hallway and into the burn ward. As she walked toward Zobell's bed, she saw him begin to smile. She said in the firmest voice she could find within herself, "I'm warning you, don't start."

The men all laughed, and Zobell slapped his hand over his mouth. Bobbi picked up a washcloth and dipped it in the water. "Hey, that water is cold now," Zobell protested.

"Yes, it is," she said. She wrung the cloth a little but left it wetter than usual, and then she slapped it on his chest.

Zobell howled with exaggerated horror and then said, "That's what I needed, honey. A cold shower. When I'm around you, I—"

Bobbi slapped the cloth onto his face. "Now I'm going to wash your mouth," she said.

The men all liked that, but Bobbi was afraid she had only made things worse. She needed to be forty years old and hard as nails—like Kallas. Right now, all she really wanted was to get out of the navy.

Bobbi and Afton rarely had trouble getting their Sundays off. Sunday was usually the lightest day at the hospital, with less surgery going on and most doctors only on call. It was the easiest day to work, so most of the nurses were happy to accept Sunday shifts. They could get a weekday off and go into Honolulu when stores were open—and stay to enjoy the night spots.

There was a small branch of the Church in Kalihi, but since it wasn't much farther for Bobbi and Afton to take the bus into Honolulu and attend the Beretania Ward in the Oahu Stake, they decided they would do that. The ward met in a chapel next to a beautiful new tabernacle with an impressive mosaic of Christ over the front entrance.

On the first Sunday Bobbi had not been exactly surprised by the mix of people—Hawaiians, Asians, Polynesians, Caucasians—but still, it had seemed strange to her, even a little uncomfortable. She had never felt so welcomed in her life, but the Hawaiian and Polynesian women, complete strangers, were so quick to throw their arms around her, and the meetings seemed almost too casual. She told herself she liked the relaxed atmosphere, but it was so different from what she had known at home that it hardly seemed a Mormon church. Worst of all were the discussions in the adult Sunday School class. It seemed more of a storytelling time, almost a social event—and here the division of the races was more obvious. The Caucasian teacher tried to conduct the kind of lesson that might have been typical in Salt Lake, but most of the islanders hardly seemed to pay attention. When they did answer a question, or make a comment, their thoughts seemed simplistic, almost childlike. Bobbi didn't want to be a snob—she liked the people in some ways—but she longed for something more familiar, more a piece of home. Since arriving at Pearl Harbor, she had studied the scriptures more than ever in her life, and she wanted to exchange some of her thoughts, her insights, but when she tried to do that now, only the teacher and the other mainlanders seemed interested.

After she'd attended for only three weeks, the bishop had asked Bobbi to teach a Junior Sunday School class—kids five and six years old—and the time with the children turned out to be the best hour of her week. She was rather relieved to leave the adult Sunday School and be with the children, who were so lovely. She didn't think much about culture and race when she was with them, and trying to explain the gospel in simple terms was not only appropriate, it was also good for her.

On the Sunday after Bobbi had had her run-in with Lieutenant Kallas, she was especially happy to escape the navy base and take the bus into Honolulu. It was a beautiful morning—as most mornings were—and the freedom to be away from the hospital was wonderful. Bobbi and Afton packed a lunch. They planned to have a picnic in the park near the palace and then wait for the late afternoon sacrament meeting.

When they arrived at Sunday School, they were greeted with hugs and *aloha*s as usual. The girls were getting to know some of the members' names now, but even people they didn't know very well were good about greeting them. In opening exercises, a large Maori brother with a British accent got a little carried away with his two-and-a-half-minute talk—and went on and on—but no one ever seemed to worry about that sort of thing. Schedules were never so rigid here as they had been at home.

In class, Bobbi had eight little children in attendance that day. They were not always easy to handle, since some of them were too eager to tell all that was on their minds, but Bobbi was patient, and the kids all wanted to lean against her and get a pat or a hug. After class, a little girl named Lily Aoki took hold of Bobbi's hand and walked out with her. She was a quiet child and usually said almost nothing in class, but she liked to be close to Bobbi.

Out in the foyer, Bobbi spotted Lily's mother, Ishi, and walked over to her. "Oh, there you are," Sister Aoki said. She was holding a little boy in her arms, but she knelt in front of Lily. "What did you learn today?" she asked.

"About Jesus," Lily said.

Sister Aoki patted Lily on the head and then stood again. She smiled at Bobbi. "That's what she always says." Sister Aoki was a young woman in her late twenties. She was always friendly but more formal than the Polynesian members. Bobbi knew that Sister Aoki's husband was in the army, and that he had been shipped out with other Japanese-American soldiers recently, but Bobbi wasn't clear how that had happened. Why were some Japanese Americans being interned and others being asked to serve in the military? But the subject seemed sensitive to Bobbi, and she hadn't asked. Bobbi didn't think much about little Lily being Japanese, but she was very conscious of it with Sister Aoki.

Sister Aoki was certainly not a first-generation immigrant. She was "AJA"—American of Japanese Ancestry—as most islanders called them these days. Her speech had a certain accent—more precise than the pidgin English of the Polynesians and yet a little hard to understand at first. Or at least it was for mainlanders—usually called *haoles* in the islands.

"Well . . . Lily's right," Bobbi said. "We always talk about Jesus."

"She loves you, you know," Sister Aoki said, and she patted Bobbi on the arm. "She talks about 'my teacher' all the time."

Bobbi looked down at Lily and gave her hand a little squeeze. "I love you, too, Lily," she said. Lily leaned against Bobbi's leg. Afton had walked over to them by then, but she stayed back a little.

"What's your little boy's name?" Bobbi asked. She really did want to be friendly.

"David," Sister Aoki said. "We named him after David O. McKay. He came here to dedicate the tabernacle last year, just before our little David was born. He was such a nice man—so good. We want our David to be like that."

Bobbi thought of President McKay, so tall and elegant. It seemed strange, although she didn't know why, that Sister Aoki would name her son after him.

"I know you two stay in town during the day—until sacrament meeting," Sister Aoki said. "Would you like to come over to my house for dinner?"

Bobbi hesitated, but Afton was quick to say, "Oh . . . actually, we brought a lunch with us. We were going to eat in the park."

"I see. Well, perhaps next week."

"Gee . . . uh . . . maybe," Afton said, sounding tentative.

Bobbi wanted to be kind to Sister Aoki, but she was uncomfortable with the idea of going to her home. She noticed, however, that Sister Aoki was forcing a smile, trying to mask her disappointment, and suddenly Bobbi was ashamed. "I'm sure we could come next week," she said. "Why don't we plan on it?"

Bobbi saw Sister Aoki brighten, and she was glad, but she couldn't get rid of her reluctance. "That will be wonderful," Sister Aoki said. "Lily will like that so much."

Lily smiled and then looked away, too shy to admit her own pleasure. Bobbi glanced at Afton, whose smile seemed less than natural.

"Have you been in the Church a long time, Sister Aoki?" Bobbi asked.

"My husband was baptized when he was fourteen," Sister Aoki said. "I joined when I was nineteen—after I met him." She smiled. "We went to the Japanese-American branch for a long time. But the missionaries are going home, and no one is coming to replace them. It's not easy to run a small branch without missionaries, so I think everyone is going to move into the other wards. It's closer, too, so it's easier for me to get here with the children. I started coming last month, and everyone has been quite nice to me."

Bobbi knew exactly what that meant, and she was embarrassed. "Of course they would be nice to you. They're great people, and so are you."

"Thank you." Sister Aoki gave a little nod that was almost like a bow. And then she said, "Well, let's plan on next week."

"All right."

Afton finally did say, "Okay."

But after, as the girls left the church, Bobbi said, "Afton, I didn't know what else to say. We really should go."

"I know. It's all right."

They walked out to Beretania Street and turned right. At the corner, they had learned, they could catch a bus to the Iolani Palace.

When Bobbi could get away from the hospital and see this island—the palm trees and flowers—she was always amazed to think where she was. If only her life weren't hemmed in by the walls of hospital wards, or by her box of a room in the nurses' quarters, she could love being here.

"I think some things are still hard for me to get used to," Afton volunteered. "I know Sister Aoki isn't the same as a Jap soldier, but golly, it's hard for me not to think about her that way. I just feel funny around those people."

"I know," Bobbi said again. "But we couldn't turn her down. Did you see how she was looking at us?"

"I know. It'll be okay. It's probably good for me to get to know her—so I won't feel the way I do so much." Afton walked by a hibiscus plant, picked a flower, and tucked it in her hair, over her ear. The girls often wore their Class A uniforms to church simply because they didn't have a lot of civilian clothes, but today Afton was wearing a pale lavender dress she had bought the week before. With her dark hair and the red flower, she looked very pretty.

"In Arizona we had lots of Mexicans and Indians, but I didn't really know them—except for men who worked for my dad sometimes. I'm not used to different races being together. My mom and dad used to say that it wasn't good—that people ought to stick to their own kind."

"We had a Japanese family in our ward when I was growing up," Bobbi said, "but they were born and raised in Utah. They didn't seem foreign or anything. Sometimes, in Salt Lake, I would see a few colored people. My dad said they worked on the railroad. But other than that, I've always lived where everyone was white."

"Don't you like it better that way?"

Bobbi had to think. The two had come to the corner, and they glanced up the street to watch for their bus. There were almost no cars moving about. It was noon now, but Sundays were lazy days here, and gasoline was hard to get. Even people who owned cars tended to use the bus system now, or walk. Most of the people in town were sailors or marines. The bars did a booming business on Sundays, and the red-light district, from what Bobbi and Afton had heard, was always packed.

"I don't know, Afton. I like all those Hawaiian ladies. It's my fault if I don't want them to throw their arms around me. I can't think why races have to stay apart—especially in the Church. If we feel funny, I guess it's our problem, not theirs."

"Well . . . my family wouldn't believe it if I told them I was eating with a Jap woman."

"I think—here—it's better to say 'Japanese,' or 'AJA.'"

"Yeah. I guess so." And for a time neither said anything more. But finally Afton said, "Bobbi, I still think about all the boys in the hospital—and what they say about Japanese soldiers. One little sailor told me he went overboard when his ship was going down, and Jap pilots were diving down and shooting the boys who were in the water. Why would *anybody* do something like that?"

Bobbi admitted something to herself. She liked Sister Aoki

and little Lily. She even wanted to love them. But she was harboring anger that she wasn't ready to let go. Still, she told Afton, "Maybe some of our boys do things like that too. War makes people do all kinds of things they normally wouldn't."

"I don't think we kill when we don't have to. We're not like that."

Bobbi wanted to believe that, but she had heard the bitterness of some of the sailors in the hospital, and she knew the war was changing the hearts of lots of young boys.

Bobbi and Afton had a nice afternoon. They even napped a little in the warm sun, after lunch, and then they took a bus to Waikiki and strolled along the beach. The sand was pretty and white, and the water was so blue it hardly seemed real. In the distance, the green of Diamond Head, with its blunt top, stood out against the blue sky and water. It was all quite breathtaking, and the only bad thing was that tomorrow was Monday and Bobbi was scheduled for five twelve-hour shifts that would probably change to six as the week went along.

Sacrament meeting was the same as always, with familiar hymns taking on a new life when sung with such spirit. But the speaker was a *baole* today, a Honolulu businessman who was on the stake high council. So the sermon had the ring of home, with little passion but solid doctrine.

There was, however, a new little excitement. Maybe five minutes into the meeting, Afton turned and looked to the back of the chapel. She kept looking for quite some time before she turned around and nudged Bobbi. "I think I'm in love," she said. "There's a navy officer back there. Take a glance over your left shoulder, at the back, but don't be too obvious about it—the way I was." She giggled.

Bobbi waited a minute or so, and then she glanced back. She saw exactly what Afton was talking about. The officer was tall and handsome, bronze in his white uniform, with dark hair.

When the meeting was over and Afton moved quickly in the officer's direction, Bobbi found herself rather glad to have someone around who was forward enough to approach the officer. What she didn't expect was such a direct assault. "Say, sailor," Afton said, "welcome aboard. We're navy officers, too."

He smiled a little and nodded. He had been moving away, apparently planning to leave the building without meeting anyone, but now he stopped. Bobbi could see he was a lieutenant—equivalent to captain in the army, and two ranks above Bobbi and Afton. "Nurses?" he asked.

"Yes."

"It's nice to meet you." He nodded politely, and then he turned to walk away.

"Gee whiz, wait a sec. Are you sure you're in the navy?"

Bobbi still hadn't said a word, and she hated to see the man leave so quickly, but she hardly knew what Afton was up to.

"Yes. I'm certain." This time his smile seemed subtle more than slight, as if he suspected some sort of gamesmanship from Afton. He tucked his hat under his arm, and stood tall. The man really *was* something to look at. Bobbi liked the way his dark hair drooped a little on his forehead, liked the strong bones in his cheeks and jaw, and she loved his pale blue eyes, set off by his tanned skin.

"When you meet a couple of pretty nurses, you're supposed to ask their names—and probably their phone numbers—and not just walk away," Afton said. "We ought to know. We're around navy men all day, every day."

"And do you give your phone number to all of them?" This was a well-placed jab, but he was smiling more now, and a soft hint of rakishness had appeared in his eyes.

Afton was up to the challenge. "I give my number to *none* of them. But I'm at church now. That's different. I'm assuming you're a nice Mormon boy."

Bobbi could feel herself blushing—mostly for Afton—and at the same time she was wishing she had worn her best dress and taken more time with her hair that morning.

The officer held out his hand. "My name is Richard

Hammond," he said. "I'm from Springville, Utah. May I ask your names? I won't be so bold as to request your phone numbers just yet."

This was all done with exaggerated politeness. In response, Afton made a little curtsy, and then, as she shook his hand, she said, "Afton Story. How nice to make your acquaintance. I'm from Mesa, Arizona."

Bobbi stepped just a little closer. "I'm Bobbi Thomas," she said. "From Salt Lake." She shook his hand too.

"Where did you take your nurse's training?" he asked her.

"LDS hospital. But I went to the University of Utah for two years before that."

"Really? I went to the U. Graduated two years ago."

"And you're not married—right?" Afton asked. She giggled.

"No," he said. "I'm not."

"But you have a girl in every port?"

"Dozens." He finally laughed a little.

"So where are you going now, in such a hurry?" Afton asked.

"Back to my ship. On Ford Island."

"Golly, don't go yet. We're going down to the beach to watch the sun go down. Why don't you go with us? I won't embarrass you anymore. I was just kidding about the phone numbers."

"I'm sorry, but I can't. I made special arrangements to get away from my ship. I have to be back right away."

"Then would you like our phone number after all? We have the same one."

"Actually, I would." He even seemed to mean it. "I may not be able to come to church all the time. But while I'm in port, it would be nice to have some friends from home."

"Does that mean Bobbi—because, as I mentioned, I'm from Arizona."

"That's still home to me."

"Oh, good." Afton found a slip of paper in her purse, and then she searched for a pencil.

"How do you like the navy?" Richard asked Bobbi.

"I don't," she said. "I don't understand all this military discipline and privilege of rank. I just want to be treated like a human being."

He nodded. "I know what you mean," he said. "But I think I understand why it's necessary. In battle, it can save lives."

This seemed just a little too by-the-book to Bobbi. On impulse, she suddenly straightened, gave him a brisk salute, and said, "Aye, aye, sir. I certainly didn't mean to insult the navy."

"I'm sorry. I just meant . . ."

But he didn't finish, and Bobbi rather liked what she had done to him. He was smiling now—really smiling—and his fine white teeth, against that tanned skin, made him very easy to forgive. "I was just teasing," she said.

"Well . . . I had it coming." For the first time he seemed to focus on Bobbi, really see her. Bobbi felt almost breathless as she felt his eyes taking her in, assessing her.

When Afton handed him the slip of paper with the phone number, he thanked her, but he still kept looking at Bobbi, and when he said, "I do hope I'll see you," he said it to her.

As soon as he walked out the door, Afton said, "Oh, wow, he is *so* cute. And I blew it. He doesn't like pushy women. I could see that. You were the one he was looking at."

"He took one look at me—there at the end. The rest of the time he was looking at you."

"Oh, good. Maybe he's nuts about me."

Bobbi laughed. "Probably so," she said. "He's probably not my type anyway. I'll bet he majored in engineering."

"Hey, that's fine with me. I wasn't planning to read textbooks with him."

"Good. He's all yours." But Bobbi *had* seen something in the way he had looked at her. And she couldn't stop thinking about his smile.

I 0

The Japanese guards had finally provided four large tents for the men on the Tayabas work detail. It was September now, and only about sixty of the original three hundred were still alive, but at least these men could stay dry at night. It was a small consolation. Wally was in trouble, and he knew it. His body ached fiercely, and when he got up each morning, his joints would barely allow him to move. He had developed a deep, raspy cough that sometimes shook his body until he nearly passed out. He was sure he had hepatitis, among other things. He could see the yellow color of his skin. He also had pellagra, which had caused open sores on the back of his hands and behind his knees. He tried to keep the sores clean, but they filled with dirt every day, and he had nothing but river water to wash in.

Wally's boots had rotted away, and so he went about barefoot like most of the other men. He wouldn't have been able to wear shoes anyway; his feet were swollen with beriberi. His coveralls were falling apart, and he knew his half-naked body resembled a skeleton. He watched the other men moving about like specters—a faraway look in their eyes, their steps deliberate and clumsy—and he knew he was catching a glimpse of himself.

The road detail was pointless now, with only a couple of dozen men still able to work and the road not progressing. Sooner or later the Japanese had to give it up, and then maybe those alive could get to a healthier place. It was the only hope.

Almost everyone was also suffering from malaria. Wally had avoided that so far, but one morning as he trudged off to work, he felt the chills and fever that he knew came first. He told himself that it wasn't malaria, just the effects of all the other diseases he was dealing with. He had been feverish many times before—just not quite so severely. By the time the sun was high in the sky, however, he was sure he had something new.

He was working next to Alan, the two of them digging to expose a root. "Alan," he finally said, "I'm getting sick. I'm okay in my stomach. It's not dysentery. But I've got a fever."

"Malaria?" Alan asked.

"Maybe."

"How bad are you?"

"I'm getting dizzy. I don't have any strength."

Hatchet, the guard, shouted a phrase in Japanese. The men had heard it often enough to know that it was an instruction not to talk.

Wally continued to work for a time, but he was feeling more and more that he might pass out. He finally leaned on his shovel and said, "I don't know if I can do this."

"You need to rest. Tell the guard."

"I don't want to go down. That might be the end of me."

"You'll be all right. You have some quinine, don't you?"

"Yeah."

But now Hatchet was coming. He yelled at them, and then he struck Alan across the back with his forearm. Alan stumbled forward but caught his balance and turned around. He pointed at Wally. "Sick," he said.

"Work," the guard said. "No sick."

Wally looked over at Alan. "It's all right. I'll work. I'll start the quinine tonight."

A man named Norm Staker stepped up next to Wally. He had once been a big-bellied little man, but he was shriveled now. He couldn't weigh more than eighty pounds. "Don't kill yourself, Wally," he said. "Take some rest, no matter what Hatchet says."

Hatchet was shouting again, but Staker turned on him. "He's *sick*," he said.

Wally put his hand on Staker's shoulder and said, "It's okay. I'll try to keep going. I'll be better off."

"I don't know, Wally. If you—"

"I'm not going to die, Norm. Hatchet can't make me do that."

Staker nodded. "We'll help you get through this, Wally—like you've done for a lot of guys."

Wally knew what Staker meant, but he also knew the truth. In the past few weeks, Wally had made an all-out effort to save some of his friends' lives. He had fed men who were too weak to feed themselves. But virtually all of them had died. The only ones who survived were the ones who kept up their own will, who simply refused to die.

"Don't push yourself too hard," Norm said. "Alan and I will stay close to you."

"All right," Wally said.

Hatchet had had enough. He kicked at Norm, caught him in the knee. Norm went down on all fours. He grunted, hesitated, and then got up. For a moment he stared into Hatchet's face. Then he picked up his shovel and went back to work.

Wally tried to do the same thing, but the effort was overwhelming. He watched the shadows, but the sun seemed stuck in the sky. He heard the whirring of insects, the scraping of shovels, but he felt as though he were hidden deep within his body, hardly part of himself. He was wet from the moisture in the air, the rain that had come and gone that morning, but he wasn't sweating. His body was raging hot.

He kept trying to push his shovel into the ground, but then, suddenly, the earth swerved upward at him. He never felt himself strike the ground, only knew that time had passed when he awakened—back in his tent. Alan was there, and he was wiping Wally's face with a torn piece of an old shirt.

"Wally, while you're awake, you need to take your quinine."

Wally nodded, and he tried to sit up, but the tent began to spin, and he dropped his head back.

"Where are your pills?"

Wally had buried them at the head of his little sleeping area, near the wall of the tent. He rolled on his side, reached, and began to scratch at the earth.

"I'll do it," Alan said, and Wally heard the words, but the next time he knew what was happening, the angle of the sun had changed. It was getting dark inside the tent.

"Wally, listen to me. You need to take a pill now, while you can sit up."

"Okay," Wally managed to say, and he did understand, but he still felt lost inside his body.

Alan hoisted him to a sitting position. "Here's your canteen. Can you take a drink?"

Wally nodded. Then he reached for the tin of quinine pills that he saw on the ground next to him.

"Let me get one out for you," Alan said.

But Wally fumbled to open the tin and then dropped all the pills in the palm of one hand—about fifteen of them.

"No, Wally. Here, give me those."

But suddenly Wally's hand came up, and he tossed all the pills in his mouth at once.

"Wally! Don't!"

But it was too late. Wally had brought the canteen to his lips in the same motion, and now he had swallowed them all.

Alan cursed. "What do you think you're doing? Are you trying to kill yourself?"

Wally didn't understand the question. The doctor had told him that he should save those pills, and if he ever came down with malaria, he should take them. And that's what he had done.

"You were supposed to take *one,* Wally." Alan sounded angry, even desperate, but Wally was slipping back into himself.

Wally slept through mealtime and all night, but he awakened early. When he did, he was not sure what had happened the night before. He lay on his back in the dirt, and he waited to feel the fever and the dizziness. It all seemed gone.

Alan's eyes came open. "Wally, are you all right?"

"I feel okay." He laughed a little. "I mean, I feel terrible. Like always. But the fever is gone."

"It'll be back. Malaria doesn't go away that easy. At least the quinine didn't kill you."

It all came back to Wally. "I took all my pills, didn't I?"

"Yes. What were you thinking?" Alan sat up.

"I don't know. My mind wasn't clear." He thought about it for a moment. "But it seemed like what I was supposed to do. And I feel better."

"Don't try to work today. Just rest. You'll—"

"No. I have to get up. I have to keep moving."

"Okay. Maybe that's right." And then, after a moment, Alan added, "Man, I'm glad you didn't die. I thought . . ." But he stopped, and Wally could see he was struggling with his emotions.

Wally got up. His joints and muscles ached; his feet hurt. The sores on his hands and legs stung with pain. But he felt no fever, so he joined the other men, and he helped cook the rice, and then he ate all he could.

Norm helped with the cooking, and he looked brighter than he had in some time. "Boy, I'm glad to see you," he told

Wally, and Wally understood. The men tried not to let the deaths scare them, but a clock seemed to be ticking on everyone, and when someone fought off death, the others had more reason to hope.

Wally went to work. He looked Hatchet in the eye, even gave him a defiant little smile, but Hatchet merely made a gesture for him to pick up his shovel. Wally didn't feel strong, but he worked all day. The whole time he monitored himself, prepared for the fever to return, but he didn't feel any sign of it.

A few days later Alan told Wally, "That dose of quinine must have done something to your system. Maybe that's what everyone should do when they get it."

"I don't think so," Wally said. He and Alan were off the road, in the jungle, and they were digging a grave. Only one man had died that day, but there were several more who wouldn't last much longer. "I think God answered my prayers. He made the quinine work."

"Wally, you'll be one of the guys who makes it through."

"You too, Alan."

"I hope so. But you've got more inside you. Everyone knows you're the man to follow."

Wally was amazed. He thought of his father, and he thought how much he would like to talk to him now, to tell him he was not giving up.

Another week went by and more men died. Rumor had it that a Japanese crew with trucks and equipment had been working on the same road, and that it was catching up. Men had heard the big rigs behind them, across the river. The speculation was that once the Japanese workers overtook them, this decimated crew would be of no help. The nightmare could finally end.

Wally didn't want to think that way. What if the crew did come but then only pushed faster and asked more of the men? Wally told Alan, "Just plan to keep working. Keep thinking of one day at a time." But Wally had heard the bulldozers himself now, and he couldn't help thinking that any sort of change would be better than continuing this daily, pointless drudgery.

Then one morning two big trucks, shifting and racing their engines as they staggered over the rough road, drove up to the work crew and stopped. Two soldiers, better dressed than the ones the prisoners had grown used to seeing, got down from the trucks. They spoke at some length to the guards, and then one of them spoke to the prisoners. "Truck. You go."

Alan whispered, "Thank God," but Wally was still unsure. Maybe the prisoners would only move to another part of the road. He didn't want to make too much of this and then be disappointed. He began to walk toward the trucks with his shovel in his hand.

But Hatchet took hold of his shoulder. "No," he said. And he pointed to the shovel. Then he pointed to the ground.

Wally dropped the shovel, and he looked into Hatchet's eyes, tried to see something there. Hatchet stood for a moment, looked back at Wally, his narrow face as stern as ever, but he made a slight, barely discernible bow. Wally hesitated, and then, without knowing exactly why, he returned the gesture. Then he turned and walked to the camp. He wanted to get his meager possessions, and he knew he would have to help some of the men onto the truck.

He called out, "Okay, guys. They're moving us out. Hatchet told me not to take my shovel, so I think it's over."

No one cheered. But some of the sick men got up, and he saw the looks on their faces. They were too weak to show much joy, but some cried, and he could see the sense of relief, of awe, in all their faces. He knew that at least some of them were saying prayers of thanks, no matter how bitter and obscene they had been throughout this ordeal. Wally never thought to count how many of them were still alive, but he knew it was fewer than fifty.

He and Alan climbed into one of the trucks. They sat down together and leaned against the wall of the truck bed.

Hatchet walked around to the back and looked in through the slats. "Where are we going?" Wally asked. "Where go?"

Hatchet understood. "Bilibid," he said.

Wally looked around. "Does anyone know what Bilibid is?" he called out.

"It's a jail in Manila," one of the men said. "There's supposed to be a hospital there."

It sounded too good to be true, but Wally took a deep breath and tried to relax. Just the thought of riding in a truck and not working for a day was almost too wonderful to imagine. "Hey, Hatchet," Wally said. "Thanks for the memories," and he laughed.

Hatchet smiled a little, and no one had ever seen him do that before. Wally was in a great mood, but he wasn't ready to forgive. Hatchet and his buddies were responsible for all those deaths, and Wally wasn't about to forget that.

The truck backed up and turned around, and as it bumped over the road the men had built, Wally looked around at the other prisoners. They had survived the Tayabas work detail, and somehow, wherever they were going, conditions had to be better. At the same time, what he saw was as sad as anything he had ever looked at. These men who had once been well-conditioned soldiers were dressed in the shreds of their uniforms or in "G-strings"—mere strips of cotton cloth held between their legs and over their loins by a strand of string. The men looked wild with their long beards and hair, their skin covered with filth and open sores. And worst of all were their emaciated frames, every rib showing, their legs and arms thin as sticks. Some of the men, clearly, would not last much longer, even with medical help.

It was a long ride, and uncomfortable, but it was a joy ride. In Manila Wally had a chance to see that people still lived in homes, were still civilized. Even Bilibid prison didn't look bad. It was a dreary place, with buildings circled like the spokes of a wheel, and the compound surrounded by a high wall, but the men were taken immediately to a makeshift hospital. They got a chance to wash and rid themselves of their old clothes. The water was cold, but there was soap. Wally received an old pair of shorts that were much too big for him. He used a piece of string to cinch them up, and even though he had no shirt, he liked the shorts better than a G-string. Medicine was in short supply, and conditions were crude, but navy doctors, prisoners themselves, examined all the men.

Wally learned that he had the diseases he suspected: pellagra, beriberi and hepatitis, and he tested positive for tuberculosis. He weighed just over one hundred pounds, down from one-seventy. When a doctor—Doctor Ahern—asked him about symptoms of malaria, Wally told him about taking the quinine.

"Well," Doctor Ahern said, "the symptoms sound like malaria, but a big dose of quinine wouldn't cure it overnight."

"It went away, and it hasn't come back," Wally said.

Dr. Ahern was a thin man who had probably lost a good deal of weight himself, but he looked robust compared to most. Wally hoped that meant prisoners in Bilibid ate fairly well. The doctor put his hand on Wally's shoulder and said, "Just count yourself lucky that the malaria—if that's what you had—didn't get any worse. With everything else you have, I doubt you would have lasted long."

"I think God made that big dose of quinine work," Wally said. "That's my explanation."

Doctor Ahern looked into Wally's eyes. His own eyes were red and tired. "I don't know, son. Maybe so. But I've seen a lot of kids die. Sometimes I wonder where God has run off to."

"I know what you mean, sir," Wally said. "But I feel like I know some things now I probably wouldn't have learned any other way. So maybe, in a way, it's worth it."

"Well . . . there ought to be a better way, if you ask me." He shoved his hands into his pants pockets, and then he added, "I will say this. In most cases, it's the boys who believe some-

thing—have some commitment—who are surviving. Even if it's
hatred a guy feels, it's something to cling to."

Wally understood the hatred, but he knew it wouldn't have
been enough to have gotten him through.

* * *

Gene and his friends were celebrating. They had beaten
West High 26 to 6 that afternoon and clinched the city "Big-
Three" football championship. Gene had scored two of the
four touchdowns for East, and he had also been the main force
on defense. The challenge now was to create adequate refresh-
ments for the celebration. Sister Thomas had bought some root
beer, but Gene wanted to have root-beer floats. Most of the
kids had managed to bring a little sugar—a half a cup or so—
and cream was no problem. So now the boys had gathered on
the front porch, and they were taking turns cranking an old
ice-cream freezer. It was a cool October evening, but Gene was
rather glad of that. It was an excuse to wear his letter sweater—
which he wore proudly.

Ralph Nielson, Gene's big, red-headed friend who played
center, had twisted his knee, but he had stayed in the game
until the bitter end. Now, however, he was lying on the porch
with his knee propped up on the love seat. Del Marshall, the
fullback, was turning the handle on the freezer. He told the
others, "You can always trust old Ralph to claim an injury just
when the work has to be done."

"Watch your mouth," Ralph told him. "You give me a hard
time and I'll hike the ball to Gene all the time."

East High used a single-wing offense. The center hiked the
ball through the air, either to the tailback or the fullback. At
tailback, Gene not only carried the ball, but he threw passes
and was the punter besides.

Max Rasmussen, who was sitting on the front steps, turned
toward Arden Schwendiman. "I think the guys who get all the
glory should have to do the work."

"That's right," Arden said. "We open up holes that my

grandma could run through, and then Gene gets his name in the paper for scoring the touchdowns."

"Hey, I've got 'swivel hips,'" Gene said, chuckling. "Don't you guys read the paper?"

The week before, after a game with South High, the sports writer for the *Trib* had described Gene as "a swivel-hipped lad who can slip through the smallest of openings."

"That's true," Ralph said. "You do walk like a girl."

This set off a round of laughter and then another series of insults. Finally the boys were interrupted by Millie Ellertson, who stepped out the front door. "What's going on out here?" she asked. "Where's the ice cream?"

"Hold your horses," Del said. "Anything good is worth waiting for."

"Yeah. Like Gene," Ralph said from his prone position.

Millie laughed. "I'll wait for Gene as long as it takes. But I'd like my ice cream *tonight*."

When Millie shut the door, Arden said, "Oh, Genie boy, that girl has it bad for you."

"Naw. She's got it bad for ice cream."

The boys kept taking turns and kept sprinkling rock salt on the ice. Gradually the crank began to require more power. "Let me try it now," Gene said. "I know *exactly* when it's done." He turned the handle a few times. "Okay. Three more turns and it will be perfect," he said, and he gave it three more cranks. Then he released the cross bar, pushed the ice aside, and pulled out the canister. The boys all followed him inside, Ralph limping slowly behind the others.

The girls were in the kitchen chatting with Sister Thomas. President Thomas was in the living room near the console radio. He was listening to the late evening news.

"Okay," Gene said as he walked into the kitchen. "I haven't looked inside yet, but I have the touch—and I know this ice cream is perfect."

"Oh, pooh! I'll bet it's still too soft," Thora Bradford said. "You boys aren't strong enough to finish it off."

But just then President Thomas said, from the next room, "Listen to this, kids." He had turned up the radio.

Gene walked to the door and held it open. He heard something about Northern Africa and knew that the expected invasion had begun. "In Algiers," the announcer said, "American troops landed with little resistance, but in Casablanca the French joined with Nazi forces to resist the Allies."

"What's wrong with those stupid French?" Gene said, glancing at his friends. "How can they fight against *us?*"

"Be quiet a minute," Dad said.

The announcer continued the account, and everyone listened. The Allies had gained a foothold, and the push into northern Africa—to reverse recent British losses—had begun. Meanwhile, on the island of Guadalcanal, in the Pacific, marines were driving forward, making steady progress against the Japanese.

Ralph had sprawled out on the kitchen floor. "Man, that's what I want to be," he said. "A marine. They're the toughest guys out there."

"No more than the airborne boys in the army," Gene said. But he was also listening as the announcer continued. In Egypt and Libya, British and New Zealander troops were pursuing General Rommel, of Germany. In Russia, German troops continued to advance through the Caucasus. And on the other side of the world, Australian troops were fighting the Japanese on the island of Buna, off the coast of New Guinea.

"It all gets confusing to me," Alice Shepherd said.

She was sitting at the kitchen table with LaDonna Bliss, who said, "I know. I can't keep it all straight."

Gene thought how different it was for him. He read the accounts of every war front, and he wondered every day where he might end up when his time came.

The broadcast ended, and President Thomas walked to the

kitchen. Gene stepped back, and his father stood in the doorway. "I think the tide is going to turn," he said. "We need to give the Germans a licking somewhere, and Africa is probably the place."

Gene looked about the room and noticed how serious everyone had become. He had noticed in recent months that a change was coming over his friends—especially the boys. All the talk was that the draft would soon be extended to eighteen-year-olds.

"They need us East High Leopards over there," Ralph said. "We'd kick the Germans around the way we did the Panthers today."

"You got that right," Del said, and the kids laughed.

"I wonder where you guys will be this time next year," LaDonna said.

"From what the newspapers are reporting," Gene said, "the Allies will probably land in Europe next year—and start pushing toward Germany. Some of us could get in on that."

"We've got to take back a lot of islands in the Pacific," Ralph said. "Some of us will be going there, I suspect." There was a long pause, and Gene felt a kind of grim acceptance in the silence. But then Ralph grinned. "I plan to learn the hula-hula from some pretty girls in grass skirts."

No one laughed—except Ralph. For a couple seconds, Gene thought someone might admit the truth, say something about the fears they all shared. But Max said, with too much volume, "When the class of '43 arrives, we'll polish off this war in no time."

"That's exactly right," Del said, and the moment passed.

Gene had talked with his friends about his regrets that the war was going to disrupt their lives. Once he had even told Ralph that he wondered how many of the guys from their class would end up killed. But never had the whole group stopped to admit their worries.

It was President Thomas who said, "I hate, more than any-

thing, to see you boys going out to fight instead of serving missions. It seems such a waste to me."

"Maybe we can go on missions later," Ralph said. There was
something rather innocent—guileless—about Ralph. He was a
huge boy, his brown V-neck sweater seeming to stretch a full
acre over his vast shoulders, but he was also a kid. It occurred
to Gene that there was something wrong with training him to
go to war.

"I hope you can," President Thomas said. "But the way I see
it, you boys are going to do your missionary work by teaching
your buddies. Who knows? The war might take the gospel to
more lands, more people, than anything else could."

"My brother gets teased about being religious," Thora said.
"Most of the sailors sound pretty wild, from what he writes us."

"Well, sure," President Thomas said. "But Wayne is still in
San Diego, isn't he?"

"Yes."

"Just wait until those boys ship out, and they face the
prospect of dying. That's when some of them will turn to Him."

"I guess so," Thora said softly. But she was clearly thinking
of her brother facing death, and not of his friends.

"We'd better get those root-beer floats going," Gene said.

Sister Thomas stood up. "Yes. Before the ice cream melts."

Gene did the dipping and Mom did the pouring, and
everyone was soon eating—and laughing again. The boys
began to talk about the football game. They traded tales of
their great blocks, their crushing tackles, and no one spoke of
the war.

Mom and Dad eventually disappeared, and the kids rolled
back the rug in the living room and danced to music on the
radio. The room was small for jitter-bugging, but they managed
it anyway, or, more often, they stayed with the fox trot. Gene
danced with Millie more than with the others, but he made a
point of dancing with all the girls. A little before midnight, the

gang all left at the same time—all except Millie. Gene would walk her home.

It was a cool night, and along the way, Millie grasped Gene's arm and pulled herself close to him. "In case I didn't tell you," she said, "I was proud of you today. There's not a girl at East High who wouldn't want to be in my shoes right now."

"You're right about that. You do have nice shoes."

She pinched him in the ribs, and he squirmed. "Gene, you hate being a hero," she said. "That's what I love about you."

Millie had been saying those sorts of things lately, and sometimes she hinted that Gene ought to admit his feelings, but Gene didn't want to get into all that. In the back of his head was always a feeling that life was up in the air, beyond his control. When the two reached Millie's front porch, she turned toward Gene and looked up at him. She put her hand on his arm and said, "Thanks, Gene." And then she waited.

Gene knew what that meant, but he said, "Sure thing. I'll see you," and he took a step away.

"I'll see you at church," she said. "Do you want to come over on Sunday, after dinner?"

"Yeah. I guess so." But he was uneasy about her obvious attachment. As he walked home, along the quiet streets, he was surprised by the sadness that came over him. He heard leaves crunching under his feet, smelled the decay, and something in the sound and the smell reminded him of the fall days when Alex, and then later, Wally, had played football at East. He missed them, and he missed Bobbi. Gene had always loved to have his family together, especially for holidays, and now he wondered whether that would ever happen again. Thanksgiving was coming up soon, and the family would hold its usual big dinner, but he knew that the three people he wanted most to see wouldn't be there.

When Gene got home he walked up the stairs to his bedroom, sat down on his bed, and took his shoes off. He was unbuttoning his shirt when he heard his dad say, "Gene?"

"Yeah."

Dad opened the bedroom door. "I thought I heard you come in. Why didn't you say something?"

"I figured you were asleep."

Dad stepped into the room and leaned against the wall. He was wearing flannel pajamas, as he always did in the winter. He shaved very early every morning, so by this time of night his beard was stubbly and dark, his jowls seeming heavier. "I don't go to sleep very easily these days."

"Too many worries?"

"I do have a lot on my mind. It's hard to keep the stake going the way I'd like—with all the disruptions." He folded his arms over his chest. "But beyond that, don't start thinking you're old enough to come and go as you please. I want you to check in with me—even if I have gone to sleep."

"Okay." Gene smiled, and then he pulled off his argyle socks, balled them together, and tossed them toward a basket he kept in the corner. The socks came apart and dropped short.

"You need to get your shooting eye back before basketball starts," Dad said, and he laughed.

This was a good sign. Gene knew that Dad wasn't really all that upset if he could laugh already. "Basketball is going to be fun," he said, "but it about kills me to see my senior year of football come to an end."

Dad nodded and said, "I can imagine," but then he introduced the topic he must have come upstairs to talk about. "Gene, I get the impression that Millie is pretty sweet on you."

"Yeah. I guess."

"And what about you?"

"I don't know. I just want to be friends."

"She *is* a wonderful girl."

"I know. But nothing's exactly normal right now. I think it's better not to make any promises."

Dad took a long look at Gene. "You know," he said, "I always had to tell your big brothers things that you seem to understand on your own. You've been blessed with a lot of wisdom."

"I thought my best quality was my swivel hips."

Dad laughed. "Well, you've got those too, and you didn't get them from me. We'll blame that on your mom."

"That woman does sashay around, doesn't she?"

Dad smiled, but his mind was somewhere else. "Son, I was proud of you tonight. You played hard."

"I just like to play, Dad."

"That's how it ought to be." Dad nodded a couple of times, and Gene saw how satisfied he was. He and his dad had become much closer since the older kids had left home. "Well, good night." He turned to leave, but then he stopped. "Gene," he said, "I love you."

"I love you too, Dad."

Dad nodded again, and then he walked out. But Gene was surprised. Dad sometimes said something like that in a blessing, or in a formal situation, but this was spontaneous. And yet it was hard for him. Gene noticed how rapidly he looked away, and how quickly he left the room.

11

Wally was improving steadily. He had actually gained a little weight, and most of the symptoms of his diseases were abating. He was eating regularly, if not all that well, and exercising. Gradually he was getting so he could walk for quite some time. He also tried to help the men who were coming into Bilibid for medical care. He especially devoted a good deal of time to Captain Bud Surmelian, an infantry officer who had lost his legs to a mortar shell in the Battle of Bataan. The captain was unable to get about, wash his clothes, and the like, and Wally liked to keep him company and take care of some of his chores.

When Christmas approached, a rumor circulated that the men were going to receive Red Cross packages—and maybe even boxes from home. Wally had never been allowed to write to his family, nor had he received any word from them, so he was eager to believe the rumor. He also listened with some hope to the other scuttlebutt going around, that American troops would liberate the Philippines before much longer. Wally was realist enough to doubt these stories, but it was hard to think that another Christmas might come around with him still a prisoner.

When Christmas morning came and no packages appeared, and when the day turned out to be exactly like every other, Wally felt the ache more than he wanted to. He knew that it was Christmas eve at home, since he was across the International Date Line, and he tried to think what his family might be doing. He wondered whether Alex might be in the service by now, and where he might be. Would the family gather at home in Sugar House on Christmas day? It was hard to imagine anything quite so wonderful as to hear all those people laughing and enjoying each other—and eating all that glorious food. He wondered what they knew about him, whether they knew he was alive.

Wally spent a couple of hours with Captain Surmelian in the morning. They talked about their homes, the Christmases they remembered as kids, and mostly about food—the subject the prisoners always talked about more than any other. It was almost masochistic to remember Christmas dinners and enumerate every specialty a soldier's mother had cooked, but it was also the memory that preoccupied everyone. Wally found it interesting that when the soldiers had been well-fed back in the days before the war, they had talked mostly about getting drunk. And always about women. But now they talked about turkey and dressing, candied yams, sweet pickles, and pumpkin pies—and they described each delicacy in detail, as though holding the idea of the food in their heads somehow saved it from extinction.

Early in the afternoon Wally found Alan, and they took a walk in the compound. They were walking down the center roadway through Bilibid when a prisoner told them to hurry to the north compound. "Tell everyone to gather there," he said.

"What's going on?" Wally asked.

"Just hurry."

Wally immediately thought of the rumor about the packages, but the north compound was the most distant from the administrative buildings; the guards rarely wandered up that far. It was highly unlikely that anything official would happen there. Still, Wally was happy to have anything out of the ordinary occur. He and Alan walked to the north end, where they saw nothing to explain what was going on. It was a nice day, the skies clear, and men were milling around, most of them confused about why they were there—and asking whether anyone else knew.

Then two men hustled along the wall, carrying a pole. They stopped, turned, and faced the men, and then they walked away from each other, unfurling a large American flag between them. By then the men could see the banner that was attached below the flag. The sign read: "WE'LL BE FREE IN '43."

An enormous cheer went up. Wally felt himself letting loose, whooping and shouting. "Yes. Yes!" Alan was yelling, and he was pounding Wally on the back.

But then someone shouted, "Guards!" and all the shouting stopped as suddenly as it had begun. Wally saw the guards running toward the crowd. He looked back to the flag, but somehow it had disappeared.

The guards approached, slowing as they neared, holding their rifles in front of them, bayonets in place, but the prisoners acted as though nothing had happened. The guards shouted questions in English, but no one answered, and so the men were ordered out of the area. As Wally and Alan walked back to their building, they laughed quietly. "I don't know who did that, but it was a good idea," Wally said.

"It's going to happen, too," Alan said. "We're going home this year."

Wally didn't know whether he believed that, but he wanted to, and so he said, "That's right. We'll be free in '43. We'll be with our families next year for Christmas."

But a little later, when he walked over to see Bud Surmelian and told him what had happened, the captain said, quietly, "I doubt it, Wally. I know a guy who hears radio reports every now and then. He says the Japs are in control of most of the

Pacific. We're just starting to make some headway against them."

And those were the words that were on Wally's mind when he went to bed that night—the night before Christmas back home. It was the first time since he had made it out of the jungle that he allowed himself to feel his homesickness.

* * *

The Stoltz family was living in an apartment in Berlin. With so many people displaced, apartments were not easy to come by, but many families were fleeing to the country, where they were in less danger from air raids. The Stoltzes found a small apartment on the top floor of a downtown building. It was not attractive to most people, since the escape to the basement was so distant and the vulnerability in a surprise attack was great, but to the Stoltzes it was a welcome change from all the dark they had lived with for so long. Peter had to sleep on a couch, but after sleeping on the floor at the Hochs' for so long, that didn't bother him.

Anna found it lovely to have a bedroom to herself, a place to be alone in the evenings. She was even thankful to have work, although she put in long hours at a munitions factory. Her father had created false papers for her and the family, and they had grown accustomed to their new names. More than anything, the Stoltzes wanted to attend church, but Brother Stoltz had contacted President Hoch—at his place of work— and the president thought it unwise for them to try. A few days after the Stoltzes had left the Hochs' home, Agent Kellerman, from Frankfurt, had visited. He was certain that the so-called Hofmann family was the family he was looking for. President Hoch had stayed with his story, but Kellerman hadn't believed him.

"The coincidence is too great," Kellerman had told President Hoch. "The family I am looking for fits the description of these Hofmanns, and these people are Mormons, just as you are."

"The Hofmanns told me they were protestants," President Hoch had told him. "That's all I know."

And Kellerman had left. But President Hoch was convinced that the man had left only so that surveillance could continue. He had seen men watching the house, and twice Gestapo agents had come to church services. "Don't contact me again," President Hoch had warned. "And don't come to church. I'm certain you'll be spotted."

So life was uneasy. Having identification simplified the Stoltz's lives, but they rarely ventured out beyond their daily journeys to school or work. Brother Stoltz thought it would be wise to eventually slip away from Berlin, but for now they were better off not to change anything. Kellerman had lost their trail.

When Christmas came, Brother Stoltz paid a terrific price to buy a goose, and the family had a nice dinner. Anna said the blessing on the food, and she prayed that the family would be protected and that the Thomas family might be blessed that day too. She also prayed that peace might return to the world, but she knew within herself that the war was not likely to end for a long time.

It was at the dinner table that Brother Stoltz told his family he had someone coming over that afternoon.

"Someone coming? Who?" Sister Stoltz asked.

"I don't know him personally," Brother Stoltz said. "I found out about him through another contact." He hesitated. "This could be a little dangerous. I need to tell you that. But it's something I need to do."

"Whatever are you talking about?" Sister Stoltz asked. Anna always felt insecure. She hated to think of her father doing something that might put them in deeper peril.

"A man came into our office seeking papers a few weeks ago—and I knew something was wrong from the beginning. He seemed nervous, and I caught him in some contradictions. So I sent him away, but then I followed him outside, and I talked to him. I told him what I suspected, and then I took a chance. I told him that I could help him. He was very relieved but unsure what to do. Finally, he told me I would be contacted."

"I don't understand," Sister Stoltz said. "What are you going to do?"

"The man coming today is a member of a group that hides Jews from the Nazis. I've told him I will help make false papers for some of these people. I have a chance to save some families from the Gestapo."

"But what if you're caught?"

"I'm not too worried about that. These people know what they're doing. The man is coming on Christmas because it's a day he's not likely to be followed. He knows all about avoiding the Gestapo, and he said he would make certain no one was watching him before he approached the house. I wanted to meet him somewhere else, but he said a visit on Christmas would seem quite natural."

Anna could see that Peter was frightened. "Papa, at Hitler Youth, we hear about these things," he said. "The Gestapo gives no mercy. To help Jews is the worst thing anyone can do."

"If the Gestapo is so much against it, it must be the *right* thing to do. Isn't that so, Peter?"

"But to be caught is to die."

"I know, Peter. But *we* were chased by the Gestapo—and people put themselves in danger to help us. We need to do what we can for others."

"Yes. But why for *Jews?*"

"Especially for Jews, Peter. You can't be polluted by what you hear at Hitler Youth. Jews are our brothers and sisters, as much as anyone is."

It was right, and the whole family knew it, but the quiet in the room communicated the depth of everyone's fear. Anna didn't want to feel this way on Christmas, when things were starting to get better, and Peter was clearly upset.

The man showed up later that afternoon. He didn't ever say his name. He was a gentle man, soft-spoken, with graying hair. He hardly seemed a clever Nazi resister; there was too much sadness in his eyes.

Brother Stoltz and the man sat in the living room for over an hour. They talked about the logistics of getting pictures and information to Brother Stoltz, and systems for getting the false papers back to those who needed them. The man seemed to know all the tricks about passing each other casually in public places, slipping materials back and forth.

Anna sat in the kitchen and listened to the conversation, and her own nervousness continued to grow. One mistake and her father would be caught, and then what would happen to all of them?

Before the man left, he asked to speak to the family. "Your father has told me a little about you," he told them. "I know, for instance, that Niemeyer is not your real name." He was standing near the door, apparently prepared to leave. He had buttoned his big black overcoat and tucked his muffler around his neck. "You must all be careful to bring no special attention to yourselves. Young man, you must never let any hint of anything slip out at Hitler Youth meetings. Just to say that you moved here from another place could be something that could be used by someone looking for you."

Anna could hardly bear to hear more of this. She was already frightened enough.

"But I want you to know, your father is saving lives. The Jews are being forced into squalid ghettoes, full of disease. They are sometimes beaten to death for no reason. We even have reports that some are being shot and then buried in mass graves. If you help a few of these poor people, then you are saviors. Think of that today, on Christmas. I know it is all very frightening, but think what it means to put yourself in danger for someone else's sake. It's what a Christian should do."

He looked around at each of them, thanked them again,

and then left. Silence filled the room, but this time Anna felt something new. She put her arms around her father's shoulders and kissed him on the cheek.

* * *

At the conclusion of jump training, the paratroopers got their "wings." The symbol was a little parachute hovering over silver eagle wings, to be pinned over their shirt pockets. They also received their airborne patches to sew on their garrison hats. Alex had proved to himself—and to some of the guys who didn't like him—that he could stick it out, and he was proud of that.

Alex's only friend was Curtis Bentley, who shared most of his values—if little else. Curtis had been terrified by his first jump and had almost backed out, but Alex had pushed him out of the airplane. After that first experience Curtis had done pretty well on the remaining four jumps. So no one in their barracks had washed out during the final stages at Camp Toccoa, and all of the men would now be moving on together for further training. After they were pinned with their wings, they heard what they had been hoping to hear: "All right, you are on leave as of right now. You have ten days. Stay out of jail, and be back in Georgia, at Fort Benning, on the fifth of January, before seventeen hundred hours."

The men were already leaning forward, waiting to run.

"Did you hear me?" the Colonel barked. "January *five.* Seventeen hundred hours. Anyone who is one second late will be drummed out of this outfit and shipped to a straight-leg regiment. No exceptions."

Finally, he said the magic words: "Fall out!"

A lot of the men lived in the South, and they would be home before the day was over, but Alex had to get himself all the way across the country. It was December 26. Alex didn't understand why things couldn't have been planned so the men could get home for Christmas. As it turned out, however, he had a better chance of getting a train and making it home now than he would have had a few days earlier.

Alex spent most of the day in a train station, and then he spent all night and most of the next day sitting up in a train, only to end up waiting in another train station all night in St. Louis. By the time he got to Salt Lake City, it was the morning of December 29, and he had to start thinking about beginning his trip back.

But he called his parents from Union Station, and they drove down to get him, the girls with them. Alex was happier to see them this time than he had been when he had come home from his mission. He grabbed each of them and held on for a long time.

"Where's Gene," he finally asked.

"Who knows?" Mom said. "He was off somewhere with Ralph. But I told him you'd probably be in this morning, and he said he wouldn't be gone long.

And it was true. When the Thomases arrived home, Gene burst out of the house and ran toward them. He grabbed Alex and practically broke his ribs with his hug. Then he stepped back. "Wow. That's some uniform. Maybe I want to go airborne."

Alex grabbed his duffel bag and tossed it at Gene. "Carry this, then," he said. "You've grown some more, haven't you?"

"Maybe. I'm not sure."

"He scored about twice as many touchdowns as you did when you were a senior," Dad said.

"Hey, I know all about it. Everyone I know has written me about his 'exploits on the gridiron.' I've got enough clippings to get in trouble for hoarding newsprint."

Everyone moved into the house, and Mom said she would start dinner. She had taken the day off from the plant to await Alex's call, and Dad wasn't going in until later. So Dad sat in his big chair and Alex and Gene sat on the couch. LaRue and

Beverly plunked themselves on the floor and stared up at Alex as though he were an angel visiting from heaven.

"So you got your wings?" Gene said.

Alex pulled on his shirt. "Right there," he said. "And I'll tell you, I earned them."

"What was it like to jump out of an airplane?" LaRue asked. Alex was amazed at LaRue. She was prettier than ever—and not just the "little-girl" pretty that Alex associated with her. At thirteen, she was looking very grown up. "Oh, it wasn't bad. Remember when we went to the Grand Canyon?"

"Sort of. I was kind of young."

"Well, picture yourself jumping into that canyon—on the trust that your parachute will open."

"Golly. That would scare me so bad."

"How was basic training?" Gene asked.

Alex knew why he wanted to know, but he didn't want to get into all that yet. "It's *terrible*. That's what it is. But what I want to know is what's going on around here."

"One good thing," LaRue said. "I got my own radio for Christmas."

"A *radio?*" Alex said. "You have a radio in your room?"

"It's just a little one."

"Yeah. And she won't let me touch it," Beverly said.

"I *always* wanted my own radio," Alex said. "Do you have one too, Gene?"

"I have Wally's. But a tube has gone out, and I can't find one to replace it. I get more static than anything else."

"I can't believe this. Three radios in one house."

"Four. Dad has one in his office."

Alex was shaking his head. "I think things are looking up around this place. Are you getting rich, Dad?"

"No, no. I saw the shortage of radios coming last summer, so I bought two extras, that's all."

"That doesn't sound like the old days."

"Well, we've done all right. But I think we did get a little carried away for Christmas. There are so many things we can't get these days, so we went overboard on things we could buy."

It was not like Dad to admit even that much. Alex thought he saw a change. LaRue's sweater looked expensive, and even though she may have worn it for his arrival, it seemed strange to see her so dressed up on a weekday.

"I want you to know, Alex," Dad added, "we still consider you a partner in the business. We aren't taking a lot of money out, for the present, but I've been putting some into war bonds for you."

"A *lot* of war bonds," LaRue said. "Sugar House was having a big bond drive and a parade and everything, so Dad walked up to this booth and gave the man a check—and the man's eyes about popped out."

"Don't exaggerate, LaRue," Dad said, but he seemed pleased. He looked at Alex. "I was buying bonds for all the kids—not just for you. I want Wally to have something to get started with when he comes home—and something for college for the girls."

Alex looked down at Beverly, who hadn't said a word. "Bev, are you going to go to college?"

"I guess so," she said. She was still such a little girl compared to LaRue, but she was eleven now.

"Do you still play with your dolls?"

"*No!*" she said, emphatically. He noticed that she was dressed like her big sister, in a straight skirt and sweater, not in the frilly girls' dresses she had always worn when she wanted to dress up.

"That's only because I tease her if I catch her doing it," LaRue said.

"It is not. I don't like dolls anymore."

Alex hated to think of that. Why did everything have to change? He looked around, trying to drink all this in so he could hold it close when he was gone again.

"Did you hear that the BYU beat the Utes this year in football?" Gene asked.

"Oh, no. How did that happen?"

"A lot of guys are in the service," Gene said. "It's the first time *ever* that the U. lost to those guys."

Alex laughed. "It's a tragedy. We can't let that happen again."

And that set off a whole discussion about sports at East and the University of Utah, and especially about the upcoming basketball season. Alex couldn't believe how good it seemed to talk about things that no one in Georgia knew anything about.

After a time, Alex got up and wandered into the kitchen. He chatted with his mom and then helped her open some canned vegetables. "So how are you and dad doing at the plant? Does he mind working with you?"

"No. Once in a while someone will walk right past him and ask me something, and I can see him get his nose a little out of joint, but he asks me as many questions as anyone. I'm the one who understands all about the government paperwork. But I have two secretaries now, and they take care of a lot of things. I couldn't keep up without them. By the way, one of them is Lorraine Gardner. She started with us last summer, and she's done a great job."

"Is she still single?"

"Yes."

"Waiting for Wally?"

"Not exactly, I don't think. She goes out quite a lot—considering how few boys are still at home—but she doesn't seem to get serious with anyone."

"You haven't gone to three shifts at the plant, have you?"

"No. But we've rented another building, next door, just as big as the first one. And a lot of days we put in overtime. Our biggest problem now is, we can't find enough help. Most of our machinists are women. Your dad feels out of place—surrounded by all those girls."

"Hey, I never had it like that."

"You didn't look at girls anyway. You've only had one in your head all along." Mom was standing at the sink, scrubbing potatoes. She glanced over at him and smiled, showing her dimples. It struck Alex that she was a pretty woman, even if a little too round—something he had never stopped to think much about when he was younger.

"I wish I could hear from Anna and know she's okay," Alex said. "There's been a lot of bombing in Berlin. If something were to happen to her, I might never know it—even when the war is over."

"Oh, Alex, I don't know how you and Anna can make it through all this." Mom lifted her apron and wiped her hands on it, then stepped to Alex, raised herself to her toes, and kissed his cheek. "It's sad to me," she said. "So many things are sad right now. Most of the girls who work for us have husbands or boyfriends off in the war. One of them got word that her husband is missing in action on one of those little Pacific islands. By now, the poor girl's pretty sure he's dead, but she just wants a definite answer. It would be so much easier to deal with that."

"Like Wally, I guess."

"No. Wally's alive. I know that."

Alex hoped she was right. He was not nearly so confident.

After dinner, Alex walked upstairs and unpacked the things in his duffel bag. He also changed out of his uniform and put on some old cords and a sports shirt. He liked the feel of that. He was sitting on the bed that had once been his, putting his shoes on, when Gene came in. "Hey, if I had a uniform like yours, I'd never take it off," he said. "The girls at East would be nuts over me."

"I hear they are anyway."

"Naw." Gene sat down on his own bed, across from Alex.

When Alex straightened up, he looked at Gene. "I'd give anything to keep you out of the service," he said. "Are you sure you have to go? Don't they have rules about how many have to go from a family?"

Gene laughed. "Dad used to tell you that you didn't have to go, and you fought him tooth and nail."

"I know. But there are three from our family in the service already. Why couldn't you work down at the plant and get a deferment that way?"

"The same reason you wouldn't. I have to do my part. All us guys in high school know we'll be going next year. Some have been dropping out of school and joining up before they graduate."

"It's not like you think, Gene." He leaned forward and spoke quietly. "You get treated like dirt. And not just by the drill sergeant. If a fellow doesn't use foul language and get drunk, the other guys give him a hard time. I've watched some good kids, from good homes, lose track of who they are."

"I won't do that."

"It won't be easy, Gene. I've been on a mission and everything. But you'll be right out of high school."

"I know. Ralph and I are talking about going together. Maybe we can end up in the same place."

"The army sends you wherever it wants to. There's never anything guaranteed. I was supposed to be in intelligence, and nothing has ever come of that."

"Is the food as bad as everybody says?"

"It's not Mom's cooking, if that's what you mean. But Gene, that's nothing." Alex didn't know how to say what he was thinking. "I really think you should stay out of it, if you can."

"I'd feel like a coward if I stayed home, Alex. All my friends are going."

"But Gene, think about Mom and Dad."

"They're used to all of you being gone now. It'll be the same with me."

Alex sat for a time, considering his words. Then he raised his head and took a long look at Gene. "This war could be very long," he said. "I don't know whether Wally will make it. And I'm in a regiment that will drop in behind enemy lines. We'll end up surrounded by the enemy, no matter where we fight. The chances aren't that good for me, Gene. I don't want to tell Mom and Dad that, but it's just how things are."

The point, of course, was sinking in with Gene, and Alex saw that the color was leaving his face. "You guys have to come home," he said.

"I hope we will. But maybe you should *stay* home, and then the family would be certain of having one son get through this."

Gene looked at the floor. "I don't necessarily want to go," he finally said. "But I have to."

Alex thought of arguing the point, but he remembered all too well the conversation he had had with his father, not a year before. Alex stood and put his hands on Gene's shoulders, and Gene looked up, "There would be no shame in it, Gene. Think about it."

The two brothers stared into each other's eyes. "I wish the war could just end," Gene said, "and we could all be back together again."

"It's going to take *years*, Gene. Years. Hitler has himself in a mess in Stalingrad, and that's going to help the Allies. I feel pretty sure we'll win—in the long run—but the price is going to be high."

"It's a rotten time, Alex. When you were my age, you had nothing but good things to look forward to."

"I *thought* I did, anyway. But look what happened."

"I know. But I really believe everything will work out." Gene seemed to know what Alex was thinking. "You and Anna are going to end up together."

Alex didn't ask why he thought so, but he was moved by the tender goodwill he felt from his brother. "I understand you have a girl too," he said.

"Not really."

But Alex saw in his eyes that he did. The two brothers looked at each other one more time, and for the first time in his life, Alex saw Gene as a grownup. The two of them were facing the same set of problems, the same realities, and Alex was deeply saddened to think of his little brother walking down the same dark path.

・ CHAPTER ・

1 2

"But Dad, I'm *almost* fourteen. All my friends are going."

"LaRue, you just turned thirteen. And I don't believe for a minute that your friends are going. You always say that. It's an M-Men and Gleaners dance, and you're a Beehive."

"That doesn't matter. It's *sponsored* by the M-Men and Gleaners. Beehives can go."

Dad was sitting in his chair, the newspaper folded over his lap and his reading glasses in one hand. LaRue was standing in front of him. "It's not fair to Beverly," he said. "She'll be here with Mom and me tonight—without one thing to do."

"We don't do anything anyway. Except listen to the radio until midnight—and then say, 'Whoopee! Happy New Year.'"

Beverly walked into the room from the kitchen, where she had obviously heard everything. "I don't care if LaRue goes," she said. "I don't want her here anyway." She continued on through the room, into the parlor, and then up the stairs to her bedroom.

President Thomas waited until he heard the door shut upstairs, and then he said, "LaRue, think about your sister. She's such a lonely little thing."

"That's her fault, not mine. And she's eleven. She'll get to go to dances when she's older."

Dad let his head fall back against his high chairback. He closed his eyes. "Somehow, sooner or later, I hope you learn to think of someone besides yourself, LaRue."

"Dad, I have to take Beverly with me to *everything*. And that's not fair. Bobbi didn't take me when I was eleven."

Gene watched all this from across the room. He was amazed at the way LaRue was holding to her guns. It seemed to Gene that Dad asked a lot of LaRue. She could be self-centered, but she did look out for Beverly. Gene also remembered too well his own early teen years when Dad seemed to work to keep him from growing up. It was as though Dad knew that his influence would soon slip away, so he held out as long as he could. This last year he had had to adjust as he let his older children take their lives into their own hands, and in some ways he was a different man, but his impulse was still to control his children.

"Bishop Evans's daughter is going. She told me so. And she's younger than I am."

"That's the bishop's business."

"Here's an idea," Gene said. Dad and LaRue both looked at Gene as though they were surprised he was still in the room. "How about if I take LaRue as my date?"

"Aren't you going with Millie?" LaRue said.

"Not really. I'll see her there, but I didn't tell her I'd pick her up."

"So you'll take LaRue, and look after her, make sure she gets home all right?" Dad asked.

"Sure." Gene knew he had hit on his dad's real concern.

LaRue's eyes widened as she realized that Dad was giving in. She began to smile, but Dad looked up at her and said, "I don't like this. I think you're too young, but if you'll let Gene take you, I'll let you go."

"Oh, thank you, Daddy. Thank you." She leaped toward him, bent, and kissed his cheek, and then she charged Gene, threw herself onto the couch next to him, and hugged him around the neck. "Thank you, Gene!" She looked back at her dad. "If he tries to kiss me good night, I'll slap his face."

"Listen," Dad said, "I want Gene to take you there and bring you home—and look out for you during the dance. We have so darned much trouble these days with boys getting drunk and then showing up at church dances." He hesitated, and then added, "And you two come *straight* home. Remember, we have a curfew law now."

"It's not fair. It's only for girls," LaRue said.

"Well, the police can't monitor all these young soldiers who are passing through, but they can sure keep our girls away from them." Gene could tell that Dad didn't like giving in. He was trying to sound firm. "Now what about Beverly?" he asked. "What can we do so she won't be miserable all evening?"

Alex's voice rang from the stairway. "Don't worry," he said, and he walked down the stairs. "I asked Bev out on a date. We're going to the Coon Chicken Inn for dinner, just the two of us. And maybe we'll go to a picture show."

"I don't want her out late—with a lot of drunks around."

"We'll start early. And then we'll come back here. At midnight we'll go *crazy* with you and Mom. We'll throw back the rug and jitterbug, just like you always do."

"Oh yes, I'm certain," Dad said, refusing to laugh. "I'm lucky to stay awake that late." He picked up his newspaper.

It was several hours later when Beverly came downstairs in her Sunday dress—pink with a big satin bow in back—and white patent leather shoes. Alex, who was wearing a suit, stood up and said, "Wow, you're the prettiest girl I've dated in years."

And she did look pretty. Beverly was not as striking as LaRue. LaRue had dark hair and blue eyes so rich they seemed almost lavender, and enticing dimples that appeared even with the hint of a smile. Beverly was more like Bobbi, with light brown hair and freckles across her nose and cheeks, but she had an innocent, round little face and pale, guileless eyes.

Beverly giggled. "Alex, you never *go* on dates," she said.

Dad stood up. "Mother, Gene," he called out, "could you come in for a minute?"

Mom came in from the kitchen, and Gene, in his blue jeans, walked down the stairs. They both made a fuss over Beverly, and she clearly liked it, although she pretended she didn't.

"Before you all leave tonight," Dad said, "I wanted to say something to you."

"Oh, no, one of Dad's meetings," LaRue said, but then she patted his shoulder to show him she was only teasing. She had her hair up in curlers and was wearing a tattered robe. She had spent an hour, it seemed, painting her fingernails dark red— much to her father's disgust.

Dad shook his head with mock annoyance. "Just sit down for a second," he said, his tone surprisingly soft. Mom and Alex and Beverly sat together on the couch, and Gene and LaRue found spots on the floor. Dad had been listening to a special New Year's Eve broadcast by Artie Shaw and his band, but he turned the radio off now. "I'm not going to give a speech, LaRue," he said. He laced his fingers together. "I just wanted to say that I'm proud of all of you tonight. You boys are doing something very good—very impressive. It hit me just a few minutes ago what fine young men you are." He looked at each of them and nodded. "You couldn't ask for nicer girls to date, either."

"That's right," Alex said, and he put his arm around Beverly.

"I was also thinking about this coming year," Dad said, his voice lowering even more. "It's hard to say where everyone will be by the time it's over. Alex, you'll be leaving in a day or two, and I don't know when you'll get home again. I doubt Bobbi or Wally will be with us for quite some time either."

"I'll be gone next year," Gene said, "unless I get a furlough—like Alex got."

Dad didn't agree to that, and Gene knew why. He was still clinging to the hope that Gene wouldn't have to go. "Well, anyway," he said, "I just thought we might have a prayer, to thank the Lord that we made it through this last, very hard year, and ask that we might make it through this next one all right."

And so everyone knelt, and Dad did something unexpected. He usually prayed at such times, but tonight he asked Mom to say the prayer. She cried, and she begged the Lord for help for Wally, protection for Alex and Bobbi, and family strength. "Lord," she said, "we don't ask that hardships pass us. We only ask thee to strengthen our shoulders, to give us the power to carry the load we are asked to bear."

Gene felt his mother's words penetrate him. He didn't want to think what the coming year might bring.

* * *

It was the first Sunday of 1943. Bobbi caught herself glancing toward the back of the chapel as sacrament meeting was about to start. She knew that Richard Hammond wasn't able to come every Sunday, but he had missed two Sundays in a row during the holidays. Maybe he had gotten leave and gone home. Maybe his ship had put out to sea. But then, it probably didn't matter either way, because he usually had to hurry off after the meetings. Bobbi still hadn't gotten to know him very well.

Bobbi glanced back again, and this time Afton said, "Gee whiz, Bobbi, what are you looking for back there? If you're not careful, you'll sprain your neck."

Bobbi laughed. "I was just greeting all my brothers and sisters," she said. "I'm very friendly, you know."

"I thought you didn't like that guy."

"*Guy?* I have no idea what you mean."

"Yeah. Sure. If he doesn't show up again this week, we're both going to bawl."

The bishop's first counselor had stood up now. "Aloha!" he said to the congregation, and everyone answered back. Bobbi had come to enjoy that beginning—even though it still annoyed her that the services never seemed to start on time. Apparently, she was more her father's daughter than she'd thought. There were right ways to do things, and starting late and then running way over at the end—because a speaker got carried away—just seemed wrong to her. Bobbi longed to be home now anyway, to go to her own ward one Sunday, to see the snow on the mountains and enjoy the decorations downtown in Salt Lake—all the things she associated with the holidays.

During the opening hymn Bobbi noticed Afton taking a look at the back of the room. Bobbi was about to tease her about it when Afton said, "Guess what? Christmas came late this year. Our package just arrived."

Bobbi resisted looking back, but she was surprised how pleased she was. And when the meeting was over, she made a point of walking directly to the foyer. To her surprise, Richard seemed to be waiting. "Bobbi, how have you been?" he asked.

"Heck, what about me?" Afton asked. "Aren't you concerned about my health?"

He smiled. "I was about to ask."

"Well, I'm fine, and so is Bobbi, but where in the world have you been?"

"Some of the senior officers had leave during the holidays, so the rest of us had to pull double duty. I haven't been able to get away from the ship."

"We're going out for our Sunday-evening walk," Bobbi said. "Would you like to go with us?"

"Yes. I think I would."

"It's a long way. We walk all the way down to the beach and then watch the sun set before we take the bus back to our quarters."

"I'm off for the evening," he said. "That sounds nice."

His response sounded polite more than enthusiastic, but it was Bobbi, again, he looked at. Bobbi soon looked away. She loved those crystal-blue eyes of his, but she didn't want him to see any interest in her own eyes. She certainly didn't want him to think that she was as forward as Afton.

As the threesome tried to leave, a Hawaiian sister stopped them. Bobbi knew the woman only as Hazel. Her last name, like so many of the Hawaiian names, was a long line of short syllables that Bobbi struggled to remember. "Bobbi dear," Hazel said. "Is this your man? He's *fine* looking."

Bobbi laughed, but she was embarrassed. "This is Brother Hammond," she said. "He's my friend. And Afton's."

Richard nodded.

"So nice to meet you. Why do you sit in back and hide from us?" She reached toward him with open arms, but Richard kept his distance. "I can't always get here on time," he said. He shook Hazel's hand.

"You should marry our Afton. Or Bobbi. One of them. You could make pretty babies."

Richard actually reddened. "Well, thank you," he said, and he laughed.

Bobbi was now trying to move away, but Hazel grabbed her. She pulled Bobbi against all her flesh, which was loose and flowing under her flowered *muumuu*. Bobbi felt herself stiffen, but Hazel didn't seem to notice. She turned and hugged Afton, too. By then some of the other members had approached. They also wanted to meet Richard, but he was retreating, nodding from a distance, saying, "It's nice to meet all of you."

"What a pretty man," one of the sisters told Bobbi. "Almost like one of our Hawaiian boys." She was squeezing Bobbi, hanging onto her. "Is he your boyfriend?"

"No. Just a friend." Bobbi pulled away and kept going this time. "Good-bye," she said. "We'll see you next week."

All the sisters waved. "Aloha," they said.

The long walk to the beach took the better part of an hour. The three chatted, mostly about home, but Richard actually said little about himself. When they arrived at Waikiki, they sat on a bench and looked out across the ocean. The sun was setting a little earlier this time of year, but otherwise it was hard to remember that it was winter.

"Was it difficult for the two of you to be away for Christmas?" Richard asked.

Afton was sitting in the middle. "Only the hardest thing I've ever done in my life," she said. "I cried half the day and was grouchy the rest of it."

"I was on duty," Bobbi said. "But it was quiet at the hospital, and I had a chance to sit down with some of the men who were homesick. It actually turned out to be kind of nice."

"So are you liking the navy any better?" Richard leaned forward so he could look past Afton to see Bobbi.

Bobbi watched the motion of a tall palm tree, a silhouette against the sunset. There was something almost unnerving about the attentive way he looked at her. "I've gotten used to most things," Bobbi said. "Except for all the mutilated bodies. I'll never get used to that."

Richard rested his elbows on his knees. "I know what you mean," he said. "I don't think there's any getting used to war." There was something softer than usual in his voice. Bobbi even thought she heard an intonation she associated with Utah County.

"Have you been in any battles?" Afton asked.

"Yes."

"Is it really horrible?"

"Sure." He waited, and for a moment Bobbi thought he wouldn't elaborate, but then he said, "In a sea battle, there's a lot of noise and confusion, and it's actually quite exciting. But when it's over, it hits you that you're sitting on this tin can—out in the middle of the ocean. You realize how easily you could have gone down." He paused, and then he added, in an even softer voice, "After a battle, most of the men try to act like they haven't been affected. But I've seen some big ol' galoots go to their bunks, lie down, and start to cry."

"We see that kind of thing too," Bobbi said. "Once a patient wakes up from the morphine, he has to accept what he's experienced. Some boys won't talk at all."

"They'll just sit and stare for hours and hours," Afton added.

Richard looked out at the ocean, where the waves were ablaze with the red and orange of the sunset. "One time," he said, "we sank a Japanese troop transport. It was loaded with soldiers heading for an island we had been bombarding. That night, I walked out to the aft of the ship. As the prop turns, it creates a phosphorescent glow in the water, and you can see deep into the ocean. I looked out over the waves, and I saw these lumps, so I walked closer to the rail to see what they were. Then I realized the lumps were Japanese soldiers."

"How awful," Afton said.

"There were dozens of them. Some were on the surface, and some down under, just hanging in the water. I'd spent the whole day hating Japs—happy to see them die. And then there they were. It was like I was looking into my own subconscious, seeing things I already wanted to forget—and knowing I never would."

Bobbi and Afton didn't speak. Bobbi was stunned by Richard's quiet, matter-of-fact tone—but also by the pain lurking behind it.

"All I could think was, 'I killed those guys.' When you sink an enemy ship, you feel this tremendous elation, like you've taken another man's piece in a chess match. But when I saw those men, I knew what I had done."

"You can't blame it on yourself," Afton said.

"Right then, it seemed like I should."

"Don't you wish you didn't have to go back out to sea?" Bobbi asked.

"Someone has to go," Richard said, and he sat up straight. "Those are probably not things I ought to talk about." Then, without seeming to feel that he had changed the subject, he asked, "Bobbi, didn't you tell me you were an English major before you went into nursing?"

"Yes."

"We have a little library on our ship. For the first time in my life, I've started reading novels. But most of them are non-sense—just a waste of time. I'd like to read some good books. What should I read?"

Bobbi was caught off guard. "It depends. What do you want from a book?"

Richard turned and leaned back against the bench. "I don't know," he said. "I majored in engineering, and—"

Afton began to laugh, and Richard stopped. "I'm sorry," Afton said, "but that's what Bobbi told me—that you were probably an engineering major."

"And I suppose that was the worst thing she could think to say about a person?"

Bobbi felt herself blush all the way to her throat. "Not at all," she said, before Afton could respond. "I just remembered that most of the boys in ROTC majored in engineering."

Richard leaned forward again, and that beautiful smile of his appeared, those white teeth. "But you didn't socialize with *that* set, did you?"

Bobbi was dead in the water. There was no right answer. She really hadn't been friends with many engineering majors. But his accusation was wrong. "I wasn't part of any *set*," she said.

He was still smiling. "Just tell me this. What should I read?"

"And I repeat my question. What are you looking for in a book?"

Afton slipped off the bench and sat on the grass, apparently tired of obstructing the view.

Richard said, "I want to be educated. I only worried about getting my degree when I was in college. But I've started to think about . . . things. I want to see what other people think."

"And feel?"

"Sure."

"One of my professors used to say that people read novels to find out where we fit in the universe."

Richard was still watching Bobbi closely, as though he thought he would understand more from her face than from her words. "Do you feel that way? Like you don't know where you fit?"

"Not exactly. But when I make a connection—in a book, or with a person, I realize how much I long for deeper relationships."

Richard finally looked away. "I've never been very good at making those kinds of connections. I don't understand much about myself—so how am I supposed to explain my feelings to someone else?"

"Sometimes, that's how it happens. You start talking, comparing—and you see yourself for the first time."

Richard nodded. "Maybe so. But it seems strange to me. Aboard ship, men talk philosophy at times. But they never make it personal."

"That's what I dislike about most men. They're so afraid to admit they feel anything."

Richard didn't say anything for a time, but he seemed to be thinking, looking for the words he wanted to say.

Suddenly Afton stood up. "You know, I think I'm going to go for a walk on the beach—see if I can find some shells, or—"

Bobbi laughed. "No, Afton. Don't go. I'm sorry."

"Nothing to be sorry about. But you know—three *can* be a crowd."

Bobbi saw Richard flinch, and she felt herself blushing again. She couldn't think of anything to say.

"So, anyway, I think I'll just—"

But Richard stood up. "Why don't we all walk a little?"

"No, no," Afton said. "Tell Bobbi how you feel about things, and . . . all that stuff."

Richard smiled, and he suddenly looked like a little boy caught doing something wrong. "Afton, what you don't know is that you just saved me. You two were about to find out that I'm nothing more than a military man and an engineer. I'm one of those guys Bobbi can't stand—who has no idea what he thinks, or what he feels."

Afton assured him that wasn't the case, but Bobbi decided it was time to keep her mouth shut. The truth was, Bobbi wasn't so sure he was wrong. He was very nice to look at, but she really didn't know whether he and she had anything to share. He certainly wasn't David Stinson.

That night, though, when Bobbi lay in bed, she couldn't stop thinking about Richard, and she kept remembering him saying that he wanted to be educated; that he wanted to read good books. That certainly seemed a good sign. And she remembered what he had said about the Japanese soldiers. He had thought a great deal about that—and felt, too—and he hadn't been afraid to say so.

On the following Sunday Richard was at church again. He came in the morning for priesthood meeting and then stayed for Sunday School. But instead of going to the adult class, he poked his head into Bobbi's classroom and said, "Could you use some help?"

Bobbi laughed. "I'll say. These are tough kids to handle."

"Oh, sure. I can see that."

There was only one large chair in the room, and Bobbi was using it. Richard walked to one of the little chairs and took a good look at it, as though he were wondering whether he could make it work. "Here, take mine," Bobbi said. "I think I can do better in the little one than you can."

"No, that's—"

But Bobbi pushed her chair toward him and laughed. "Those legs of yours are just too long," she said.

Richard looked down at the kids. "My legs are long enough to reach the floor," he said. "And that's exactly the right length, if you ask me." The kids laughed, although Bobbi was not entirely sure they understood his joke.

After class, Bobbi walked to the foyer with Richard, and

they waited for Afton. When Afton appeared, she beamed. "I see you two found each other," she said.

"He came in and helped me with my class," Bobbi said. "The kids loved him."

"Who doesn't? Golly, Richard, why do you like Bobbi more than me? The first time I saw you, I said how cute you were. Bobbi just said you weren't her type."

Bobbi looked directly at the floor. "Afton, you don't have to reveal *everything*, all the time," she said.

"I know. I'm sorry. My dad always says I should shut the gate before the cows get out. But my cows are track stars. They get out before I remember there *is* a gate."

"My best bet is to change the subject," Richard said.

Bobbi told him, "Good idea."

"What are you two doing for lunch?" Richard asked.

"We brought our lunch with us," Afton said. "And I noticed that Bobbi packed more sandwiches than the two of us could ever eat. I'm not sure why she did that."

"Maybe that's how she picks up sailors. She carries extra food."

"I prefer Marines," Bobbi said. "They're more manly."

Richard rolled his eyes, but he let the little insult go. "I have to be back to my ship in less than two hours," he said, "so I don't have a lot of time."

Just then Bobbi saw Sister Aoki, with Lily. "Oh, hi," she said.

Sister Aoki walked across the foyer to them. "Lily told me a handsome man in white clothes came to her class today. I thought maybe a prophet of old had appeared. But now I see who it was. Hello, Brother Hammond."

Richard nodded and shook hands, but he didn't say anything.

"I'm Ishi Aoki. You met my daughter."

"Yes, I did."

"Well, anyway, Lily thinks you're handsome in your

uniform." She looked down at Lily, who pushed her face against her mother's leg.

"Hey, watch it, Lily," Afton said, and she gave the little girl a nudge. "Bobbi has first dibs on him."

Bobbi shook her head and laughed, but when she glanced at Richard, he was looking surprisingly serious. He had taken a step away.

"Why don't all three of you come to dinner with Lily and me next Sunday?" Sister Aoki said.

"I'm not likely to have Sunday off again next week," Richard said, "but thanks."

"We'll come," Afton said, and Bobbi nodded.

"Well then, we'll plan on you girls, and Lily will have to wait for the man in white clothes to come some other time."

Richard nodded, but he said nothing.

Bobbi retrieved her picnic basket from a corner where she had left it, and she was quite forceful about getting out the door—without hugging everyone. She knew Richard didn't have much time. At the corner, the three of them caught the bus to the Palace park.

Bobbi found herself wishing that Afton might find something else to do one of these Sundays so Bobbi would have a chance to get to know Richard better—without all of Afton's joking. But Richard had never suggested the possibility of a date or a visit during the week. In fact, except for the way he looked at her sometimes, Bobbi saw no clear sign that he was interested in anything more than having friends he could spend a little time with. Bobbi wondered whether he had a girlfriend at home, maybe even a fiancée.

At lunch, the conversation turned toward home again. Afton talked about her family, and she laughed about her sheltered childhood. Then she said, "I've learned a lot of things by coming over here. I didn't think I could ever be friends with Ishi—you know, because she's Japanese. But Bobbi and I just love her now. She invites us over for dinner all the time."

Richard offered no response.

Afton waited for a time, and then she said, "Richard, you don't want to go to Sister Aoki's, do you?"

Richard looked at the grass, not at Afton. "No, I'd rather not," he finally said.

"Do you know that her husband is in the 100th Regiment that got sent to the mainland for training? Everyone in the regiment is AJA, and they're going into battle—*for us.*"

"I do know about that unit. I didn't know he was in it."

"Sister Aoki is the nicest person in the world. Can't you forget the color of her skin? I didn't think I could, but I did."

It was a bad moment. Richard looked away. No one spoke for quite some time.

"I know we're fighting the Japanese," Afton finally said, "and maybe it's different for someone actually out there—"

"Afton, anything I say is going to sound wrong. I have nothing against Sister Aoki, but right now, I just can't sit down to eat with her. I don't know any way to explain that to you."

Richard's face was expressionless, as though he were working very hard to hide what he was feeling. Bobbi didn't think he was hateful or bitter, but she found herself thinking that she might never really get to know him. He was hiding things away.

· C H A P T E R ·

13

During the winter and spring Wally's strength had continued
to build. It was May now, and he had begun to receive work
assignments. Some days he unloaded ships at the Manila docks,
or loaded boxcars at the train station. These were good details
since he could sometimes scrounge a little food. One day he
hauled canned peaches that had been left behind when the
American troops had moved into Bataan. Now he finally got
his share. He and the other men opened cans when guards
weren't watching, and they ate their fill—enough so that Wally
was sick of peaches before the day was over.

But it had been a glorious day, with so much to eat, and the
vitamins had to be good for him. The best thing was, the men
had been able to eat on the spot and not take the chance of
smuggling cans back into Bilibid. Anyone caught with contra-
band was beaten, at best. If the guards were in a sadistic mood,
they would make an apprehended prisoner stand at attention
in the sun for hours, or they would force a man to hold his
arms out wide and not drop them. When the pain became so
terrible that he let his arms come down a little, the guards
would beat him until he forced them back up.

One afternoon a group of prisoners was brought in
through the front gate. They seemed in decent shape, much

better than the usual walking skeletons or bloated beriberi victims who normally arrived. As it turned out, the group was only stopping for the night. They were from a camp near the town of Cabanatuaan, north of Manila, and they were on their way to a work detail in southern Luzon.

Prisoners were always hungry for information, and so that evening the Bilibid POWs gathered around in groups with the men from Cabanatuaan, and they shared what they knew. Wally had spotted a man he thought he remembered. "Weren't you in O'Donnell?" he asked him.

"Yeah. In the beginning. My name's Wendell Paxton."

"Wally Thomas." The two shook hands. "I was there for a while too. When did you get moved?"

"Last year. In May. They closed up O'Donnell and sent all of us who could travel up to Cabanatuaan. The ones who couldn't travel, the Japs just left to die."

Wally told him about the Tayabas work detail, and Wendell remembered the day the group had left. "I had a buddy on that detail. Atterly. Did you know him?"

"Sure. He lasted a long time, but he got worn down with malaria, and then he got dysentery. He died toward the end."

Wendell swore. "I wish I could kill just one lousy Jap for every one of us they've starved to death."

"The guards out there in Tayabas were bad," Wally said. "They worked most of the men to death, and they knew they were doing it. They didn't care."

"None of these Nips care," Wendell said.

The prisoner next to Wendell used some foul language to curse the guards, and then he said, "Sometimes I dream about strangling those guys to death—one after another. Just squeezing until their eyes bug out."

Wally didn't particularly like the image—but mainly because it reminded him of some of the ugliness he was storing inside himself. "Actually, you guys look pretty good," Wally said. "It must not be so bad up where you've been." He squatted down by the men. Three of the visitors were sitting in a line, leaning against the building. Their clothes were shabby, but they had more flesh on them than the Bilibid prisoners did.

"Yeah. We were just telling these guys, Cabanatuaan ain't half so bad as O'Donnell was. The Japs have a big vegetable garden up there. They keep everything clean."

"So do you eat pretty well?"

Wendell laughed. "Not really. The Japs ship all those vegetables out to their own troops. They might stick a little chunk of sweet potato in your rice at night, but they serve that runny rice water for breakfast, and more rice for supper—the same as they did at O'Donnell. The only difference is, once in a while you can grab a turnip or a leek or something out there in the field while you're weeding. That makes a difference."

"I had a couple of air corps buddies—Warren Hicks and Jack Norland. Do you happen to know them, or know if they ended up in Cabanatuaan?"

"Doesn't ring a bell." He looked over at the other men.

One of them said, "See that guy down at the other end of this building—the one in the middle with the hat on? He's air corps. Ask him."

"Okay, thanks." Wally stood up and walked to the other group of men. They were talking, so Wally waited. But after a time, he said, "I understand you're in the air corps."

"Yeah."

"You weren't at Clark, were you?"

"No. I was over at Nichols."

Wally hunched down in front of the guy. "But you were at O'Donnell, right?"

"I sure was." He grinned. "It was a nice place to visit, but I wouldn't want to live there on a permanent basis."

All the men laughed.

"Do you know a couple of guys from Clark? Warren Hicks and Jack Norland?"

"Sure." The man nodded, solemnly.

Wally thought he saw what was coming, and his impulse was to walk away and not ask. All the same, he said, "Are they all right?"

"No. They both made it up to Cabanatuaan, but Norland was sick by then, and he kept on going downhill. One night—I don't recall just when it was—he musta lost his head or something. He took off a-running, and he tried to crawl out under the barbed-wire fence. The Japs beat up on him, awful bad. I didn't see it, but from what I heard, they broke about half the bones in his body. He died in the morning—after a real bad night."

Wally felt the strength go out of him, but he asked the other question. "What about Warren?"

"Well . . . them two—Hicks and Norland—buddied up all the time. And it seemed like something went outta Hicks after Norland passed on. He got sick, and the Japs stuck him in that barracks where they take people to die. Not too many are dying in that camp, but the guys who get sick don't have much of a chance. Hicks only lasted a day or two down there, and then he was gone."

Wally stood up. He nodded. "Thanks," he said.

"I guess you were buddies with them guys?" the man said.

"Yeah."

"Well, I'm sorry to have to tell you what happened to them." Wally was hanging on, trying not to let this take him down. But he felt as though his insides had been scooped out. "I wish I could get hold of those guards who beat up on Jack," he said, but he couldn't even manage to sound very angry. Tears had also begun to fill his eyes. So Wally left, and he walked to his building, went in to his spot on the floor, his mattress, and he lay down. He told himself he wasn't going to cry very long, not give way to this, but he needed to let it out for a minute or two. And so he pushed his head into his dirty, smelly mattress, and he cried. And then, after a time, he rolled onto his back and tried to think about home, about something he could hope for. For so long, he had trusted that Warren and Jack were still out there somewhere, fighting to stay alive. He had always assumed they would end up in the same camp again, and the three of them would do some good scrounging.

Wally understood Warren—how he must have felt with both his buddies gone. But he had always been so strong. If Warren could give up, anyone could lose heart. Wally knew he had to concentrate on the things he was living for. He tried to remember Salt Lake—Sugar House in the spring when the trees were budding out. He pictured the craggy peak of Mount Olympus, drives up the canyons, dances at the Rainbow Rendezvous, his first date with Lorraine when they had driven into the foothills and looked out at the lights in the valley.

Sometimes he could almost picture Lorraine's face, but it always seemed to slip away just as he was getting it into focus. Still, he needed to keep her alive in his mind. He tried to imagine himself holding her on the dance floor, his hand on her back, her hair against his cheek. The smell of her. He absolutely had to believe that someone like her would be there for him someday.

But it all seemed so far away. It was hard not to think of all the days ahead, the months, maybe years. Suddenly he got up. He needed someone who could help him. He went looking for Alan, and he told him about his friends. Alan didn't say anything that made any real difference, but he understood.

"Well . . . we just gotta keep each other going—like we've been doing," Alan said.

"That's right. No matter what happens, we'll stick together."

Another two weeks went by, and word began to spread that those who could work would be shipped out to Cabanatuaan. Wally was pretty sure Captain Surmelian had been pulling what strings he could to keep him and Alan around, but he also knew his luck couldn't hold much longer. So when an officer told Wally he was being transferred, he felt the shock of fear run through him, but then he was relieved to

hear that he was going to Cabanatuaan. It hadn't sounded too
bad.

"Alan is going too, isn't he?" Wally asked.

"Who?" the officer asked. He was a Major named Searle.
He was the American whom the Japanese used as their liaison
to the prisoners, and he made a lot of decisions about transfers.

"Alan West."

"No. West is staying a few more days, and then he's going
on a work detail down south."

"But he was at Tayabas. He shouldn't have to—"

"Look, the doc gave us a list of those in the best health. He
was on it. I can't change the list now."

"But the two of us have been through a lot together."

"I'm sorry. I know how that is. But I can't do anything about
it." He walked away.

Wally was numb. He told himself not to let this throw him.
Cabanatuaan was okay. He would be all right.

As Wally turned to go back to his quarters, he saw Alan
coming toward him. He had obviously gotten the word. The
two stopped in front of each other, and each nodded, as if to
say, "Yeah, I know."

"They told me it's a short detail," Alan said. "Then I'll
probably end up at Cabanatuaan, the same as you."

"Good." But they both knew that promises of that sort
meant nothing.

"We'll be all right," Alan said.

"I know."

It was embarrassing to feel so much for each other, to be so
terrified by the separation. Neither could say anything. Not
knowing what else to do, Wally reached out and shook Alan's
hand. "Thanks," he said. "You know . . . for everything." But
that was not enough, so Wally hugged his friend and patted
him on the back.

The train ride to Cabanatuaan was hot and dirty and miserable, but at least not as crowded as the trip he had taken the

year before to O'Donnell. And the march to the camp, a former Filipino training camp, was actually rather enjoyable. It had been so long since he had been out in the open country.

From the outside, the camp looked anything but inviting. Heavy wire fences surrounded the big compound, and tall lookout stations, on stilts, lined the perimeter. At the gate to the camp, a crudely printed sign, in English, read: "Anyone attempting to escape will be shot to death." Inside, however, Wally was relieved to see long buildings, like barracks, built of bamboo and thatch. They looked solid enough to protect against the rains that were coming every day now, and the compound looked clean and orderly. He tried to tell himself this would be all right, but the numbness hadn't left him. He saw only endless days stretching ahead, and loneliness.

Wally was standing outside the headquarters building, waiting to be directed to the air corps section of the prison, when he heard a voice behind him. "I don't believe it. East High's track star!"

Wally turned around. He was looking into a face he was sure he knew, but a body that was skin and bones. And then he remembered. It was Chuck Adair, the star of every sport at East. "Chuck!" Wally almost shouted.

"I can't believe I'm happy to see you, Wally. I thought I was going to hate you forever."

Wally knew exactly what he meant. When Wally had quit the track team, most of the guys had held him responsible for losing the city championship. "You should hate me," Wally said, laughing. "I let you guys down."

"For some reason, it doesn't seem all that important at the moment," Chuck said. He laughed, and Wally saw that his teeth had decayed badly.

"How did you end up here?" Wally asked. "I didn't even know you were in the service."

"I joined about a year after you did. I got shipped over here just in time for all the fun."

"I can't believe I'm looking at you."

"There's another Salt Lake guy in here. I don't know whether you know him. Art Halverson."

"Sure. He's a year younger than us. He lived over by Mel. Hey, I want to see him. I want to see anything from home."

"Are you doing okay?"

"Well . . . yeah. Not too bad now. I was on a work detail in Tayabas. I barely made it out."

"We heard about that detail. Anyone who made it through that one had to be made of good stuff."

"I guess I don't quit as easy as I used to."

"Oh, man. It's good to see you." Chuck took hold of both of Wally's shoulders and gave them a good shake. "We'll come over and see you tonight, okay? I'll bring Art."

Wally was led away to his section of the compound, but he felt lighter, better. He might not see these guys all that often, but just to chat with them once in a while was going to make everything easier.

Over the next couple of weeks Wally learned the crucial techniques for survival at Cabanatuaan. As he bent over to weed the garden, where he worked most days, he would harvest a vegetable for himself, move it along on the ground, knock some of the dirt off, and then spot the guard and make sure he had time to take a quick bite. One day he was so intent upon a guard nearby that he didn't notice one coming up behind him, and he came within a breath of getting caught with a half-eaten turnip in his hand, but he managed to slip it under his shoe and press it into the dirt until the guard had passed.

Wally watched one other day as one of the prisoners, caught eating, took a terrific beating from two guards. In English, one of the guards had reprimanded the man for his "dishonor"—for stealing from the imperial government. Then, without warning, he drove the butt of his rifle into the prisoner's sternum. When the prisoner dropped to the ground, both guards kicked him and battered him with their rifles.

Wally found only satisfaction in his hatred at such moments. But gradually Wally was beginning to understand the way the Japanese army operated. He found out that many of the guards at Cabanatuaan were Formosans who were looked down upon by the Japanese officers. One day Wally looked up from his work to hear a Japanese officer screaming at a Formosan guard. Wally had no idea what the dispute was about, but the exasperated officer finally picked up a two-by-four and slammed it over the head of the young guard. The man dropped to the dirt and didn't move. Wally had no idea whether he had died immediately, but no one helped him, and that afternoon his body was still lying in the sun, flies buzzing around it. Wally knew that the lowliest guards wanted some-one they could punish—to pass along the ill treatment they got from their superiors. But to Wally, that didn't excuse any of them.

Each morning Wally would receive a work assignment. Most days he labored in the sun all day, out in the garden. It wasn't terrible work, but it was tedious and tiring. He preferred the wood detail because he could get outside the camp, and that always opened up the possibility of making contact with natives. A worse detail was carrying water—because the buckets became so heavy as the day progressed. But worst of all was the "honey" detail. The work was not terribly strenuous, but the humiliation was almost more than he could stand. A work crew would carry the contents of the outhouses to the fields, and then they would spread the human waste around the plants in the garden.

All the prisoners found it enraging to spend their days nur-turing the garden only to see the vegetables harvested and shipped away. They continued to live on cast-off, filthy rice. Each night, before a man could eat, he had to dig the white worms out of his rice and watch for rocks and rodent droppings. The barracks seemed almost civilized in appearance, but the bunks were constructed of bamboo, and inside that bamboo lived lice and fleas. At night they bit the men, who were usually exhausted enough that they slept anyway, but in the morning they found little bloody spots all over their bodies.

What kept Wally going now were his two friends, whom he would often see after dinner. They talked about Salt Lake and about their days at East High. Wally didn't remember Chuck as having been active in the Church back then, but he now talked a good deal about his faith. On Sundays, even though the prisoners worked all day, the same as any other day, the three Mormon men would hold their own meeting. They prayed, and they talked about the things they believed. They couldn't remember the exact words of the sacrament prayer, so they didn't take the sacrament, but they did bless each other at times and called on the Lord to sustain their little group. They even wrote out the words to hymns, as best they could remember them, and then sang together. Wally had never expected to find such pleasure in singing those familiar old hymns. Over and over, they sang "Come, Come, Ye Saints."

Wally's old friend Don Cluff was also in the camp. More often than not, he met with Wally and his friends at their little "church" meetings. He even learned the hymns, and he asked lots of questions about their beliefs.

For the first few weeks in the new camp, Wally hoped to see Alan soon. But as summer approached, and he didn't show up, Wally turned more and more to Chuck and Art. Still, he prayed every day for Alan and hoped he was well.

One Sunday evening, Art came to the meeting with a story. One of the Japanese guards—a man everyone called "Bug Eyes"—had been trying to raise carrots, which didn't do very well in the soil at Cabanatuaan. He had brought Art and a boy from New York City, Frank Pineda, over near his living quarters, and he had pointed to the weeds in his own little garden. "I could see the carrot tops growing among the weeds," Art said, "and I told Frank what to look for. Then I started at one end, and Frank started at the other. I didn't pay too much attention to what he was doing, but Bug Eyes came walking over, and he set up a howl. Poor Frank never had a garden in his life, and he just couldn't tell the carrots from the weeds."

"How bad did Bug Eyes beat him?" Chuck asked.

Art was sitting on a bunk in Wally's barracks. He had been a big kid at one time, but now he was a beanpole. He was bending forward with his elbows on his knees, his long bones seeming to stick out in all directions. His voice was rather high-pitched, but now it sounded almost tender as he said, "That's the strange thing. I thought for a minute the Jap was going to cry. He bent down and showed Frank which ones were carrots and which were weeds. He hardly knew a word of English, but he kept showing ol' Frank and jabbering away. It was almost like he was saying, 'Oh, son, look what you've done to my lovely little carrots.' I've never heard a guard sound like that."

"And he never did beat him?" Wally asked.

"No. Frank kept saying, 'Gee, I'm sorry,' and Bug Eyes kept nodding like he understood. And then he motioned for him to go back to his weeding, and he watched, just to make sure Frank got it right."

"Why would he do that?" Don asked.

"Well, I'll tell you," Art said. "I know this sounds funny. But it hit me all at once. Bug Eyes is probably a pretty regular guy back home. These guys must get filled with all this hatred and resentment, and this whole philosophy about our being worthless cowards who don't deserve respect, and they think they have to treat us bad. But if you could know one of them, man to man, they're probably about like everybody else."

"I don't believe that," Chuck said.

"Well, look how our guys are. They wouldn't talk the way they do here back home. Everything changes in a war." When neither Chuck or Wally replied, Art added, "Anyway, that's

what I want to believe. I don't want to spend all my time hating."

Wally was moved by that. But later that week a Japanese
guard went crazy because a prisoner had stepped on some kind
of plant in the garden. He ran at the prisoner, knocked him to
the ground with his rifle, and then kicked the man in the stomach and chest, over and over. Wally watched, and he tried to
think about the things Art had said. But it wasn't easy.

* * *

Mat Nakashima had been working for a year to get his
brother Ike released from internment camp. Ike was from Sugar
House, the same as Mat—had grown up in the Thomases'
ward—but he had been working for his uncle in Fresno,
California, when Pearl Harbor was attacked. Soon after,
Japanese Americans along the West Coast had been rounded
up and jailed, and then shipped to hastily established "relocation camps" in inland areas. At least a dozen times Mat had sat
in the offices of government officials and made his argument:
"I live in Utah, and no one arrests me. I continue to work and
grow fruit. I'm a productive citizen. My brother happens to
spend a little time in California, and suddenly he becomes dangerous. Why can't he just come home and work with me? How
could that hurt anything?"

"We can't get into all that," the men would say. "We don't
know which ones might be spies and which ones not. And we
can't start letting some go and not the rest. They're being fed
well, and they're getting along just fine. I've been at those
camps, and the people are happy and having a good time."

One man even suggested that Ike wouldn't have been
heading off to California if he hadn't had some spying in mind.
When Mat suggested that thousands of Utahns had gone to
work in California during hard economic times, the federal official had looked Mat in the eye and said, "Yes, and most of them
were white. White people didn't attack this country. It was
Japs, like you."

Mat had stood up, hat in hand, and said, quietly, "I suppose I'm mistaken. I had the idea that Hitler was white. And Mussolini. But I guess maybe they're Japanese, too."

"Now don't start all that with me," the man had said. "Maybe you're the one who ought to be cooling his heels in one of those camps until this war is over. You sound like a troublemaker yourself."

And so Mat had given up. But he did want to see Ike, and so, before the cherries came on, he took a bus to Bakersfield, California, and then hitchhiked into the mountains to the internment camp at Manzanar. The long rows of wooden barracks didn't look so bad from the outside, but the place was surrounded by barbed-wire fences, and at the gates, soldiers with rifles guarded the entrance.

Mat knew he was breaking the law, but he didn't care. He wasn't supposed to travel more than twenty-five miles from home. He had worn a hat when he purchased his bus ticket, pulled it down over his eyes, and done the same in boarding the bus. In California, a man had picked him up, but once he had gotten a good look at Mat, he'd had almost nothing to say. Mat didn't care. He wanted to see his brother—and his new sister-in-law. Ike had met a girl in the camp, and the two had gotten married a few months before.

As it turned out, when Mat got inside the camp and asked for his brother, Ike was out in a field, working. Much of the food for the interned Japanese Americans was raised within the camp. An older man took Mat out to Ike, and when Ike saw that it was Mat coming toward him, he ran across the field and threw his arms around him. "Mat," he said, "it's so good to see you. You said you might try to come, but I didn't know when to expect you."

"Well, I thought I'd better come before the cherries come on. I'll be busy after that, for the rest of the summer." The two backed up a little and looked at each other. "You look good," Mat said. "Are you treated all right?"

"Oh, sure. It's not so bad." But Mat saw the look in his eyes, the humiliation. "It's just that . . . it doesn't make any sense. I don't know what we're doing here."

The two walked back to the barracks, and for the first time Mat met Betty, the girl Ike had married. Betty was a pretty girl with wonderfully bright eyes and long, rich hair. She was third-generation American and sounded like any kid from California. She and Mat lived in the same barracks with her family and some other families.

"It's strange," Ike said, as he sat on his narrow bunk. "This is not where we want to be. But if I hadn't been here, I wouldn't have met Betty, so—you know—it's funny how things work out."

"But this is terrible, living like this—so many together."

"I know." Mat reached his arm around Betty. "We don't have a lot of privacy. That's for sure." And then he smiled. "But we have some news."

"What?" Mat could guess what was coming, and he could hardly believe it.

"Yup. We're going to have a baby. We haven't told anyone yet. We weren't really sure until a few days ago."

"That's good, Ike." Mat looked down at the floor. It struck him as sad that a child had to be born in a camp like this—a prison—and yet life was continuing. He was proud of his brother for holding up so well. "Will everything be okay?" Mat asked. "Can you manage here?"

"Sure. We're used to how things are."

"Aren't you angry?"

"I try not to think about it. Nothing makes any sense at all, as far as I'm concerned, but if you think about it, you could go crazy. We just have to be good citizens so everyone will know that we're Americans. Some people believe they'll let us out before too much longer—maybe before the year is over."

"I don't know, Ike. I've been talking to any government official who will listen to me, but I can't get anyone to admit that a mistake was made, or that people could be released on a case-by-case basis—or anything else. They just keep saying they have no choice but to hold you until the end of the war."

"Well, maybe."

"We'll be okay," Betty said. "Ike's going to build a crib, and it's no problem to get diapers and the other things we need."

"I know. But . . ." Mat looked around at the crowded building, the rows of bunks, with blankets hung up for partitions, or crudely built walls that didn't even go all the way to the ceiling. He saw how hard the people were trying to make everything nice, to keep the place clean—even decorated—but there were simply far too many forced into such tight confines.

"One thing I want you to know," Ike said. "Some of us younger men are talking about joining the service. And it looks like they're going to let us in."

"*Why* would you do that?"

"What better way to prove that we're loyal, Mat? After this war, I don't want anyone to doubt that I was willing to stand up for my country. I want to look people in the eye."

"Is that how everyone in here feels?"

"No. Some guys are mad. The government sent a man here to talk to us about joining up—an AJA. And some of the boys in here tried to go after him. If some of the rest of us hadn't stopped them, he would have gotten himself roughed up."

"But you want to go?"

"Not exactly. But I will. I want my name—our name—to be respected."

That was something Mat could understand. But he knew he would never do that. He would make the best of things, and when the war was over he would do all he could to show what kind of man he was, but he wasn't going to leave his wife and children to prove something he shouldn't have to prove.

1 4

In late May Alex and his entire regiment—the 506th Parachute Infantry Regiment—took a train to Sturgis, Kentucky. There the troops were to participate in highly realistic war games—a necessary preparation for the combat that lay ahead. From the little train station, where Red Cross girls served doughnuts and coffee, the battalion marched into the country and set up tents. That night they received the army's favorite dinner: creamed chipped beef on toast. The soldiers made all the standard jokes, but Alex didn't mind the stuff—he was hungry. He didn't even mind sleeping on the ground. What he dreaded was making a parachute drop into this hill country, where winds were tricky, and open drop zones were hard to find.

That night Lieutenant Summers called E Company's Second Platoon together and explained the plan. The "five-oh-six" was designated red and would fight against blue troops, who were infantry units, not airborne. Alex's squad had the assignment to drop behind enemy lines, to secure and then hold a bridge on a little creek. Alex listened to the plan and noted the landmarks, but he didn't think much about the operation. Sergeant Foley, the squad leader, was the one who would have to worry about the details.

At the end of jump school a group of noncommissioned

officers had been assigned to the company. Ernie Foley had taken over Alex's squad. All the guys from Alex's barracks stayed in the same squad, but some new people had been added. One of them was a fellow named Calvin Huish. He had three years of college behind him and was a little older than most of the recruits. He was witty but caustic, and most of the younger guys didn't like him. Alex didn't particularly take to him either, but at least the man could carry on an intelligent conversation.

Sergeant Foley was from the boot heel country of Missouri. He was a big man with red hair and freckles—and a permanently confounded look on his face. He had been in the army longer than the trainees, but Alex could think of no other reason he had earned his rank.

The next morning, early, the men ate breakfast and then double-timed to a little airfield. After that, for reasons no one could explain, there was a long delay. Finally, at about eleven o'clock, the men boarded a C-47 that was hot inside from having sat in the sun all morning. And then, predictably, there was another delay. Curtis was sitting next to Alex, the last two men in the twelve-man "stick."

"What are we waiting for?" Curtis asked. He was obviously nervous. At Toccoa, the drop zones had been flat and clearly designated. This would be their first drop into rough terrain. The troops were also fully outfitted this time, not only carrying their rifles but also packs, ammunition, grenades, shovels, and all the rest. It seemed more than a parachute could handle.

"We're waiting because we're in the army," Alex said. "We were supposed to drop about four hours ago."

"At least it's not a night drop. I'm scared about that."

"Stick around. That'll be next."

"Are you hot?"

"Melting."

All the gear and webbing felt like a straitjacket, and no air was moving inside the airplane. Alex was sick already, but he was hardly prepared for what came next. The C-47 finally lumbered down the runway, lifted into the air, and then almost immediately began to bounce and twist as it caught the air currents coming off the surrounding hills. The men had experienced turbulence in Georgia, but nothing like this.

The airplane hadn't been up for more than ten minutes when Alex realized he was getting sick. He kept breathing deep and trying to control himself, and he held out fairly well until Sergeant Foley shouted over the noise of the engines, "We gotta circle back and come at the drop zone again. There's a lot of wind, and we gotta allow for that."

The C-47 banked left, pushing Alex back in his seat, and then, just as the craft came level, it took a sudden drop. Alex was still resisting, but suddenly Curtis jerked his helmet off, bent forward, and vomited into it.

The smell hit Alex and he was gone. He grabbed for his own helmet, but it was too late. He was already losing his breakfast on the floor in front of him. And now almost everyone was doing the same thing. Splats were hitting the floor, or men were hunched forward, their faces pushed into their helmets. The stench was overwhelming, and Alex lost control again. He got his helmet off this time but then decided against using it. The floor was a mess anyway, and he saw no reason to fill his helmet.

Foley was the only one who showed no signs of being sick, and gradually the others lost all they had to lose. They were looking white and miserable, but most were staring ahead, and Alex was sure they were feeling the same thing he was: he just wanted to get outside, into the air.

After a few more minutes, Foley shouted, "Clear those helmets. Put them on."

Now Alex was glad he hadn't used his. Poor Curtis decided to do what others were doing. He dumped the contents of his helmet on the floor, shook it, and then stuck it on his head, but the very act of doing so set him off retching again.

"Stand up and hook up!"

Alex, with the rest of the men, stood and snapped his fastener over the line, jerked it a couple of times, and then inserted the cotter pin to secure the fastener on the cable. The jumpmaster opened the door. The rush of air and the roar of the propellers filled the airplane. "Check equipment," Foley called out.

It was a pointless little exercise. The men had checked their shoulder straps—and each other's—a dozen times, at least. But each took a tug at the straps on the guy in front of him. Then Alex, as the last man, called out, "Twelve okay." And up the line the shouts came. "Eleven okay. Ten okay. Nine okay."

As the men shuffled forward, they clung to each other and worked their way over the slippery floor to the door—as awkward as first-time ice-skaters. Sergeant Foley made it to the door and assumed the jump position: left leg forward, right foot back and ready to drive forward, hands on the sides of the door. The second man, Lester Cox, shuffled in close and set his foot at a right angle to Foley's back foot—to brace him.

The green light by the door suddenly came on, and the jumpmaster yelled, "Go!"

Foley screamed, "Geronimo!" and leaped out the door.

Alex's insides were still in an uproar, but when he finally made it to the door and jumped into the slipstream, he felt better almost instantly. He twisted left to make the quarter turn that he had been trained to execute; he held his chin down, so the risers wouldn't catch his head; and he clutched the reserve cord.

"One, one thousand . . . two, one thousand . . ." Wham! The chute blossomed, and he felt the tremendous jerk on his shoulders. The risers were squeezing the sides of his helmet, but he glanced up at the white canopy, and he was thankful to see that it was wide open and catching air. But then he saw that the men who had gone out ahead of him were drifting too far north. He could see the creek below and the hill they had all been told to spot. But they were supposed to land south of the hill and the creek, and they were actually going to be strung out on a line beyond the hill or, as in Alex's case, somewhere on it.

Alex pulled hard on his risers and tried to hold himself as far south as possible, but the wind was strong, and he was drifting fast. The ground was already rushing toward him, and he could see that he was going into a heavily wooded area on the south slope of the hill. He pulled hard to the left and avoided a little grove of oaks, but he crashed into some low brush. The parachute yanked at his shoulders and doubled him over and then dragged him through the brush—scratching his hands and face.

When he came to a stop, he was caught—helpless—in the brush with his feet off the ground. The chute was billowing ahead of him, pulling hard, and he had no way to collapse it. He flailed about for quite some time before he could get his hand to his leg and pull his knife out. Then he slashed his parachute cords. Once he had done that, he sank a little in the brush and got his feet on the ground. It took some work, but he managed to stand up, and he released the harness and threw it off. By the time he had worked his way clear of the deep brush and got under some oak trees where the undergrowth was thick but more manageable, he had begun to wonder where everyone else was.

"Alex," he heard someone shout.

Somehow Alex wasn't surprised to see that Curtis was hanging from a big red oak a little farther up the hill. "Just a minute," Alex yelled to him. "I'll get you down . . . one way or another."

Alex trudged through the bracken to the base of the tree. By now he could see that the problem was not so great as it had seemed. He was able to grip a low limb, swing up onto it, and then climb high into the tree, where he grabbed the lines of the parachute and pulled Curtis to a place where he could get a limb under his feet.

"Okay, release your harness and work your way over to the trunk of the tree," Alex told him. Alex was above him, and so he waited for Curtis to move—more slowly and cautiously than seemed necessary. And then the two climbed down.

The problem now was that they couldn't see anyone else, and Alex knew that most of the squad was on the wrong side of the hill, far from the creek and the bridge. "Aren't some of the blue guys camped over on that side?" Curtis asked. But now he had taken a good look at Alex. "Hey, your face is all cut up."

"I got into some briars over there." Alex wiped his hand across his cheek and then looked at the blood on his hand. "It's not as bad as it probably looks."

"I'm still a little sick."

Alex laughed. "That's better than being a lot sick."

Curtis pulled his helmet off. "My hair is full of puke," he said. "It was even running down my face." He grabbed some leaves, which he used to wipe at his face and hair and then to run over the liner of his helmet. "What are we going to do now?" he said.

"I don't know. The two of us can't take that bridge by ourselves."

"If our guys came down in the middle of enemy troops, they probably got taken captive."

"Maybe." Alex was thinking. "Why don't we work our way over the top of the hill and see if we can find anyone? We might have to free those guys from the enemy. If we can get them loose, maybe we can still take the bridge." For the first time this all seemed rather fun to Alex—like the games of war he had played in the foothills above Sugar House when he was a boy.

"Why don't we go to the bridge? Then Lieutenant Summers will know we got to the right place, even if the rest of the squad didn't."

"What good does that do? We won't get the bridge that way. Not two of us. We might as well try to finish our mission."

Curtis was looking up the hill, which was covered with thick growth. The heat was terrible. "That's a big hike," he said.

"Not for us. We're paratroopers." Alex grinned. He knew he was in the best shape of his life, but he had never bought into the Superman image the airborne tried to sell to its troops. What he liked was the thought of pulling off a commando raid and freeing the other men in his squad. If the blues "shot" him, so what? It was only a game.

So Alex and Curtis worked their way up the hill and eventually found a path that cut through the heavy growth. Along the way they found two of their own men, who were sacked out under a tree. "Hey, what are you doing?" Alex asked them.

The two troopers—Huff and McCoy—jerked and then got quickly to their feet. Alex saw Huff relax when he saw who it was. He was a small kid, a guy who strutted like a street fighter and always bragged about his exploits back home in Ohio—his conquests with girls, along with his fistfights. He also took every chance he got to catch some sleep. "Most of our guys got dropped over there," he said, pointing to the north. "We're waiting for them. We have to go back the other way anyway."

"That area is all held by blues," Curtis said. "I doubt our guys had much of a chance."

Huff shrugged. "So what are we supposed to do?"

McCoy said, "Let's go take the bridge. Four of us can do it. Those blue guys are just straight legs."

Alex smiled. McCoy loved being a paratrooper. He and Huff came back from every leave with another story about fights they had gotten into with infantry troops.

"We'd be better off if we could get the rest of our squad together," Alex said.

"Yeah, but how can we do that?" McCoy asked. "The plan was to have that bridge by tonight. If we give it a try, at least we'll get credit for that." McCoy was a powerfully built man with heavy black eyebrows over brooding eyes, but he was about as straightforward as anyone in the squad. He didn't defend Alex when others started in on him, but he never had anything to say himself. Huff, on the other hand, never passed up a chance to give Alex a hard time.

"That's right," Huff said. "We can take that bridge. The two of us were going to do it if those other guys didn't show up soon."

Alex thought of making a crack about finding them asleep, but he decided he'd better not get anything started. "That's fine with me," he said. "What do you think, Curtis?"

"I don't know. I'd like to find Foley. He's the one who's supposed to decide."

"Yeah, and your mama is supposed to tuck you in at night, Bentley. But she ain't here."

The four of them stood for a moment, as though waiting for someone to make the decision, but it was Alex who finally said, "Let's do it. The guys at the bridge won't expect us to come in from this side of the creek. Let's stay above them and get a look at how they're deployed. Maybe we can take them by surprise."

"Sounds good," McCoy said, so the four started down the path, and it was Alex who led out.

Over the next hour or so, Alex worked his way along the hillside, staying in the trees, and he guided the men to a point where they could see into the valley. "You were right," Curtis said. "All their troops are on the other side of the bridge."

"Yeah, but there's a bunch of them," McCoy said.

Alex was thinking the same thing. The rules of this kind of game also made things tough. Alex and his men couldn't snipe at the troops from a distance and shout, "You're dead." To claim victory, they had to rout the unit with overpowering gunfire.

"Here's what I'm thinking," Alex said. "We could send one guy across the creek, and he could move into those trees on the other side of the bridge. He could draw some fire and pull a patrol in his direction. Then three of us could move in close to the creek. One guy could lay down covering fire while the other two charge across the bridge and take them by surprise."

"Who died and made you the president?" Huff said.

"No one. Have you got a better plan?"

"I don't know. Maybe . . ." But he offered nothing.

McCoy said, "Sounds good to me. I can probably make it across that creek as easy as anyone. The current might be pretty swift, but I can buck it."

"Hey, I can do that," Huff said.

"You're too short," Alex said. "You might get your rifle full of water."

"What are you talking about? I can—"

But McCoy cut him off. "He's right. I'll head straight down from here and get across. You guys work your way toward the bridge. How soon should I start firing?"

"Whenever you get in place and ready, start shooting. We'll be ready."

"All right. But if there are troops anywhere along the river, I might have to make a wide circle to get into place. I could even get bumped off."

Alex looked at his watch. "If we don't hear anything by 1500, we'll figure you got taken. Then we'll just have to do the best we can without you."

"All right." McCoy started off through the woods, down toward the river.

Alex led the way along the hillside. When he reached a safe point, with good cover, but where he could see the bridge, he halted. "Let's wait here now," he whispered. "We can move in closer when we have to."

Huff swore. "I can't believe you, Thomas. You're just a trainee, the same as the rest of us."

"Okay. Go ahead and take over," Alex said. "You decide from this point on."

"Hey, I'm not saying that. I just don't think you have to act like you're the squad leader."

"Someone has to lead," Curtis said.

"Shut up," Huff whispered, and he cursed. But then he sat down in some tall grass and lay back. "I don't care what we do. The way you said is all right. Thomas, you and me can make the run across the bridge. Bentley can put down the cover fire." He shut his eyes, and in a few seconds he seemed to be asleep.

Alex kept watch on the bridge. It was a humid afternoon, and he was sweating profusely under his uniform and gear. The wait was tedious, but when he figured McCoy should soon be in place, he gave Huff's boot a little kick and said, "Okay, let's move in." The three got up and worked their way down the hill. They stayed low and watched for any sign of movement. The blue troops on the other side of the stream seemed bored. Some of them were sleeping, and others were sitting in a little circle on the grass, playing cards.

"We should charge them when they're not ready," Huff said. "As soon as McCoy shoots, they'll all sit up and pay attention."

"There are too many of them. If McCoy can pull some away, we have a better chance."

"I wish we could take them for real. We could handle 'em hand to hand, no problem."

Alex doubted that, but he didn't say so. He waited until the first shot echoed through the valley. Immediately the men at the bridge jumped to their feet and ran to the creek bank. They jumped over the edge, where they had some natural cover.

McCoy moved a little and fired a couple more times. Then, after another minute or so, he fired from a third spot.

"Hold tight," someone shouted. "This looks like a feint. Second Squad, move across the bridge and cover from the other side."

Huff swore. "Hot idea you had, Deacon," he said.

"Okay. We'd better charge. Run as far as you can and then

drop and start shooting. Let's catch that squad coming across the bridge, while they're out in the open." Suddenly Alex jumped up. "Let's go."

The three men charged hard and then dropped into some long grass not far from the bridge. As the squad hit the bridge, they opened fire with their blanks. The men in the squad suddenly came to a stop, confused, and then ran forward again. As far as Alex was concerned, they were all erased. He jumped up and shouted, "Head for the bridge," and off he ran.

"Watch those trees," someone was screaming from across the bridge, and Alex guessed they were still wary of another attack from the south side of the creek. He charged across the bridge firing his M-1, with Huff next to him. Curtis had stopped by the bridge and was laying down covering fire—or at least a lot of noise—at the men who were in full view along the riverbank.

What followed was a good deal of confusion, but it all ended with Alex and Huff standing at the south side of the bridge and McCoy charging from the woods. "I'd say we have you," Huff shouted. "This bridge is ours, straight legs."

A huge argument followed, but it was a young lieutenant for the blues who finally said, "I guess you're right. We did that all wrong."

Alex and Huff looked at each other and began to laugh.

The exercise ended the following day. When the rest of Alex's squad wandered into their base camp, they looked bedraggled and embarrassed. When Foley saw the four men who hadn't been taken captive, he said, "Where have you guys been?"

Huff, of course, was the one who took the credit. "Hey, we took the bridge and held it. We covered your butt, Foley."

"Don't give me that? Where were you?"

"We did take the bridge," Curtis said. "Alex planned out a surprise attack. We overran those blue guys."

Huff protested that Alex's plan had actually backfired, but

he didn't go so far as to admit that it was the incompetence of the blues that had worked most in favor of the four attackers. What soon circulated through the platoon, however, was the word that "Deacon" had been the guy who had gotten the job done.

And that's probably why Lieutenant Summers came looking for Alex at the bivouac camp that night. "Thomas, I need to talk to you," he said, and he turned and walked away from the other men.

Alex had been cleaning his rifle. He got up from where he was sitting, near his pup tent, and walked with the lieutenant away from the tents. When Summers stopped, he turned and looked at Alex. He crossed his long arms over his chest and said, "You did a good job out there. I think you're becoming a soldier after all."

"Sir, the truth is, we got pretty lucky," Alex said.

"Listen, I need you. I need your leadership. I want to make you a corporal and assistant squad leader."

Alex took a breath. He liked the idea of doing well, of being advanced, but he didn't want to be drawn into leadership.

"I'd rather not, sir," he said. "I don't feel ready for a real battle."

Summers moved his hands to his hips. "That's just the trouble. No one is ready. But you have some sense. I need someone who can back up Foley—take over if he goes down. We're going to be in this war before long—right in the middle of it. And we're going to be thrown into impossible situations from the very beginning. I'm searching desperately for men who can step forward and lead."

Alex had assumed an "at rest" position, but his body was tense. "Sir, the men wouldn't want me as a leader. You know how they feel about me."

"They may not be buddies with you, but they respect you."

Alex knew what Summers meant. The men in the squad—

especially Duncan—had watched as Sergeant Willard had kept the pressure on all during basic training. The sergeant's expectations had been uniformly unreasonable, his punishments excessive. Alex had run twice as far as anyone, had pulled more KP, had listened to more corrections, more insults. But the results hadn't been so bad. Alex felt the hardness in his body, and in his mind, and he knew that the other men stood in awe of what he had put up with.

Certainly their view of him had softened some, and at times Alex noticed hints of goodwill from some of them. But Duncan had tagged him with the nickname "Deacon," and everyone had taken it up. They made fun of him for all he wouldn't do—drink and party and fight—as well as for what he did: go to church when he could and study his scriptures in the barracks. Worst for Alex, however, was the estrangement, the loneliness. If it hadn't been for Curtis, Alex doubted he could have survived.

"I'd rather be a rifleman, sir. I don't want to—"

Lieutenant Summers suddenly swore. "Thomas, you still don't know which side you're on, do you?"

"Yes, sir. I do know that," Alex said.

The lieutenant stepped a little closer. "Tell me why you don't want to lead, then."

"Lieutenant Summers," Alex said, "when I signed up for airborne, the recruiter told me there was a need for guys who could speak German. He said I would probably end up in an intelligence unit."

Summers let that sink in for a moment before he said, "You're telling me you wanted to back up the troops, put them in the right places so they could do the killing, but you don't want to kill anyone yourself."

"Sir, I didn't say that."

"Well, then, what *are* you saying?"

But Alex was face to face with his own logic, and he knew that Summers was right. He didn't know what to say.

"You joined up," the Lieutenant said. "You told yourself—and everyone back home—that you were ready to do your part. But you haven't made the commitment. You still don't want to get your hands bloody."

"I'll do what I have to do."

But that wasn't good enough for Summers. He cursed Alex. "You don't get it, soldier," he shouted into his face. "We have to win this war—and you don't have any idea what it's going to take to do that."

Alex felt the truth of that—the fear.

That night he lay in his tent, deathly tired but unable to sleep, and he was quite sure he had made a mistake to come this far. He should have stayed home and built parts—little gadgets that didn't look dangerous but played their own remote role in the killing. He had found that work difficult, but it was nothing compared to what he would face in battle. He kept hearing Summers' accusation: you don't want to get your hands bloody. That was exactly right, but Alex couldn't help it. He knew the enemy, and that knowledge was something the other men didn't have to carry into battle, like an extra field pack—immense and loaded.

· CHAPTER ·

15

Gene was sitting on an almost-empty trolley. As it bumped and rattled over the tracks, he stared ahead, lost inside himself. He wondered what he could expect. It was the day after his high school graduation, and he had just left the marine recruiting office, where he had enlisted. Almost all the guys in his graduating class, including Gene, talked about their eagerness to get into the war, but now, alone, and knowing that he really was going, he felt nervous.

As a marine, he was almost sure to go to the Pacific, and he wondered what kinds of exotic places he might see. He tried to think of the adventure of it all, but a picture kept returning to his mind. At a movie one night, he had watched a "March of Time" newsreel and had seen a squad of marines dug in on an island. They were sitting in foxholes, eating from mess kits. Now, as the image returned, the whole idea—leaving home, living in barracks or in foxholes—made his stomach uneasy.

Gene had always liked his comfort. He had liked camping out with the Boy Scouts—for a few days—but after, he had been happy to get back to his own bed and his mother's cooking. He didn't sleep well in a sleeping bag, and he liked to take a nice warm bath before he went to bed at night. It was hard to imagine himself in a bunk on a rocking ship, or rolled up like a potato bug in the dirt. Once, on a hike, he had gotten into some poison ivy, and he had been miserable for days. He was pretty sure that jungles had all sorts of insects and snakes and poisonous plants; he worried about the misery of life in a place like that.

He and Ralph had talked for a long time about joining up together. But Ralph's bum knee was keeping him out. He had tried every branch of the service, and no one wanted someone with a leg that was unlikely to hold up. Gene knew he would feel a lot better if the two of them were going off together, and the truth was, he sometimes felt a twinge of envy that Ralph could avoid the service without any dishonor. He believed in the war, was committed to doing his share, and when he listened to news reports and heard about the atrocities of the Germans and Japanese—or when he thought of Wally—he sometimes became impatient to get into the action.

But today he was feeling apprehensive. He didn't think about death or wounds or even battle. He sensed only that he was giving away more than he had realized, more than he wanted to give. He had turned himself, like a parcel of goods, over to the government, it seemed, and he sensed that he wouldn't get the package back in its original condition.

When Gene got off the trolley on Twenty-first South, he didn't walk home. He walked to Millie's house instead. He knocked on the door, and then, when Millie appeared, he said, "Come outside for a minute. I want to tell you something."

"You signed up, didn't you?" she said. She pushed the screen door open and stepped outside. "I look so awful. I'm embarrassed for you to see me."

She was wearing jeans and saddle shoes and a man's white shirt that was much too big for her. Gene tucked his hands into his pants pockets. He had worn his Sunday suit to the recruiter's office, although he didn't know why. Maybe it had made him feel older. "Actually, you look good," he said. He saw her blush, instantly, and he knew it was because he so rarely said anything of that kind.

"So what did you decide?" she asked. "Navy or marines?"

"Marines."

"Oh, Gene, why?"

The two of them had talked about this a lot lately. Millie was pretty sure the navy would be safer, and she couldn't understand why Gene would even consider the marines. "I don't know," Gene said. Then he laughed. "Wally's in the Army Air Force, Alex in the paratroopers, and Bobbi in the navy. I just figured there ought to be a Thomas in the marines. How else are we going to win the war?"

But Millie looked worried. "Don't marines get the most dangerous duty?"

"I don't know. They're supposed to be the best; that's what I like."

"That's not why you're going into the marines. I know the real reason."

"What's that?"

"Because you know you'll be in the Pacific. And you have it in your head that you'll be fighting to get Wally free."

Gene looked past Millie. "Well . . . yeah. I would like to fight in the Philippines—and help liberate those prison camps. I don't know if I'll ever get that chance, though."

"You miss him all the time, don't you?"

"Sure I do."

Millie looked into his eyes as though she were trying to understand something inside him, but Gene tried not to let her in, although he couldn't have said why.

"Why don't you take your coat and tie off?" she finally said. "You look hot."

It was a pretty June morning. A light rain had fallen the past couple of days, and the storm had cleared the air. But it was warming up today. Gene pulled his coat off, and he sat down on Millie's front step. Out front were two big weeping willow trees that seemed to guard the house and cut it off from the street, the world. Gene had sat on these steps so many times, but this morning he was feeling that his former life was over, and everything familiar to him would soon be taken away.

"When do you leave?"

"Three weeks from yesterday."

"Are you worried?"

Gene looked away. "Naw."

"Come on, Gene. You have to be a little nervous, at least."

"Well, yeah. A little. I've heard that boot camp is awfully hard."

"You'll do fine there. It's the war I'm worried about." She waited for him to look at her again, and when he did, he was struck with how pretty she was. Gene preferred the way she looked when she was serious, when her dimples were subtle and her eyes soft. She reached over and took hold of his hand. "I hope you end up in an office somewhere typing letters for a general."

A robin fluttered down onto the lawn. Its head jerked back and forth, and then it took a couple of tentative steps before it looked this way and that again. Gene was amazed at the way he was noticing things this morning. He had watched robins all his life, without a second thought, but now he wondered whether there would be robins where he was going, whether there would be anything familiar to him. He glanced at Millie again.

"Gene, I'm going to be here," Millie said. "I'm going to wait for you—no matter how long you're gone. I want you to know that and never doubt it."

But Gene didn't want this. He had thought a lot about it, and he didn't think promises were a good idea. "Millie, let's just . . . see what happens. We're friends, and—"

"Gene, I love you. I've been in love with you since I was a little girl, and I'm going to love you through all eternity. There isn't even another possibility."

She was grasping his hand, but he didn't look at her. He didn't want this to happen.

"I don't expect you to say the same thing to me, Gene. I know how you are. But I just want you to know that I'm going to be here when you get back."

Gene continued to look toward the lawn, saw the robin bob its head and peck at the grass. "Let's just be friends," he said. "Let's write to each other—and you can tell me what's happening around here. Stuff like that."

"Gene, I know you don't feel as strong about me as I do about you. And I don't want you to feel trapped. But I can't help it. I feel the way I do, and I'm not going to change."

He knew what she wanted him to say, but he just couldn't. He was sorry he had stopped by. "When do you start work?" he asked.

"Monday. I'm helping Mom with some cleaning today."

"Do you want to do something Friday night?"

"Yes. And Saturday too." She smiled, and her dimples deepened. "And I want to see you at church on Sunday, and have you come over Sunday evening. And I want to see you every other minute that I can have you until you leave. I know I'm being too forward to say all that, but it's true."

"Well, I . . . want to spend time with you, too."

"Wow. For Gene Thomas, that's almost a profession of love. I'm going to write those words in my diary tonight—just so I can check back and be sure I've remembered right."

Gene got up. "I'll see you Friday," he said.

"What about tonight?"

"I don't know. I could come over, if you want."

"I want."

She grasped his hand tightly again, and she stood close to him. He knew she was hoping for a little kiss—since he had kissed her good night a few times lately—but he wasn't about to do anything like that, not outside in broad daylight where someone might be watching.

* * *

LaRue and Beverly cooked dinner that night. Mom had told them that would be their assignment for the summer. She and Dad had a hard time getting away from the plant, and one or the other often returned in the evening to make sure the second shift was doing all right. President Thomas sometimes had church duties in the evening, and with so many women employees, Sister Thomas was especially effective at teaching the use of the machinery. She had a great knack for helping new hires relax and gain confidence. Mom also felt it was good for LaRue to take over more of the household chores and learn from the experience.

LaRue actually liked that idea—especially the pay she and Beverly would get for it—but she was always bigger on ideas than she was at carrying things out. Gene was impressed by the dinner the girls had prepared, but he wondered how long they would keep putting out that kind of effort. Beverly was easily distracted, and Gene could almost guess that the two girls would soon be upset with each other, with LaRue assuming herself to be the boss. Still, the table was set very nicely, and except for the lumpy mashed potatoes and a rather odd taste to the gravy, everything was fine. He even said so.

"Holy cow, Gene," LaRue said, "you're not leaving for three weeks. You don't have to start being nice quite yet."

"He'll be happy if he can get a meal like this in a few weeks," Dad said.

Gene had heard far too much about the lousy food in the military. It was one of his great dreads. "The recruiter said we'll eat better in the marines than in the army."

"I don't get it," LaRue said. "All we hear about is food shortages at home—so we can feed the boys in the service. If we have to go without everything, how come soldiers don't eat any better?"

"They turn it all into K rations," Dad said, and he laughed. "It's hard to put good food in a can."

Gene felt something strange in all this good humor. Everyone seemed to be trying a little too hard. But after a few moments, Mom said, more wistfully, "I'll have to stop downtown and get another banner. There aren't many four-star families in this valley."

"That's something to be proud of," Dad said. "I could have claimed I needed Gene at the plant. I know the draft board would have let him stay."

"Then why didn't you do it?" Beverly asked. She usually said so little that it was surprising she would ask the question so forcefully.

"I would have. But Gene and I talked about it, and that's not what he wanted. He wants to do his part, the same as the rest of the family."

"Me and LaRue aren't doing anything."

"Oh, yes you are," Mom said. "Collecting scrap metal. Storing up cooking fat. Saving string and tin foil. Even doing this cooking for us this summer. That sets your dad and me free to do what we have to do."

"I wish I could go shoot some Japs," LaRue said. "That's what I'd like to do."

"LaRue!" Mom said.

But Gene laughed. "I think you'd better let me handle that part," he said.

After dinner, Dad sat by the radio with the news on and with his newspaper in front of him, and Gene volunteered to help Mom with the dishes—since the girls had cooked the meal. LaRue thought that was wonderful, but she accused Gene again of trying to be too nice.

Actually Gene wanted to talk to his mother, although he didn't know exactly what it was he wanted to say to her. As he cleared the dishes from the dining room table, he heard bits and pieces of the war news. The Germans were on a new push in Russia, trying to recover from their devastating losses the winter before, but they were no longer having their way as

they had in the beginning of the eastern campaign. In
Germany, the American and British bombers were blasting
Dusseldorf, Cologne, and some of the cities on the North Sea.
Every day the bombing continued, and Gene wondered how
the Germans could hold out against the constant barrage.

In North Africa and in the Mediterranean Sea, the fighting
continued as well, and a fierce battle was going on in the
Solomons: islands Gene had never heard of until recently.
Gene studied maps in the newspapers and tracked the battles
all over the world. Lately, he had wondered which of the fronts
he would join, but he supposed, by the time his training was
finished, the fighting would shift to new islands, maybe even
to the Philippines. What he didn't fear any longer, as he had
the year before, was that the war would end before he could
get to it.

"Mom," Gene said, as he stood next to her and dried the
dishes she washed, "I thought I might walk over to Millie's in a
little bit."

"Haven't you told her yet?"

"Yeah, I did. I stopped over there this morning."

"It sounds to me like you two are getting pretty thick.
You're seeing her a lot more than you used to."

"Well . . . I'll be gone pretty soon."

"How are you going to handle it if she finds someone else
while you're gone?"

Gene was wiping off a dinner plate. He stepped to his
right, reached up, and placed the plate in one of the kitchen
cabinets. "I don't know," he said. "I guess whatever works out
will be best."

"For two years now you've been telling me you two are just
friends."

"We are. Mostly."

"Oh, Gene." Mom swished her washcloth through a drinking glass and then set it in some hot rinse water in a dishpan.

"You don't say much, but you're not very hard to read. I think you like that girl a whole lot more than you let on."

"I do like her. I've never said I didn't."

"What about that other little word—the one that also starts with an 'l'?"

Gene didn't answer. He was drying utensils now, rolling several of them around in his dish towel at the same time. Finally, he said, "Mom, I don't think it's good to make a lot of promises right now. It's better to wait and see how everything turns out."

Mom turned and looked at Gene, studied his eyes. Then she took Gene into her arms. He was much taller than she, and he still had a fistful of utensils in his hand, but she pulled him close anyway. "Oh, Gene, don't you think it's time to go ahead and let yourself feel whatever you feel? Millie is nuts over you. I see it in her eyes every time you two are together."

Gene let his mom hold him for a time, but he was having some difficulty, and he realized he didn't want to talk to his mom after all. He finally pulled back a little and she let go. But he did say, "I hope she does wait. I hope we get another chance—you know, when we're older."

"Oh, Gene, you ought to be starting college this year—having fun up at the U. You ought to be doing all the things I did at your age. This war just ruins everything."

"I wish I could play football," he admitted.

"I know. You'd be a star. You'd have your pick of girls, too—if that's what you wanted."

Gene didn't know about that. And the truth was, he didn't want his pick. He would just like to keep dating Millie. And play football and basketball both, maybe even run on the track team. He had broken Alex's city record in the 440 that spring, and the track coach—along with every University of Utah coach—had talked to him about accepting a scholarship. "I guess you'll be going into the service," they would say. "Well, when you get back, we'd love to have you play for us." But how could anyone think that far ahead? Life was on hold now. Everything was "for the duration," which only seemed another way of saying "forever." He didn't know how to think about life after he got home.

When the dishes were finished, Gene walked up to his room and sat on his bed. He had thought to tell his mother about the uneasiness that had been on his mind all day. He simply wanted to admit to someone—someone who would understand—what he was feeling. But Mom was not the one; he should have known that. She would only worry all the more.

That night, after Gene had left, Lorraine Gardner stopped by the Thomases'. Dad had gone back to the plant, but Sister Thomas was home, and she answered the door. "Oh, Lorraine," she said, "Come in."

"I have some very good news," Lorraine said.

Sister Thomas's immediate thought was that Lorraine had gotten engaged. She told herself to be happy for the girl, but that wasn't what she felt.

"Is President Thomas home?" Lorraine asked.

"No. The girls and I are the only ones here."

"Would you call them down, Sister Thomas? They'll want to hear this too."

Lorraine was holding a postcard in her hand—gripping it with both hands in front of her, and she seemed excited. Sister Thomas called to the girls, and in a few seconds they appeared at the top of the stairs, saw Lorraine, and then hurried down. Everyone then walked into the living room and found seats, Lorraine next to Sister Thomas on the couch. "You remember Chuck Adair, don't you?" Lorraine said.

"Yes. Someone told me he's also a prisoner in the Philippines."

Lorraine nodded, and she was beaming. "His family lives over by me. When I got home from work tonight, Sister Adair was at my house, and she had this card. It's from Chuck."

"Oh, my goodness, how wonderful. Does it say he's all right?"

"Yes. There are boxes to check off. 'I am well'—that sort of thing. But there's space for a short message. And look what he wrote. She handed the card to Sister Thomas."

At the bottom of the card, Chuck had written: "Wally Thomas is here with me. He's all right. Tell his parents."

Sister Thomas tried to read it out loud, but she couldn't get all the words out. LaRue and Beverly got the idea, however, and they rushed to see the card themselves. Then everyone cried together, including Lorraine.

"I always knew it. I *always* knew it," Sister Thomas kept saying. "But it's good to hear it from someone."

"Sister Adair would have brought it over to you herself," Lorraine said, "but she thought I'd like to give you the news."

"When will he come home?" Beverly had asked three times by now.

"Honey, we don't know," Sister Thomas said. "This just means that he's alive and he's okay."

"Why won't they let Wally send his own card?"

"I have no idea, Bev." Sister Thomas looked at Lorraine. "I've written to him once a week this whole last year. Most of the letters come back. But some don't, and I don't know whether that means they're getting through or not."

"I wish we could get a letter from him," Lorraine said.

Sister Thomas looked into Lorraine's eyes. "I know. But here's how I feel about it: At least we know he's sticking this thing out. I think he's going to come home a stronger man than we ever knew before."

Lorraine's eyes filled with tears again. "I've seen pictures of men who escaped the Japs on some of the islands. They looked like skeletons."

"I know. And Wally may look like that too. But he's not giving up. And that means he wants, more than anything, to get back to us."

"Sister Thomas, I never wrote to him after he left. Not until he was in prison. And every letter I've sent has come back. I doubt he thinks about me at all anymore."

"Oh, Lorraine, you know Wally better than that." Sister Thomas took Lorraine's hands into her own. "I'm sure it's thinking about you—as much as anything—that keeps him alive."

"He probably thinks I'm married. I gave him no reason to think I would wait for him."

"He might think that. But that doesn't change what he feels for you. I know Wally. It's remembering life at home, going dancing with you, going to shows—all those memories you two stored up together—that's what he feeds on now."

"What if they're breaking him down? He was always so fun. Maybe they'll take all that away from him."

"I don't believe that for a minute. Wally is Wally. He may be a little more serious when he gets back—and that won't hurt anything—but he'll still be Wally." Sister Thomas pulled out a hanky from her skirt pocket and dabbed away the tears on Lorraine's cheeks and then the ones on her own. "Are you hoping to see him again, date him, when he gets back?"

"I don't know, Sister Thomas. I sent him packing. He's probably never forgotten that. I doubt anything would come of it. But he was my good friend for such a long time. I just hope he'll be all right."

"Could I keep this card long enough to show it to Al? I'd run down to the plant, but I don't have a car at home."

"Let's go together. Dad told me I could use the gas in the car tonight and he'd take the bus to work this week."

"Oh, good. Let's all go. Al is going to be so pleased."

"Can we call Bobbi and Alex on the telephone?" Bev wanted to know.

"Oh, no, dear. But we'll write tonight and send the letters first thing in the morning. Everyone is going to be so cheered by this."

"Let's go to Millie's first—and tell Gene," LaRue said. "He'll be the happiest of all."

"Oh, yes. That's right," Sister Thomas said. "We need to tell Gene right now. He needs this tonight. He signed up with the marines this morning. He wouldn't admit a thing to me, but I know he's nervous about leaving home."

16

Bobbi and Afton were working the same shift at the hospital. That didn't mean they saw much of each other, but on a nice day in July they did manage to take a break at the same time. They walked outside and sat in chairs that looked out toward the harbor. Big gray battleships were docked there, but Bobbi chose not to look at them. She liked the color of the water, and closer, the red ginger plants and bougainvillea, the palm trees.

"So have you seen your doctor today?" Bobbi asked.

"My doctor. I'm sure I don't have my own private physician. Whatever could you mean?"

"Well, there's certainly one who gives you a thorough examination every time you walk by."

"Bobbi!"

"He *looks*. That's all I'm saying."

Afton was blushing, but she was also laughing. "Goll, Bobbi, don't you think he's luscious? He's like guava or fresh pineapple."

"Passion fruit, I do believe."

"You're terrible, Bobbi. It's not like that. He's a perfect gentleman with me."

"So far."

Afton turned in her seat and looked directly into Bobbi's

eyes. "Why do you say that? He respects me. He knows what my standards are."

"I just know what the other nurses say. He's got quite a reputation."

Afton folded her arms and turned straight in her chair. "They're jealous. He's the best-looking single guy around this place, and every nurse wants to get her hands on him."

"And vice versa."

"Bobbi, would you stop that!"

"Okay. But I do think you need to be careful. Dr. Brown Eyes has dated half the nurses in this hospital. I don't think all the things they say could be made up. Dolores said he was completely proper at first, and then he turned into an octopus—all tentacles."

The doctor's name was actually Julian Brown, but he did have deep brown eyes with long eyelashes, and the nurses, behind his back, had all begun to call him Dr. Brown Eyes. He was a young surgeon who had only recently completed his residency. He had an innocent look about him, but a number of nurses had told Bobbi that he rarely dated anyone for very long, and he made the most of any opportunities nurses provided for him.

"Bobbi, can I talk to you seriously about him for a minute? I mean, really?"

"Sure. But let me ask you one thing first."

"What?"

"What about Lowell, who used to make your knees weak, back in Arizona? I thought you were going to die if you didn't end up with him."

"Bobbi, he was just a boy. He's a private in the army somewhere."

"I get your point. It is hard to marry beneath your rank."

"Come on, Bobbi. Be serious for a minute. Let me tell you what I'm thinking about all this."

"Go right ahead."

"Okay." She gripped her hands together and looked at her lap. "Every girl around here is after him, and some of them really throw themselves at him. They all want to marry a doctor, and especially one who's so good looking."

"No doubt."

"Well, I think he hasn't always been as good as he should be, but I also think he would be—if he fell in love with someone he respected."

"Afton, think what you're saying. Is he going to join the Church? Is he going to take you to the temple?"

"I don't know. That's what I need to find out. You dated a nonmember—very seriously."

"Yes. And it didn't work out at all." But Bobbi was amazed at what she was saying. Was her father's voice coming out of her mouth? "David was interested in the Church," she added. "He thought very seriously about joining."

"Well . . . that's what I hope Julian will do. He's so dreamy I can hardly stand it. Golly, if you ask me, he's an angel; he just doesn't know it yet."

"That's why he's acting like a little devil."

"Bobbi!" Afton gave Bobbi's shoulder a slap. "You know how these nurses are. A lot of 'em have no morals at all. Marsha—the girl I work with in post-op—told me she stayed a couple of nights in a hotel with an officer last month. Before he shipped out, they just took off together on a two-day pass."

"Now let me see whether I understand this." Bobbi twisted so she could look at Afton straight on. "You're telling me that the good doctor is pure as the driven snow, but he can't control himself with all these evil nurses tempting him all the time."

"I'm not saying that. But men are kind of like that. A woman can get them excited, and then they can't help themselves. He could reform and stop being like that."

"Oh, brother."

"Well, it's true."

"It's an excuse men use, Afton. A lot of them go around seducing all the women they can. And they use big, innocent-looking eyes—brown, in some cases—as their favorite weapon."

"Bobbi, that's a nasty thing to say. You snapped up the only Mormon guy we ever met, and now you're being mean about the one guy I've found."

"Snapped up? Oh, certainly. I see Richard about twice a month—at church. He's never even called me."

"Maybe so. But I see the way he looks at you."

"How does he look at me?"

"Like he's so . . . *interested* . . . in every word you have to say."

"Oh, wow! Isn't that romantic?"

"Well, it is. You're *fascinating* to him, Bobbi. I'd give anything to meet a guy who cared that much about what I have to say."

"Afton, I want something more than talk."

Afton began to laugh. "Well, at least you admit it. Now who's sounding dangerous?"

"Me, I guess. But Richard is no threat. He's never even touched my hand—except to shake it."

Afton giggled. "Gee, mine's a devil and yours is a saint."

Bobbi laughed too, but then she said, "I don't know what Richard is. He likes to think, and to talk about ideas, but as soon as I try to find out what he—himself—is all about, he shuts up like a clam. I'd give anything just to feel some closeness to him."

"Bobbi, you've fallen for him."

"I wouldn't say that." Bobbi leaned back and stared at the horizon, where the sky and the water seemed to blend. "He's nice looking, and he's a good person. He's even funny sometimes, and interesting—but I don't understand him. He lets me get a peek inside once in a while, and then he closes the window and pulls down the shade."

Afton laughed. "But you do want to have a good look—right?"

"Of course I do. But he's the one who holds back."

"So what are you going to do?"

"Do? What can I do? He'll be shipping out one of these days, and he's certainly not saying anything about the future— not even that he wants to see me again."

"He will, Bobbi. I'm sure he will."

But Bobbi didn't think so. She stood up. "Come on. We'd better get back to work," she said.

Afton didn't stand up, however. "Bobbi," she said, "what about David Stinson? Do you still think about him?"

"I think about David every day. And his letters make me cry. He's the one man I've known who understands me. But there's nothing I can do. There's no way I can marry him." Bobbi tucked her hands into the pockets of her white skirt, and she turned toward the harbor. "Maybe I just want Richard to be the right one. I'm probably giving him qualities he doesn't even have."

"Am I doing the same thing with Julian?"

"I hate to say it, Afton, but I think you are."

They didn't look at each other. Bobbi was afraid she had hurt Afton. But after a time, Afton said, "Probably so. But it's so hard. I want someone."

"I thought we were going to enjoy our freedom over here," Bobbi said.

"That's what we said. But Bobbi, I need someone to love me. No one has ever loved me."

"I guess that's what I want from Richard, too."

"Well . . . if you want him, go after him."

"I've tried. A little. But any time I get personal, he gets scared. That's when he shuts up."

Twice now, after church, Afton had claimed that she had other things to do, and she had left Bobbi and Richard alone. They had gone for walks, and Bobbi had enjoyed the time together. So had Richard, it seemed, but he had never said any- thing that implied they were becoming more than friends.

Afton stood up, and she looked directly into Bobbi's eyes. "Richard is probably just being careful—being sure, before he says anything. And you're doing the same thing." She put her hands on her hips and cocked her head to one side. "Maybe it's time to take a step forward. Tell him how you feel. Or just kiss him and see what happens."

"Oh, sure. He'd jump in the ocean and swim to San Francisco."

"Naw. Richard would never go AWOL. He's too reliable to do something like that."

Bobbi laughed, and then she began to walk toward the back doors of the hospital. Afton got up and followed along, but just before they walked inside, she said something that haunted Bobbi afterward. "If both of you keep waiting for the other to say something—or do something—he'll be gone, and neither one of you will know how the other one feels."

That same week, on Thursday, after Bobbi got off work, she walked next door to the nurse's quarters. She had put in a twelve-hour shift, from six in the morning until six at night, and she was exhausted. She walked down the hall in her robe, took a shower, and then returned to her room. Afton had apparently been held over at the hospital. That happened sometimes in post-op.

Bobbi decided to wait for her before she walked to the mess hall to eat. She was lying on her bed when a little knock came at the door. "Bobbi," a voice said, "there's an officer down at the front desk. He said he wanted to see you."

"Officer? What officer?"

"Lieutenant Hammond is his name. He's a tall guy. Nice looking. He said something about—"

"That's all right. I just need to throw something on. Could you tell him I'm coming?"

"Wow. Sounds pretty exciting."

Bobbi couldn't believe this. But she was suddenly up and moving. She tossed on a little cotton flowered dress and then slipped on a pair of sandals. In five minutes she was heading out her door. But she slowed as she approached the stairs, and she tried to appear rather casual about Richard's being there. "Hi," she said, from the stairway, and he stood up.

"Hello," he said with that mellow voice of his. He waited for her to approach. He was actually wearing a Hawaiian shirt—white, with blue and yellow flowers—and sunglasses. "I got a chance to borrow a car—and I thought it would be a nice time to take a little drive. I didn't know what shift you were on, or whether—"

"I'd love to go for a drive."

"Have you ever seen the north shore?"

"No. I've been dying to drive up there. I've never even had a chance to see the temple."

"Do you need to . . . get anything?"

"No. But I ought to leave a note for Afton. Or did you want her to go with us?"

"Well, actually . . . I hadn't had that in mind."

"Okay." Bobbi fought hard not to smile. "I'll just run up and leave her a note. She hasn't come in yet. We both worked the day shift today."

"Sounds good." He smiled.

"Okay." And this time she smiled fully, with more satisfaction than she wanted to grant this guy who had never come around and had now shown up without warning.

Bobbi hurried to her room and actually worried that Afton might show up before she could get away—and Richard, out of politeness, would ask her to go along. But she merely wrote, "Gone with Richard for the evening. Don't think it, and don't say it when I get back. It's just for a ride."

But that's not what she was thinking. The truth was, he looked awfully good, with his hands in his pockets and his flowered shirt draping over his slim hips.

The car was something of a relic—an old Ford—but it was

a convertible, and of course perfect for the weather and for a drive of this kind.

"I'll bet you're really beat," Richard thought to say as he opened the door for her. "Do you have to be to work at six in the morning?"

"No. Tomorrow is my only day off this week."

"Well, you're luckier than I am. I have to be up early in the morning."

"We don't need to go clear out to—"

"No. That's all right. I've been wanting to get off the ship for a long time." He was talking as he walked around the car, and then, when he got in, he looked over at her and smiled. "I think our flowers clash a little," he said.

Bobbi looked into those blue eyes, which seemed almost silver in the late-afternoon light, and somehow couldn't think what he had said. "What?" she finally asked.

"My shirt and your dress."

"Oh." She laughed. "We look like a garden, don't we?"

He started the car. "I'm a little self-conscious wearing something like this," he said. "I had to borrow it from one of the other officers. He told me that's what I had to wear if I was going to drive a car like this."

"You look great, actually."

Richard looked away, shifted, and then backed out of the parking spot. "I know this car is a jalopy, but the air feels great." He drove slowly to the exit gate. Once out on the highway, however, Bobbi felt the flow of the air in her hair, and she did love the freedom she suddenly felt.

Richard drove on the little highway through Honolulu and then continued toward Diamond Head and around the east side of the island. He took his time and let Bobbi enjoy the view. It was also easier to talk when they didn't drive too fast. They stopped for a few minutes to look at the Blow Hole, near Koko Head, and then continued around Makapuu Point and on north. By the time they reached Laie, the sun was going down, but the temple looked beautiful in the fading light, with the reflecting pools glowing.

After, they drove on to Waimea Bay. It was dark by then, but a bright moon was coming up, and Richard parked the car. "Let's just go out and sit on the beach for a few minutes before we start back," he said.

"I'm worried that it's getting too late for you."

"That's okay. I've gone two or three days without sleep sometimes. I get by all right. This is the closest I've been to freedom in a long time. I don't want it to end."

But Bobbi was pretty sure he was talking only about the beach and the lovely air—the sound of the waves. As usual, he had not said anything very personal all evening. He did sit fairly close, however, and for a time he gazed out at the reflection of the moon on the waves. "This is one thing we could have used in Springville," he said. "A nice ocean."

"What about Utah Lake? Wasn't that good enough?"

He laughed. "Well, I'll tell you what. This is a beautiful place, but I'd trade straight across, right now, if I could go home and stay there."

"Is that where you want to live after the war? In Springville?"

"Not necessarily. But probably in Utah."

"And do what?"

"Maybe go back to college."

"I thought you were finished."

"I was. But I don't want to stay in the navy now, and that was always my plan. And I'm not that interested in engineering."

"So what would you study?"

"In a way, I'd like to be a teacher, but it's hard to raise a family on a teacher's salary."

"Is that what you want? A family?"

"Of course."

Bobbi heard the finality in his voice, as though he were

saying, "But I don't want to talk about that." And so she moved back to the first subject. "What would you teach?"

"Math, maybe. But I doubt I'll do that. Nothing is very clear to me right now. The end of the war doesn't seem real to me. I can't seem to think that far into the future."

"I used to think about teaching at a college."

"Literature?"

"Yes."

"Why don't you do it?"

"I don't know. One part of me says that I'd rather read novels and poetry—and not deal with the real world. Other times, I feel like nursing is the right thing for me. Today a young sailor left the hospital—a boy named Stanley. He had gotten burned in an explosion on his ship, and he really didn't want to leave. But he told me I'd helped him through all these awful weeks he's had to survive. That made me feel like I'm doing something worthwhile."

"Is he going to be okay?"

Bobbi heard a surprising amount of concern in Richard's voice. "Well . . . it's going to be rough for him. He's really quite disfigured."

"It happens all the time, you know," Richard said. "A lot of sailors get burned. I think I'd rather die than have my body mutilated like that."

"Don't say that. Stanley is such a nice kid. After I got used to how he looked, I didn't think much about it. People will just have to take the time to get to know him."

"But it's one thing for a nurse to handle that sort of thing. Do you think a girl could ever fall in love with him?"

"I don't know. I think so."

Richard seemed to let that run through his mind for a time. Bobbi glanced at him, saw the silhouette of his face in the moonlight. Suddenly she didn't want to talk. She wanted him to kiss her. But Richard said, "I think you should be a teacher. Or a professor. You'd be good at it."

Bobbi was frustrated. She knew he was only looking for something to say. "Maybe," she said, "but on a day like this, after what I experienced with Stanley, I don't want to think as much as I want to touch."

Richard chuckled.

"I didn't mean it *that* way," she said, and she laughed at herself. "It's just that I've always thought so much about everything. I wish, in a way, I were more like the Hawaiian women in our ward. They seem to savor life now, not worry themselves to death about the future."

"But it's hard to savor life, the way it is now. And who knows how many of us will even have a future? Or how many will end up like your friend Stanley."

That stopped Bobbi for a moment. She finally had a clue to Richard's reticence. "But that's just it," she said. "The war should force us to look at the basics. Life and death. Isn't it better to experience the good things than to put everything on hold?"

When Richard didn't say anything, Bobbi kept waiting; she wanted to hear his answer. Richard shifted his weight so that he was leaning mostly on one arm and a little closer. "Bobbi, I have this sense that a kid named Richard Hammond once lived in a place called Springville, Utah," he said. "But both the boy and the town are gone now. And it doesn't seem possible to get either one of them back."

"I don't see that. The war will end. That's why we're fighting—so we can have all the good things we remember."

"But I've seen things I never knew existed. It's hard to believe I'll ever be the same person again."

Richard lay back on the sand, and Bobbi turned to look down on his face, visible now under the moonlight. Her impulse was to drop all this talk and to follow Afton's advice: just kiss him and see what happened. But she couldn't do that, so she asked, "Don't you have to keep believing in good things? You believe in the gospel, don't you?"

"Sure. And I try to keep that perspective in my head. I also try to believe that Richard Hammond is still in me some-where—and will return. But it's a fight for me right now."

"Springville is still there. I saw it not too long ago."

He laughed. "I left a girl in Springville. She promised to wait for me forever. But she fell a little short. She didn't last six months."

Bobbi felt some relief to hear that, but the words had some sting in them too. "So that's made things worse, I guess."

"No. I don't think so. At least now, when I go back to sea, I won't have to worry about her. Last time out, I always won-dered, if something happened, how much it would hurt her. I think it's better, when you go into battle, not to leave any con-nections behind."

He looked at her intently, and they both knew what he was saying.

"Will you be shipping out soon?"

"I don't know. And if I did, I couldn't say. But it can't be too much longer."

Bobbi wanted to challenge him, tell him that "connections" were the only thing that mattered. But she could see in his face that he wasn't going to say anything more than he had said. What she did sense was that he knew more about his feelings than he claimed; he was *choosing* not to reveal what he knew about himself. She was almost sure he cared for her, too, but he was not going to say so.

They stayed there together for quite some time, Richard lying back on the sand and Bobbi looking out at the waves. Neither said a word. Bobbi felt her frustration turning into sad-ness. There were so many ways to be a casualty of this war.

· C H A P T E R ·

17

When the air-raid sirens sounded, Anna didn't panic; in fact, she rolled over in bed and groaned. But then she remembered, and fear stopped her breath. All through the latter part of July and into August, Hamburg had been devastated by an unprece-dented torrent of bombs, and now Berliners were expecting the same kind of attack. American and British bombers had struck Hamburg night and day for well over a week. So many phos-phorus bombs had dropped that at times the flames sucked all the oxygen from the air, causing hurricane-force windstorms that fanned the fires into white heat. The pavement in the streets had burned, turned into rivers, like lava. Tens of thou-sands of civilians had died.

Then, on August 1, Allied planes had dropped leaflets on Berlin with a warning for women and children to leave the city. Everyone assumed that Berlin would be next—and many chil-dren were sent to the country. But how could women leave? They were the ones keeping Berlin running, the ones staffing all the war production factories.

Anna slipped out of bed and gathered up her light summer *Feder Decke*, and then she hurried down the stairs. She and her parents and Peter, without saying anything, walked to the cor-ner of the basement. Other families from the apartment building were finding their way to their own usual spots. The basement was cooler than their third-floor apartment on this hot August night, and really quite pleasant. Anna curled up on top of the feather tick, but she didn't fall asleep as she sometimes managed to do. She waited and listened. Peter was next to her in the dark, and she couldn't see him clearly, but she heard his breath, coming unsteadily in tense bursts.

And then the bombs began to drop—closer than usual tonight but still a mile or more away. Anna wasn't frightened by these first explosions. She had been through these raids many times; she could judge the distance. She knew that a single bomb would probably not reach the basement unless it was a direct hit. What she feared was that these bombs were the first of thousands, that the firestorms would begin here— and destroy the entire city.

The explosions had a kind of rhythm, and Anna had learned to read the patterns. The bombers were moving past, not toward them. That was good, but a parallel pattern was likely: more planes, dropping bombs along another strip. The Stoltzes lived on the edge of town, and not very close to any major railroad lines or factories, which helped, but the choice of targets was not easy to explain. However much Anna disliked what Hitler and the Nazis had done to Germany, she still struggled to understand why the British and Americans bombed residential areas. She knew, of course, that Germany was doing the same thing in England, and perhaps had even started the civilian bombing, but it was still infuriating to see whole neighborhoods destroyed without a strategic target anywhere close.

"Is it beginning?" Sister Stoltz whispered to her husband, and Anna knew what she meant, what she feared.

"I don't know. It seems quite the usual thing, so far," Brother Stoltz told her.

"They're a long way off," Peter said with confidence, and Anna knew he was trying to show that he wasn't afraid. In the past few months he had finally grown taller, and soft hair was appearing on his cheeks and lip. Anna loved the way he was trying to assume his role as a man, which for him seemed to mean that he had to be brave—a protector to his mother and sister.

Anna lay still and kept listening for more bombers. The airplanes seemed a kind of enemy themselves, like birds of prey, coming in hordes. The irony was, the effect of all this bombardment was to unify Germans. No matter what people felt about Nazis, resolve to keep the defense plants operating was only heightened. Anna had seen her own munitions factory blown apart and three days later, after a monumental effort by employees, open again. Conditions were terrible, with rebuilding still going on as assembly lines operated, but the workers, without pressure, seemed to raise their level of effort.

Anna, herself, wanted this war to end in a way that would bring her old Germany back, and she knew that would require the Allies to win, not the Nazis, but she also loved the dedication that kept things going, and the people's loyalty to each other. She wondered whether the victors, these men in the bombers, could ever understand that.

At least when the bombs fell, everyone hunkered down together. At all other times, the Stoltzes had a bigger worry: that they might be recognized for who they really were. There were no further reports of Kellerman poking his nose about in Berlin, but the Stoltzes still dared not attend church, and Brother Stoltz always told the family to stay together, to avoid personal friendships, and to be careful about anything any of them might say. Worst of all, Brother Stoltz was working with the underground on a steady basis now. He said little about it, but Anna knew he was constantly making false papers for Jews who were hiding in the city, and somehow he was getting those papers to his contacts. At any time he could be caught, and the Gestapo would strike at the family quickly and decisively.

So all the world seemed an enemy. The bombs that dropped may not have been intended for Anna, personally, but they might as well have been. And most Germans would report the Stoltzes if they somehow learned their actual story. Certainly Brother Stoltz was a traitor by almost everyone's definition, and his family was just as bad for supporting him.

The raid didn't last long that night. It was not the beginning of the long siege Anna had feared. She was soon tramping back upstairs, where she fell asleep again almost instantly. But at breakfast, she felt numb. She would work a twelve-hour shift that day, and spend it typing and processing paperwork. All of it was so routine and uninteresting to her. And the irony never exactly left her that she was helping to make bullets that could possibly be used against the man she wanted to marry. In the night she had felt her anger toward those bombers, but when she could think beyond her immediate danger, she feared even more the German or Japanese soldiers who might be shooting at Alex somewhere else in the world.

"Papa," Peter said, as he sat across from his father at the breakfast table that morning.

"Yes."

"How long do you think the war will last?"

"I don't know. Maybe the Allies will cross the channel this year—and the Russians seem to be pushing our troops back in the east again. But I don't see an end in sight."

Peter was leaning forward, his hands on his forehead. He wasn't eating. "When can we be normal people?" he asked.

"We're normal. We merely have to be careful."

"I have no friends. I have to stay home all the time."

Brother Stoltz leaned back in his chair. "I know, Peter. It's difficult for you. But we can't help what's happened to us. We're lucky to be alive."

"*Blessed* to be alive," Sister Stoltz said.

Peter didn't move. After a time, he said, "I want my own

name back. I want to say what I think to someone. I'm sixteen, and I have to live like a little child—always home."

"Peter, I'm sorry. But what can we do?"

"You don't have to work for the underground—helping *Jews*. At Hitler Youth they tell us all the bad things Jews have done. I don't know why we have to take chances for them."

"Do you believe what you hear there, Peter?"

"I don't know." Peter sat up straight and looked at his father. "I have to say what they say, or they will know what traitors we are. I say it and say it, and after a while, I don't know what I think."

"Peter, we are not traitors," Brother Stoltz said.

"Of course we are," Anna said.

"We're not traitors to our people. We're traitors only to the Gestapo, to Hitler."

The room was silent. Everyone knew all this. But Anna understood how tired poor Peter was, how much he needed to be accepted somewhere by someone.

"I'm sorry," Brother Stoltz finally said, "but I'm going to keep helping the underground. If I can save a few lives, I'm going to feel much better about myself when this war finally ends. Or if I die, I'll be able to face the Lord."

It was a noble thing to say, and Anna agreed, but she looked at Peter, and she was sure she knew what he was thinking. He didn't want to die. He didn't want his father to die. And he also didn't want to go on living this way.

A few days later Anna came home a little after the others. When she walked in, she could see that Peter and her parents were upset about something. They were sitting in the living room, and Peter had a resolute, angry look in his eyes. He had grown so much in the past year, changed so much; he looked more combative, more determined than she had ever seen him before.

"*Was ist los?*" Anna asked. What is wrong?

"Papa wants to bring Jews into our house," Peter said, rather too loudly.

"Please. Be still," Brother Stoltz said, and Anna heard her father's anger. He looked at Anna. "It's an emergency. They may not have to stay long. We could keep them in the attic for a time, just as the Hochs kept us. Peter seems to have forgotten that without the Hochs we would not be alive now."

"I haven't forgotten that. But if we're caught, we'll *all* be killed. Why can't someone else take them?"

"Who? There are so few who are willing—few who can even be asked. And we have this attic. We have enough food. We can do it."

"What about bombing raids?" Anna asked. "The attic is the worst place to be."

"I know that. But it's also the last place the Gestapo would expect to find them. And these people have no choice. They have to take the gamble."

"Peter's right about the danger," Anna said. "But I think we should do it." She was looking at Peter, trying with her eyes to say to him, "Don't be selfish. Rise to this."

Peter slumped down in his chair. "They're *Jews!*" he said. "They're not like us. I don't want them here."

This was stunning. Brother Stoltz jumped to his feet, and for a moment Anna thought he was about to strike Peter. But Brother Stoltz said, "Have you forgotten our friend, Brother Goldfarb? Can you remember how he cried and thanked us—only because we gave him a few vegetables? And what did the Gestapo do? They took him away and locked him up—for nothing. For being a Jew."

"Peter doesn't mean what he said," Sister Stoltz said. She got up and walked to him, and then she knelt by his chair and touched her hand to his hair. "He hears so many things. It's all very confusing."

Peter pulled his head away from her touch, but he didn't say anything, and Anna was sure he *was* confused.

"The simple fact is, they are coming tonight. Soon," Brother Stoltz said. "And Peter, you will treat them with the respect they deserve."

Peter said nothing.

It was Anna who said, "How can they be brought in without being seen? Shouldn't they wait until after dark?"

"The people I work with know about these things. Moving about at night is the most dangerous thing a person can do. The family will walk through the front door, in daylight, and not look suspicious."

"Won't our neighbors notice that they haven't left?"

"Only if they get suspicious. That's why it all has to seem an ordinary visit."

Anna thought about that. She often saw people come into a building, but she didn't really watch to see whether they left unless she had some reason to notice. But the idea of it—harboring Jews—was terrifying. There was no surer way to draw the vengeance of the Nazis.

As the Stoltzes ate their evening meal, they spoke very little. Peter was being sullen, maybe even stoic, but he still looked unhappy, and now that Father had taken his stand—and had quieted Peter's objections—he seemed nervous himself. So was Mother.

The Stoltzes were still at the table when the knock came—quick and light. Brother Stoltz started and then got up quickly. He hurried to the door and let the people in without saying a word. Anna saw that the family was young—a couple with a little boy.

"Welcome," father said. "Are you all right?"

The man and woman stood stiff and unsure, and they glanced around. The little boy was leaning against his mother's legs, his face against her skirt.

"We're called the Niemeyers," Brother Stoltz said. "It's best if you know us by that name, I suppose." He was trying to sound friendly, but the tension was obvious in his voice.

"We're the Rosenbaums," the young man said. He was very Germanic looking, with light brown hair and a strong jaw. His wife was small, pretty, with dark hair and eyes. She was wearing a simple gray dress and was carrying a purse strapped over her shoulder. "This is Benjamin. My wife's name is Hannah. Mine is Herbert."

"Please. Sit down. We'll make a bed for you in the attic later, but stay with us here for now."

"Thank you," Hannah said, but she seemed tense as she led her little boy to the couch. Little Benjamin leaned against his mother, pushed his face against her side.

"Is there any way to look out and see whether anyone is watching?" Herbert asked.

"Yes. Of course," Brother Stoltz said, and he walked to his bedroom, which looked out on the front street. When he returned, in only a few seconds, he said, "I couldn't see anyone out there. I don't think we need to worry about that."

"That's not certain," Herbert said. "They know better than to show themselves."

"Yes. We know about that. We've been in hiding ourselves."

"You're not Jewish, are you?" Hannah asked, and Anna heard some concern in her voice. But maybe, right now, everything worried her.

"No. We're not. But Jews are not the only ones hiding these days," Brother Stoltz said.

Sister Stoltz walked over to Hannah and patted her shoulder. "We do understand what you are going through," she said.

Anna saw some relief come into Hannah's face, her wide eyes softening. "We were able to bring only what I have in my purse," she said. "And Herbert has a few personal things in his pockets. A razor and—"

"It's all right. We have enough," Sister Stoltz said. "And gradually, we can get some things you will need."

"We're not to stay here long," Herbert said. "That's what we were told."

"Probably not," Brother Stoltz said. "We are not perhaps the safest people to be with . . . in the long run. But everything should be fine for now."

"We had to go somewhere," Herbert said. "Neighbors had gotten suspicious where we were."

No one seemed to know what else to say. Peter was sitting straight in his chair, and he was avoiding eye contact with anyone. Anna had been standing behind him, but now she walked over to the couch. She sat down next to little Benjamin. "Good evening, Benjamin," she said. "May I be your friend?" He peeked at Anna, and then he tucked his head against his mother's side again. "How old is he?" Anna asked his mother.

"Three. He's shy at first. But he likes to be noisy, once he relaxes a little. It's been so hard to keep him quiet. He doesn't understand, of course."

"That's so difficult," Anna said. "By the way, my name is Anna, and my brother is named Peter. Those are our real first names. You might as well know them."

"You're so beautiful," Hannah said, and her voice seemed natural for the first time.

"Oh, thank you," Anna said, "but that's exactly what I wanted to tell you."

Anna felt something good between the two of them. She knew that Hannah wasn't much older than she was, and Anna had been cut off from almost all contact with young women. She liked the idea that the two of them might be friends, at least for a time.

"Benjamin," Anna said again, "we're happy you came to stay with us." He continued to hide his head.

"Could I get you something to eat?" Sister Stoltz asked. "Have you eaten tonight?"

"Actually, no," Herbert said. "We hate to impose, but I do believe that Benjamin is hungry."

"Oh, of course. I know you must be thirsty, too, in all this heat. Will you come into the kitchen? That might be easiest."

And so the Rosenbaums went to the kitchen, and so did the others, except for Peter, who stayed in his chair.

Sister Stoltz was more in her element now, serving food and fussing over the Rosenbaums. The tension began to ease. Little Benjamin ate rather heartily and began to look around at the Stoltzes, even if he still wouldn't say anything.

After everyone had eaten, Sister Stoltz climbed a ladder into the attic, and Hannah followed. Anna went along too, and they arranged a bed on the floor. There was a small window, which was now emitting the last of the day's light but seemed to let in almost no air. "I'm afraid this won't be very comfortable for you," Anna told Hannah.

"It's fine. I can live with the heat if we can only stay safe."

Sister Stoltz said, "I wonder whether we couldn't let you sleep in our living room. The couch would be better for you, and Peter could come up here."

"No," Hannah said. "If someone came in the night, we couldn't hide fast enough."

"We spent many months in a basement," Anna said. "We were cramped, but we're still alive."

For the first time, Hannah let her emotion show. She blinked away some tears. "It's Benjamin I live for. If I can keep him alive, I can accept . . . anything else."

"But no one would take the life of a little child," Sister Stoltz said.

Hannah gave her a quick, surprised look. "Oh, Frau Niemeyer, you have no idea what is happening now."

Anna felt a chill run through her. The thought of anyone hurting little Benjamin was too appalling to think about.

When the women climbed down from the attic, Anna found that the men were talking about the same thing. Brother Stoltz looked at his wife and said, "Herbert tells me that all the Jews being arrested are now being hauled on trains to Poland."

"I thought they were doing that before."

"Yes. Here. But now they're being transported from France and Italy and Denmark—anywhere the Nazis have power."

"Where are they keeping so many people?" Sister Stoltz asked.

"They're not keeping them," Herbert said.

Everyone knew what that meant. But Sister Stoltz said, "Surely, they can't. . . ." She didn't want to say it. "Not so many people."

Herbert spoke softly. "We hear things. We don't know everything. But in Poland, people are being dragged from all the ghettos, and they aren't coming back."

For the first time Peter spoke. "This could be lies. How could so many people be killed?"

"It's not lies," Herbert said. "People have watched Jews being forced onto trains. And some of the Poles who are trying to do what they can to help us—people like you—they know the whole story. They say that at some of the camps, Jews are shot down—men and women and children—and buried in mass graves. In other camps, the Nazis are using gas. They keep the young people, who can work, but they kill the rest, and then they burn their bodies in ovens. They say the ovens are going all day and all night—every day."

Peter was sitting up very straight now, his eyes trained on Herbert. "In Hitler Youth, they told us that such stories are lies—stories told by Jews to make the Führer look bad."

"Peter, I haven't been there," Herbert said. "I haven't seen it. So I cannot say for certain. But you know as well as I do that very few Jews are left in Germany. Where have they all gone? And *why* were they taken away? Hitler means to rid the world of us. He says we're mongrel dogs who must be destroyed. And he doesn't mean only me and my wife. He means little Benjamin, too."

Anna saw Peter take a long look at Benjamin.

"Peter," Herbert said, "I'm an ordinary man. All my life I've lived in the Jewish section, in Berlin. That was not exactly my family's choice, I suppose, but we were content to be there. So was Hannah's family. We never harmed anyone in our lives. I was learning the jeweler's trade, and I wasn't making much, but Hannah and I got married, and we were managing to get by. The only thing we want is to raise a family, be decent people—the same as anyone. Now tell me, what's our crime? Why do we have to hide? And tell me Benjamin's crime. How could anyone want to hurt him?"

"What kind of people could hold so much hatred in their hearts?" Hannah asked. She put her arm around Benjamin, but she was looking at Peter.

"We won't let it happen," Sister Stoltz said. "We'll keep you safe."

"I wish it were that easy, Frau Niemeyer," Herbert said. "But the Gestapo never . . ." He stopped and glanced at his wife. "But maybe the war can end before too much longer."

The problem was, everyone knew that wasn't true. The better part of a minute passed before Peter got up and walked to a desk at the end of the room. Anna was worried. She didn't know whether Peter was clinging to the things he had heard at Hitler Youth. She thought he was going to pull out his school-work and turn his back on the Rosenbaums. But he got something from the desk drawer, and then he came back. He walked toward Hannah and Benjamin, and he knelt down in front of them. Peter had a little toy truck in his hand. "Benjamin," he said, "would you like to play with this?"

Benjamin looked at him for a time, and then he nodded, and he took the truck in his own hand. But he only looked at it.

"Come with me," Peter said. "We'll play."

Benjamin nodded, and then he slid off the couch.

"Where did you get the truck?" Brother Stoltz asked.

Peter took Benjamin's hand, and they walked to the end of the room where Peter's desk was. "I found it in the bombed-out house where we lived. I just . . . decided to keep it."

Anna knew he was embarrassed to admit to this; he was too

old for such toys. But he knelt down with Benjamin, and he made a sound like the roaring of a truck. Benjamin laughed, and he pushed the little wooden truck across the hardwood floor.

Bobbi hadn't seen Richard for more than a week. He hadn't come to church, and he hadn't called or stopped by since the night they had taken the drive together. On the way back from the north shore that night he had chatted casually with her, but then, at her door, he had said, carefully, "Bobbi, I wish I had met you at a different time." That was all. If he had added, "And I hope I can see you when I get back" or "after the war," she wouldn't have felt so bad. But he had merely walked away, and now he had made no attempt to get in touch. She wondered whether his ship had already sailed.

Then, on a Friday afternoon, she got a call from him at the hospital. By the time she was able to walk to her station, Mary Pindetti, the nurse who was sitting at the phone, told Bobbi, "He couldn't wait. But he wondered whether he could take you to dinner tonight. At seven."

"He couldn't *wait?*"

"No. But he sure has a nice voice. He told me, 'Tell her seven. I don't think she knows what time 1900 is.'"

Mary laughed, but Bobbi didn't. "What did you tell him?" she asked.

"I just said I'd give you the message. Who is he, anyway?"

"He's just a friend of mine. An officer. I should call him and tell him I won't go."

"Hey, no girl ever got that mad at a *friend*. If you don't want to go, I will." Mary was not one of the girls with "a reputation" around the hospital. In fact, she was quite a straight-laced Catholic. But she knew as well as anyone how hard it was to find a nice fellow to go out with—who wasn't either married or nineteen years old.

All afternoon Bobbi huffed, and she thought about things she wanted to tell Richard. And then, when he didn't get there until seven-thirty, she was fuming.

But when he finally arrived, he stood, officer's hat in hand, looking repentant—and he smiled. He was wearing his khakis, not his dress whites, but he still looked good in uniform. "Sorry I'm late," he said, "but you don't know how close I came to getting stuck on board tonight. You can't believe how busy we are."

"Well . . . as long as you think it was worth the trouble."

"Ooooh. You're mad at me, aren't you?"

"I don't get mad at my friends." She thought of adding, "If you were my boyfriend it might be different," but she didn't.

"There's a place in town that serves real Hawaiian dinners. Poi and all the rest. I thought it might be fun to try some of the genuine stuff."

"Afton and I have eaten Hawaiian food. A lot of it I don't like."

"Oh . . ."

"But that's all right."

"Uh . . . we also have to take the bus. I couldn't get a car."

"That's fine." Bobbi walked out ahead of him.

But on the bus she was soon regretting her childishness. He talked, in his gentle way, about the ship and how pressured he was, and gradually Bobbi began to get the picture. He was shipping out. She found herself more disappointed than she wanted to be but also less harsh in her judgment. Still, he didn't admit he was leaving, and he seemed especially careful to stay on neutral subjects. He talked about a letter he had gotten from home. A friend of his from high school had been killed in the invasion of Sicily. "He wasn't one of my closest friends," he told Bobbi, "but I played basketball with him. He was a nice enough guy, but he was kind of a big talker, always bragging about what he would do in the war. But he's not bragging now."

"A boy from my neighborhood is missing in action in the Solomons," Bobbi said. "He's just a kid. It seems like only the other day he was going on Scout trips with my little brother. Mom says his parents don't hold out much hope that he's alive."

"Sometimes MIA means that he's been taken prisoner."

"I remember when it only meant Mutual Improvement Association."

Richard smiled and nodded. "I wish it still did."

Bobbi looked out the window of the bus. It was "boat day," one of the days when the ocean liners arrived in port from the mainland. Hawaiians turned it into a big celebration, with music and leis for all the new arrivals, even though they were mostly military people now. As the bus passed through the streets of Honolulu, Bobbi could see the crowds down by the beach.

When the two got off the bus they had a couple of blocks to walk. Bobbi hoped, just a little, that Richard would take her hand or show some little sign of affection. But he didn't, and it angered her that she couldn't give up the hope. At the restaurant, after they had ordered, they talked a little but said nothing of any importance. Finally Bobbi couldn't stand it. "Are you shipping out?" she asked.

Richard took a long look at her, his eyes full of confusion. "That's not something I can discuss," he said. "You know it's classified information."

"But you didn't say, 'No, I'll be around for a while yet.'"

"No. I didn't say that."

Bobbi let her eyes go shut. "Richard, I can't do this. I don't operate this way. I need to know what you're thinking."

"I don't know what you want me to say."

Bobbi shook her head. She picked up her butter knife. "If I stab you before this night is out, don't be surprised."

"Why?" He tried to laugh.

"I want to know what's going on between us—if anything."

"Bobbi, it's hard to talk about that now. Maybe I'll get back here. Or maybe I'll see you in Utah, and then . . . you know . . . we could . . ."

"What? Do you *want* to see me? Do you want to pursue this, or are you just my old buddy from Utah—someone to kill a few hours with?"

He didn't answer. He looked at her for a time, and then he let his eyes drop.

"Okay. Let me start," Bobbi said. "I don't really know you. You only let me see you in little glimpses. But every now and then I get the idea that I could like you very much. I even get the impression that you like me. What I don't understand is why you keep your guard up all the time."

Richard nodded, and he looked at her for a long time, but he still didn't speak.

"I take it all back," Bobbi finally said. "I hate you."

"You're right. It *is* pleasant to share our feelings." He smiled.

"Look . . . I know you're going into battle, but so what? Everybody is just sort of passing through right now. Nothing is permanent for anyone. That's simply the reality we have to live with. I don't agree with what you told me last week. What's so wrong about leaving some *connections* behind?"

Bobbi was out of breath—and *very* embarrassed. If he had said, immediately, "Oh, Bobbi, you're right; I'm nuts about you," she might have been all right. But he said nothing.

She remained quiet while some slow seconds passed and he continued to avoid her eyes, and then she said, "Say, Richard, what do you think about this weather we've been having? And by the way, do you think the Yankees will win the pennant this year without DiMaggio?"

He finally looked at her. "Bobbi, I can't do this. I just want to leave things the way they are."

"Then why did you call me? Why didn't you just leave?" Bobbi crossed her arms and stared hard at him, but he looked at her only in glances.

"I just wanted to see you one more time."

"Were you going to say good-bye?"

"Not exactly."

"What were you going to tell me?"

"I don't know. I hadn't thought that far ahead."

"Do you think that's fair?"

"Bobbi, listen to me," he said, and he leaned forward and looked into her eyes. "Above all, that's what I'm trying to do. Be fair. I think you actually understand that."

Bobbi told herself to give up. She knew what he meant, perhaps, but she didn't agree. Richard had an outer layer, like armor; maybe there was something under it, but she would never know. She leaned back and tried to seem relaxed. The restaurant was elegant, full of flowers, with one side open onto a garden. Most of the diners were in uniform, and they all seemed happy. In the garden, a little Hawaiian band was playing, and a man was singing "Lovely Hula Hands." It was like something out of movies Bobbi had seen, but right now she would have given almost anything just to escape the place.

Richard was still watching her. "Bobbi, I'm sorry," he said. "It was selfish of me to ask you out tonight. I know that. But I didn't want to leave without seeing you."

Bobbi could make no sense of this. "Richard," she said, "I don't understand what you're up to. Everything you say implies that you're interested in me. Don't I have a right to know what you have in mind? Do you *want* to see me when you get back?"

He sat for a very long time, and Bobbi wondered whether he was ever going to answer. But finally he said, "I do want to see you, Bobbi. I really do. But it's the getting back I'm not sure about. And I have good reason to feel that way. I think it would be unfair to say anything more than that." Those crystal eyes of his had filled with tears, which surprised Bobbi more than anything that had ever happened between them.

About then the waitress arrived with the food, and Richard was quick to cover his emotion. Bobbi had no idea what to say, what to think. Where was he shipping off to that he was so doubtful about his future? She wanted to disagree with him, to tell him that she could deal with *anything* better than his silence, but she was sure he wasn't going to change his mind.

When the waitress left, Richard talked about the food. Clearly he had decided that he had said enough, and he was returning to small talk. Bobbi tasted the pork and didn't mind it, but the poi, and especially the taro, almost made her sick; she was not in an emotional state to handle it. She said almost nothing. All of the sentences that came into her head were questions, and clearly he didn't want her to ask.

She was actually relieved when she and Richard got on the bus and headed back to the base. She knew that the days ahead would be painfully drab, but she also knew she could change nothing, so she wanted to get away from him and start getting used to life the way it would be now. What hurt more than anything was that she was finally admitting to herself what she had really known for a few weeks now: that she *was* in love with him.

When they got off the bus, they walked quietly in the mildness of the Hawaiian night; they reached the front door to Bobbi's quarters without saying a word. She stopped and said, "Thanks, Richard. I hope you get back to Springville someday, safe and sound."

"Bobbi, I'm sorry. I've wanted to get to know you, but I haven't dared. I think you understand that, don't you?"

"No. I don't."

"I tried to explain. As much as I can." He stood for a

moment, obviously struggling to think of something to say in parting, but finally he merely held out his hand. Under the porch light at the doorstep, he looked tan, wonderfully handsome, but very much in pain. She wanted so badly to take him in her arms and cling to him. But she only took hold of his hand. He held it for a few seconds, and then he nodded, let go, and walked away.

Why?

Bobbi felt as though she were about to be swallowed up in that same emptiness she had felt when she'd had to leave David in Chicago. Why couldn't anything ever work out right in her life? She didn't turn to go inside; she simply stood and watched him pace away with those long, resolute strides.

Then he glanced back. When he saw her, still standing by the door, he stopped. She nodded and he turned around. And then he stood and looked at her. She could read nothing in his face, and as the seconds mounted, she wondered why he didn't just end this. She was crying now, tears running down her face, and his standing there was only adding to the pain.

Then he began to walk again, but this time toward her.

When he reached her, he didn't grab her. He merely took her gently by the shoulders and pulled her to him, held her next to him and wrapped her in his arms for the very first time. He didn't say a word, and she was still not clear what he was thinking.

"Bobbi," he finally whispered, "I do want to have this bit of time. But it seems so selfish."

"It's all we have," she said.

"Do you have to work tomorrow?"

"Yes. But no. I'll get off somehow. I'll bribe someone to take my shift. I'll do . . . anything."

"Okay. I only have tomorrow, but I'll get away, too. And maybe I can borrow that car again. We can go back to the north shore. All day."

"All right. I'll go AWOL if I have to."

"Bobbi, it's just the one day. I can't say exactly when I'm leaving, but tomorrow is the only day I can get away from my ship."

"One day is so much better than what we just had."

He stepped back enough to look into her eyes, and then, finally, he leaned forward and kissed her. It was the lightest of kisses but the loveliest of Bobbi's life.

Bobbi didn't let him go. She pulled him back, kissed him again, longer this time, and then she nestled against him and felt engulfed with joy and relief, even though she knew already that so much torment lay ahead.

Richard picked up Bobbi early the next morning. She had agreed with Iris Smithton to trade two shifts for one over the weekend, which meant she would miss church, but at least she would have her day with Richard.

He seemed more relaxed, happier than she had ever seen him, as he drove through the mountains, up over the steep Nuuanu Pali road and then north through Laie and around to Waimea Bay, where they had been before. This time they did go swimming. They swam against the waves and then let the surf carry them back, and they played in the shallow water, splashing each other, teasing, laughing. There had been no chance to pack a lunch, so they bought pineapples, guavas, and mangos at a roadside stand, and they returned to the beach. They found a shady spot, a little away from the beach, and they cut the fruit with Richard's pocketknife. The fresh pineapple was luscious, but Bobbi always seemed to find a way to let the juice run all over her. She laughed. "I'm making a sticky mess of myself," she said.

"Me too," Richard said. "Maybe we can get stuck together, and they won't be able to ship me out."

It was the most flirtatious thing he had ever said to her, and she was taken by surprise. "I think I'm starting to see a whole new side of you, Richard."

He laughed. "Well, you've certainly seen the more serious side of me up until now."

"Why?"

"Are you going to make me serious all over again?"

"Temporarily. I'm curious to know." But that's not exactly what Bobbi was thinking. It had all been very fun, and Bobbi liked Richard this way, but he actually hadn't revealed any more of his feelings than before. He had not kissed her again, hardly touched her all day, and he'd said nothing about the future.

Richard was still wearing his swimming trunks, but he had also put on an old shirt, light blue, which he had left mostly unbuttoned. He pushed his bare feet into the sand and leaned forward, his arms on his knees. "When I came back from our last tour of duty, I wasn't in a very good state of mind. A lot of terrible things happened."

"Are you talking about those Japanese soldiers you saw in the water?"

"Well, yes. But there was a lot more than that. We got hit by dive bombers and took some heavy damage. We were lucky to stay afloat. And a lot of people died. One of the officers, a good friend of mine, got burned over most of his body. He lived, but now I think he wishes he hadn't."

Bobbi suddenly understood a few things Richard had obviously been thinking about. "It must be horrible for you to go back out there."

"Of course it is. But it's not just the danger. It's everything to do with the war. In port I started to feel human. But now everything starts again."

"Richard, tell me something. Why didn't you want to have dinner with Sister Aoki?"

"Isn't that obvious, Bobbi? When you're trying to kill human beings, it's not good to think of them as people like yourself. Sister Aoki only reminds me that the Japanese are cultured, kindly people. That's not a good thing to have on my mind when I'm bombarding Jap troops on some little island."

"And what about the Dear John you got? How does that fit into all this?"

Richard looked at Bobbi directly, accepted her own gaze. "I didn't want to get close to you, Bobbi. I liked you the first time I met you. I knew immediately that you were bright and interesting and—"

"Just not gorgeous."

"Oh, Bobbi, one of your best qualities is that you have no idea how pretty you are. You've got this fresh, wonderful quality. You seem so sophisticated, and then you smile, and you look like an eleven-year-old kid."

"Is that good?"

"It's perfect. You're this wonderful blend of everything I want. You're smart and pretty and thoughtful—and yet you're not conceited. You're good, Bobbi—really, really good. And lately I've had a hard time believing in goodness."

Bobbi's breath was gone.

"But I didn't want to hurt you. And I didn't want to go through the same thing again. Margie—the girl in Springville—sent that letter to me after I had worried so much about her. I wanted to be free of concerns this time. Then if something happened, there was no one who would have to feel the pain."

"And no one for you to lose?"

"That's right. But when I left home, it never occurred to me that I might die. Even when we got into our first action, it seemed impossible that anything would happen to me. But then we got hit, and all these guys were dying—a lot of them with girls back home—and it became very clear that I might not get my chance to be married and raise a family and do all the things I've always wanted to do. So I vowed not to get involved with anyone again until I knew for sure I was going to get through the war."

"It's funny. I vowed almost the same thing. I was engaged once, and I got my whole family upset with me when I backed out. Then I fell in love with a guy who wasn't a member of the Church, and I scared my parents half to death. It was all way too complicated, so I joined the navy and told myself I would stay out of any more attachments—until life got back to normal."

"Normal. What is that? I'd give anything for those days in high school when I'd never heard of most of these islands in the Pacific."

Bobbi slid a little closer and took hold of his arm. "What were you like then? In high school."

"I was pretty shy, actually. I spent a lot more time with my buddies than I ever did with girls. I hunted and fished a lot, practiced basketball all year round. But I don't know; I can hardly remember who I was back then. I don't think I ever had a serious thought about anything."

"Most guys are like that in high school. Girls, too, I guess. But I thought about *everything*. I asked so many questions I drove myself and everyone else crazy. There always seemed so much to discover, and none of my friends seemed to care. I couldn't find anyone who looked at the world the same way I did."

"It's good we didn't meet in college, Bobbi. I was really practical, and I got my education, but I was always complaining that I saw no reason to study history or art—or anything of that sort—when I was going to be an engineer."

"So how do you feel about that now?"

"What I really want is to curl up in a library somewhere and read every book on the shelves. I have so many things I want to think about. For one thing, I need to study the scriptures and try to put some things in perspective. There's just too much that doesn't make sense to me right now."

"I'm moving the other way, Richard—trying to respond to life and not think about it quite so much. I want to *feel* the Spirit and not depend so much on my own perceptions."

"Well . . . maybe we can meet halfway."

Bobbi suddenly twisted and got onto her knees. And then she looked into Richard's eyes, her face only inches away. "I'll always love to read," she said. "Let's make a date. When the war is over, let's read together. And talk about everything."

He smiled, slowly and fully. "That does sound good. But it wouldn't be a fair compromise. Maybe we could do a little of that touching you were talking about the other night."

"Careful, buddy. I was talking about caring for the sick."

"Hey, I'm just talking about holding hands while we read."

She smiled and took hold of his hand. "That sounds wonderful."

"Maybe we could even steal a little kiss between chapters."

"That sounds better." And then, without warning—even to herself—she was kissing him, clinging to his neck and pushing him backward onto the sand. And after the kisses, he lay next to her, holding her, and finally he whispered the words back to her. "It's a date. When the war is over."

It was a good day. They swam some more, and they talked and talked. But it was also a horrible day, with the dreadful reality becoming increasingly clear. It was the last day, and nothing was guaranteed after that. When Richard took her back to her quarters, late that night, they didn't want to part, and so they sat on the lawn and talked most of the night. And kissed.

"Will you write to me?" Bobbi asked him, when it was almost morning and they were finally standing in front of the door to her quarters.

"Sure. But there's no predicting when letters will come through. You might get several at once and then nothing for a while. Don't let that worry you."

"It will worry me."

"Well . . . I know. That's why—"

"No. It's okay. I want to worry about you. Richard, I've never been so sad in my life. But I wouldn't have missed this day for anything."

"Day and night," he said, smiling.

"I'll write to you, too, but will you get the letters?"

"Eventually."

"Can you tell me anything about where you're going?"

"No."

"It's dangerous, isn't it?"

"Yes."

"*Very* dangerous?"

"Possibly. It's hard to say for sure."

"Richard, can you tell me what you're feeling for me? You still haven't told me that—not exactly."

He took her in his arms, there under the porch light. "Bobbi, I love you. I want you to be here—or back home—and I want to come home to you. I want you forever. But I shouldn't even say that. If I don't—"

"Richard, I love you, too. I'm going to wait for you. We're going to be together. I don't care if that makes it worse for both of us; it also makes it better."

But she was crying now, and so was he. He kissed her again, and then he said, "I can't tell you when I'm leaving, but it's soon. Don't tell anyone I said that. I know I won't get off the ship between now and then. Or even be able to call. But I'll write soon."

"I will too."

"But let's not hurt each other with our letters. Let's not talk about being apart. Let's not even talk about the future. Let's just keep each other going."

They kissed one more time. And then he walked away, as he had the night before, taking those long strides. He did glance back once, and wave, but he didn't return. Bobbi was sobbing, but she was so glad he had come back the night before.

Bobbi didn't bother to go to bed. She went upstairs and showered, and then she watched the sun come up. When Afton woke up, she tried to tease Bobbi about being out all night. But Bobbi began to cry again, and she told Afton how much she was in love with Richard. Then they cried together.

The day was very long, and Bobbi seemed in a daze. She wanted more than anything to be called to the phone—just to hear his voice one more time. But he didn't call, and she knew he couldn't. When Bobbi got off work that evening, she had expected to go directly to bed, but she wasn't sleepy after all, and she was so empty that she felt she had to get away from her quarters and do something—anything. And so she took the bus to Honolulu, and she walked to Ishi's house.

"Oh, Bobbi," Ishi said when she opened the door, "is something wrong?"

"No, no. Not at all. I was just in town, and I thought I'd stop by to say hello." And then she began to cry.

Ishi took her inside, hugged her. "What is it?" she asked again.

"I'm in love," Bobbi said, and she tried to laugh.

"Who doesn't know that?" Sharon said. "Is Brother Hammond shipping out?"

"I can't say. It's a secret."

"Yes. Just like your love is."

"Oh, Ishi, what am I going to do?"

Ishi stepped away, had Bobbi sit down, and then sat next to her on the couch. "Well, for one thing, you can come to see me all you want. The kids would love that. And I need someone who understands what I'm going through. It looks like my husband is finally going into battle."

"Do you know where?"

"No. But in his last letter, he said the army has finally agreed to let the Japanese boys fight. The government stuck them in Wisconsin for a long time." She smiled. "Almost froze them to death. And now they're in Mississippi. All they've done is train until they're sick of it."

"When do you think you'll see him again?"

"Who knows? I doubt the army would send Japanese sol-

diers to the Pacific. He's probably on his way to Africa. That's
what people here think."

"How are we going to get through this, Ishi?"

"I don't know. I wish I could do something, say something,
that would help you, but I'm feeling all the same things you
are."

"It helps to have someone who understands." Bobbi took a
breath, tried to compose herself, and then said, "Where are the
kids?"

"Out back. Playing in the yard."

"Could I go out and see them?"

Ishi stood up. "Of course," she said.

Bobbi wiped her hand across her eyes and then fumbled in
her pocket for a handkerchief. "Wait just a minute. I need to
stop crying."

"It's okay. Children understand crying better than anyone."

"I know, but . . ." Bobbi found her handkerchief and wiped
her eyes. "I don't want them to feel bad. It's a happy time, really.
He told me he loved me." She forced herself to smile. And then
she went outside, and she played with Lily and David. She
forced herself into it with a kind of intensity that was supposed
to drive all her other thoughts away. But all she could think was
that she wanted the months and years to vanish, to have
Richard home, and to have her own children—his children.
She saw no irony at all in the idea that these dear children she
loved so much—and for the moment, represented her own—
were Japanese.

- CHAPTER -

19

A few days before Christmas of 1943 the same old rumor began to circulate that the men in Camp Cabanatuaan would receive packages from home. Wally tried not to think it possible. How many times had he heard it before? But this time men claimed to have seen the packages, to have unloaded them from trucks themselves.

There was always so little to look forward to, and the grinding work in the garden, out in the hot sun, was like an eternal punishment—some level of Dante's Inferno. Gardening work was much better than the labor Wally had known in the Tayabas jungle, and he tried to remember that, but the sameness, the boredom, were hard to deal with when no end was in sight. The new motto this year, spread among the men, was "Mother's Door in '44," but a year before the hope had been to be free in '43. The fact was, no one knew how long the war would last.

A few days before Christmas the guards called the men together, and they announced that packages actually had come. They read off the names of a number of prisoners— twenty or so—and the men marched forward and received their gifts from home.

Each of the men looked exultant as they returned to the

group with parcels in their arms, but everyone who received nothing, like Wally, had to struggle not to resent the ones who had been on the list.

But the guard said, "More tomorrow."

No one knew what that meant. Why would the guards hand out some and not all of the packages? But then, why did the guards do anything they chose to do? There was never any predicting.

The next day, and again the day after that, the Japanese distributed boxes. And everyone who didn't get one continued to wait and hope. It was cruel, and maybe that was the point. Wally could accept the idea that he hadn't gotten anything, if he just knew, but the wait each day was excruciating.

The following day he received nothing again, and the division among the men was becoming obvious. Everyone who hadn't received packages longed for the next day—anxious but afraid to hope—while the resentment built toward those who had gotten all the good things from home: food and clothing, personal care items, medicine. Wally was sure he would get a box of Ginger Snaps, if he got anything at all, and he lay awake at night imagining the taste.

Finally, on Christmas Eve, Wally heard his name called out. He was afraid for a moment that he had heard wrong, but several prisoners turned toward him and said, "That was you, Wally."

And so he stood up and walked to the front, and a guard placed a good-sized box in his arms. But now he had to go through the same routine as the others. He had to open his package in front of a guard, and the guard had to inspect everything inside. Wally hated this intrusion. He wanted to take the package back to his barracks and open it alone, and then look at everything slowly and carefully, one item at a time.

But the guard rummaged through the box quickly, and Wally saw most of what was there. Then he closed up the box and took it back to his barracks. Chuck walked with him. He had received a package a couple of days before, but Art still hadn't gotten one. The three had agreed to share what, if anything, they received. Now they were happy to have another package to work with.

"I got my Ginger Snaps," Wally told him, and Chuck laughed, but then Wally sat on his bunk and took out the items one at a time. He had some towels and washcloths. He touched them to his face and loved the softness, but he caught the smell of home, and a rush of homesickness passed through him. He clung to the towels and kept sniffing, saw all sorts of images, thought of the bathroom at home and the nice tub, the hot water.

There were also several bars of Palmolive soap, and that was a glorious thing to sniff and hold in his hands. He would have to use the bars carefully and make them last as long as possible. The same with the toothpaste. And then he found a toothbrush, and he could hardly believe his joy. It was something he had gone without since the beginning. He also discovered a safety razor and a leather autostrop to sharpen blades—plus a dozen packages of blades. He thought immediately how many men would be able to get a good shave with these. It was a treasure.

Wally laughed when he looked at the undershorts his family had chosen to send. They were his old size—with a 32-inch waist. They would almost go around him twice now, but still, he could do a little stitching on them and make them work somehow.

He also found sacks of candy: pink wintergreen mints and lemon drops. He wanted to break the packages open immediately, but he told himself, "One a day. Make them last."

On the bottom of the package was a large envelope. He hoped there was a letter inside. He opened it slowly and pulled out several pictures—but no letter. Apparently, letters had not been allowed. No one else had gotten them either.

The pictures, though, were wonderful. One was of the family, taken two years before, when everyone but Wally had still been home. Wally studied the faces, tried to get them back in his mind. It had been so hard at times to keep the images clear. But he wasn't prepared for the pain the pictures caused him. He found school pictures of LaRue and Beverly, and one of Gene in a marine uniform. The girls were so pretty, so grown up, and Gene looked confident and mature, but Wally hated to think of him going off to war. It seemed impossible that he could be old enough. There was also a picture of Alex in an army uniform and Bobbi in navy dress whites. It all told a story, one that said the family was broken apart this Christmas.

Wally studied the pictures carefully, and he learned what he could. In the background, in the snapshot of Bobbi, were beautiful, exotic flowers, and Wally had to think she was in Hawaii or on some other island. Gene's picture had been taken outside a newly built barracks, and Wally had to believe it was at a boot camp somewhere in the states. Alex was wearing his pant legs tucked inside high boots, which was not the usual thing to do, and he was wearing a silver insignia—maybe wings—on his chest. He had to be in some sort of special service unit.

But everyone was in the service—all but the little girls, who weren't little girls anymore—and Wally had to wonder what would happen to all of them in the next few years. He went back to the group picture, with everyone together, and he liked thinking about them that way. He hadn't been home since the summer of 1940, when he was not quite nineteen. Three and a half years had gone by since then, and he was twenty-two. He had missed three Christmases; tomorrow would make four.

Wally didn't realize he was crying until Chuck said, "Hey, Wally, are you okay?"

"Yeah. Sure," Wally said, and then he showed the pictures to Chuck. Chuck knew President and Sister Thomas and was somewhat acquainted with Alex and Bobbi. He studied the pictures with Wally, and they talked about the changes that must be taking place at home.

Finally, Wally opened the Ginger Snaps, and he and Chuck each ate two, for Christmas Eve. "We'll open one of the packages of candy on Christmas morning," Wally told Chuck.

"I've got some stuff to eat, too. You and I and Art and Don will have us a little feast."

"We've also got to give some of this stuff to the guys who didn't get anything."

"I know. I've thought about that. That's what we'll do for Christmas."

Chuck had to head back to his own barracks. When he was gone, Wally went through his box again, one item at a time. Then he lay on his bunk, with the towel against his face. He shut his eyes and breathed deeply, taking in the smell of home.

* * *

Bobbi and Afton went to Ishi's house for Christmas. They took presents to the kids—two books and a toy each—and they ate Japanese food. "I wanted to cook a turkey for you girls," Ishi told them, "but I couldn't get one."

"Shrimp is better than turkey any day," Bobbi said.

But Afton seemed to be struggling more than Bobbi. She always had a harder time trying new foods, and she'd seemed a little depressed the past few days. Bobbi assumed she was homesick.

After dinner, Lily and David, who had gotten up early, both fell asleep. Bobbi and Afton and Ishi sat down together in the living room. "Did you hear anything from Richard this week?" Ishi asked.

Bobbi had been trying not to think about that. "I got three letters, all on the same day," she said, "but he didn't say where he was or what was happening. There was even a section in one letter that had been razored out by the censor. Maybe he hinted too much about what was going on."

Ishi laughed. "How would you like to write a love letter to

your girl and know that some other officer on your ship was going to read it?"

"They weren't love letters," Bobbi said, although she could feel herself blushing. "They were just—you know—mostly to say hello and tell me he's okay. But I was glad to hear something."

"Were the letters written quite a while ago?" Ishi asked. "That's how mine always are."

Bobbi thought she heard some uneasiness in Ishi's voice. She was sitting rather primly, straight up, as she always did, so differently from most Hawaiians, even most Japanese Hawaiians, who were rather quick to open up to others. The neatness of this little house, the Japanese watercolors on the wall—so much of what Bobbi felt here—said that Ishi had stayed close to her heritage. And yet her husband had gone off to fight for what he and Ishi were—Americans.

"All three of those letters were written before Thanksgiving," Bobbi said. "Things could have changed by now."

"At least he's not landing on beaches. I think the navy is safer than the marines—or the infantry, where Daniel is."

"What have you heard from Daniel lately?"

"Old news. His regiment got shipped to North Africa. That was in the paper. But in his last letter, he didn't even tell me that. Maybe they wouldn't let him. Right now, from what I'm hearing, the 'one-puka-puka'—do you know what that is?"

Afton had been sitting back listening, but she was curious enough to say, "No. What?"

"Daniel's in the 100th Regiment. In Pidgin English, people say 'puka' for 'zero' when they give a telephone number. It really means 'hole.' So 'one-puka-puka' is one hundred. But anyway, the newspaper says the 100th is still not in the fight. But that's all Daniel wants. Every letter I get, he says he wants to get to the front lines."

"Why, Ishi?" Bobbi asked.

"Our boys want to prove themselves. Daniel was in ROTC

at the University of Hawaii, and then he was an officer in the Reserves. When Japan attacked us, he was called up, like all our boys, and they were ready to fight. Then, all of a sudden, the government took their guns away and made them feel like they were traitors—just because they were of Japanese descent."

"Then why did they get shipped to the mainland?" Afton asked.

"No one knew what to do with them. They were in the military, but no one wanted to fight next to them. The government hid them away for a long time, and then President Roosevelt finally told the army to give them a chance."

"I don't understand," Afton said. She leaned forward, put her elbows on her knees, and looked closely at Ishi. "Why were the AJA in California arrested and the ones over here left alone, or even drafted?"

"There were too many of us here. If they arrested all of us, there wouldn't be enough people to work. Everything would have been shut down."

"It's too bad President Roosevelt stepped in," Bobbi said, and she laughed. "Daniel could have sat out the whole war."

"I know. That's the way I look at it. But it would have killed his pride. The only problem now is, every AJA in the army thinks he's got to be a hero—to show everyone that he's loyal to his country. Daniel's the same way. He's a teacher—just a very nice man—and now he thinks he has to be a warrior."

"And that scares you, I'm sure."

"Of course it does."

Ishi was friendly but not one to reveal her feelings easily. This was the first time she had expressed her concerns so openly. Bobbi had been fighting her own worries all day, and Ishi's words seemed to turn her anxiety into a kind of ache. She wished so much that she'd had more days with Richard, that they had made the best of their time together—sooner. She had also been thinking all day about her family, and she felt her homesickness come on again as the mood changed.

On the way home that evening, neither Bobbi nor Afton had much to say, and it wasn't until they were back in their quarters that Bobbi quit thinking about herself long enough to realize that Afton was having a hard time. She had lain on her bunk as soon as the girls had come in, and now she had turned away.

"What's wrong, kid?" Bobbi asked. "A little homesick?"

"Yeah."

Bobbi walked over and sat down on the bed next to her. She patted her shoulder. "Me too," she said.

"Oh, but Bobbi, you have someone to wait for."

"What's going on with you and the doc? Isn't he willing to convert?"

Bobbi was trying to keep things light, but Afton began to cry. "Don't even mention that . . . *ape* . . . to me," she said.

"What happened?"

"I don't want to talk about it."

"Okay."

"I slapped his face. That's what happened."

"I don't have to ask why."

Afton rolled onto her back and looked up at Bobbi. "He is so smooth, Bobbi. He just kept telling me how much he respected me, but he was always pushing for more than I would give him. And then, the other night, he decided to get what he wanted—whether I liked it or not."

"Really? I can't believe he would do that."

"Darn it to heck, Bobbi, don't say that. You told me he would. Just go ahead and say 'I told you so,' and get it over with."

Instead, Bobbi said nothing. She was actually surprised the guy would get *that* aggressive.

"I should have hit him with something harder than my hand."

"Yeah. Like a bedpan."

Afton was still crying, but she suddenly grinned. "That's a

good idea. I might do it yet—in front of a whole ward full of patients. Then I'll announce to everyone, 'This guy has rushin' hands and roamin' fingers.'"

Bobbi laughed, and finally Afton did too.

"Hey," Bobbi said, "at least you didn't make any mistakes you could be regretting now."

"Yes I did. I trusted him, and now I'll never trust anyone again."

"Yes you will. Just watch out for Romans and Russians."

And the two laughed again. But neither one could make the laughter last very long.

"Bobbi, I'm never going to find anyone," Afton said, and she rolled onto her side again. But Bobbi wondered which would be worse—not to find anyone, or to lose the one you had found.

* * *

The Stoltzes prepared a nice Christmas dinner to share with the Rosenbaums. Little Benjamin was gloriously happy to have Peter home all day. But everyone was tired and rather disheartened. Throughout the night, on Christmas Eve, another massive Allied bombing attack had kept them awake.

In recent weeks everything had changed in the Stoltz household. The Allies had finally targeted Berlin for all-out destruction, and bombing raids had come with increasing frequency and intensity. "Carpet bombing" had replaced the usual raids, and little was left of central Berlin. A thousand airplanes would strike the city, sometimes continuing both day and night, and dropping up to two thousand tons of bombs. The area near the *Tiergarten* and the *Unter den Linden* section of the city were almost entirely flattened. The Stoltzes lived on the edge of town, and so their neighborhood had been hit only three times. Their own row of apartments had so far been little affected. Still, with each new raid, it seemed likely that their luck would run out.

The bombing had been a mixed blessing for the

Rosenbaums. Brother Stoltz had had to take a chance; he told his neighbors that the Rosenbaums were the Glissmyers, a refugee family from central Berlin. Refugees were everywhere now, with over a million Berliners homeless, and neighbors knew that Brother Stoltz worked at a job where he might well meet such a family and bring them home—as he claimed. The change in identity meant that the Stoltzes could bring the Rosenbaums to the cellar during bombing attacks. The chaos in the city also lessened the danger that anyone was bothering to look for hideaway Jews.

At the same time, both the Stoltzes and the Rosenbaums had to watch every word they said, and little Benjamin had to be kept under control. To speak his name might well tip someone off. The bombs, the firestorms, were enough of a fear, without the constant worry of detection.

Most days Brother Stoltz still traveled into the city, although some days busses and trolleys couldn't get through, and he would have to walk long distances through the rubble. His building had been struck by bombs twice, with the upper floors mostly destroyed, but the offices didn't close, and the work went on. Berliners seemed almost like ants in a disturbed ant hill; no sooner would the destruction stop than they would scurry out to set things right again.

Today was Christmas, and that should mean a reprieve, a little peace, but Anna wondered whether the bombs would begin to fall again, even today. Terror had become so much a way of life that she had become fatalistic, expecting the worst and relieved each time she survived another pounding. At night, when the thudding sounds of the bombs were distant, she took comfort that she and her family were safe, but as she made her way to work, she often saw the results: the fires; the buildings in smoking ruins; the wide-eyed children clinging to their parents; and sometimes the bodies being carried from the buildings or lying under blankets in the street. One morning she had crossed through a bombed-out area, hiking because no transportation could get through, and she had seen a little arm protruding from the fallen blocks of an apartment building. The arm had haunted her ever since, and she found herself struggling to forgive the Allies, no matter what their justification might be.

And yet she and her family, and the Rosenbaums, made the best of things. Peter had bought Benjamin a wooden train for Christmas with cars that could be disconnected and rearranged. He got down on the floor with Benjamin after dinner, and the two pretended to be engineers. They drove the train about and stopped to load and unload it. Peter, in his deep voice, pretended to ask for various items he wanted loaded on his train, and Benjamin would giggle each time and pretend to fill the order. Anna felt sure that Peter was having as much fun as Benjamin. He was far too old to play on the floor with toys, but Benjamin provided him an excuse to do so. Besides, Peter was always alone, and this was his chance to have a friend, and an adoring one, even if he was just a little boy.

Anna had watched what was happening to the Rosenbaums over the past few months. It was what she had known during her months in hiding. The tedium and purposelessness, combined with the horror of the bombing raids, was wearing them down. Brother Stoltz always tried to get war news, and in some ways it was encouraging. According to German radio, all was going well: The Germans were winning great victories in Russia and Italy, and the Japanese were dominating in the Pacific. But British radio, played softly and carefully, told another story. the Germans were bogged down badly in Russia, suffering terribly from cold and cut-off supply lines. Many thousands had been taken captive. Kiev had now been retaken by the Russians. And in Italy, where the Italians had already bowed out of the war, German troops were being pushed steadily back, up the peninsula, in hard-nosed mountain fighting. It was discouraging to think of all the German boys being killed, all the agony and exposure they were suffering. At the same time, to Brother Stoltz it was becoming ever more clear that Hitler could never win. Ultimately, that had to be good news for the Rosenbaums, but it was hardly anything to find much joy in.

In the Pacific, battles were taking place in the Solomons, the Marshall Islands, and the Gilberts. Raging battles in little places like Tarawa Atoll or Bougainville left thousands dead, but American and Australian troops always won in time, and Japanese control of the Pacific was slowly giving way.

What Anna wondered was whether Alex was in one of those places: Italy perhaps, or on one of those islands. With so many dying, could she hope that nothing would happen to him? She was caught by this war, with no way to feel any sense of victory, no matter what happened.

Anna had received a pretty, cloth-bound diary for Christmas, and that afternoon, while Peter and Benjamin played and her mother and father talked with the Rosenbaums, she started her first entry. She wanted to say everything, express all her feelings, and then someday share it all with Alex. But the trouble was—and her father had warned her about this—she had to be very careful what she recorded. If someone were to get hold of it somehow, a document of that sort could be dangerous for all of them. She couldn't tell who she really was or where she had come from. She couldn't record her genuine fears and worries, even her hopes for the future. And so she wrote about her testimony of the gospel—without explaining why she couldn't go to church—and she wrote about the man she loved, without saying who he was and where he lived. She tried to say as much as possible, in hidden, careful ways, but she was soon frustrated, and she set the diary down. The Nazis had a way of controlling everything; they were not even allowing Anna to be Anna.

* * *

Alex ate at the mess hall—a nice Christmas dinner of canned turkey and reconstituted potatoes. Actually, the meal tasted pretty good, but as usual Alex was alone. He and Curtis had spent some time together that morning, but in some ways Curtis wasn't a true kindred spirit. Their conversations always came back to the same topics and then wore thin rather quickly. Curtis had finally lain down to take a nap, and Alex was actually glad for the peace—but he was still very lonely.

Alex had been in a camp in Aldbourne, England, since September. Aldbourne was a little town about eighty miles west of London, and the men of his regiment were living in Nissen huts set up on a "football" field. Some of the men had passes and had gone to the city. A couple of them asked Alex whether he wanted to go along. But for Alex that would have meant spending long hours in some London pub with men who had no interests other than drinking and chasing skirts. The amazing part was, these young guys seemed to have a lot of success with British girls. English troops complained that the Yanks were "oversexed, overpaid, and over here." They resented the way Americans threw their money around and used their brash confidence to charm the local women. In response, the Yanks told the limeys, "You're undersexed, under-paid, and under Eisenhower," and then, if everyone was in a good mood, a rousing fight might follow.

Alex wanted none of that, of course, so now he sat in an almost empty barracks, listened to Curtis snore, and wrote a letter to his parents. All day he had been thinking about Christmas at home. He imagined his family, his grandparents and uncles and aunts, gathering and talking about all the cousins who were now spread around the globe. No one in the Thomas or Snow family had been killed or wounded so far, but the ones Gene's age were still in training, and before long sev-eral would probably be in harm's way. Rumor in England was that a landing in France would happen that spring. Alex's unit, the second battalion of the 506th Regiment, had now been attached to the 101st Airborne Division—the "Screaming Eagles," as they were known—and there was little question that the whole division would be part of it. So the coming year would be the telling time, and chances were not good that all the family would make it through. It was chilling, that thought, just the consideration of the odds.

Alex didn't talk about any of that in his letter, however. There were some things he wasn't allowed to write home about, and many things he didn't want to say. He hesitated to let his family know how lonely he was, and he wasn't anxious to have a censor read that information either. And so he wrote a few upbeat things about his health and his commitment to the cause, and he joked about the miserable weather in England. He wasn't allowed to say he was in Aldbourne, or even that he was in the southern part of the country. He only mentioned that he'd had a chance to visit London and found it very interesting.

When he was finished with the letter, he decided to write to Anna. It was a pointless thing to do since he had no way to post a letter to her—not even any idea where she was. But he liked the idea of telling her his feelings and giving her a few details about his life. It was something he had done a few times before. If he ever saw her again, he would give her all these letters, and she would at least have some sense of this time in his life. Otherwise, it would all be lost to them.

But the attempt was quite unsatisfying. He knew he was writing to some future Anna, not to the Anna he longed to see. At times like this he chided himself for even hanging on to such a hope. He got out her picture and looked at it, but it was no longer easy to bring back the powerful feelings he had once known. He looked at her pretty face but saw it like some picture in a magazine. He was losing his sense of *her.* So he got out that one letter he had from her, and he read that. He knew every word of it, but he told himself that their promises to each other still meant something, that those feelings couldn't be killed by the tedious ticking away of time. And yet he wondered whether she still felt the things she had said in the letter. By now she must have passed through some terrible ordeals.

He lay back on his bunk and looked at the chipped paint on the open rafters. He wished the day would move by more swiftly. A training exercise, or work, or almost anything was better than all this time. It would even be nice to admit to someone other than Curtis that he had a girl in Germany; but the men would not have taken kindly to that, and so he never spoke her name.

* * *

Gene was at the Quantico Marine Base in Virginia. He had completed his boot camp, but now he was taking training in amphibious assault. Time and again he had heard about the huge losses units would take when they hit the beaches. And there were plenty left to land on. Most of the guys bragged about all they would do to the Japs, but Gene wasn't one to talk that way. He tried to focus on the training, do what he had to do, and not worry too much about what lay ahead.

Gene still dreamed of liberating his brother, but he knew the truth. The Philippines would be a target before too much longer—probably before he got there—and even when the Philippines were taken, the war would still be far from over. He had grown up considerably in the past few months, was seeing the realities ahead with clearer vision.

One of the problems for Gene was that he felt so lonely in his platoon. There was another Utah boy, a fellow named Floyd Jeppesen from Tooele, who might have been a pretty good friend. He was a Mormon, but he seemed to have forgotten it already, and he was doing a lot of drinking. He was worse than anyone for giving Gene a hard time about being a "Sunday School boy." The fact was, Gene had not had a single chance to go to church since arriving in Virginia, and Floyd, in one sense, was right: Gene would have loved to go to Sunday School if he could have gotten the chance.

Gene enjoyed a better-than-usual dinner at the mess hall,

but by evening he was having a hard time. Everyone had five-day passes, and most of the guys from the East and the South had headed home. Those who were still around the base had taken off and gone into town, or were at least gone for the day. Gene thought about writing some letters, but he was in no mood for it. And so he did something on impulse—even though he was worried his dad might be upset with him. He walked to a pay phone near the headquarters building, dropped a nickel in, and told the operator he wanted to make a long-distance call to Utah—collect.

By the time the phone rang, he was scared to think what the call might cost. But the first person to pick the phone up was LaRue, and she squealed, "Oh, yes. Yes. We'll accept the charges." And then Gene was actually saying hello to her, hearing the wild excitement in her voice.

"Mom, it's Gene. It's Gene," LaRue screamed, and then, just as loudly, she shouted into the phone, "Are you all right? How are you doing?"

"You don't have to yell. I can hear you all right," Gene said, laughing. "Merry Christmas."

"Merry Christmas to you, too. Did you get the stuff we sent you?"

"Yes. I liked the pictures best. And the articles from the paper about East High football."

"We sent a package to Wally, too. The Red Cross said they might be able to get it to him this year."

"That's good. You haven't heard from him, have you?"

"No. But we got a package from Bobbi—grass skirts and leis and all this other stuff. It was nifty. And we got a letter from Alex. He's doing just fine."

"Is everyone there?" Gene could hear all the noise, the cousins, all the family gathered for the big Christmas dinner.

"Yes. Here's Grandma. She wants to say hello to you."

And so it began. Grandma and then Uncle Everett, and then cousins and more aunts and uncles, Grandpa, all of them asking the same questions, and all of them yelling as though they thought they had to give their words a boost to slide them through the lines all the way to Virginia.

Eventually Dad got on the line. "Merry Christmas, Son," he said. "How are you doing?"

"Is it okay that I called? It was collect."

"It's fine. Don't worry about it. How are you?"

"All right. You know—a little homesick today."

"Well, that's only natural. We're missing you and the other kids an awful lot. Are you keeping up your standards, Gene?"

"Sure. I can't get to church very often—not our church anyway. But I go to services on base."

"You aren't letting those marines influence you in the wrong direction, are you? You're keeping your speech clean, and you're not smoking—or any of those things?"

"Gee, Dad, is this my stake president's interview?"

Dad laughed. "That's exactly what it is."

"Well, I'm doing okay. I called my M-1 rifle a bad name the other day, but it had it coming. It smashed my thumb."

Dad laughed again. "I'm sorry for the interrogation," he said. "I know I don't really have to ask. Well, we'd better not make this last too long. Here's your mom."

"Gene?"

"Hi, Mom."

"Oh, honey, it's so good to hear your voice. Tell me the truth—are you okay?"

"Sure."

"What are you doing today?"

"I'm just . . . well, it's been kind of a hard day . . ." The one thing he had told himself was that he couldn't cry. He swallowed, but he couldn't get any more words out.

"Oh, Gene, I'd give anything to have you home for a day or two. Do you think you'll get leave after your time out there?"

But Gene couldn't answer. He was crying hard now, holding the mouthpiece away, trying not to let her hear. "I don't know," he managed, finally, to tell her.

"Everyone is gone this year. It's so hard. It's just so hard." And now she was sobbing too.

The two of them spent at least a quarter of a dollar that way, but Mom did manage to say, in time, "I'm sorry, Gene. I'm sorry. We're all fine. And we're going to get through this and look forward to the year when we're all back together."

"Okay, Mom. I'd better get off the phone now."

"We pray for you every day, Gene. For all of you."

"I pray for everyone too, Mom. I love you."

"Oh, Gene, I love you, too. Just say good-bye to Beverly. She hasn't had a chance to talk to you."

But Gene only managed to say, "Hi, Bev," and then he was sobbing again. And poor Beverly, who had always loved Gene so much, could hardly get a word out.

20

By March of 1944 everyone knew that the invasion of Europe had to be coming soon. Alex's regiment had trained all winter in England, but a new intensity was emerging. On March 23, two battalions made an inspection jump into a drop zone in southern England. From a specially prepared grandstand, Winston Churchill watched along with Generals Dwight D. Eisenhower, Omar Bradley, and the new commander of the 101st, Maxwell Taylor.

As soon as Alex hit the ground, he collapsed his chute, shed it, and raced to a parade ground to fall in for inspection. While running at full speed, all the paratroopers assembled their rifles, which had been broken down for the jump. In a matter of minutes, over a thousand men had jumped, landed, and hurried to the formation. Alex had to believe that all the dignitaries were impressed.

He stood at "parade rest" and waited, and before long he saw, out of the corner of his eye, Churchill and the generals walking along the formation, stopping occasionally, talking to this soldier and that. And then the entourage appeared before Alex's platoon. General Eisenhower stepped up to a soldier at the front, in the first squad. "Where are you from, soldier?" he asked.

"Oregon, sir," the soldier answered, with more volume than seemed necessary. He was a man named McCloskey.

"What did you do before the war?"

"I was a student, sir. At the University of Oregon."

"So how did the Oregon and Oregon State football game turn out this year? I didn't hear."

"I'm sorry to say, sir," McCloskey said with a laugh, "Oregon State came out on top."

Eisenhower laughed too. "Well, Oregon must have sent its best boys to the war."

"I'm sure that's true, sir."

Alex couldn't believe he was this close to Eisenhower, and to Churchill, who was standing back just a little, wearing a big black overcoat. Eisenhower, at this point, turned to the prime minister. "Anything you would like to ask?" he said.

Churchill asked, in his familiar raspy voice. "Well, son, how do you like England?"

"I like it very much, sir. I enjoy English history and literature. So it's a memorable experience for me to be here."

Churchill nodded and removed the big cigar from his mouth, held it between gloved fingers. "We'll get you back home just as soon as we can—so you can go about your studies."

"Thank you, sir."

The dignitaries walked on by. General Eisenhower glanced toward Alex, even seemed to make eye contact with him for a moment. Alex liked his smile, his confidence. This was the man in charge of the coming invasion. It was an imposing responsibility, and yet the general seemed very much a regular fellow. Now Alex was impressed.

During the next few weeks the training continued to intensify. The 101st made several training jumps, all of them at night. It seemed obvious that the airborne troops would land in the dark, and it was rather a frightening prospect.

Alex wondered how the Brits must feel about all this

activity going on around them—the noise of airplanes at night, the movement of troops in trucks. All of southern England was filling up with soldiers now, the towns and roads constantly clogged with Jeeps and trucks and artillery, the pubs filled with hard-drinking boys. There were hastily built barracks in some areas, tent towns in others, and many of the troops were even bivouacked in English homes. The families had to feel pressured into this, but the women had a way of becoming "mums" to the soldiers, and in spite of the recklessness of all these young men, seemingly everywhere most of the British accepted them well. "After all," one old fellow told Alex, "we know you don't want to be here either. Every one of you will be putting your life on the line—as much for us as for yourselves."

Alex knew at least part of what the English were feeling. Early in the year the Germans had begun a bombing campaign on London. The "little blitz," as some people called it, was not as intense as the constant bombing Londoners had experienced in the blitz of 1940 and '41, but people were weary, and they hadn't expected this new round of raids. London operated amazingly well, considering what the people had gone through for so many years, but everyone was ready for the invasion and what people hoped would be a quick end to all the terror.

One night in April, Alex's squad was scheduled to make a night drop near the coastline. A major exercise was to take place, and Alex knew that Captain Morehead wanted his company to come through this time. The truth was, the previous night drop had resulted in too much confusion. The first challenge was merely for the soldier to find his own unit after he hit the ground. Then a bridge or imaginary gun emplacement was usually designated for squads or entire platoons to locate and attack.

What troubled Alex was that Sergeant Foley struggled to read a map correctly, or lead out in the dark, and yet he was quick to take offense when anyone—especially Alex—tried to give him advice. He was a big guy, imposing, and a little older than most of the men, but he made decisions too quickly, probably trying to appear decisive. Twice now he had led his men in the wrong direction and then wandered about before he got them to their target, very late. Both times it had been Alex who had finally given him the advice that had gotten the squad where it needed to be, and Alex had felt the resentment.

When Alex jumped into the dark this time, he felt the usual momentary disorientation until his shoulder harness snapped him straight, and then he caught a glimpse of the stars overhead. What followed were those few seconds of quiet, with only the whistle of air through his parachute and the occasional expletives of some paratrooper struggling with his lines. But then the ground—a black presence not clearly defined— rushed up at him. He felt the jolt on his feet and into his knees sooner than he had expected, and he tried to roll forward, but as he did, his shoulder struck something hard. He was stunned for a moment, but he tried to roll over and get control of his parachute. The wind was billowing the nylon, and his harness was pulling hard on the shoulder he had just injured.

Alex got up and fought with the lines until he managed to collapse his parachute. Then he released his harness and worked the straps free from his left shoulder. But his right arm would hardly move, and he feared that he might have broken a bone. It took all his effort, and some force against the pain, to slip the other side of the harness off. By then, however, he was fairly sure that nothing was broken. The pain was in the muscle, and the joint seemed to function all right. He thought he had probably just bruised himself.

Around him, however, he was hearing other men, the grunts and profanity. Men were crash-landing into rocks, not into the grassy field that had been the intended target. Alex rolled up his parachute, and then he stumbled toward a man who was down on the ground, moaning. "Who's there?" Alex called out.

"Campbell," the voice said. "I've hurt my knee."

"Can you get up?"

Campbell cursed. "Yeah. Just a minute."

Alex had taken hold of Campbell's shoulder, but the man was resisting for the moment.

"Hey, over here," someone was yelling. "Foley is down, and he's not talking."

Alex left Campbell and worked his way toward the sound. He could see a little better now, as his eyes adjusted, and he spotted two men, hunched in the dark. "He's moaning, but he doesn't seem to hear me," one of the men said. Alex recognized Rizzardi's voice.

"Don't move him," Alex said. "Let's make him as comfortable as we can and then get a medic over here."

"Alex, I think he's hurt bad," Curtis Bentley said. "It looks like he hit his back on these rocks."

In the next few minutes the squad gathered, but the men were a group of walking wounded. Almost everyone had slammed an arm or leg into the jagged rocks. "I'm bleeding like a stuck pig," Lester Cox told Alex. "My leg is sliced wide open."

"We're all sort of banged up," Alex said, "and we don't have a squad leader. Where's McCoy?"

"Right here. I can't walk very good though. I twisted an ankle."

"Do you need to stay here and wait for the medics?" Alex asked.

"I don't know. I guess not."

"Well, then, take over." McCoy was the assistant squad leader.

"I am taking over. Lay off, Thomas; you don't have to tell me what to do." But he was quiet for a few seconds before he said, "Does anyone know where we are?"

Silence followed. The sky was unusually clear, with the stars out, but the waning moon didn't offer much light, and in the damp cold and the dark—and now, with all these injuries—no one seemed exactly gung-ho to get going. Alex had already been thinking things over and had an idea what had gone wrong, but he didn't want to push himself into the lead.

Duncan called out, in his blaring voice, "The wind was taking us east. We must be east of that grassy area we were supposed to hit."

No one disagreed. "Okay, that sounds about right," McCoy said, slowly and with no confidence.

Alex couldn't let this happen. "I don't think so," he said. "I think they had us jump a little too soon. We're closer into the shoreline than we were supposed to be. That's why we're into the rocks."

"Come on, Deacon," Duncan said, "you don't know that for sure." But he sounded half-convinced.

"That's true," Alex said. "But it makes sense." He decided to say nothing more.

No one said a word. McCoy obviously had no idea what to do. "Let's look at the map," he finally said. Each man carried a simple map of the area. Alex already had his out, but he decided to let McCoy make the decision. He sat and rubbed his shoulder—and waited.

Someone found a match and lit it, and everyone gathered around McCoy. The match didn't last long, but Huish took a look over Huff's shoulder and said, rather tersely, "See, that's where the rocks are—along the coast. Thomas is obviously right."

No one would have admitted it, but everyone knew Alex and Huish were the men most likely to know what they were talking about. "Okay. That's probably where we are—south of the target," McCoy said. "Let's head north."

"What I'm looking for is a pub on this map. And I can't find one. Maybe ol' Deacon can figure that one out." This, of course, was Duncan's way of backing off from his first opinion, but it also showed a change of attitude. At times Duncan was almost friendly with Alex, even if he made fun of him every chance he got.

"Strike another match," McCoy said, "and I'll take a look at my compass."

"McCoy, just look at the sky," Huish said. "There's the north star right there."

"Well, yeah. Right. Let's move out, men. We'll send someone back to get Foley as soon as we make contact. My ankle is feeling better. Are you guys all right?"

Alex didn't want to say anything more, but he was worried about Foley. "Wouldn't it be better to get on the radio and call the medics in?" he asked.

"I guess we could."

"I think he's hurt bad," Curtis said. "The back of his head is bleeding."

"How are you doing, Cox?" Alex asked.

"I need a little help with my leg," he said. "If I can get it bandaged, I think I can walk all right."

Alex had watched Cox change a lot over the past year. He had been a brash, arrogant kid in the beginning. But as the real battle got closer, most of the guys had dropped their big talk.

Alex got out a bandage that was tucked in his leg pocket. He quickly cut away Cox's trousers with his knife, and then he wrapped the wound. Rizzardi was the radio man, and he got hold of a medical unit, but then it was Alex who got on and told the man how to locate the site. He told the medic they would leave someone with Foley to look after him and to help the medics find him. "Who's going to stay with Foley?" he asked McCoy when he got off the radio.

"Oh, let's see. Maybe you should."

But Huff, McCoy's good friend, said, "Thomas had better come with us, Dale. He knows where we're going."

"Hey, I know where we're going." But Huff turned and said, "Cox, you stay here. You're cut up anyway."

McCoy spun toward Huff. "That's enough of that. I'm in charge here." But he didn't change the order.

The men moved out to the north. They found the grassy

drop zone about a mile ahead. And beyond that, they found the road they were looking for. By then they had located a rock fence, shown on the map, and they knew that they needed to head a little west to reach the intersection. Duncan didn't say anything to Alex, but he told Rizzardi, loud enough for everyone to hear, "I *knew* we had to be east of our target."

At the intersection McCoy told Pozernac and Gourley, two recent additions to the squad, "You guys set up your machine gun emplacement over there." He pointed to the northwest corner of the intersection.

Alex couldn't believe it. The sun was beginning to glow in the east just enough to allow some sense of the surrounding terrain. Alex stepped over to McCoy and said, softly, "They won't have a view of the whole intersection there. They need higher ground." He pointed to the opposite side.

"Look, if you think you know everything, you do it," McCoy told Alex.

"Never mind," Alex said, and he walked away. But he noticed a few minutes later that the MG team was setting up where Alex had suggested.

There was nothing to do after that, but when Lieutenant Summers showed up, he seemed relieved to find the squad in place. He looked over the machine gun emplacement and said, "Good job." And then he asked, "Where's Foley?"

McCoy stepped forward. "He's down, sir. We got dropped in some rocks. He's hurt pretty bad, we think. We called in medics and left a man with him."

The lieutenant cursed. "Where is he?"

"South of here a couple of miles. The medics might have picked him up by now."

Alex knew it was at least three miles, but he didn't say so. "Stay put. You'll be picked up in the next hour or so," Summers said. He climbed into his Jeep and drove away.

The squad was picked up by a troop truck not long after daybreak and then hauled back to Aldbourne. They ate a quick breakfast and were allowed a little sleep, since they had been up most of the night, but then the platoon was called together, and Lieutenant Summers reviewed the exercise. He wasn't pleased.

Most of the men had missed their drop zones, which was not their fault, but it had led to problems. The flat area north of the coast had offered little in the way of landmarks, and some of the squads had gotten themselves badly lost. Summers told the men that Captain Morehead had chewed him about the panic and absence of discipline, the lack of initiative to make the best of the situation. "When you men don't do your job, I hear about it," Summers told the men. "And I don't like that. But one of these days this is all going to be for real, and then it gets down to men losing their lives because someone else did- n't do his job. That's not going to happen in this platoon."

Toward the end of the session, held in a Nissen hut that was entirely too full of men—and smelled it—Summers told the platoon, "We had a few casualties. Sergeant Foley broke his back and sustained some head injuries. I don't know whether he's even going to make it. Private Alex Thomas has been pro- moted to sergeant, and he's going to take over Foley's squad. I want to see Sergeant Thomas as soon as we're finished here."

Alex was stunned. He was only a private. How could he suddenly be made a sergeant? What about McCoy?

When everyone else filed out of the hut, Alex walked up to Summers. The lieutenant told Alex, "I talked to some of the men. They told me you were the one who got them to the right spot last night. They said McCoy didn't know what he was doing. Believe it or not, they told me you were the one who ought to be the squad leader."

"I'm good at maps, but that doesn't mean I ought to take over the squad."

"I didn't ask you what you wanted to do. I don't have that luxury any longer. We've got a job ahead of us, and I can't mess around. So are you going to lead these men or not?"

"I will, but I'd rather not."

"Thomas . . ." He swore. "Listen to me. I need a man who won't go to pieces when things get tough. And I know that's you. But are you going to kill Germans or not?"

Alex didn't know. He had tried all during training to predict what he would be like when the firing started, and he just didn't know. But that's not what he said. "I'll hold my own out there."

The lieutenant cursed again. "Why doesn't that convince me? I know you can find your target, and I know you can set up an MG emplacement. But I have no idea whether you'll kill anyone."

Alex didn't answer.

"God is *not* on Hitler's side, Thomas. If you want to bring your religion into this thing, you better fight on the same side God's on—and fight like everything good depends on it."

"That's how I do feel, lieutenant. I agree with that."

"So what happens when you face your first German? Are you going to kill—or get yourself killed?"

"Kill," Alex said, and he felt the enormity of the word. For all these months he had continued to tell himself that somehow he wouldn't have to face that decision. Maybe he would get pulled into Intelligence after all. But this was it, and now he had announced his decision.

"All right. You'll get your stripes. I never thought this would happen. A year ago, I thought some of those men would kill you before you got this far. But soldiers have a way of sensing who their leader is, and they all know it's you."

Alex didn't know what to say to that. And so he merely saluted and then walked to his barracks. When he entered the door, Duncan laughed. "Here comes our sarge," he said. "Ain't he nice looking? They ought to use him for a recruiting poster, not put him on the battlefield."

Duncan was just mouthing off, as usual; he didn't sound upset about the promotion. But Alex still wondered what these guys really thought of him. "I didn't ask for this," he said. "Let's just make the best of it. Let's pull together."

This brought a huge laugh from Duncan and most of the other men around the barracks. "Golly gee, Deacon, you'd make a swell cheerleader," Duncan said. "Maybe you could go into battle wearing a little skirt and carrying a megaphone."

Alex had the good sense to laugh. "Well, anyway, you know what I mean."

* * *

Bobbi walked from the burn ward and noticed that down the hallway a tall marine in his brown uniform was smiling at her. And then, suddenly, she realized it was Gene. She ran toward him, and he grabbed her up in his arms and hugged her, but he set her down rather quickly. Bobbi could see he was embarrassed by all the attention the two of them were getting.

"I didn't expect you yet," Bobbi said, out of breath.

"I know. We got here sooner than I thought we would." He had written her a couple of weeks before and told her he was stopping in Honolulu—if all the rumors were right—and he would try to contact her if he got a chance.

"When did you get in?"

"A couple of hours ago. I was on my way to Tripler—the army hospital—before the cab driver told me I could have just walked over here in the first place."

"So how long will you be here?"

"I don't know. They don't tell us much. I have to be back to the ship by 2200 tonight. But I don't know whether I'll get another chance to see you."

"Oh, dear. Let me see what I can do. Maybe I can get off early. Do you want to go swimming at Waikiki?"

"I don't know. I don't have any trunks."

"We can get some." She suddenly laughed. "You're so handsome in your uniform. Look at those nurses staring at you."

Gene grinned, that familiar, boyish smile of his. And he

turned a little red. "They're just saying, 'Bobbi must be an old lady to have such a big little brother.'"

"You watch your tongue." She hugged him again. "We could buy you a swimsuit over in town if you—"

"Naw. Let's just go see what it looks like. I don't care if I swim or not."

"All right. Let me see what I can do to get out of here. Just wait here a minute."

Lieutenant Kallas was never pleased by disruptions, but she was in a decent mood today, and Bobbi told her the burn unit was in good shape, with fewer patients than usual. "Make your rounds again," Lieutenant Kallas said, "and let someone know what's going on so someone can cover, and then go ahead. Are you sure this kid is only going to be here a short time?"

"Yes. He said this might be the only day he gets off the ship. He doesn't know for sure."

Bobbi was already heading out the door. She hurried back to Gene, where a couple of nurse friends were talking to him. She told him he could wait in the front lobby and she would be ready in half an hour.

"Hey, leave him here," one of the nurses, a girl named Verna, said. "We like these younger boys. We can raise them up the way we want them."

"I'm afraid you'll lead him astray. He's a good boy."

Gene was grinning again, but then he turned and walked down the hall, taking long steps, like Richard's.

Bobbi didn't finish quite as soon as she hoped, but in an hour she and Gene were on a bus, headed into Honolulu. "Do you know where you're going when you leave here?" Bobbi asked him.

"The only thing I know for sure is that I'm not heading straight into battle." He rubbed the palm of his hand across his forehead. "It's humid here," he said.

"Not any worse than Virginia, is it?"

"I was there mostly in the winter." But then he came back

to the question. "We're supposed to do some more amphibious training before we hit our first beach. Some of the guys think we'll be on the big island of Hawaii—or maybe on Maui."

"Neither island is far at all."

"Well, maybe I'll be close for a while then. But I don't know whether I could get over here on a pass."

"Find out as soon as you can. If you could come for a weekend, I know a lot of people you could stay with. You could go to church with me."

"That'd be nice. I've only gotten to Mormon meetings a couple of times in the past year."

"You'll find churches on the big island, or Maui. There are a lot of Mormons in the islands."

"That's good."

Gene had never minded church as much as Wally, but still, Bobbi was impressed, maybe even a little surprised, at his desire to go.

When the two got off the bus, they strolled down to the beach. There were actually very few people out on the sand, and most of them were probably military personnel on their days off. Tourism in Hawaii had almost come to a stop since the war had begun. All the ships were transporting soldiers, and Hawaii now meant Pearl Harbor—and war—to most people.

Bobbi tried to lead Gene out onto the sand, but he protested that he would ruin the shine on his shoes and have to work on them before he could go back to his ship. So they walked on a boardwalk along the edge of the beach, and then they found some lawn to sit on, near the Royal Hawaiian Hotel. They looked out at the pretty breakers and the deep blue water.

"No wonder people like to come here," Gene said. "Ralph's brother was on a mission over here, and he loved it."

"That's where you ought to be heading, not going off to war."

"Yup." But he was quick to change the subject. "Mom wants me to ask you all about this Richard guy and give her a full report in my first letter."

"Are you kidding? The only thing I told her was that I had met a fellow from Springville and he was a nice man. I think I even told her he was mostly just a friend."

"Well . . . you know Mom. She thinks she can read between the lines, and she's sure that he's your new *beau*—to use her word."

"That's just like Mom."

"Oh oh."

"What?"

Gene laughed and then set his hand on Bobbi's shoulder. "I notice you're not denying a thing."

Bobbi knew she was blushing—she could feel it. "Oh, Gene, I'm in another one of my messes."

"Messes? Why?"

"I'm really nuts over this guy, and he's a navy officer. He's out there somewhere, right in the middle of everything, and I hardly ever hear from him. It's been five weeks since I got his last letter, and the worst part is, if something has happened to him, I don't know how I would find out."

"He's probably all right. Those navy boys just deliver us. We're the ones who stick our *leather* necks out."

"Gene, don't say that. It scares me so bad."

Gene pulled at his tight collar. He had filled out so much since Bobbi had seen him last. He looked like a man now, so changed from the way Bobbi remembered him.

"It's so awful to have all four of the guys I care most about in danger," Bobbi said. "Wally's situation must be awful, and I know Alex will be landing in Europe before much longer. Now you're heading out there somewhere with Richard. I think I'd rather go myself than to wait and worry."

Gene smiled. "Take my uniform. I'll stay here and do the worrying."

Bobbi laughed. "I wish you *could* get assigned here somehow, with a nice, safe office job."

"What I'll be is a replacement. I'll hook up with some unit that's already taken a lot of casualties. I'll be landing on some island in the next month or two, if everything goes the way they tell me it will."

"Tell me what you're feeling about that, Gene."

"Well . . . I'm okay about it." Gene leaned back and folded his arms over his chest, and he smiled. "You and Mom and Millie are the only ones who ask that. Guys never do. It's best just to take what comes and not think too much about it."

"I'd be *terrified* if I had to land on an island—with people shooting at me."

Gene looked out toward the ocean again, and his smile faded. "I got to know this guy at boot camp," he said. "He wasn't religious at all. But one day he said to me, 'I wish I believed in heaven. Then I wouldn't be so scared.' He was just kidding around, but it hit me—he was right. All my life I've been going to Sunday School and everything, but I think that was the first time I ever just said to myself, 'Okay. I do believe in heaven. So everything will be all right—no matter what happens.'"

"I know, Gene. I try to think of that too. But I don't want to lose anyone yet. We're all too young."

"I think about that too."

Bobbi slid closer, and she took hold of Gene's arm. "You're still this little kid to me, Gene. I can't think of you any other way."

For a long time after that the two sat silent. Gene was obviously thinking about a lot of things he wasn't saying. He had always been that way.

"Somehow," Bobbi finally said, "it all has to come out all right. I just have to believe in that, or it's all so frightening."

"I'm sure it will," Gene said. "So quit making me think about it. I thought we came down here to see some hula girls. Don't they have any of those around here?"

"No tourists—no hula girls."

"What a dirty deal. I came all this way, and no one will even dance a hula for me?"

"I could give it a try, but I doubt you'd get much of a thrill out of it."

Gene laughed in that familiar chugging style of his, and for the first time, he really did seem the same old Gene.

2 1

It was Easter time. It was also Passover. So Sister Stoltz bought horseradish to use for bitter herbs, and she and Hannah Rosenbaum baked unleavened bread for a Seder feast. The Rosenbaums had no copy of the ceremony, and it was dangerous—probably impossible—to find a copy anywhere, but David wrote out the words he could remember. "On all other nights of the year, we sit or recline, but on this, the holiest of all nights. . . ."

They broke the unleavened bread, shared it among them, and Peter grimaced as he ate the bitter herbs. They didn't dare leave their apartment door open, not when they were doing something so audacious, but they left a bedroom door ajar and left a place at their table for Elijah to arrive and take his seat. And finally, they ate a good meal. It wasn't quite the feast it would have been in the Rosenbaum's own home, or in their parents' homes when they were growing up, but it was good food, and fitting, if not exactly kosher.

The Stoltzes were actually a little ashamed they had so much to share. With three adults in the family working, they managed much better than many families. They had to pay high prices for food, but with little else to spend money on, they were able to do all right. More and more foods were rationed these days—or simply not available—so their diet was often little more than bread, potatoes, and milk, and a little cabbage when they could get it. But at least they had enough.

Much of Berlin was now nothing more than heaps of debris. Tens of thousands had died, and hundreds of thousands had migrated from the city, but work crews continued to replace train tracks, clear rubble, restring electric and telephone lines, and, above all, keep defense plants going. That meant continued work for those who stayed. And then in March the Allies seemed to find other targets more important. Attacks persisted, but not as often and not with such huge armadas of airplanes. The Stoltzes and Rosenbaums were very aware of their blessing that their little corner of the city had survived, and that they were all right, warm, and eating well.

A celebration feast was fitting for both families, but the Seder dinner was especially meaningful to the Rosenbaums. "Benjamin should learn our traditions," Herbert told the Stoltzes. "But we have had no way, these past two years, to do anything like this."

"We know how you feel," Anna told her. "We've not been able to go to our church for such a long, long time."

They had eaten their meal, and yet everyone was lingering at the table, where they had had to crowd together for all of them to have a place—and to leave a place for Elijah. Hannah was holding Benjamin on her lap. He was more docile than usual tonight, as though he sensed how important this dinner was to his parents. "I know that you had trouble with the Gestapo," Herbert said, "and I understand it's just as well that Hannah and I not know your past, but can you tell me this much? Why would you, as Christians, put yourselves in such danger for our sakes?"

Brother Stoltz was tired of being careful. He said, "Others helped us when we were running from the Gestapo. In that sense, we are only returning the favor. But it's also what religious people should do. I hope you don't think that this evil being done to your people comes from Christianity."

"No, we understand. People who hate come from every background," Herbert said. "We've heard you say that you are Mormons, but we know nothing of this religion. Can you tell us anything?"

Brother Stoltz told the story of their conversion, and he explained the Restoration. Then he said, "The young missionaries who visited us, back in 1938, asked me one night what it was that Germans had against Jews. I was hesitant to answer, and so I asked them what the Mormon attitude toward Jews was. One of the young men answered promptly, 'They're our brothers and sisters.' I was very surprised by that, but now I understand."

"What did he mean?" Hannah asked.

Brother Stoltz was about to answer, but before he could, Anna said, "We're *all* brothers and sisters, sons and daughters of God, no matter who we are."

Brother Stoltz nodded, but then he said, "But there's more to it than that. We believe that God has made special covenants with the children of Israel. When a person becomes a member of the Church of Jesus Christ, he or she takes on those covenants and is adopted into one of the twelve tribes of Israel."

"But most Christians blame Jews for Christ's death," Herbert said.

"Very few of the people who lived at the time of Christ actually accepted him as the Messiah. And it was the Romans, not the Jews, who officiated over his death."

"But Hannah and I have not accepted him as the Messiah. Doesn't that offend you?"

"Not many people on this earth believe that Joseph Smith was a prophet. All we ask is respect and the right to believe as we choose. So why shouldn't we accord the same respect to people who believe differently from us?"

"Yes, of course. But so few seem to feel that way."

"Maybe more than you might suspect. But in this country, people are frightened. They see Jews disappearing, being mistreated, and in their hearts they know this is wrong. But they don't dare do anything about it."

"Are there many in Berlin doing what you are doing? Helping Jews?" Herbert asked.

"I help create false papers for people," Brother Stoltz said, "and so I know something of what's happening. There are dozens of people involved, working underground, trying to save lives—but we are doing little compared to what needs to be done."

Hannah held Benjamin close to her. "If the war continues for a long time," she said, "I'm afraid all of us will be found."

Brother Stoltz nodded. He wanted to be honest and not make any false claims. "Perhaps. But in some ways, things might get easier. The bombing interferes with organized searches. If officials begin to see that Germany is losing the war, they may also concern themselves less and less with carrying out Hitler's orders." He hesitated. He didn't want to frighten them more than he had to, but there were things they had to know. "I must tell you that we are still being sought. If the Gestapo should catch up with us, you could be caught in the same net."

"Is there some safer way for us?" Herbert asked.

"I've been thinking," Brother Stoltz said, "that we all ought to get out of Germany. It's very dangerous—but it's taking one great chance, and then we would all be free."

"How could we do that?" Sister Stoltz asked.

"I can make new papers for all of us. There's an office in our building that issues travel passes. Sometimes military officers have taken vacations in Switzerland, and they receive permission to take their families. Maybe I could pass Herbert and Hannah off as my son and daughter-in-law. I'm not certain the travel office would approve that, but it's worth trying to find out."

Peter had been listening quietly all this time, and Brother Stoltz saw how nervous he was becoming. "Papa, how could you pretend to be a military officer?"

"I don't know." Brother Stoltz slid his chair back a little, and he folded his arms over his chest. "If I could get hold of the proper forms—so I could create a new identity—I could claim to be a wounded or injured officer who needs rest in the Alps. It's been done before. The problem is, I don't have travel forms in my own office. I would have to find a way to steal some."

"It's too great a chance," Sister Stoltz said. "It could be that one mistake that would destroy us all."

"Or our only chance."

"But why, Heinrich? Why can't we continue as we are?"

Brother Stoltz hadn't wanted to say so much, but he decided it was probably time to do so. "Tell them, Peter," he said.

Peter leaned on the table with his elbows, and he looked at his plate. "At Hitler Youth, our leader told us that a new plan is coming. Whole battle groups will be called directly from Hitler Youth into the army. It could happen this year."

"But you're only sixteen," Sister Stoltz said.

"Even younger boys might be called," Peter said. "Fourteen- and fifteen-year-olds. This is what our leader says, and most of the boys are eager to go."

"Hitler is running out of troops," Brother Stoltz said. "The BBC says that he's lost a million men in Russia—killed or captured—and he's occupying too many countries. He needs more troops to fight the Americans and British, who will certainly be attacking across the English channel this year. Some say he will soon be drafting older men. I could be called up, too."

"Not with your injuries."

"Frieda, don't you understand what I'm telling you? If I'm called up, my identity won't hold up. Nor will Peter's. I made him a year younger on his false papers, but that won't help now. I haven't wanted to say too much until I looked further into the possibilities, but the fact is, our only chance may be to get out of Germany—if I can find a way."

No one said a word, and Brother Stoltz hated what he saw in all the faces. He wanted to believe that somehow he could save everyone, but what he was beginning to feel was that he had led them into a trap he couldn't get them out of.

"I suspect, for you, Herbert and Hannah," he added, "that it might be better to separate your futures from ours."

"Herr Niemeyer, I feel good about our chances with you. You have access to papers, and you are planning carefully."

"I think, however, we should get you somewhere else for a time. I know that a Gestapo agent has searched for us in Berlin and lost our track, but it wouldn't take much for him to locate us again, and if he did, you see the danger."

"Moving is also dangerous."

"Yes. I know. Let's see what we can do."

The silence returned. All this was so wearing: the never-ending worry for one's existence and the constant dread for the children. Even little Benjamin sat wide-eyed and apprehensive, as though he understood the peril he was in.

During the following week Brother Stoltz intensified his effort. With so many deaths in the military all the time, it was hard for the bureaucracy to keep up with the creation and retirement of personal identity numbers. A man named Max Ingelstadt, an *Oberstleutnant*—a rank comparable to a captain—had died in Russia, but Brother Stoltz had found his papers in a file that had been misplaced and never processed. He used the name Ingelstadt to create papers for his family even though the officer had actually had four sons and no daughters. A thorough check would reveal the falsehood of the papers, but what Brother Stoltz needed was only a set of papers that would get his family across a border, where such a thorough check might not occur as long as he had travel papers.

Doing something for the Rosenbaums was more complicated. Herbert, too, needed a military background, or there would be no explaining someone his age not serving. He was also a little old to be Brother Stoltz's son. He was not too old to be Ingelstadt's son, however, and Brother Stoltz was sure he could pass for being a few years older. Still, papers that would allow both to leave the country might be questionable. What Brother Stoltz needed was to get his hands on some actual travel papers so he could see what regulations might be involved.

Brother Stoltz had to be very careful. On a couple of occasions he dropped by and tried to chat with an older woman who worked in the office that granted travel passes, but he found her stiff and unresponsive. Finally, he decided he would have to take a more direct approach. He stopped by one afternoon and said, "Frau Schaeffer, I have a man in my office who asked me a question I couldn't answer. Perhaps you can help me."

"I can try." She looked up from her desk, which was neatly arranged. Around her were extensive shelves filled with the large binders used to file official papers or to store forms.

"This man has returned from the Russian front, wounded. His personal papers were lost, and I'm taking care of that, but his doctor has advised him to take a rest cure for a few weeks. He asked whether he could possibly travel to the Swiss Alps, and I told him I would ask what the requirements were for travel of this kind."

"There's no need for it. He can go to the Black Forest. We aren't approving foreign travel—not without some overriding need for it."

"Such as?"

Frau Schaeffer was clearly annoyed. "One can rest here in Germany," she said.

"Yes. But it seems he knows an officer who took holiday in Switzerland—so he believes it's possible."

"I'll tell you how that happens. It's the high-ranking men who make these special arrangements. Someone knows someone. And then we get a phone call, and some general tells my supervisor to grant such a pass. Otherwise, it's only for business or military demands that these passes are granted."

"Maybe he knows someone."

"Don't tell him I said that. Tell him merely that he should not give it another thought."

"What sort of forms must be processed? Are there request papers he can fill out just on the chance that—"

"No." Frau Schaeffer took her wire-rim eyeglasses off and set them on her desk. "Herr Niemeyer, such a request will *not* be granted. I told you this. We have forms here." She reached to the right of her desk and patted the spine of a binder. "But it wouldn't matter what he said; I will not grant such a pass— nor will my supervisor."

"Unless he knows someone who can make a phone call."

"I told you already—"

"*Ja, ja.* I know." Brother Stoltz laughed, and then he left. But what he had learned was important. He needed the form, and then he needed official stamps and signatures. At the border, no one would have to know why the papers were approved; the important thing was, occasionally they were approved.

For the next few days, he took every opportunity to walk by Frau Schaeffer's office, and he learned something about her routine. She rarely left her desk, but when she did, she asked an assistant to come out from a back room and sit in her place. The chances of getting into the shelves didn't look promising. Brother Stoltz was beginning to think he might as well forget that possibility, but then one day he heard air-raid sirens— something that hadn't happened often in the daytime lately. He hurried from his office, down the stairs, and to the travel office. He stepped through the door and said, "Did you hear the siren, Frau Schaeffer?"

"Yes, yes. I'm leaving." She was filing away a slip of paper in one of her desk drawers.

"Did those in the back room hear the siren?"

"I'm sure they did."

"Let me make certain." Brother Stoltz walked to the door at the back of Frau Schaeffer's office. He pulled it open and called, "Air raid. Did you hear the siren?"

Two young women were already walking toward the door. "Yes, of course," they said, in the same terse voice their boss always used. Brother Stoltz was simply not seeing the opportunity he wanted. He held the door for them and tried to stall. By now, the supervisor had come out of his office. "I have enough to do without this," he mumbled.

The supervisor walked to the main office door and held it open as everyone filed out. He gave Brother Stoltz a curious glance, but he said nothing. Brother Stoltz waited until last, walked to the door, and then stopped in the doorway. "Oh, my goodness," he said.

"What is it?"

Brother Stoltz hesitated. "I can't believe I did that." He was stalling, letting Frau Schaeffer and the two young women reach the stairway.

"Please. Come out."

"I just brought a form to Frau Schaeffer, but now it occurs to me, I needed one more signature. I must take it back."

"Yes, of course. Come back after—"

"Let me pick it up now. Then I won't forget later. I'm afraid I do forget things." He laughed and continued to stand in the doorway. Then he turned. "Let me see. I believe she put it right here." He stepped to her desk but stood rubbing his chin.

"Please. Hurry."

"All right. Let' see . . ."

"Pull the door shut when you come out," the man said, and he let the door go shut as he hurried to the stairs.

Brother Stoltz took a deep breath of relief. He stepped to

the shelf, pulled down the binder Frau Schaeffer had pointed to on his previous visit, and got out two copies of the travel forms he needed. He folded them neatly and tucked them inside his suit coat, and then he hurried out of the office and down the stairs to the basement. He made certain that Frau Schaeffer and her boss saw him there, but he didn't approach them. He didn't want the supervisor to say anything that might give him away.

When the warning ended—without anyone hearing any bombs drop—Brother Stoltz hurried back to his office, and there he filled in the necessary information on the travel forms. What he lacked, of course, was a signature of approval and an official stamp. He would need to see the supervisor's signature so he could forge it, and he needed access to the stamp that Frau Schaeffer surely kept control of. That was going to be a much bigger challenge.

Another week went by, and in spite of Brother Stoltz's many attempts to observe the goings-on in the travel office, he saw no likely way into Frau Schaeffer's desk. The one thing he couldn't do was get in a hurry and make a mistake. He had to trust that if he kept watching and kept his patience, he would find a way.

He was working at his desk one morning when an elderly man came in to obtain new papers. "My wallet was stolen," the man said. "I believe Jews are doing this. They will do almost anything to get Christian identification papers."

Brother Stoltz handed the man a set of forms. "You must fill these out," he said.

The man was elderly and thin, with white hair and a yellowish mustache. He took a look at the papers and said, "I must give you all this information? I can't remember so much."

"You may take the papers with you. Perhaps someone can help you—or maybe you write such things in your family Bible."

"Yes, yes. And then another trip here again."

"I'm sorry."

The man stared at Brother Stoltz for a moment. On his desk was a nameplate that said, "Niemeyer." "I know some Niemeyer's in the west part of the city. Is that where you're from?"

"Yes, but—"

"What's your Christian name?"

"Horst."

"Is that so? I knew a Horst Niemeyer. He was killed in a bombing raid. He and his family. Are you related to that one?"

"No. It's a common enough name."

The man nodded. "I suppose so," he mumbled. "What if I can't answer every single question on this paper? What then?"

"Get some help. I'm sure all the information is available. You may have to go to the city records department."

"Oh, what nonsense," the man mumbled, and then he left.

But from the back office, where the door was open, Brother Stoltz heard his boss say, "Horst, come here a moment."

Something in his tone was wrong; Brother Stoltz felt an alarm go off inside him. He walked to the door. "Yes?" he said.

"Sit down. I need to relieve my mind of a concern."

"Certainly." Brother Stoltz sat down.

"What this man said just now—that a Horst Niemeyer died with his family. He said it was on the west side, and that is where you were bombed. No?"

"*Doch.* That is true."

"Is it possible that another Horst Niemeyer was also bombed, and this one died with his family—just as our records showed?"

"I suppose so, Herr Lindermann. Or maybe this man had the name wrong. He was quite old."

Herr Lindermann stared at Brother Stoltz. "There are other things wrong. I noticed long ago that your dialect isn't right. Your papers say you were from the east, from Dresden, I think."

"Yes. But I also lived in Frankfurt for a time."

"You never mentioned that before."

"I try not to think much about the past."

Lindermann seemed nervous. His voice was tighter than usual, and he had begun to tap his pencil across the palm of his hand. "There is something else. One day, I heard you tell a man, 'Yes, that's what my wife tells me.' But you have no wife."

"It was a slip of the tongue, I suppose. I should have said that she always *told* me that."

"Maybe. That's what I thought at the time. But there are too many things I don't understand. You seem an educated man—perhaps a university man. You can't hide that, and yet you tell me that you only attended trade school."

"I like to read. That's all."

Lindermann continued to tap the pencil. "I don't like this," he said. "This isn't adding up. I don't want an impostor right under my nose here—not in this office, of all places."

"Certainly. I understand how careful you must be."

"What if I call in the Gestapo or the SD—and have them question you? Would you be afraid of that?"

"No. Of course not. I have no reason to be afraid."

"Good." He picked up the phone. "You understand, I must cover myself. If you are caught here, I'm in great trouble."

Brother Stoltz waited, just to see whether Lindermann was bluffing, but he was dialing. "Wait a moment," he finally said.

Lindermann stopped, thought for a moment, and then put down the phone. "Yes?"

"It might be better for both of us if I disappear. As you say, you could also be in trouble."

Lindermann looked thunderstruck, his face suddenly white. "Horst, what have you done to me?"

"Give me a little time and then report that I haven't shown up for work. I'll get far away by then. If you say nothing of these other matters, they will have no reason to check on me. I would merely be a missing person."

"Are you a *Jew?*"

"No. Give me time to leave. That's all I ask of you."

"How do I know what you have been doing here? You have access to all sorts of official papers." Lindermann stood up.

"I've done nothing that would hurt anyone. My conscience is clear about that."

"What does that mean?" He reached for the phone again.

"Please. Let me leave."

"I like you, Horst. You've done good work for me. But I can't protect you. I'm not willing to die for you."

Brother Stoltz got up. "Just let me go. And give me some time." Lindermann was still holding the phone. He didn't promise anything. "Please. I do have a family. Let us get away, and we'll hurt nothing, no one. Please."

Brother Stoltz walked from the office. But his mind was running fast, and he was already organizing his next steps. He stepped to his desk, pulled out a drawer, and reached under some old files where he had hidden the travel papers. He thought immediately of some false identity papers he had been working on. He didn't want them discovered, so he grabbed those, too, and he stuffed everything into his pockets. He also had a set of identity papers for his family in case something like this happened. He pulled out a drawer and got those. Lindermann had not followed him, but certainly he could hear him going through his desk.

Lindermann wasn't telephoning—not yet—and that was a hopeful sign. Brother Stoltz had to get home; he had to warn the Rosenbaums—get them out. Then he had to find his family, and somehow they all had to lose themselves in this city again.

But his thoughts stopped there. Now, more than ever, he had to get his family out of Germany, and that meant he had to have the proper stamps on his travel papers. He hurried down the stairs. A plan, one he had thought of before and rejected, was taking shape as a last-chance approach.

He marched into the office and stopped in front of Frau

Schaeffer. "You've done it this time," he said. "I'm angry, but Mauer, downstairs in the *Anmeldung* office, wants your head."

"What are you talking about?"

"You can't shove things past us, no matter how long you've worked here."

"I've done no such thing."

"Tell that to Mauer. He's calling your boss. He says he's going to have you fired."

She was aghast, her face and neck suddenly blazoned red, but he could also see the bewilderment in her eyes.

"If you deny it, I would talk to him this minute—before he calls. Walk down there with me right now."

"I have nothing to deny. I—"

"Then come with me. Let's talk this out, for once."

She stood up, considered for a moment, and then stepped to the door to the back office. "Please come out here, one of you," she called, and she stormed from the office.

Brother Stoltz followed her to the stairway, but then he stopped. "I'll catch up with you. Just one moment."

He let her walk down a few steps, and then he dashed back to her office, hurried past her desk, and opened the door. "Never mind," he called to the young women in the back. "Frau Schaeffer is helping me. She came back."

One of the women was on her way to the door. "What is wrong out there?" she said, and stopped. Brother Stoltz pulled the door shut, and then he stepped to the desk. He wanted to work furiously, but he couldn't leave a trail and let anyone know what he had done. He pulled open several binders until he found what he needed: one that was full of papers signed by the supervisor. He extracted one from the middle of the binder, neatly, and put the binder back. Then he stuffed the sheet in his pocket.

Now he needed the official stamp. He opened the top drawer, saw nothing, but pulled out the deep side drawer and saw the box immediately. Every German office had a stamp to press an official symbol into government papers. He wanted to grab the thing and run, but he knew he couldn't do that. He pulled the box out, took out the stamp, got the papers from his suit coat pocket, and stamped them both. Then he put everything back as it had been, and he shut the drawer. He walked from the office, down the stairs, half expecting to meet Frau Schaeffer coming up, but he didn't, and suddenly he was outside, with one impossibility taken care of and so many more still ahead.

Brother Stoltz hurried down the street to a hotel that had so far survived the bombings. Taxis sometimes waited there. He would normally have taken a bus, but he had to hurry now. He was leaving a trail, perhaps, but it didn't matter. Lindermann had his address. The point was to get there before Lindermann lost his nerve and made the call.

A taxi was waiting, as it turned out, and the driver made the midafternoon drive quickly, even though he had to take a route around a bomb-damaged part of the city. In the taxi Brother Stoltz continued to work on his plan. He had recently walked past the bombed-out area where he and his family had hidden the year before. The block had been cleared of most of the debris, and the standing walls of the buildings had been knocked down, but the basements were intact, and it was still a good spot to hide. He decided to tell the Rosenbaums to get out of the apartment and wait in a park, or somewhere inconspicuous. He could do that in a moment and then head to Peter's school. Peter could go after Anna, and he, himself, would find his wife. Everyone would meet that night.

Brother Stoltz had the driver stop one street away from his apartment. He paid the man and then hurried away, but he thought better of running and forced himself to walk. He was watching for Gestapo agents, but he saw nothing. And then he reached the corner by his apartment, stopped, and peeked around. Instantly he threw himself back around the corner, against the building. In front of his apartment house was a man in a dark leather coat.

What now? Was the Gestapo already in the apartment? He had to hope that the Rosenbaums were safe in the attic. No one was looking for them. The Stoltzes would be the only ones being sought at the moment. Maybe the Rosenbaums could stay put until the Gestapo or SD, or whoever it was, had given up on the family coming back. Then he could sneak back and find them. But all too often, now, the Rosenbaums stayed in the apartment during the day so Benjamin wouldn't be so cooped up.

Or maybe that man in the coat was not what he seemed. Brother Stoltz took another look, but when he did, he was stunned. The man he had seen before was crossing the street, and two men had just come out of the building. They each had one of the Rosenbaums by the arm, and Herbert was carrying Benjamin, who was crying and clinging to his father.

Brother Stoltz stepped out from behind the building in full view of the men. He thought of bolting toward them, trying to fight them all. He wished for a gun, for help, for some way to stop this. But one of the men turned toward him, and Brother Stoltz knew he had to get away, go help his own family. And so he turned, and as best he could, he ran.

Brother Stoltz knew that he had to think fast. He ran halfway down the block and cut left into an alley behind his apartment house. Then he did the last thing the agents would expect him to do. He entered his own building through the back and hurried down the stairs to the basement. He slipped into a little storage area and hid in a dark corner.

He had made a good choice for the moment. There was no way he could have outrun those men. But now he was trapped. If more agents were being called in, some might keep a watch on the house. He had the feeling that his best chance might be to get out the front door now that the agents were probably searching in the back, and so he took a bold move. He waited long enough to catch his breath, and then he walked up the stairs and strode to the front entrance. Another man was standing out front. Brother Stoltz walked out, looked at the man, and said, "Good day."

"Excuse me," the agent said. "Do you know Herr Niemeyer?"

"Yes. Of course. He lives upstairs."

"Have you seen him today?"

"Yes. I saw him leave for work. He leaves about the same time every morning."

"But not since then?"

"No. What's going on?"

"It doesn't concern you."

"That's fine. Good day, *Mein Herr*." And Brother Stoltz walked away, slowly, casually, even though he wanted more than anything to run. When he reached the corner he crossed the street, and then, once out of sight, he hurried to the next corner, where he caught a bus to Peter's school. It was only a few blocks down the street, and he got there quickly. He knew he had to gather his family as fast as possible. Lindermann knew nothing of his wife or children, but the Gestapo would be asking questions, and they would certainly try to track his family down once they got information from others in the apartment house.

At the school Brother Stoltz spoke to a woman in the headmaster's office, asked that his son be called out of class— because of an emergency. And once he had Peter outside, he told him, "Go to Anna, quickly. Hide out somewhere for the day, and then, after dark, go back to the basement where we hid last year. Make sure no one is watching before you enter, even if you have to wait until very late."

"Papa, what's happened?"

"Never mind. I can tell you everything later. For now, hurry to Anna."

"Will I be able to go to school? Can I—"

"Please, just hurry."

Peter nodded, but Brother Stoltz saw how crushed he was. Peter's life was falling apart one more time. He took a few steps away and then turned back. "Papa, what about the Rosenbaums? Are they all right?"

Brother Stoltz couldn't look Peter in the eye. "They've been taken," he whispered.

"Benjamin?"

"Yes." Brother Stoltz saw Peter's eyes fill with tears. "I'm sorry," he told him. "But please, you must hurry, or we will all be caught."

Peter dashed away.

Brother Stoltz wished he could move as quickly. He had to take another bus, and then he had to ask, very calmly, for his wife, and once again, he had to tell her that all their troubles had returned, that they were back where they had started.

Brother Stoltz knew he had to make one more contact. He was not without help this time. He had a telephone number and a code word. He called the number from a telephone station in a post office, and he heard the voice of his underground contact. "The packages you left with me have been removed," he said.

A long silence followed. "Do you think they are lost?" finally came the question.

"Yes. Taken away."

"Have the senders been traced?"

"No. But the receivers are known."

"Perhaps it's time to call a meeting. Have you time today?"

"Yes. In the place where we spoke before."

"At the accustomed time?"

"Yes."

And so Brother Stoltz took his wife to the little park where he and his contact had sometimes met. It was after four when they arrived, and the contact would be coming at six. The time passed slowly, and after the hurried discussion in the beginning, there was little to say to his wife. Brother Stoltz knew how much she was grieving for the Rosenbaums, and he saw that her courage was giving way. They had been through too much. He knew she—*and* he—couldn't survive much more of this.

Brother Stoltz also had time now to blame himself. He thought of Benjamin, hardly more than a baby, and dependent on him for his life. What could he have done differently? Why hadn't he moved the Rosenbaums to another hiding place as he had always expected to do? Maybe he shouldn't have stayed with his job so long but used his papers to move to the country somewhere. All these people were under his protection, and his mistakes were turning destructive, maybe even fatal.

As six o'clock approached he strolled to a little pond, where he watched the ducks and swans. When a man stood a few feet away, Brother Stoltz didn't look at him.

"It's a nice day for the ducks," the man said.

"Yes. They seem to be well fed."

"Go to your assigned location. Tomorrow morning, at four, a milk wagon will pick you up. Come out quickly and get into the back. Cover yourselves and wait. We'll get you out of Berlin."

"That's good."

"Was it Gestapo?"

"Yes. I think so."

"How did they know?"

"They didn't know. But my false identity was discovered. They went to look for me—and found them."

"We took too great a chance this time. But we couldn't help it. There are so few who dare to help us now."

"Will they die?"

"Maybe not. They're young and strong. The Nazis will surely put them to work for now."

"What about the little boy?"

"I don't know. It's hard to say. But good luck to you. Thank you for helping."

"I made mistakes."

"We all make mistakes." He turned and ambled along the pond for a time and then walked away.

Brother Stoltz walked back to his wife and sat down by her on a bench. "They will pick us up early in the morning and get us out of Berlin," he said.

"Pick us up where?"

"At our hiding place—in the basement. It's the place where I told them I would be if anything ever went wrong."

"Where will we go?"

Brother Stoltz heard his wife's lifelessness, her desolation. He knew he had to sound confident. "I don't know exactly," he said. "But we'll be better off outside Berlin."

"Do we have to wait now?"

"Yes. Until after dark."

"I'm so afraid for Anna and Peter."

And that, of course, was what Brother Stoltz was also thinking. It had been a warm April day, but now, with the sun angling lower in the sky and a breeze coming up, he felt the cold. It would be uncomfortable in the basement that night; he was glad they would not have to stay long. But he wished he could hurry there now and see for himself that his children were safe.

It was after nine o'clock, however, when Brother Stoltz and his wife walked down the street to their hiding place. They walked by once and looked about for observers, and then they came back and hurried around the remnant of the old building and entered through the back stairway. Peter and Anna were not there. "I told them to wait until late," Brother Stoltz said. "I was being cautious. But don't worry. I'm sure they're fine. They know how to handle these things."

Still, however, Brother Stoltz was more worried than he admitted. He and his wife sat on the old couch, in the dark, and they listened and waited. They talked a little at times, but mostly about Peter and Anna and what they might be doing. It was almost eleven o'clock when they finally heard footsteps. "Anna. Peter," Brother Stoltz called out.

"Yes. We're here," came the answer.

"Oh, thank God," Sister Stoltz said.

"Yes. Yes. That is exactly what we must do," Brother Stoltz told her.

And so, once the children were inside, the four knelt together, and Brother Stoltz did thank the Lord for delivering them one more time. And he asked that all would go well in their escape the next morning. Then he prayed for the Rosenbaums, that somehow they might survive.

After the prayer, he explained what was happening, and he told the children to get some sleep while they waited.

"Papa," Anna said, "can't anyone help Herbert and Hannah—and Benjamin?"

"My friend in the underground told me that the SS will use them as workers."

"What about Benjamin?" Peter asked. "They wouldn't kill a little boy, would they?"

"No. I wouldn't think so."

"Heinrich," Sister Stoltz said, "we have no proof that Jews are being killed. It's all rumors. I still don't think German people would do such a thing—not even Nazis."

Brother Stoltz didn't know for sure either. But the reports were very convincing. "Let's hope the rumors are wrong," he told his wife, and then he added, "This was my fault. Herr Lindermann figured out that I wasn't who I said I was."

"You couldn't help that," Sister Stoltz said. "You were fortunate to last as long as you did."

Brother Stoltz looked into the dark, not toward the voice. "I've never wanted to kill, but if I could have killed those men today and saved the Rosenbaums, I would have done it. I stood there, powerless, with absolutely no way to stop them."

"You would be dead now had you tried to do anything."

"I know. I knew that then, and I knew I had to get to all of you. But it doesn't change how I feel. I'm tired of this helplessness. I want to fight back."

"Others can do the fighting," Anna said. "Hitler is losing his war. At least when it's over, we'll know we tried to help."

"Yes, of course," Brother Stoltz said, but it was not what he was thinking. He wasn't going to be satisfied until he did something more.

At four in the morning the Stoltzes were waiting and watching, huddled close to the ground in the dark. They heard the old milk wagon coming long before they saw it. It was a horse-drawn wagon, and the horses' hooves made a resounding noise on the cobblestones. As the wagon came nearer, the Stoltzes moved out to the street, and then, as soon as it stopped, they all scrambled into the back.

"Lie down," the driver whispered. "I'll cover you at my first stop."

And so the Stoltzes lay in the back and listened and waited as the two big horses clip-clopped down the street. It was a slow way to escape, and nerve-racking, but Brother Stoltz had no question that the underground planned such things carefully.

After a time the driver stopped the wagon and got down. Then he appeared at the back. "Lie flat," he said. "I'm going to cover you over with boards. I'll be stacking milk cans on top. Don't worry, you'll have plenty of air, and there's not much danger anyone will check us. Just don't make any noise, and don't panic if someone does decide to look in the back. We have to pass through a guard station, but it's not a big concern."

The man sounded rather old, and certainly experienced,

but the hiding place would be obvious to anyone who checked very carefully. Brother Stoltz hoped he hadn't gotten his family into another mess.

The man put the boards in place, leaving no space at all to move. Then the wagon jostled as the driver piled milk cans on top of the boards.

Four more stops followed, and each time, the driver thumped more milk cans onto the boards. Eventually Brother Stoltz could feel a bending board press a little against his chest. He felt almost claustrophobic, closed in that way. He knew that if anything went wrong, he wouldn't have a chance to make a move to save his family.

He could feel his wife on one side of him, close, and Peter on the other. Both breathed regularly, but not with the relaxed sound of someone resting. No one said a word. And then, finally, the horse's hooves slowed, and Brother Stoltz heard the driver say, "Good morning."

Outside, from a distance, a muffled voice said, "What do you have?"

"Milk. The same as I do every morning."

The voice was closer to the wagon when it sounded again. "Get down. We must check in the back."

Another voice, still in the distance, said, "It's only old Engelmann. He comes through every morning."

"Yes. That's true," the driver said, and he laughed. "I haul milk to the creamery down the road—every day, God willing."

"We still must check. That's why we're here."

"Certainly. It's not a problem."

Brother Stoltz felt the wagon shift a little as the old man climbed down. And then he heard the canvas cover at the back of the wagon, as someone tossed it aside. What Brother Stoltz knew was that even in the dark, it would be easy to see that with the false floor, the cans sat too high.

"I guess you get all the milk you want," the driver said. "That's one thing good about being away from the war front."

"We never get milk," the guard said. "Not even a little to have with the mush they serve us."

"You mean you have to eat your mush dry?"

"Yes. We certainly do."

"What a pity. That's one thing I always have enough of—plenty of milk. I wouldn't say that I pour a little out for myself from time to time—since you might report me—but it seems to come from somewhere." His laugh came from deep in his throat, and it set him off coughing.

"How about a little for us then?"

The old man laughed and then coughed again. "I couldn't possibly give you any," he said. "But you are guards, and you should check one of the cans—to make sure I'm not a smuggler. You may even have to pour a little milk out to be certain. These things are sometimes necessary for officials like yourselves."

"You're right. Pull one of those cans down. I must check. You look like a smuggler to me. I'll find something to pour the milk in."

Both men laughed, and then some time passed before the guard's voice sounded at the back of the wagon. "Pour a little right in there, and let's see whether it's really milk or not."

Brother Stoltz heard the old man grunt as he pulled the top off the can. Then he heard the milk spilling out and the guard saying, "Fill it right up to the top. I need to test plenty of it. It could be poison you're carrying to the creamery."

"Yes, yes. I'm a saboteur."

In another minute or so, the can thudded as it dropped back into the wagon, and the guard said, as he was walking away, "Go on. Move on through. But I may have to check your milk again in a day or two. I don't quite trust you yet."

"It's fine," the old driver said. "I understand what it's like for you men. I was in the Great War, back in 1914."

And the wagon rolled on. Two or three minutes went by before the driver said, "Sorry, my friends. I wasn't expecting that. It happens with new guards. We don't have far to go now. In twenty minutes you'll be out of the wagon."

It seemed longer than twenty minutes, but after a rather rocky ride up an apparent dirt lane, the driver got down and began pulling milk cans out of the back of the wagon. And then he lifted the boards and set the Stoltzes free. When they climbed out of the back, a woman was waiting. "I'm Frau Riedel," she said. "You can call me Inge. Come with me. Quickly."

"Everything good, I wish you all," Herr Engelmann said.

"Thank you so much," Brother Stoltz said. "You were very clever with that guard."

"They always want milk," he said, and then he climbed back onto the wagon.

Inge was leading the way, and Brother Stoltz hurried to catch up. She walked to the back of her farmhouse and on to a barn. She opened a wooden latch and pulled the door open, and then she walked a few steps inside. "Here's the ladder," she said. "You can't see it very well now, but it will soon be light. Climb up to the loft. I have bedding up there. For now, you can get some rest."

"Will we stay here long?" Anna asked.

"I don't know, my darling. I only take people for as long as needed. I don't ask questions, and I usually know very little. I can take you into the house later, perhaps, if you stay that long, but for now we have to be certain that you haven't been traced."

"Are you putting yourself in danger?" Sister Stoltz asked.

"I suppose. But it doesn't matter. What will they do to an old woman?"

"We can pay you something," Brother Stoltz said. "We have a little money."

"Keep that. You might need it. But I'm alone. My husband has been dead for some time now. Some who stay here are able to give me help with the farm, and that I appreciate."

"We'll help," Peter said.

"Yes, I know you will. But hide for now. And rest. I'll bring you some food after a time."

And so the Stoltzes climbed into the loft, and they found blankets and feather ticks. But no one seemed sleepy now. Gradually the sun was coming up, and light was seeping in through the cracks of the boards on the barn walls.

"One more time we've stayed alive," Sister Stoltz said. "But now what? Where can we go from here?"

"Maybe we can stay," Peter said. "We can work and—"

"Yes," Sister Stoltz said, "and how long before someone starts asking questions? Who are we this time?"

Brother Stoltz heard the discouragement in her voice, and he didn't blame her. He was feeling the same fatigue. "It's not quite so bad as it seems," he said. "I made new identity papers for us before I left. I prepared them in case something like this happened. I also have travel visas—with official stamps. I think it's possible we can get out of Germany."

"Where would we go?"

"Switzerland, I'm thinking. And if we get that far, maybe there's a way to get to England."

"Or to America?" Anna asked.

"I don't know, Anna. I'm not sure what country would let us in. But if we could get out of Germany, we could wait out the war much more easily."

"Oh, Heinrich, I don't know. How can we keep doing this?"

It was the same old question. But there were no easy alternatives. That decision had been made long ago. "Frieda," Brother Stoltz said, "we can rest a little now, and then we'll feel better. We must keep finding ways—and not give up."

"This time we've lost *everything*. At least I had my little plate till now."

"I lost my diary," Anna said. "And my picture."

Brother Stoltz knew she meant her picture of Elder Thomas. He put his arm around her shoulders, and she turned to him and began to cry. Her pain seemed somehow a reproach, although he knew she didn't mean it that way.

"Papa, we prayed for Herbert and Hannah, and for Benjamin," Peter said. "Why didn't the Lord help them—if he helped us? Or is it all just luck?"

"I have no idea why things happen the way they do," Brother Stoltz said. "But maybe the Lord will save them yet."

"Let's at least pray again for them," Peter said.

Brother Stoltz heard the desperation in his son's voice. "Yes," he said. "Let's do that now."

So they prayed again. And after, Peter lay on his bedding. Brother Stoltz heard him crying but trying not to let the others hear. Brother Stoltz knew the anguish that Peter was feeling for his little friend. He wished he could cry, too, and get some relief, but his anxieties seemed to fill up his heart.

2 3

President Thomas was in charge of the paper drive in Sugar House. All the shipping of weapons and food and equipment to soldiers required a tremendous amount of paper and cardboard. Most scrap metal had already been scavenged, and discarded tires had been collected, but newspapers continued to circulate, and everyone had some sort of paper in the house that could be turned over to the drive. President Thomas set out to pull off the drive with a minimum of vehicles—to avoid gasoline use. He asked kids to get out their red wagons, and he instructed people to bind their paper in bundles that could be easily carried. He set up a receiving station in the center of Sugar House on Twenty-First South and Eleventh East. He recruited Bea and LaRue and Beverly, along with some of his stake leaders, to separate the paper into several categories and then pile it onto the trucks that would transport it to Union Station.

But all that was to happen in the afternoon, and his factory still had to operate. It was April 29, a Saturday, but there was no letup in the long days or the six-day-a-week work schedule. The huge demand for parts and munitions had actually slowed a little as the nation, at full production, was finally meeting the demands of the war. Some people thought they even saw a light at the end of the tunnel with the Allies gradually getting the upper hand.

But all that was only talk to President Thomas. The great push of the war was still ahead. Europe had to be invaded, and Germany and Japan had to be fought in their own lands. So far, he saw no falloff in the demand on his plant. Some fly-by-night operations had opened at the beginning of the war, and failing to meet the deadlines and specs of the big defense companies, they had gone under, but a company like President Thomas's, which made excellent parts, still had all the work it could handle.

Even though President Thomas never admitted it, he was getting rich. He was putting away more money than he had ever dreamed of having. So far, his life hadn't changed much. He was still careful with his money, and he refused to spoil his children, but he had begun to think a little differently about the future. Sometimes it crossed his mind that he, or perhaps one of his sons, might want to go into politics. The Thomases had a good name in the Valley, and if they had the backing of some wealth, why not have some influence on the direction the state—maybe even the whole nation—would take after the war?

The last thing President Thomas wanted was to grow proud, or to let his family be corrupted by a sense of self-importance, and so he said little to them about the accumulating savings. But he thought, often, about a day when everyone would be home again and he could see the fruition of all this work. He longed to see his children in nice homes, raising his grandchildren, holding leadership positions in the Church.

It was all a distant dream, with so much to get through in the meantime, but it was what kept President Thomas going. His life was pressured and busy, and he sometimes felt overwhelmed by all the things people expected of him. But if America could get this war won, and his children all made it safely home, he could look forward to better days.

Bea had told him one morning, when just the two of them were at the breakfast table, "Al, I don't think you'll ever slow down. You'd rather work than play."

"I do enjoy work," he told her as he chomped down his eggs and toast. "I like to get things done. But I want to ease off a little one of these days. When the war ends, you and I are going to take a boat to the Hawaiian Islands and see if it's as nice over there as Bobbi says it is."

"Really, Al? Do you want to do that?"

"I do. I want to see the Holy Lands, too, and maybe Greece, or . . . I don't know . . . a few other places."

"Al, I would give anything to have a little time to relax. I wouldn't even have to go anywhere. I'd just like to know what a full day is like when I didn't have so much to worry about."

"Well, we can't think too much about it yet," President Thomas told her. "But better times are ahead for us."

The whole idea seemed too good ever to be true, but President Thomas thought of it every day. And Sister Thomas mentioned it often. If they could just get through this war, and their children could be kept safe, better times were waiting.

But this particular Saturday was a busy one. Early that morning Sister Thomas got the girls out of bed, and the whole family drove to the plant. President Thomas had a "B" card for gasoline, because his factory was involved in the war effort, and he therefore got enough gas to drive to work. Sister Thomas usually didn't stay as many hours, and so, most often, she took a bus home. Until the war, she had never driven, but that had gotten awkward, and so she had finally taken the test for her driver's license. Now and then President Thomas actually let her take his beloved '41 Nash—the last model produced before the wartime pressure had shut down the production of cars. Today, however, they would all drive back together, park the car at home, and then walk to the receiving station in town.

LaRue and Beverly usually helped out at the plant on Saturdays. LaRue had learned to operate some of the machinery, but most often she worked in packaging, where she packed parts for shipping. Beverly normally ended up sweeping or picking up scraps.

President Thomas hired a number of high schoolers, who came in on evenings or Saturdays. The boys, until this year, had treated LaRue like a kid sister, but at fourteen she was "blossoming into womanhood," as her mother liked to say. The older boys were definitely taking notice.

On this particular morning, a young man named Nolan Sharp was working, and he soon managed to trade places with a friend at the packaging table, where he could stand across from LaRue. "I didn't think you would be here this morning," he told her. "I read in the *Trib* that your dad was in charge of the paper drive out in Sugar House. I thought you'd all be out there."

"Gee whiz, I didn't know you could do that."

"Do what?"

"Read."

He smiled. Nolan was a boy from Pennsylvania whose father was stationed at Fort Douglas. Before the war, there had been few "outsiders" in Utah, but now, with the new Hill Air Force base near Ogden, the new Steel Mill in Provo, and all the defense installations up and down the Wasatch front, people were moving in from other areas.

Nolan was a tall boy with a sly smile that suggested mischief. LaRue and Beverly had talked many times about how cute he was, and clearly, even though he was seventeen, he had taken an interest in LaRue.

A radio in the package room was playing Johnny Mercer's hit "G. I. Jive." Nolan snapped his fingers to the rhythm a few times and let his head bob. "Sweetheart," he said, "I can not only read. I can also sign my name."

"Well, you eastern boys simply don't receive a proper education the way we do in the more refined western states."

Nolan laughed at that. "When I told my friends that I was

moving out here, they wanted to know whether I'd have to worry about getting scalped by wild Injuns."

"And what did they say about living around Mormons?"

Nolan had filled his box, and now he closed the top and began to tape it. He concentrated to get the tape straight, holding one eye shut, and then he looked back at LaRue, who was waiting for an answer. "They told me the truth," he said. "They said that every man had a dozen ugly wives, and every one of them went around with long faces, singing hymns all day."

"Come, come, ye Saints," LaRue began to sing, solemnly, with a gloomy look on her face.

"See. It's true."

"You'd better go back East, where the girls are pretty."

He stopped and looked at LaRue. "I'll tell you the truth. In all of Pennsylvania, cross my heart and hope to die, I never saw a girl as cute as you." He unleashed that wily smile of his, and LaRue was absolutely at a loss for words. She ducked her head and worked on her package again, and about then President Thomas stepped into the room and said, "LaRue, I have something I need to have you do."

LaRue was saved but not sure she wanted to be. She gave Nolan a quick glance, which he was waiting for. He winked at her and said, "See you later, LaRue."

She didn't say anything, but she felt herself blushing. And then she followed her father to his office.

"LaRue, I want you to sort through all these invoices," he told her. "Stack them according to vender, and then put them in order, by date. We've needed to do that for a while, and we've gotten behind. Can you do that for me?"

"Sure." But she caught a little stiffness in his manner, and she knew there was more to this than he was admitting. "You wanted me out of the packaging room, didn't you?" she said.

He was almost to the door, but he stopped and turned around, and then he shoved his hands into his pants pockets.

He was wearing a white shirt and tie, with suspenders, but he had taken his suit coat off. "Well . . . yes."

"I was getting my work done. We were just talking a little."

"LaRue, I could hear everything you two were saying. You were flirting with him, and you're too young for that."

"Maybe he was doing the flirting."

"No question. But you were too, honey, and you don't know what you're toying with there."

"He's not a Mormon. That's what bothers you."

"That *is* part of it." President Thomas walked back toward his desk, where LaRue was beginning to sort through the invoices. She was looking down, avoiding his eyes—her way of showing that she was irritated with him. "Nolan is a good worker. But he's cocksure of himself, and I don't know what kind of standards he's been taught. These people come in here from back East or California, and they think—"

"Dad, I was only talking to him. He hasn't asked me out on a date or anything."

"But how long until he does? And the kid is a junior in high school. I'm not going to let you go."

LaRue actually had been hoping Nolan would ask her out, and even though she had been fairly sure what her dad would say, now she had forced him into taking a stand. She gave her father a hard look, one she knew would sting him, but she said nothing.

"LaRue, you're the most self-willed of all my kids, and you're too pretty for your own good. I hate to think of the trouble you can get yourself into." But his voice softened as he said, "Honey, I have to look out for you. I'm your father."

"You don't give me credit for having any sense at all, do you?" She knew what she was up to. She had always been able to work her dad into corners.

"You're fourteen, LaRue. You have a lot to learn, and I don't want you to learn it the hard way. I know you've talked to your mother, but it's one thing to talk to Mom, and it's another thing to be with some boy who . . . well, there's just more to it than you know."

"Dad, I know about *everything*. How young do you think I am?"

President Thomas shook his head. "Just sort those invoices. And if Nolan asks you out, you have my answer. Tell him you're too young—that your bad old father said so."

"Fine. You're the boss. Let me know when I can take my hair out of pigtails, all right?"

Dad groaned, and then he walked away, and LaRue actually felt some guilt—but she was also angry. She didn't worry about boys "taking advantage" of her; what she worried about was never getting a chance to have a date with Nolan before he went off to the stupid war. So many boys were now signing up for the service before they ever got out of high school.

When LaRue was almost finished with the invoices, her mom came in and gave her some other assignments. Clearly, Dad had told her to keep LaRue busy—and away from Nolan. LaRue was still fuming over that when Lorraine Gardner stepped into the office. She had started out doing secretarial work for the Thomases, but she was now in charge of all the secretaries and bookkeepers. "Hi, LaRue," she said. "What does your dad have you working on?"

"Anything to keep me out of the packaging room."

Lorraine smiled. "Dads are all alike," she said. "But I can't say I blame him in this case."

LaRue looked up. "Why? What's he so scared about?"

Lorraine laughed. "*Older* boys," she said, and then she added, "You look just like Wally when your temper flashes like that. Your eyes are exactly like his."

"It was my dad who always made him lose his temper—the same as me."

"That's true." Lorraine smiled and stepped a little closer, but then she added, quietly, "But Wally always wanted more freedom than he was ready for."

There was something so serene about Lorraine. Nothing seemed to ruffle her. It was a quality LaRue admired without really envying. "Wally left home as soon as he could. Maybe that's what I'll do. Then Dad can't make my decisions for me."

"Oh, LaRue, be patient about growing up. Sometimes, now, I wish my parents would step in and decide a few things for me. I have some hard decisions to make."

"Like what?"

"I have a chance to go to Seattle and work for Boeing. There's a guy we work with up there—he's been down here a couple of times. He offered me a job at a really good salary. It sounds exciting—and I'd sort of like to get away from home for a while. But it's scary, too. I don't know anyone up there."

"So what are you going to do?"

"I don't know."

Lorraine was so beautiful and so likable. LaRue wanted her to be at home when Wally got back. "I hope you stay here," LaRue said. "I'd miss you if you left."

"Well, thanks. I'm glad to know you'd miss me. And just remember, you'll be my age in no time, and then it won't be as easy to leave home as you think."

LaRue tried to think what it really would be like. All she knew was that everyone seemed to be on the move, heading to one part of the world or another, and she couldn't even go out on a date. The thought made her angry all over again.

The Thomases went home in time for an early lunch, and then they walked to the receiving station. They spent the afternoon sorting and processing all the donated paper that people were carrying in. Everyone, of course, knew the Thomases. President Thomas spent half his time that afternoon talking with members of the stake—whispering quietly, settling problems, giving advice.

"What do you hear from Bobbi and the boys?" was the most common question everyone asked Mom.

She would say, "Wally's still a prisoner of war in the

Philippines, but the last we heard, he's all right. So we feel good about that." And then she would tell about Alex being in England and Bobbi and Gene in the Hawaiian islands.

There was something to say about everyone except LaRue and Beverly. Nothing exciting ever happened to them. When LaRue's older brothers and her sister had been her age, they hadn't been tied down by all the rationing. Activities could never be as fancy now, whether at school or church. And always for the same reason: "Hey, there's a war on, don't you know?" Or, "We can't do that—not for the duration." And the list of things they couldn't do seemed to get longer all the time.

When old Sister Bryan, from the ward, came by with some school notebooks, apparently left behind by her children long ago, she asked Mom about the family and got the same report. LaRue turned to Beverly and whispered, "Maybe we could put this on a phonograph record and just play it all afternoon."

Beverly laughed.

Sister Bryan sighed and said, "I'm happy to hear they're all right. I lost a grandson in Italy just recently." LaRue saw tears fill her eyes. "I have too many grandchildren," she said. "Too many the wrong age. I have five more in the service—and more coming up—and I can't stand to think that any more of them might be taken. They were all with us, all here close by, and now they're scattered to the four winds."

LaRue saw the pain in Sister Bryan's face, and suddenly she felt bad. She remembered what she had felt on Sunday when she had looked at the big banner on the wall of the chapel. It displayed a blue star for each of the ward members who was serving in the military—like the banners in the windows of homes. Each Sunday LaRue counted the numbers as they grew, and now there were more than forty. What she also looked at were the gold stars at the bottom. Three young men from the ward had died now, and others had been wounded. What she hadn't thought of were how many grandchildren and cousins and friends there were—whose stars were on someone else's wall.

LaRue put her arm around Sister Bryan's back. "I'm sorry," she said, softly.

"Oh, thank you, sweetheart. You're such a dear young woman."

When Sister Bryan was gone, Sister Thomas took hold of LaRue's shoulders and looked into her eyes. "That was very kind, LaRue."

LaRue knew that her mother worried about her, about her whining and complaining, about her "attitude." And LaRue found herself wondering which was her real self: the one who felt sorry for Sister Bryan, or the one who resented not having decorations for school dances? Both, she supposed, because her moods jumped from one to the other every day—every hour.

At the end of the big project, when the last of the trucks had been sent off, Dad said something astounding. "Why don't we walk over to the Marlo this evening and see a picture show?"

LaRue wondered whether that would work. The movie at the Marlo was "Best Foot Forward," with Lucille Ball and Harry James. It was a lot of singing and dancing, which Dad usually didn't go for. "Me and Bev saw that one already," she said. "But we could go downtown."

"Well, all right. You kids look at the paper when we get home. Pick something out. We'll drive downtown."

"What's going on?" LaRue asked.

"What do you mean?"

"You never want to go to movies."

"I know. But if we go home, you girls have a way of wandering off with friends, and I read the paper and listen to the news while Mom reads or sews or something. We just need to spend some time together."

LaRue saw it all. Dad wasn't feeling good about the "chat" he had had with her that morning, and he wanted to show her, in some way, that he was sorry. Several times lately he had apologized for being gone from home too much, and he had admitted one Sunday at dinner that he had demanded too much of Wally, hadn't let him grow out of his rebelliousness. He had also told LaRue a number of times that she was a lot like Wally. Dad was trying to do the right thing, and LaRue was touched by that.

"You don't have to ask twice," Mom said, and so they all went home and cleaned up, and then they ate a quick supper: homemade soup that Mom had bottled the year before when so many vegetables in their garden had been ready at the same time. She hadn't baked bread much lately, with all her busyness, and so she put Wonder Bread on the table. Dad usually had something to say about that, but he didn't complain tonight—and he certainly ate plenty of it.

LaRue and Beverly picked a double feature at the Paramount. "Chip off the Old Block," with Donald O'Connor, was just as much a song-and-dance picture as the Lucille Ball movie, but the second feature was "Memphis Belle," a documentary put out by the war department, with actual combat films. The girls thought Dad would like a war picture, in Technicolor. Dad didn't pay much attention to what they told him, however; he was looking through the newspaper, and he merely said, "That's fine, girls."

By the time they got downtown, they'd missed the first part of "Chip off the Old Block," but the usher helped them find seats, and it didn't take long to catch the idea. All of it was really quite silly, but LaRue loved it, and Beverly couldn't stop giggling. Dad hardly reacted at all, and the girls joked between themselves about him being such an old stick-in-the-mud. At the end of it, he said, "We don't want to see another one, do we? It'll be awfully late."

"The other one was the one you wanted to see," LaRue said.

That was not exactly true, of course, but Dad sat back and

didn't argue, and they stayed—for a while. But "Memphis Belle" was about a flight crew on a bomber. Dad watched for about half an hour, and then he said, "Girls, I don't really want to see this. Let's just go."

Mom said, "I think I'd rather leave too."

LaRue was interested in the picture and resisted, but before long Dad stood up and said, "Come on. I can't do this." LaRue had no idea what he meant. Everyone was in the car before Dad said, "I'm sorry. I didn't mean to ruin things for you."

"Why didn't you like it, Dad?" LaRue asked.

He backed the car from the angled parking space and then shifted gears and started forward. "There's something you might as well know," he said. "The paper tonight said the invasion might be starting."

"What invasion?" LaRue asked.

"The invasion of Europe. The D day everyone has been talking about for such a long time."

"Girls," Mom said, and she twisted in her seat to look into the back seat. "The paratroopers will probably go in first."

"Oh," LaRue said, and the significance of Dad's concern finally struck her.

"So far, it's just a lot of bombing," Dad said. "The invasion could still be weeks away. No one knows. But tonight there was a picture on the front page of a Jeep being loaded on a glider— getting ready for the landing, probably in France. That means the airborne troops are getting ready to go."

"Alex will be all right, won't he?" Beverly asked.

There was a long silence, and finally Dad said, "We certainly hope so, honey."

But LaRue felt his dejection, heard it in his voice. No one said another word all the way home.

24

The Stoltzes now had the paperwork they needed. Or at least they hoped so. As it had turned out, leaving Germany was much more complicated than Brother Stoltz had known. But his friend from "Uncle Emil"—the code name for the underground—knew much more, and one member of the group was a master printer and an expert at creating false papers. Based on the papers Brother Stoltz had already made, the printer had created passports and identity cards. Now the Stoltzes were on a train heading for Switzerland—except that they planned to stop in Frankfurt. Anna wasn't sure that was wise, but she felt the same way everyone else did—if they were going to leave their homeland, perhaps forever, she wanted to see her home one more time.

So when the train pulled into Frankfurt, late in the afternoon on Monday, May 29, the Stoltzes first took a streetcar to their old neighborhood, and then they walked down the street where they had lived. They knew they were taking a chance, but it was one they couldn't resist. They stood a little way off and gazed toward the apartment house. It was not a romantic castle or a country manor; it was merely a blocky gray building, but to Anna, it was magical. It represented a time of life when fear and tension hadn't consumed their attention. It was also the place where the elders had first come to teach them. She remembered the day when Alex and Elder Taylor had stopped to talk to her, there on the street, not far from where they were standing. She had known by then how much she liked Alex, but she had never imagined that a relationship would actually grow between them.

"It doesn't seem real," Peter whispered. "I can hardly remember what it was like to live here."

Everyone knew what he meant. He was the one who had been so young then, and he was the one who had changed the most. He was filling out, looking more and more like a man. He was seventeen, and yet he had been little more than a child when he had left this home.

But the Stoltzes couldn't linger very long. They couldn't be recognized by old neighbors who might happen to know that they were being sought. They only looked at the windows that had been their apartment and wondered who might live there now. Sister Stoltz did admit one element of her pain: "I wonder who got all our things. My dishes and the furniture."

"I wish we had all the pictures," Brother Stoltz said.

But these were thoughts almost too painful to harbor, so the Stoltzes walked to the corner and waited for a streetcar, and they took a little journey through the heart of the city. Large sections of Frankfurt had been bombed, but it was operating pretty well. Much of the bombing was on the outskirts of town where there were factories and military installations. Along the Main River, the beautiful old cathedral was still standing, along with the ancient *Rathaus*, but some of the bridges were gone.

Finally, they did something bold, but something they all wanted to do. They took the streetcar to President Meis's apartment house. They studied the place and walked by once, just to make sure no one was watching, and then they stepped into the building and walked up a flight of stairs, where they rang the doorbell. In a moment Sister Meis appeared at the door. She looked at the four of them for a second or two before the full realization seemed to strike her. "Oh, my goodness," she said. "Please come in."

She took Sister Stoltz into her arms, held her for a moment, and then called for her husband. "Are you back with us?" she asked Sister Stoltz. "Will you live here again?"

"No, no," Sister Stoltz said, but she didn't explain anything more than that.

Brother Meis had apparently been eating. He came from the kitchen, still holding a napkin in his hand. He stopped and stared for a moment, and then he grabbed Peter, who was closest to him. "My goodness, boy," he said, "you have grown twice the size you were."

Brother Stoltz stepped to him. "Go a little easy on me," he said. "I've never mended quite so well as I might like." But he was laughing, and he hugged President Meis.

"Please, tell us what's been happening to you," President Meis said. "We knew from the branch president in Berlin that you were apparently there—but he wouldn't say much. And then we heard nothing. We feared the worst."

And so the Stoltzes sat down and rehearsed their story, or at least the parts they could tell.

President and Sister Meis were astounded by all they heard. "But what now?" President Meis asked.

"We're not likely to see you again," Brother Stoltz said. "But it's better if I not say exactly what we have planned. That way you have nothing you would have to hide, should you be questioned."

"But that means you are still being pursued."

Brother Stoltz nodded. The others in the family were sitting on a couch, but Brother Stoltz had chosen a wooden, straight-backed chair, which was easier for him to sit on. "Agent Kellerman—the one who harassed you—will never stop chasing us, I'm certain. We know that at one time he was looking for us in Berlin."

"Someday—when it's safe—will you let us know where you are?" Sister Meis asked.

"Oh, yes. But that will only come when the war is over."

"You were right all along about Hitler," Brother Meis said. "He's led us into disaster. War on too many fronts. And now we're going to pay for it."

"The British and the Americans are getting ready to cross the channel," Brother Stoltz said.

"I don't doubt that," President Meis said, "and Russia is having its way, more and more, in the east. When those two great forces come at us from both sides, I hate to think what will happen to us."

"Is this what others think? We never dare talk to anyone."

"I'm never sure. No one speaks out, but everyone can see what's coming. I hear people complain about the bombing, curse England and America—and I feel that way myself at times—but I think most people know by now that we never should have let Hitler get us into this."

Sister Meis, who was sitting next to her husband, took his hand in hers. "We lost our Günther," she said. "He was on the Russian front. He died in all the cold, last winter."

"Oh, no," Sister Stoltz said. Anna wondered that young Günther could be old enough to go to war, let alone to have died.

"He was only seventeen," Sister Meis said. "We didn't want him to go—but there was nothing we could do."

"Where is Alene?"

"That's our great blessing. She married a nice young man—a member of the Church. She lives here in Frankfurt, and she has a little girl. Her husband is in the army, of course, but for now, he's not in danger."

"He's in France," Brother Meis said. "I doubt it will be a safe place for much longer."

"It's all so terrible," Sister Meis said. "One of the Richter sons was also killed, and Sister Zander's son lost both his feet to frostbite—also in Russia. The Müllers were bombed out of their house. They weren't hurt, but they lost everything. And . . . oh . . . you don't know about Sister Goldfarb."

"No. What?" Brother Stoltz asked.

"She was taken away—she and her daughter. Ernst kept in touch with her, helped her a good deal. But one day he went there and she was gone. A neighbor wouldn't say much, but he did admit that someone—SD or Gestapo, or someone—had come and taken the two of them away."

Brother Meis said, "The neighbor told me, 'I suppose you know that she had married a Jew,' as though that were explanation enough."

"I won't say much about this, Ernst," Brother Stoltz said, "but we were involved in hiding Jews, in Berlin." He looked down at the floor. "We were tracked down, and the young couple and their little boy were taken. We got out, but they didn't. We are all brokenhearted about them. You know what the rumors are about the Jews, don't you?"

"I hear things. But I don't believe it."

"I have no proof, Ernst. But I have strong reason to believe that it's all true."

President Meis looked at the floor. He didn't argue. "How can all this happen?" he asked. "How did we *allow* it to happen?"

"It's too late to worry about that," Brother Stoltz said. "For now, we're merely trying to stay alive."

President Meis was sitting in an old, worn upholstered chair. He leaned back and let his gaze drift away. "Brother Stoltz, how much longer until men our age are inducted? I always thought my age would keep me out, but Hitler is taking older men all the time."

"And younger. Those Peter's age are manning antiaircraft guns now. That's one of the reasons we're on the run."

"But Peter will have to go," Brother Meis said. "It's just a matter of time until they take him."

"Maybe not."

"Then you must be planning to leave Germany."

"It's better not to say."

"Oh, Heinrich, that's so dangerous."

"Everything is dangerous these days."

"Yes." President Meis looked at Brother Stoltz for a moment and then seemed to drift into his memories. "I long for the days when our branch was going strong and the missionaries were with us. I wonder now how many of them are fighting in this war. Most of them, I suspect."

Anna thought back on her days in the branch. So many things had been so lovely when she and her family had first joined the Church—when she had taught the small children in Sunday School and the branch had met in those little upstairs rooms.

"Do you still hold branch meetings?" Anna asked.

"Oh, yes. It's not always easy. Travel is not possible for those who live outside the city, and many of the members are suffering such hardships. But we have meetings every week, and we try to keep everyone's spirits up. I visit the members as much as I can, and I try to make sure no one is going without food. I know we have some terrible times ahead, but we hold out hope that all this will finally end and things can someday get back to where they were."

Two hours slipped by quickly before Brother Stoltz said, "We should go now. I'm afraid we could put you in danger."

"When are you leaving Frankfurt?" Sister Meis asked.

"In the morning. By train."

"Then stay the night. We have beds now, with our children gone."

The Stoltzes protested a little, but not long, and as it turned out, they stayed up very late that night, talking and remembering. And early the next morning the two families knelt together and prayed. President Meis prayed for the Stoltzes, that they might be kept safe, and he prayed that they all might one day see each other again. "And Father," he said, "let the gospel be preached in this land again. Give us the opportunity to help in spreading the truth."

By the time the Stoltzes were back on the streetcar, heading toward the train station, Anna was feeling a loss she had almost forgotten. She had lived with fear so long that the thought of escaping Germany had become an obsession. Now, however, she felt a renewed sense of what she had given up the day she chose to fight back against Kellerman. In one sense, Germany no longer existed, but if it returned, she would not be part of it anyway. If her family failed to make it across the border, all was lost; if they made it, much was lost all the same.

Two days later the Stoltzes were finally approaching the Swiss border. Twice, in southern Germany, the train had been attacked by Allied airplanes. All passengers had been evacuated into the woods during the attacks, and then, the second time, several hours had passed before the repairs on the track and train had allowed further progress.

All the nostalgia about leaving was gone now, and the tension was in Anna's throat. She kept watching her mother, who was white with fear. Anna hoped that all their rehearsing would pay off. Brother Stoltz, with the advice of his friend in the underground, had chosen to cross the border at Basel, and to show tickets for Bern. But once in Basel, the plan was to buy tickets for Zürich. This would break the trail, and Zürich was a large city where a person could get lost more easily. Getting into Switzerland was a major step toward freedom, but it was not exactly a safe haven. Brother Stoltz had been warned that Switzerland was swarming with German spies, and a runaway "enemy of the state" could not feel secure, if known.

As the train arrived at the border, it pulled to a stop. Just as the Stoltzes had been told to expect, German border guards got on. A stout little man walked to the Stoltzes, who were sitting together in a pair of facing seats. "Your papers," he said.

And then, as they all handed over their passports and travel papers, he asked, "Are you Germans?"

"Yes," Brother Stoltz said. "I'm an officer in the *Wehrmacht*. Home from Russia. I was hurt there. We're taking a little holiday." He had kept his voice light and friendly, and Anna was impressed by how natural he sounded.

"Russia? What regiment were you with?" The man was studying the papers.

Brother Stoltz had prepared all this information. He gave the number of his regiment, his rank, and the campaign he had been involved in near Kiev. "I was in a truck that ran over a mine," he said. "I wasn't hit by shrapnel, but I was thrown out of the vehicle, and I broke my shoulder and knee. My doctor said I needed some time to rest and recover, and my regimental commander was good enough to get permission for me to take a trip to Switzerland. My son will soon be old enough to enter the military himself, and so we're having one last holiday together."

"And where are you from?"

"Saarbrücken."

This all sounded friendly, but Anna hoped the questions stopped soon. She could feel her heart beating, hear it in her ears.

"I am going to keep these papers momentarily," the man said, without changing his tone. "I want someone else to talk to you."

He walked away.

Anna felt the panic. She wanted to bolt from the train now, while they had a chance. She saw the terror in her mother's eyes, too, and in Peter's. But Brother Stoltz was saying, "Don't lose control. We can't make a mistake."

"Why is he doing this?" Sister Stoltz whispered.

"I don't know. He is merely being careful, I suspect. But if we act nervous, he may pull us off for questioning. Everyone *must* seem natural."

Maybe two minutes went by, and the whole time Anna's mind was racing, her pulse, too. She kept trying to take long, steady breaths and not look frightened, but she could feel that her upper lip was sweating as well as her forehead, and her mother was rigid with fear. Anyone could see that.

Anna saw a man in a black uniform—Gestapo—step into the car. He followed the little border guard to the Stoltzes. "Good day," he said, sounding official but not unfriendly. He was a slender young man, erect, with a narrow face and clear, focused eyes. "I'm a little confused by your papers," he said. He lifted the travel papers and studied them over for a time. "I hope you won't mind, Herr *Oberstleutnant* Ingelstadt, if I ask you a few questions."

"Of course not, young man," Brother Stoltz said.

"I mean no discourtesy to an officer, and certainly not one who has only recently returned from the front, but these trips are not allowed anymore. Earlier in the war, officers sometimes took holiday in Switzerland, but we have not seen this in the past year."

"Yes, I understand." Brother Stoltz laughed. "Sometimes it helps to know the right people."

"Could you tell me who arranged for this?"

"I told you. An *Oberst*, my commander. You see I have the proper papers, and I doubt that you need anything else."

"You have to understand, if someone passes through with false papers, I must answer for that. Is there someone I could contact—to verify these arrangements?" The man was obsequious—on the surface—but behind the words Anna thought she heard a challenge. He was watching for her father to make a mistake, and he kept eying the rest of the family at the same time.

"I understand your position," Brother Stoltz said. "Think of this, however. If I telephone certain of my contacts and explain that you showed an officer of my rank disrespect, that would also be something you wouldn't want to answer for. I have proper permission for this trip, and I see no reason for further discussion. Would you please give me your name?"

"I am Agent Reinert. Excuse me for not introducing myself," the young agent said. He looked around at the Stoltzes, focusing on one of them at a time. "Your wife seems nervous," he said carefully, obviously probing again.

"She's not well. This train has been warm, and twice we've been held up by those stinking British bombers. We're all very tired. That's one reason I want no further delay here." And then he softened his voice. "You understand, don't you?"

Reinert nodded, and Anna could see that he was considering. "Not many survived your campaign. I thought most were taken prisoner last winter. How did you get out?"

"My injuries occurred in January, before the battle turned so much against us in the Korsun Pocket. I spent some time in a temporary hospital at the front, but I was shipped back by train. I was in a hospital in Nurnberg until recently. I am only now moving about some. But this is the first time since my return from battle that I have had to suffer insults."

"No insult, Herr *Oberstleutnant.* I don't intend such a thing. But I have a job to do, the same as a Wehrmacht officer."

And still he stood his ground. "Where, exactly, are you going? Would you please tell me that?"

"Certainly. We are traveling straight on to Bern if this train ever moves again, and we will stay at a small resort hotel outside Bern, in Spiez, on the Thuner Sea."

"And what is the name of the proprietor there?"

"Herr Kaufmann, I believe it is. The inn is called *Hotel Adler.* Check there, and you will find that we have a place reserved."

Anna knew that such a hotel did exist. Her father had prepared all this information ahead of time. He had even made the reservation, just in case something of this kind happened.

The agent was jotting down the information, and Anna thought she saw a change in his manner. "I'm very sorry to have bothered you, *mein Herr*," he said. "I hope you and your family have a fine stay."

"It's only four weeks," Brother Stoltz said. "And then I'll be happy to return where I belong—on the battlefront."

The agent nodded again. "I admire you," he said. "It's such devotion that no one can defeat."

"That is right, young man. We each have a role to play. I don't blame you for playing yours. Heil Hitler." He gave a Nazi salute.

The agent responded with his own salute and then handed the papers back to Brother Stoltz. But before he left, he took another look around, as though he were trying to remember everyone's appearance. He studied Anna longer than seemed necessary. "Have a fine holiday," he said to her, and then he and the guard left the car.

Anna felt her body relax, finally, but Sister Stoltz was letting go. She was quivering and taking quick breaths.

"Frieda, please don't do this. Sit quietly. Don't call attention to yourself. We'll soon be in Switzerland."

Anna glanced around at others in their railroad car; most were looking at the Stoltzes, at least in glances. Anna knew her family had to continue to be careful.

"Will they telephone the hotel?" she asked.

"I hope they do. We have a reservation. All is in order."

"And what if they call in a day or two and we're not there?"

"We'll be in Zürich, and we have another set of papers. We'll be using other names."

"Won't they start looking for us if we're not there?" Peter asked.

"It's not that easy for them," Brother Stoltz said. "Germans don't have free run of Switzerland. If the Gestapo comes after us, they have to do it with infiltrators—spies. This young agent can travel into Basel, to the train station, but he has no authority beyond that."

"So we're not safe yet when we cross the border?" Anna asked.

"Not entirely," Brother Stoltz said. "But we have passed the big test. From all I have been told, we now have little left to worry about. So smile." He smiled himself.

Anna thought she would feel better when they left Basel, but she was breathing more easily now.

The train jerked, inched forward, and then gradually began to roll. It had just begun to pick up speed, however, when it slowed and stopped. It had crossed the border, but now Swiss authorities stepped on and checked all the papers again. This time the inspection was cursory, however, and soon the train was moving again.

Peter let out a little whistle, and his father laughed. "Not quite so easy as I'd hoped—on the German side—but not bad," he said. Sister Stoltz had lost her stiffness, but she looked bedraggled. All the pressure the family had gone through in the past few months had built up, and Anna knew her mother was close to a breaking point.

In a few minutes the train stopped again, this time at the Basel train station. The Stoltzes gathered up their luggage, and they hurried quickly from the train. Anna was relieved to get off. But they had only walked a short distance along the platform, amid the crowd of people, when Anna heard someone call, "Herr Oberstleutnant!"

All the Stoltzes stopped and looked back. It was Reinert. He had stayed on the train with them.

"Why are you getting off the train?" Reinert called. He stepped down.

Peter took a quick step, as though he were about to break into a run, but Brother Stoltz grabbed his arm. "No. Don't panic. I'll talk to him. We'll be fine." He turned back and looked toward the agent, who was fighting his way through the crowd. "What do you mean by this?" Reinert asked as he approached. He seemed genuinely surprised.

"I believe we change trains here. That's my understanding. Am I mistaken?"

"Yes, of course. You know that. This train continues to Bern."

Brother Stoltz felt in his coat pocket for the tickets, and pulled them out. He studied them for a few seconds, and then he said, "Oh, of course. You are right. Thank you so much for the assistance." He looked around at his family. "We need to get back on the train," he said.

"No," the agent said, and he stepped closer to Brother Stoltz. "I don't like any of this. Something is wrong here. I want you all to come to our office in the *Bahnhof*. I must do some checking before you can go on."

"Young man, this is absolutely unnecessary. I told you already that—"

Reinert grabbed Brother Stoltz's arm, and he leaned closer to him. "I told you, you must come with me. All of you."

"Of course. I'm not saying we won't. I simply hate to miss our train."

"I cannot help that. Come with me, immediately." He still held Brother Stoltz by the elbow, and now he was pulling him, rather roughly.

"That's perfectly all right. I'm coming," Brother Stoltz said. "But don't walk too fast. I'm still not well."

"You others go first," Reinert said. "We will follow. Walk into the station."

Anna stepped ahead, taking her mother by the arm. "It's all right," she whispered. "Don't let him scare you." But the fact was, Anna was terrified, and her mother grasped Anna's arm so tightly that it hurt.

But Anna told herself to keep control—and to help her mother do the same. The two continued along the platform toward the main hall of the station. The crowd had cleared a good deal now. Peter was behind Anna and his mother. Anna glanced back to see that her father, at the rear, was still being escorted by Reinert. But just as she looked forward again, she heard a loud grunt. She spun to see that her father had shoved the agent toward the edge of the platform. Reinert was teetering on the edge, but he was still clinging with one hand to her father's arm. Brother Stoltz slammed his arm across Reinert's wrist, but the young man held on and was fighting his way back, trying to get his balance. And then, suddenly, Peter charged him. He slammed his shoulder into Reinert's chest. Reinert's hold broke, and he fell backward, off the platform.

Anna heard him hit with a thud, heard him cry out, and she glanced over the edge to see a look of terror in his eyes. He had fallen across the tracks, struck his head perhaps, or his neck. She saw his eyes roll back and his body go limp.

"Hurry," she heard her father say. "But don't run." They all walked rapidly inside the station. Anna looked back and saw that two men were kneeling on the platform, looking down at the agent, but she had no idea whether they would soon follow. Others had turned to see what had happened but seemed uncertain what to do. As the family entered the station, Brother Stoltz said, "Walk normally. Continue on through the station. Leave by the big doors across the way."

"Aren't we going to Zürich?" Peter asked.

"We don't have time to buy tickets. We must get out of the train station." He stepped forward, with his arm around Peter's shoulder. Anna and her mother walked close behind, arm in arm. Each was carrying a little travel valise, but Anna realized that her father and Peter didn't have theirs.

Anna looked back to see a policeman—Swiss—step into the big hall from the platform they had just left. He was staring about, but clearly he didn't know whom he was looking for.

"Smile at me," Anna said to her mother. And Anna laughed.

"What?"

"Say something to me. Anything. Act natural. Papa, look back at me and laugh."

Brother Stoltz turned and nodded, laughed a little.

Anna laughed louder. "It *has* been a nice day," she said.

And then they were at the doors, out of the building and into the dusk—into a city with more lights on than Anna had seen in a long time. She actually wished it were darker.

"Let's get away from here," Brother Stoltz said. "The local police might look for us. They have no idea why we . . . did that. If Reinert has come to by now, the police might have a description of us. There's a hotel up the street. Let's go there."

And so they kept moving fast. As they turned and walked into the hotel, they all looked back. Anna saw no sign of anyone following, no police cars coming up the street. The little hotel seemed classy, very well kept. A pleasant young woman—a little heavy, with rounded cheeks—looked up at them as they crossed the small lobby. She smiled and said, "Good evening."

"Good evening. We would like a room for the four of us, if you have something."

"We have two small rooms close together."

"Yes. That would be fine."

"Do you have your travel cards, please?"

"We have passports. We are German."

Anna saw a sternness come into the woman's face as she sat up straight, and in a less friendly voice she said, "You must have travel papers."

"Yes. We have those." Brother Stoltz placed his papers on the desk.

The young woman glanced over them, but then she said, "I'm sorry. These are not Swiss papers. I cannot help you."

"But we—"

"I'm sorry. You must have permission to travel in Switzerland."

"Young woman, I will tell you the truth. The Gestapo is pursuing us. We are considered enemies of the state in Germany. We have opposed the Nazi Party. These papers say that I'm a military officer, but I am not. We need a place to stay for a night or two, and then we'll move on. But if you send us back to the streets right now, you may be sending us to our deaths."

For a few seconds she seemed to consider. She looked at Anna, and then she looked at Sister Stoltz, who had begun to cry. "Please help us," Sister Stoltz said.

Anna saw the woman reach her decision. Her eyes softened, and she leaned forward. "It's all right," she said. "You may have the two rooms."

And so Brother Stoltz paid with the Swiss francs he had obtained from his underground contacts, and the Stoltzes climbed the stairs to the rooms. But for the present they opened only one door, and they all went inside and sat down. Anna could see that everyone was undone. The stress was finally coming home.

Peter sat on one of the two single beds and stared at the floor. "Will the police keep looking for us?" he asked.

"I don't know," Brother Stoltz said.

"Did I kill that man?"

His mother got up and went to him, sat by him and took him in her arms. "You only did what you had to do," she said. "You saved our lives."

"I don't care if I killed him," Peter said, but his face looked gray, and his eyes were wide and fixed, as though he were in shock.

Anna saw that her mother was finding her strength now. She obviously knew that she had to help Peter through this.

"I was the one who made the decision to fight—to hurt him if I had to," Brother Stoltz said. "You only came to my aid."

"What will happen to us now?" Peter asked, his voice still hollow.

"We'll try to disappear in Switzerland, if we can."

"Aren't we going to Zürich now, the way we planned?" Anna asked.

"I don't know," Brother Stoltz said. "I dropped my valise in the struggle. Our false papers—our Swiss identity cards—were in it. That makes travel difficult, but it also makes for other problems. By now, the Gestapo must have the papers, with our pictures. It won't be long until they make the connection and determine who we are."

"But you said they couldn't come after us here," Anna said.

"Officially, they can't. But if Kellerman learns of this—as I assume he will—he may not be willing to give up the chase."

"So what can we do?" Sister Stoltz asked.

"I don't know. Switzerland won't give us asylum. That would compromise their neutrality. Maybe we can find an American or British consulate. Maybe they will help us. That's the only thing I can think to try."

Everyone was silent. Anna knew they were all thinking the same thing: the nightmare they had been living for such a long time was still not over.

2 5

Brother Stoltz didn't sleep well. He considered every aspect of the predicament he had led his family into. Over and over, as he lay awake, he thanked the Lord that his wife and children had made it this far. And all night, he pleaded for further guidance.

He was relieved when the sun began to rise, but it seemed forever until his exhausted family awakened. He hurried them along at that point, and they all went downstairs and ate in a little breakfast room. Then Brother Stoltz stepped to the front desk and asked whether there were a British or American consulate in Basel.

"The British consulate is not far from here," the man at the desk said. And he gave Brother Stoltz directions to Bahrfusser Platz and a large old mansion nearby.

The nearness of the consulate seemed providential, and so Brother Stoltz waited again, feeling his nervousness build. But at nine o'clock he left his family at the hotel and walked out the front doors. He glanced around, saw no one paying attention to him, and walked to the consulate. He stopped to look into store windows along the way, and each time looked back to see whether he was being followed, but he saw nothing suspicious. When he reached the consulate, therefore, he strode up the front walk and rang the doorbell. In a moment a young man opened the door. "May I help you?" he asked in English.

"Yes," Brother Stoltz said. "I must speak with someone. I need help. My family is in danger."

"Are you Swiss?" the man asked.

"No. German."

"What is it you want?"

"Could I come in?" Brother Stoltz asked. "Could I speak to someone in authority? I need help, but I also have valuable information to give you."

The young man hesitated, but then he stepped back. He was wearing a handsome pin-striped suit that seemed a bit too big for him, as though his frame couldn't quite fill up the wide shoulders. "Yes. Come in. You might have a bit of a wait before someone can see you."

"That is understandable."

But the wait lasted nearly half an hour and seemed twice that long. Eventually, however, the young man led Brother Stoltz up a flight of stairs to an office door. A tall, well-dressed man of about forty stood up and came around his desk. "Come in, sir," he said in German. "Tell me your name." There was something sagacious in the way he looked at Brother Stoltz, as though he were taking everything in, making an assessment.

"Heinrich Stoltz. I escaped from Germany only last night," he answered in German. "My wife and two children are with me."

"Please. Take a seat." The man walked around the desk and sat down. He didn't shake hands, didn't introduce himself. He seemed cordial enough, but wary. "Why would you come to us?"

Brother Stoltz took a breath and then took hold of the arms of his chair. "I must take a moment and explain, if it's all right."

"Yes. Please do."

Brother Stoltz decided to start from the beginning. He told

about Kellerman's attempted rape, about the years of hiding, and he told about harboring Jews in Berlin. Then he described the harrowing escape from Germany and the Gestapo agent he and Peter had knocked from the platform in the Basel train station. Finally, he said, "We intended to hide out in Switzerland, where we thought we might be safe. But now we have no travel papers, and after our trouble with the Gestapo agent, I'm not certain the Swiss government will allow us to stay. This is the only place I could think of where we might look for help."

"This is difficult," the man said. He crossed his arms and cocked his head to one side, and he remained in that position for some time. "Here is the problem," he finally said. "Most Swiss hate the Nazis—especially these Gestapo agents who strut about in the Basel train station—but the government must protect its neutrality. Local police, if they find you, may feel that they have to turn you over to Germany. You've entered this country with false papers, and you've attacked an official— one who does have authority within the confines of the train station."

"What can we do, then?"

"I'm not certain. Why did you think we might be able to help you?"

"We have been fighting Hitler, the same as you. I have intelligence you can use. I know about the underground in Berlin. I have firsthand knowledge about the treatment of Jews in Germany. I know where defense installations are in Berlin. Some are camouflaged very well, and your bombers are missing them. I could draw maps to show you where they are. Perhaps, in exchange for such information, you could help us get papers so that we can stay in Switzerland."

Again the man sat with his arms folded. He was wearing a dark brown suit, with a vest, and a well-starched white shirt. Something in his formality, his correctness, was very worrisome to Brother Stoltz.

"Herr Stoltz, let me be very frank with you. We have had

354 • D E A N H U G H E S

other Germans come to us. Some of them have been spies. They offer us bits of information, and they all claim to be Nazi haters. They usually want our help in attaining permission to stay in Switzerland. But the simple matter is, we have virtually no way to give you asylum here."

Brother Stoltz nodded. "I understand," he said. "Please, though, try to think what we're facing. It should be easy enough to check our story. We did fight with a Gestapo agent in the Basel train station, and we did injure him. He may be dead. That puts us in league with the Allies. If we can't turn to you, whom can we turn to?"

The man leaned forward and for the first time appeared sympathetic. "Let me speak to someone," he said. "While I'm gone, please begin to sketch out the maps of Berlin and the defense installations you spoke of. Will you do that?"

"Yes. Certainly. But I hope you understand what I'm doing. I know people who work in these factories. If you bomb them, I am putting their lives in danger."

"And if we don't bomb them, British lives continue to be in danger. Tell me *now* which side you are choosing. If you can't do that, you might as well leave."

Brother Stoltz had long known that it might come to this. He never wanted to be an enemy to his own people, only to Hitler, but the choice wasn't that easy. And so he said, "I'll give you the information," and the official left the room.

Brother Stoltz sketched the maps as best he could. He told himself that when the raids came, the workers would move into bomb shelters, but he knew the advanced warning wasn't always adequate. He pictured the bombs dropping, the noise and chaos of it all, the danger to innocent people, and what he felt was a deep sense of guilt, no matter how he justified his actions.

The consulate officer was gone for a long time. When he came back, he sat in his chair behind his desk again. "We have contacts in the local police department," he said. "They verify your story. The Gestapo agent you pushed off the platform is not dead, but his back is broken. He's in very serious condition. The Swiss police have pictures of you—from the false papers you lost—and they have promised to search for you. They may not be terribly committed to that search. I don't know. But I would suggest you get back to your hotel immediately—before your family is located."

"But what can we do?"

"Here's the problem. This building is watched closely by Swiss security police. They are always nervous about spy activity—because of their neutrality. When you entered this building, you were certainly observed. If someone recognized you, you may be picked up as you leave and then turned over to the Gestapo. It's true that the Swiss see that the Allies are taking control of the war, which works in your favor, and I have tried to convince the local police to leave you alone—but I can't promise anything."

"Is there a way to get papers, or to lose ourselves somewhere in the country?"

"That's the other matter I've considered with my superiors. We simply don't feel you are safe in Switzerland. Even if the police don't turn you over, German spies will try to track you down. We can provide you with temporary travel papers but nothing more. We suggest you use the papers to get to Geneva, and that you leave Switzerland and enter "free France.""

"But the Vichy government cooperates with the Nazis."

"Yes. We're not suggesting that you do this officially. What we can do—and we have to be careful about this—is to put you in touch with the French Resistance. We know people who can guide you across the border into France and then hide you. This is what downed British pilots do. The usual route from there is a long hike, with a guide, over the Pyrenees mountains. Crossing Spain is not difficult, and once you reach Gibraltar, we have contacts who can get you to England. We want your information, but we don't think you should stay here long. If you could get to Geneva soon, perhaps by tomorrow, the Resistance can meet you and take over from there."

"As I told you before, I was beaten severely by the Gestapo. I have never recovered entirely. I don't know whether I could make the hike over the Pyrenees that you speak of."

"Yes. I thought of that. In your case, we might have to go about this in a different way. The Resistance has been known to hide people for lengthy periods, when necessary. As everyone in the world knows, the Allies will soon attack across the channel. The landing is likely to be in the north. Most experts guess that it will be across the Pas de Calais. German troops may begin to abandon the south, and then—we hope—travel across France will be much easier."

"In any case, you think we will be safer in France than in Switzerland?"

"Not exactly. But we can't hide you. That would get us in trouble with the Swiss. The Resistance people aren't worried about pleasing Petain and the Vichy government."

"How will we do this, then?"

"First, finish your sketches. Quickly. And I have some questions I want to ask you about the underground in Berlin. Then we'll try to take you out a back way, in an automobile. We'll drop you off within walking distance of your hotel—but not directly by it. Before the day is over, someone will contact you with travel papers and a prearranged meeting place in Geneva. We'll also have the name of a contact you can make in England, should you get there."

"How should we travel?"

"Don't go back to the train station. That's the last place you want to be seen. There are buses you can take. We'll buy tickets for you."

"Thank you." Brother Stoltz felt tears filling his eyes. "We've only made it this far by a series of miracles. Now, we need a few more."

"Or at least some good luck. I wish you that."

An hour later Brother Stoltz was back at the little hotel. He was relieved to find his family nervous but well. Later that day a messenger brought the information and papers the Stoltzes needed. The plan was to leave the next morning, early. The bus departed at 7:40. The trip was only about 250 kilometers, but it took most of the day, with many little stops along the route.

All evening—even all night—Brother Stoltz waited for a knock on the door. He hadn't told his family everything; they didn't know about the danger of local police cooperation with the Gestapo. But the night passed slowly away, and for a time Brother Stoltz actually slept. At six, however, he got everyone up. He had purchased rolls and butter and marmalade the night before, so the Stoltzes ate quickly and then exited the hotel by a back entrance into an alley.

They looked nervously about, saw no one, and then began the walk toward the end of the alley, where it intersected with a main street. The city was quiet at this early hour, and sounds carried long distances. When Brother Stoltz first heard footsteps, he hoped they were an echo of their own. But he looked back and saw two men. They both appeared to be laborers, perhaps city employees, in coveralls. But where had they come from?

"Just keep walking," Brother Stoltz said. But he didn't like the feel of this. The men were walking in their direction, a little faster than the Stoltzes.

And then two men in suits and hats entered the alley ahead of them. Brother Stoltz turned and grabbed the back door to a building, but the door was locked. He spun and looked both ways, but now the men were closing in fast from both directions. There was nowhere to run.

"Stop right there," one of the men said. His hand was in his coat pocket. He raised it toward them, and Brother Stoltz could see the shape of a pistol barrel. "You will go with us," he said. His dialect was German, not Swiss.

"Who are you? What do you want?" Brother Stoltz said.

"My name is Breitinger, if you wish to know. We are agents of the Gestapo." He smiled, and his satisfaction was obvious. He was a square-jawed, athletic-looking man.

The man next to him, also wearing a suit, seemed less secure. His dark eyes kept darting about. "Come. This way," he said.

"You have no authority here. You can't do this."

"We have something better than authority," Breitinger said. "We have guns." He pulled out his pistol—a Lüger—to prove his point, and then he tucked it back into his pocket. "We can shoot all four of you and be gone before anyone sees us. Is that what you want, or would you rather walk to the train station with us? In Germany at least you will receive a trial. Perhaps the women and this young man will receive mercy."

Brother Stoltz knew better than to trust Nazi mercy, but he also knew that the agents were not bluffing. "All right. We'll go to the train station with you." He put his arm around his wife's shoulder. "It's all right," he said to her, although he knew that wasn't true. He saw the sad acceptance in her eyes, saw Peter's look of desperation, saw Anna's heartbreak, and he knew he had to think of something. He was the one who had promised to keep them safe.

"Go back the other way," Breitinger told the two men in coveralls, and then he motioned the Stoltzes toward the end of the alley. "Walk ahead. This way," he said.

Brother Stoltz walked with his arm around his wife, his children in front. Breitinger and his partner walked close behind. They reached the *Bahnhof* in only a few minutes, and they entered through the big front doors. By then Brother Stoltz had something of a plan in mind, but it didn't fall into place until he saw two Swiss policemen standing in the middle of the large, almost empty hall. As the group entered the hall, Breitinger said, "Turn right here."

Brother Stoltz suddenly called out, "Police! We need your help." And then to his family. "Go to them. Walk fast."

"Stop here," Breitinger commanded.

But Brother Stoltz said, "Keep walking." Then he called out again, "Help! Police."

The two policemen walked toward them, closing the gap. Both had rifles, which they simultaneously pulled off their shoulders, ready for use. Brother Stoltz had gambled that the Gestapo agents wouldn't shoot, but he felt the terror that any second he would hear the bullets, feel them in his back.

It didn't happen, and the three groups came together in the large open hall. "These men are Gestapo agents," Brother Stoltz said. "They came outside the train station and arrested us illegally."

"These are the people who pushed our agent off the platform," Breitinger said. "We are taking them back to Germany for a trial."

"Don't let them take us," Brother Stoltz gasped. "We have resisted the Nazis in Germany. They want to take us across the border and then kill us."

The policemen looked confused. They glanced back and forth from Brother Stoltz to the two agents, who had stepped up alongside the Stoltzes. One of the policemen was a small man, older, with bushy gray eyebrows. "Is it true? Are you the ones who pushed the agent onto the tracks?"

"Yes. We escaped Germany. We fought the Gestapo agent and knocked him off the platform. We admit to all that. Arrest us for our crime. Keep us here. If you send us back to Germany, you know what they will do to us."

Brother Stoltz saw the older policeman glance toward the younger, bigger one. But no decision passed between their eyes. At the same time, Brother Stoltz heard footsteps behind him, and then a voice. "So. Family Stoltz. So nice to see you after all this time." There was no mistaking the voice. It was Kellerman, with the horrible scar across his face, who stepped up next to the policemen. "I've gone to a good deal of trouble to be here," he said. "I received a call last night—after your pictures identified you—and I drove all night. But it's well worth the trouble. I can't tell you how much I've wanted to see you."

Kellerman turned toward the Swiss officers. The Stoltzes were bunched tightly together, Kellerman to their left, the other two agents to the right, and the Swiss policeman straight across from them. The group formed something close to a square, but Brother Stoltz didn't like the formation. The three agents could all too easily step in and cut off the Stoltzes from the police.

"Tell me your name, officer," Kellerman said to the older man.

"Kissel," the officer said.

"Herr Kissel, we'll take care of this. The crime was committed against our people. These are German citizens who have entered your country illegally. The entire matter belongs to us."

Kellerman looked at Anna. "It's especially nice to see you," he said. "It's something I've been looking forward to. You're prettier than ever." He nodded and lifted his hat, as if to give her a clearer look at the scar across his cheek and lips.

"This man tried to rape my daughter," Brother Stoltz said. "She cut his face, as you see, and he has never stopped chasing us."

Kellerman smiled, his lip curling into a grotesque shape. "Herr Kissel, these people are liars," he said. "You know about the agent they attacked. The man may be paralyzed for life. Our duty is to return the entire family to Germany, where they will receive a fair trial."

The little policeman was about to speak when Brother Stoltz said, "You know we will never receive that. Consider us defectors. We have British travel papers." He pulled them from his pocket.

"Officer Kissel, you have no rights in this matter,"

Kellerman told the policeman. "Those papers mean nothing." He reached to take hold of Anna's arm.

"Don't touch anyone," the little policeman said, with surprising power.

"I will not only touch them; I will take them with me," Kellerman said. "These two agents both have pistols in their pockets, and you see mine right here." He put his hand on his holster. The agents slipped their hands into their coat pockets. "We don't want to use our weapons, but we will, if we must."

Kissel had been pointing his rifle toward the floor, but now he brought it up, aimed it at Kellerman. "Let me look at these papers," he said. At the same time, the other policeman had raised his rifle toward the other agents, and now, with a loud click, he swung the bolt and drove a bullet into the chamber.

"I've already told you, you have no—"

"I'm going to look at these papers!"

Kissel took a long look, and Kellerman waited. Brother Stoltz saw the weakness in Kellerman's eyes, the fear. He seemed almost desperate.

"These papers are in order," Kissel said. "I cannot let you take these people."

"They are criminals."

"That may be true. So I'm arresting them. Switzerland will try them for their crimes."

"But the crime happened *here*, where we have jurisdiction."

"*Joint* jurisdiction."

Kissel snapped the bolt and sent a round into his own rifle's chamber, and then he stepped a little closer to Kellerman. "My country may be neutral, but let me say this. Crimes against the German state make these people heroes in most parts of the world—perhaps even to me, personally. If you did try to rape this young woman—and this is not difficult for me to believe—then I am only sorry that she didn't kill you. Now, step back before I do it for her. I am arresting this family."

"Don't either of you move," the other policeman said to the two agents.

Then Kissel told Kellerman, "Move over there with the other two."

"You can't get away with this," Kellerman said. "My country can *crush* yours any time it chooses."

"I believe your country has all it can handle right now. Before long it will be Germany that is *crushed.*"

"You shoot me, and you have created an international incident. The Führer might think again about your *neutrality.*"

"Oh, I doubt that. Even Hitler, degenerate madman that he is, wouldn't bother about someone like you."

"You've gone too far now. I won't let you get away with this."

But Kellerman didn't make a move for his weapon, and again Brother Stoltz saw the fear in his eyes. Anna moved back a little, pushed in closer against her mother. Peter was pressed against Brother Stoltz's side, the four of them stiff, tense, all locked together.

Kissel stepped forward, watching carefully, and then he commanded, "Get over there with the others."

Slowly Kellerman moved to that side. But he said to his comrades. "Go ahead. Shoot them both. Pull your triggers."

Brother Stoltz saw the indecision in the agents' eyes. Breitinger seemed to be measuring his chances. The other agent looked close to panic.

The big policeman had raised his rifle to his shoulder, and he had his finger on the trigger. At any moment, everything could explode.

"I want you to lie down on the floor," Kissel said. "I'm taking these people away. Get down. Now."

"Shoot them," Kellerman said, but not with strength. He was begging.

Ten seconds went by. Fifteen. And no one moved.

"Pull your hands from your pockets and lie down. Now!" Kissel said.

And the big policeman, in a deep voice, echoed the command. "*Now!*"

"These people aren't worth it," Breitinger whispered to his partner. He pulled his hand free from his pocket and began to bend his knees in a slow descent toward the floor.

Kellerman looked frantic. "Shoot them!" he said. But the other agent pulled his hand from his pocket, and he also crouched toward the floor.

Kellerman stood his ground, but he didn't make a move for his pistol, which was buckled into his holster.

"Get down," Kissel demanded.

"You don't have the courage to shoot me," Kellerman said. "*I* do," the young policeman said. "I would enjoy it."

It was said matter-of-factly, simply, and Kellerman seemed to accept the words at face value.

"For the last time, get down," Kissel said.

Slowly, Kellerman sank to his knees. But he stopped at that point, and his ugly lip curled back again. "I'll track you down yet. This isn't the end. I promise you."

"But it is," Brother Stoltz said. "You are so pitiful I don't even hate you anymore."

"Get down," Kissel demanded one more time, and Kellerman lay on his chest.

Kissel nodded to the Stoltzes. "All right. Let's go. You're under arrest," he said. They all walked briskly toward the front doors. But at the doors, Brother Stoltz looked back.

The young policeman was still standing over Kellerman and the others, with his rifle ready. Two more Swiss policemen were hurrying toward the scene. Kellerman's head was up, his distorted face full of rage. When he saw Brother Stoltz looking back, he cursed him and then let his face rest on the floor.

Once outside, Kissel looked at Brother Stoltz. "Do you know where you're going?" he asked.

"Yes."

"All right. Then go. I won't arrest you, but I also can't help you at this point."

"We'll be all right. Thank you so much," Brother Stoltz said. "You didn't have to believe us."

"I had to make a choice," was all Kissel said. "Good luck."

· C H A P T E R ·

2 6

It was Sunday, June 4. Alex's regiment had been trucked to a temporary camp that was set up in a field next to an airstrip in southwestern England, about ten miles from the coast. The nearest village was a little place called Uppottery. Barbed-wire fences encircled the camp, and armed guards stood at the gates. Soldiers couldn't leave for any reason now, couldn't make phone calls or send letters, and only authorized personnel were allowed to enter. All the security was to protect the secret: the invasion was finally about to begin. D day.

But a driving rain, whipped by a hard wind, was beating against Alex's tent. He kept thinking that a night drop was frightening enough without weather conditions like this. The airborne units would be jumping into Normandy ahead of the infantry, which would hit the beaches at six in the morning. The paratroopers would board their planes at about ten o'clock that night, take off before midnight, and then circle until they could link up with a massive air fleet of C-47s. A total of 13,400 troops from the 82nd and 101st Airborne Divisions would parachute or land gliders in the Cotentin Peninsula behind a beach that was code-named "Utah." The name had seemed appropriate to Alex when he had first heard it, but now he wished he could get all this over with so he could return to his own Utah.

During the afternoon, General Maxwell Taylor had circulated through the compound and stopped anywhere he saw groups of soldiers. He stepped into the mess tent and brought everyone to sudden attention, but then he shook hands with all the men. "Sergeant," he told Alex, "I need three days and nights of hard fighting from you and your men—and I need you to meet your objectives. After that, we'll pull you out and let the ground troops take over." Alex hadn't met a lot of generals. He stood erect, and he told General Maxwell, firmly, that his men would give it all they had. But later, what Alex told himself was that three days didn't sound so bad. He could do that.

All day everyone had been packing equipment, cleaning rifles, sharpening knives—and then starting all over, just to kill time. The men were smoking so much that Alex had to step outside the tent into the rain at times, just to clear his lungs. Some of the men tried to cover their tension with tough talk, and some shaved their heads and painted their faces green and black—to look like war paint, they said—but most had grown quiet, and an unusually high number had attended church services that morning. Alex did use charcoal to shade his face, but he still had a hard time imagining that he could be a fierce warrior. All the training—all the war games—had been one thing, but he had no idea how he would react when the fighting started.

Alex was bivouacked with his entire squad in a large, pyramid-shaped troop tent. Cots were crowded close, and with the bad weather, the men were cooped up all day. Still, there was little of the usual hassling and joking. General Taylor had spoken to the troops the day before and detailed the landing. "A good many of you will sacrifice your lives in this invasion," he had told them, and every man must have thought, as Alex had, "Will I be one of them?" Alex's inner trust was that somehow he would survive, but he knew that others felt the same way—and the truth was, some were going to die before their feet touched the ground, and many more would be gone before the sun came up.

Like most of the men, Alex was overstuffing his uniform pockets, his pack, his musette bag, and the special leg bag that the jumpers were using for the first time. He was carrying a flashlight, maps, K rations, socks, underwear, a compass, a razor, an emergency ration of candy bars, a pocketknife, and ten French francs printed in America. In the leg bag, which would be attached to his parachute harness with a twenty-foot rope, he had packed ammunition, two fragmentation grenades, a smoke grenade, an antitank mine, and a Gammon antitank bomb. When he got ready to go, he would strap on his canteen, shovel, first-aid kit, and a .45 pistol, and then he would don his jump jacket and pull his parachute harness over that, with the main chute pack on his back and a reserve chute in front. He would also strap his M-1 rifle under his reserve shoot, diagonally across his chest, so that he could keep his hands free to work the risers on his parachute. Then he would tie his gas mask on one leg and a jump knife on the other, and sling his musette bag on so it hung over his chest. On top of everything else, his Mae West life jacket would have to fit somehow.

The men's long underwear and uniforms were impregnated with a substance that was supposed to protect the soldiers from chemical attacks, but the stuff stank, and it made the uniforms hot and itchy. Alex kept switching equipment around, and with all the effort he was sweating badly. All the men were doing the same—and that didn't help the smell in the tent. Everyone had a different opinion about how best to pack, but what Alex knew was that discussing equipment was infinitely better than talking about what they could expect that night. The men had been through a lot together, and now they were going to depend on each other for their lives. Personality differences now seemed rather insignificant compared to what they were about to face.

Alex had come to like these men—even if they were annoying at times. They had pushed themselves through months and months of hard training, and they were linked to each other in a way that Alex had never before experienced. He had now been in the army almost as long as he had been in the mission field, nearly two years, and he had kept most of these same companions all the way through. What worried him was that in the next few days he would make decisions that would affect their lives.

Early in the evening Alex decided to stop fussing with his equipment and write some letters. He had to be realistic, and so he told himself that if he didn't come back, he at least wanted a letter to get to his parents, to Bobbi, to Gene, eventually to Wally, and, of course, to Anna. He decided he would simply address Anna's letter to his home, and then, if things didn't turn out well for him, she might at least receive this last word someday. "I believe I'll see you again," he told her, "and that we will be married. It's all I've wanted for five years now. I'm aware, however, that something could happen to you or to me. If it does, I hope we can be together in the next life. . . ."

But he tore that letter up. It wasn't fair to her. If he died, maybe she would feel she couldn't marry anyone else. He knew he couldn't ask that of her. So he wrote another letter, softened it a little, told her he loved her, admitted his concern that he might not see her, but didn't speculate about the future.

Austin Campbell had stopped fidgeting with his equipment and had lain back on his cot. He had been quiet for a long time, but Alex knew he wasn't asleep. When Alex finished his letters, he began to address the envelopes. Campbell said, "Hey, Deacon, I sure hope you're praying for us." He laughed.

"Don't worry, I am," Alex said in the same tone.

But Tom McCoy walked over and stood at the foot of

Alex's cot. "Thomas, do you really believe in heaven?" he asked, and he seemed serious.

"Yes, I do."

"With angels and harps and all that? People floating around in the clouds?"

"No."

"What then?"

"It's a lot like this life. People keep learning."

"Who gets in?" Duncan asked. He was at the far end of the tent, and he spoke in his usual booming voice. "Just guys like you, who don't drink and smoke and chase dames?"

Alex sat up straight and looked at Duncan. He didn't want to sound pious. "I can only tell you what Mormons believe," he said. "Christ died for all of us, and everyone will be resurrected. So we *all* get in. But people who accept the gospel and live a righteous life will receive the highest glory."

Duncan didn't say anything for the moment. He was looking down at his pack, which was lying on the floor. When he finally did speak, his voice didn't carry any acrimony. "So are you the only one in the squad who's going to this place of glory?"

"God decides that, Duncan," Alex said. "I have enough problems of my own to worry about—without judging others."

"What problems have you got, Deacon?"

Alex was being drawn in a direction he wasn't sure he wanted to go, but he answered. "I don't always treat people the way a Christian should." He smiled. "Like the time I slugged you in the nose."

Duncan laughed, quietly, but then he said, "But tonight, if some Kraut gets in your way, you're supposed to cut his throat. Is that what Jesus wants you to do?"

All the men stopped what they were doing. Alex knew these were boys who, for the most part, had been raised in religious homes. He suspected that they also had their regrets about the way they had been living since they had left home.

All of them had to be thinking not only about the danger they were facing but about killing for the first time.

"I'm sure Christ doesn't want us to kill," Alex said. "He must be sick to see his brothers and sisters destroying each other this way. But there are times when people have to fight for what's right." He hesitated, not sure whether he should say it, but then he added, "In the Book of Mormon there are some great warriors who fight against evil—and they fight with the spirit of God in them."

"Is that what you're going to do, Thomas?" Duncan asked. "Fight with God inside you?" His tone was not sarcastic but certainly challenging.

"I don't know, Duncan," Alex said. "I hope so."

"If that's what it takes, most of us guys are in trouble," Lester Cox said, and he tried to laugh.

No one else commented, and a long silence followed. But this worried Alex. These guys might have to kill tonight—or be killed. "Look, you guys," he said, "I don't think we have to analyze this thing to death. We know what we're fighting for, and we're well trained. We have clear objectives, and we'd better make sure we get those accomplished—no matter what it takes."

"But you still want to kill Germans and not hate them, don't you, Thomas?" Duncan said.

"Yes," Alex said. "I don't want to hate anyone."

"Well, I may go to hell then. And you may go to heaven. But I'm going to hate the Krauts, and I'm going to kill all I can. And I think that's what it's going to take."

"So you're still not sure I ought to be leading you guys?"

"I'm not saying that. You're probably the best guy to figure out where we're going and how to get there. And you'll remember all our training. But I think you'll be dead before long—unless you forget all this love stuff." He cursed the Germans in some very foul language and then added, "We need to hate tonight, no matter what Jesus might think of us."

Alex was chilled by the thought, and he wasn't sure what to say. He thought of trying to make a distinction between hating evil and hating people, but he wasn't at all sure he could live by that standard himself.

"Here's my plan," Duncan said. "I'm going to leave a path of destruction. I ain't going in scared. And I ain't going to ask a lot of questions. I'm going to kill every Jerry I can, and I'll worry what God thinks of me after it's all over."

Calvin Huish had been lying on his cot during all this, showing no apparent interest. "I don't think anyone knows what he'll do until he gets there," he said with his usual tone of superiority. "It's easy to make claims. We'll know tomorrow night who has a stomach for killing—and who doesn't."

"You'd better hope one of us doesn't have a stomach for killing *you*," Duncan said. "I've thought about it a lot of times." Duncan laughed loudly, and so did the others. But strangely, Duncan and Huish had actually become friends. Huish made fun of Duncan for his ignorance, but when weekend passes came out, Huish usually tagged along with Duncan and Rizzardi. Maybe he felt protected when he was with them, or maybe he liked getting drunk with some guys who knew how. Alex had no way to explain the strange friendships that had formed.

"My plan," Curtis said, "is to go in scared and stay scared till I get my feet back on some red Georgia clay. If you guys are looking for a hero, it ain't going to be me."

This seemed to release some tension. Dale Huff, who was sitting on his bunk near the door to the tent, said, "Duncan can be our hero. We'll send him out first to blaze his path of destruction. Then we'll move in behind him."

This set off a brief exchange of insults, but it didn't last long. The soldiers went back to their repacking and smoking. Alex used the chance to say, "Men, I just want to tell you one thing." He waited until everyone got quiet. "We don't need heroes. We need to get the job done, and we need to keep each other alive. Let's all make it through together. That's something we can all believe in."

"I'll buy that," Duncan said.

"From what I hear," Rizzardi said, "a good unit, fighting together, has the best chance of making it."

This was not the sort of thing Alex expected from Rizzardi. Everyone seemed changed today. But it was Campbell who surprised Alex even more. "Sergeant Thomas," he said, "you're going to pray before you get on the plane tonight, aren't you?"

"Sure."

"I was just thinking you could maybe say a prayer for all of us while we're here together." He laughed, sounding embarrassed. "You know—you're the Deacon."

"I don't know whether everyone would want that, Campbell," Alex said.

No one said a word. Alex looked around at the men, and one after the other, they nodded, even Duncan. Only Huish refused to look in Alex's direction. But he raised no objection. "Do you want me to do that now?" Alex asked.

A couple of the men said, "Sure."

And so they sat on their cots, or some knelt when Alex did, and Alex asked the Lord to go with them, to give them courage and the ability to accept what came. "We ask that we all might live and return to our families," Alex said, "but we realize that some of us may be asked to offer the ultimate sacrifice. Please, Father, accept this gift if we are called upon to give it, and bring us to our heavenly home, to dwell with thee."

When the prayer was over, no one said a word. The men went back to what they had been doing. But they turned increasingly inside themselves as the time for boarding approached. Alex felt the tension around him, and he felt it in his chest, but he kept telling himself not to think, to do what he had to do, and simply rely on the Lord for the outcome.

And then Lieutenant Summers stepped into the tent. "Boys, I'm sorry to tell you this, but the invasion is off for tonight. The weather over the channel is way too bad for the LSTs to land on the beaches. We'll probably go tomorrow night."

Alex felt a momentary sense of relief, and then the thought of waiting for another twenty-four hours hit him. He wondered whether he could stand it. All the men seemed to react the same way. They stood in stunned silence for a few seconds, and then these same guys who had wanted to pray not long before began to curse their fate in the most vile language they knew.

* * *

The Stoltzes crouched in a little thicket of trees and waited. It was Monday morning. Rain was pelting down rather hard now, and everyone was soaked through to the skin. Anna was wearing a man's heavy wool jacket, but her jaw kept trembling from the cold—and maybe the fear. She wondered how many more times she and her family could deal with such danger and continue to survive.

"All right, listen to me," the guide whispered, in excellent German. He had told them earlier that he was French, by birth, but he had grown up in Switzerland and spoke German and French equally well. "The weather is miserable—but it helps us. The guards don't like to walk about in the rain any more than we do. They stay closer to their sentry stations. Follow me in a line, but leave about ten paces between each of you. Peter, I want you to come last. You can help your father, if you have to."

"How far off is the border?" Brother Stoltz asked.

"Not far. Two hundred meters, perhaps. The sentry stations run all along the border, every hundred meters or so. The guards walk a path between the stations, just inside France. Once we cross the path, we are not out of danger, however. The Germans sometimes send out patrols. One never knows when they may show up."

"What do we do if we meet up with guards?" Brother Stoltz asked.

"Each case is different. Simply do what I do. Follow me, try to be absolutely silent, and stop whenever I stop. If I take cover, do the same. Find something—a rock, a tree, a bush—and lie down flat behind it. We'll be in trees at first, but at the border there's an open meadow. If I wait for a long time, trust me. I know what I'm doing." He laughed softly. "If something goes wrong, head back the way we came. They can't pursue us very far into Switzerland."

"Will you tell us if—"

"I won't speak at all. We must be quiet. If we make an accidental noise, I usually make a sound like a crow—for cover. But crows have better sense than to come out in weather like this. The sound of the rain will have to be our cover today."

That explained one thing. When the Stoltzes had made contact with this man—at a cafe in a village called Bure—he had told them it was just as well they not know his name. "Call me Crow," he had said. "That's how I'm known to those who do this work." He had also admitted, quite frankly, that he hadn't been overly happy to help Germans. But he added, "They told me that you knocked a Gestapo agent off a railroad platform and broke his back. I liked you immediately after that." He laughed, and he looked at Anna as though *she* were the one who had knocked the man down. Anna didn't like to think of the Gestapo agent, perhaps paralyzed, but she couldn't help smiling at Crow, who was so unabashed in his partisan loyalties.

Crow was a dark-eyed, small young man who seemed too forthright to be so cunning, but even at the cafe Anna had noticed how he moved—as though he walked on paws. Now, as he motioned for them to follow, he slipped stealthily through the trees, and he seemed a panther.

At first he worked his way steadily ahead. But as he approached the border, he began to stop and listen. Sister Stoltz was following him, and Anna came after her. Anna glanced back from time to time at her father and Peter. Peter would nod each time as if to let her know that he was confident, not afraid. Anna knew how much he wanted to show that he was grown up. Brother Stoltz would also nod, but Anna could see the pain in his face. They were in a thick growth of fir trees now, and getting through sometimes meant crouching below the limbs. Bending was not easy for her father.

Crow moved to the edge of the woods and waited. Beyond him, Anna could see an open area. It seemed clear, and while she feared moving into it, she wished they could get this most dangerous section of their journey behind them. But the wait continued, and then, suddenly, Crow dropped to the ground and hid in the undergrowth on the edge of the forest. Anna saw her mother drop too, and Anna did the same. She lay on her stomach in the shadows of a fir tree, where she could see slices of light through the forest, but she saw nothing ahead, heard nothing. She couldn't imagine what had alarmed Crow.

He didn't move, however, and a long time passed—ten minutes or more. Anna could hear her own heart pounding in her ears. And then she saw what Crow had detected. She spotted a German soldier, in a gray uniform, walking across the meadow, coming from the right, passing not five steps in front of Crow's hiding place. Anna knew very little about weapons, but she saw that the soldier was carrying a small machine gun, not a rifle.

On he walked, slowly. He kept looking back and forth along the edge of the woods. And then he stopped. Anna dropped her face into the fir needles on the ground. She didn't think the guard could see so far back into the woods, but his gaze had seemed trained in her direction. She had caught only a brief glimpse of his face, but she was struck with the realization of how young he was—much younger than herself, she thought.

Anna waited for a couple of minutes before she looked up. By then the guard had walked on and was out of sight. But Crow was still waiting. Five or six minutes passed, and then Anna understood. The guard came into sight again, from the left, returning along the path. He seemed less attentive this time. He moved through the opening twice as fast, and then he was gone.

Crow waited another couple of minutes, and then Anna saw him rise to his feet. Sister Stoltz got up, too, and so did Anna. Crow looked back and made a quick little motion with his hand, and then he moved out of the brush and into the open. He walked across the path and into the meadow, where there was almost no cover. He looked back at Sister Stoltz, who was walking fast, catching up with him. He held his palms down, signaling for her to slow, and he held his finger to his lips. Anna knew what Sister Stoltz was going through. The temptation was to run, but Crow knew best. Even in this rain, they couldn't make any noise.

The walk across the meadow was downhill and only a matter of perhaps fifty meters, but it seemed ever so much longer. Anna kept glancing back, terrified that the guard would reappear with his machine gun. When she finally entered the woods, at the bottom of the meadow, she saw Crow and her mother standing in the shadows. She hurried to her mother and grasped her around the waist; then she looked back. Her father was approaching the woods. Peter was nowhere in sight.

And then a dog barked.

Brother Stoltz broke into a run and reached the woods, but then he spun around. "Where's Peter?" he asked, much too loudly.

"He stopped on the other side of the guard's path," Crow said. He must have heard something. He's all right. I'll go back for him when I can. Hurry, now. Follow me." But for the first time, Anna heard fear in his voice.

Crow moved off through the trees, pushing through the lower limbs, moving quickly but carefully. The Stoltzes followed in a line, but now the dog was barking more stridently.

Anna was at the back, with her father, helping to push limbs aside for him. But she pulled him too hard, and he stumbled and dropped to his knees. She pulled at his shoulder, and he expelled a little gasp of pain. He was up quickly and moving again, but Anna could hardly stand not to take off running on her own. The noise they were making seemed loud enough to call in every guard on the border, and the dog was clearly on their trail. Its bark seemed crazed, and it was getting closer.

Suddenly there was a popping noise that came in three quick bursts, and something crashed through the tree limbs. Anna knew that it was machine-gun fire, and she felt herself losing control, fighting ahead faster, pulling too hard on her father.

Then she saw Crow stop and let her mother go by him. As Anna approached with her father, Crow said, "This is the path. Stay on it. Help your father. Run as hard as you can."

Anna stepped into the path. It led straight down the hill. It was covered with wet fir needles and was slippery, but there was nothing to hold them back now. She held her father's arm, and they ran down the hill. They quickly caught up with Sister Stoltz, who was holding her skirt up to her knees, running as best she could, slipping a little at times. Anna didn't know what had happened to Crow.

A hundred meters, two hundred, passed by quickly now that the going was easier. Ahead, Sister Stoltz reached a rock fence with a wooden gate. She grabbed the handle and pulled it open. Just as Anna and her father reached the fence, they heard gunfire and a dog's yelp. Then, nothing.

"What's happening? What can we do for Peter?" Sister Stoltz asked, her voice full of desperation.

Brother Stoltz didn't answer. He stood in the opening and held the gate open. He was looking up the path. "You go on ahead," he said. "Run on down to that thicket of trees."

"What are you going to do?" Sister Stoltz asked.

"I don't know. Maybe Crow needs help."

"Papa, you can't go back up there," Anna said. She stepped

closer and looked up the hill. At any moment the guard, with his machine gun, could appear. They needed to keep moving.

"I can't just leave him," Brother Stoltz said, and he began to stride up the path. "You two go on ahead."

But just then a figure burst from the trees and onto the path. Anna cringed for a second—and then realized that it was Crow. Something in his motion told her that he wasn't being chased. As he loped on down the path, he waved for them to go on through the gate.

Brother Stoltz stepped through the gate, and Crow called ahead, "Run to those trees."

But they all waited, and Brother Stoltz said what everyone was thinking. "What about Peter?"

"Don't worry. I'll go back when I can."

Everyone hurried down through a large pasture. Halfway there, Crow passed the others and called out, "Follow me."

Once they reached the little copse of trees, Crow stopped, and everyone gathered in around him. They were all breathing hard, and for a time no one spoke. The rain was still driving hard, and the wind was stirring the trees. Anna was no longer cold, but she couldn't stop shaking. She watched the gate at the upper end of the pasture, and she wondered, still, whether she would see soldiers chasing after them.

Crow caught his breath faster than the others. "I'm sorry for the scare," he said. "Those guards are not easy to predict."

"How do we get Peter?" Brother Stoltz asked.

"I can't go back yet. I killed that guard—and his dog. I waited, and the fool walked right to me. He must be new. But now everyone will be on alert. Peter was smart enough to stop where he was safe. He'll be smart enough to head back along the path to Bure. I'll go up there once things calm down, and I'll bring him across."

Anna was still thinking about the guard. "Did you have to *kill* him?" she asked.

"Oh, no." He smiled. "I could have let him kill me—and

then perhaps kill you. It didn't strike me as a very good option, however."

"I heard him fire at you," Brother Stoltz said.

"No. When I shot him, he jerked and pulled the trigger on his machine gun, but the bullets fired in the air."

"Are we safe here?" Brother Stoltz asked. "Shouldn't we move on?"

"The guards who find their friend won't come down this far—not after they've seen one of their men ambushed."

"What if they found Peter? Maybe another dog was—"

"No. I rarely see dogs here. There wouldn't be two." He turned and pointed down the hill. "You see that farmhouse down below," he said. "Go to the cowshed behind it. Get inside, out of the rain, and then wait. Someone will come before long. Philippe Allemann. He'll take you to his farm. He and his family will look after you. You'll never eat so well in your life. Later today, I may try to cross again, to look for Peter. But it could be a day or two. Don't worry too much. I'll keep looking."

"Thank you so much," Brother Stoltz said. He held out his hand.

Crow laughed. "*Auf Wiedersehen,*" he said. And then he added, "I'll see you at the Allemann's. I'll bring Peter there. Now you go on ahead to the cowshed."

And so the Stoltzes trudged down the hill in the rain. Anna was exhausted, and she knew everyone else was too. She hadn't had a good night's sleep in a long time, and this latest ordeal had taken the last of her energy.

The wait at the cowshed was not long, but there was time enough to stand about in deep cow dung and become very cold. Anna was shivering by the time a man appeared at the open door, nodded, and said, "Stoltz?"

"Yes," Brother Stoltz said.

"French?"

"*Un peu.*"

"A little is enough," he said in French. "I am Philippe Allemann. Come with me. We'll get you warm." Anna knew that much French herself.

The Stoltzes followed the man to a little car that was waiting on the side of a country road. Anna was trying to tell herself that they were safe now, that Peter would be all right, but she was sick at the thought of his being up there alone. And she couldn't help wondering whether he had been caught. Sister Stoltz was exhausted, wide-eyed and pale with worry. Anna kept holding on to her.

The drive was longer than Anna had expected. Allemann drove through a village named Sochaux and then entered a larger town called Montbeliard, where a section of town had been bombed. Some sort of factory lay in rubble. Beyond the town Allemann stopped his car at a farmhouse with a neat garden out front. He led the Stoltzes around the house and in through the kitchen.

The kitchen was warm and full of wonderful smells. A white-haired woman turned from her stove to greet them. She spoke in French and said something about having German relatives. Anna didn't understand it all, but she knew the woman was accepting the Stoltzes even though she normally considered Germans her enemy.

Madame Allemann motioned for everyone to sit down, and then she served a wonderful stew, with home-baked bread. In a few minutes a young man came in through the back door, just as the Stoltzes had done. "I am Marcel Allemann," he said in German. "It's good to see you. We feared the worst."

"Why?" Brother Stoltz asked.

"The Germans, for some reason, put on a special alert this morning. They doubled the guard. By the time we found out, it was too late to warn Paul."

"Paul?"

"The Crow. You were very fortunate to make it across.

Twice as many guards were moving back and forth along the border, and Paul had no way of knowing it."

"My son didn't make it," Brother Stoltz said. "He got caught on the other side."

Marcel suddenly looked more serious. "Is Paul going back?"

"Yes. When he can."

"Paul won't give up. He'll find him—if anyone can." But Marcel didn't sound nearly so confident as Crow had.

27

The C-47 was bucking and rolling, and Alex was struggling not to give in to his airsickness. An enormous fleet of aircraft was approaching the Cotentin peninsula from the west, heading for designated drop zones. The 101st Airborne troopers were to land in an area southeast of St. Mere Eglise and then move east toward the beaches. They would take and hold four parallel causeways. These causeways were the exit routes from Utah beach. The Germans had flooded the fields in order to make an invasion more difficult, and these four roads were the only gateways inland for the troops of the Fourth Infantry Division, who would be landing on the beach at dawn.

The storm had abated, and the invasion had received the go-ahead from Eisenhower on Monday, June 5. Alex and his men had repeated their preparations, and all day they had worried that the delay would be extended. But this time the armada had gathered in the air over England and then crossed the channel. Under a three-quarter moon, Alex and his squad had looked down at the water and seen *thousands* of wakes from all the ships carrying troops to the beaches of Normandy. It was an overwhelming sight, the most massive military invasion in the history of the world. Alex was filled with a sense of the greatness of the moment, but it didn't take away his personal fears—or his airsickness.

As the airplane approached the peninsula, passing between the islands of Guernsey and Jersey, the jumpmaster opened the door and removed it. That way, if they were hit by antiaircraft guns, the men still stood a chance of getting out. The rush of cold air was bracing—and took away some of Alex's nausea. It seemed to arouse the men a little, too. All of them had taken airsickness pills—something new this time—and maybe the pills were helping some, but they also seemed to make the men drowsy.

Then everyone was suddenly jarred wide awake. As the C-47s reached the peninsula, they slipped into a bank of low clouds and were engulfed in darkness. The pilot of Alex's airplane, obviously concerned about colliding with others in the tight formation, suddenly dove and veered to the left. By the time the fleet broke from the clouds a few minutes later, the formation was gone and airplanes were scattered.

And then the flak began to fly. Antiaircraft fire began to burst around the airplane at a furious pace. The plan was to fly in low, at slow speeds, and to spot drop zones that would be marked by pathfinders who had made their jumps earlier. But none of the pilots had flown in combat before, and against orders they were taking evasive action. Alex's airplane was lurching and bouncing, and Alex wondered whether the pilot was even looking for the drop zone. Outside, tracer bullets—blue, red, green—were streaking through the sky. They were like fireworks, beautiful in a way, but terrifying.

"Stand up and hook up," the jumpmaster yelled over the tremendous noise: the rush of air through the open door, the roar of the airplane engines, the booming explosions outside.

Just as the men were struggling to their feet, the craft took a hit. Alex was thrown on the floor with everyone else as the airplane started into a roll. But then it held, righted itself, leveled out. The men, hanging onto each other for balance, clambered to their feet, and they helped each other hook up to the static line.

"We've lost an engine," someone was shouting.

Other voices were pleading, "Let's get out of here!"

Alex was to be the last man out, and he found himself doubting whether he would ever make it, but he screamed at the men, "Calm down! Move to the door."

During all the confusion, the green jump light had come on, but Alex doubted that they were over their drop zone. The pilot was probably as anxious as anyone to get the men out before the airplane got into bigger trouble. The line of men moved quickly to the door, and troopers began tumbling into the night. With only three of them left to go, however, Alex heard a rattling sound like rocks in a tin can, and he realized that machine-gun fire was crashing through the fuselage. He saw Tom McCoy, in front of him, hunch and then stumble forward.

"Are you hit?" Alex screamed.

"I'm okay," McCoy said, but Alex saw blood oozing through McCoy's pantleg in the back of his thigh.

"Unhook," Alex shouted.

But McCoy stepped to the door. "I'm going," he said. And he leaped out the door.

Alex tossed his leg bag out and jumped after it. The slip stream hit him with violent power, and then his body jolted as his parachute opened. But something was wrong. He had felt a tremendous jerk on his leg strap—and then nothing. Now he knew that his leg bag had broken loose and was gone. The pilot had been flying too fast, and Alex had jumped with too much weight.

He was only just realizing what had happened when he saw trees coming up fast in the darkness. The wind was bringing him in at a steep angle. He picked up his legs and barely missed the top of a tree but then hit the ground hard. His feet touched first, but his chute jerked him forward and slammed him onto his chest. For a moment everything spun, but his training took over. He worked his way onto his knees, collapsed the parachute, and then managed to release his harness.

For a few seconds he couldn't get his breath. But he couldn't waste time. He had no idea what was out there in the dark. He saw the silhouette of a line of low trees and realized he must be looking at the famous "hedgerows" of Normandy, but he saw nothing else, heard no one. Where had his squad come down? How in the world was he supposed to find his leg bag? Most of his ammunition was in it.

Alex unstrapped his M-1 and loaded a clip. He was about to make a run across the field to where he thought his leg bag might be when he heard something crash through the nearby hedge and hit the ground. It took him a second to realize that another trooper had landed maybe thirty or forty yards in front of him. He heard a great gasp and then a stream of profanity as the man fought with the lines of his parachute.

Alex jumped up and ran to the man. "Flash," he whispered, and got no answer. He grabbed the lines and cut them with his knife. "Thanks, man. Thanks," the man gasped. "What is it I say? Lightning?"

"Be quiet!" Alex whispered. "Move back—"

Suddenly a burst of machine-gun fire cracked from across the field, and bullets whizzed past Alex. He dropped on his chest, and so did the other soldier. Alex had never been shot at before—not for real—and the sound of those bullets was paralyzing. For several seconds he didn't move, and his impulse was never to move again.

Alex could hear the other trooper, breathing hard. "Are you hit?" Alex whispered.

"No. Are you?"

"No. But we need to move away from that machine-gun emplacement. It's up there at the corner, where the hedgerows come together. Let's crawl to the hedge straight behind us."

"Just a sec. I've got to get my rifle unstrapped." The soldier rolled onto his back and worked his rifle loose. Then he rolled back onto his chest. "Okay," he whispered. Just then another burst of fire began pounding into the ground not far ahead of them. Both scrambled toward the hedge. It was not a long crawl, and Alex had no short supply of energy. He crossed the space quickly. Another burst sent bullets popping into the field, but Alex didn't think the Germans could see much. They were firing toward the point where the trooper had landed.

Alex and his new partner crawled close to the hedge, where the shadows were very dark, and then they sat and breathed. "What's your name?" Alex whispered.

"Private Milt Cooper. I'm just a rifleman. What are you?" The man had a heavy southern accent.

"Buck sergeant. Thomas is my name."

"Where are we?"

"I don't know."

"What regiment are you with?"

"Five-oh-six," Alex said.

"What's that? Hundred and first?"

"Yeah."

Cooper cursed. "We're not even in the same division. I'm with the 82nd. What's going on?"

"I think my stick got scattered. And one of us—either you or I—has to be way off his drop zone. Maybe both of us."

"So what do we do?"

"I used a leg bag and it tore loose. I've got a lot of ammo in it—and grenades and mines. I'd like to find it, but I think it's across this field, back to the west."

"Forget that."

Alex was thinking the same thing, but he felt naked out there with only a couple of clips for his M-1. "I guess you're right," he said. "Let's move along this hedgerow, away from that MG emplacement, and get out to where we can see something. We have to figure out where we are."

"But you and me ain't heading to the same place."

"Don't worry about that. You can go east with me—if we're anywhere near my drop zone. We'll work our way toward the causeways. We're bound to pick up more men along the way—and I can get more ammunition. Have you got your clicker?"

"Clicker? What's that?" In the dim light, Alex could see that this was a good-sized kid, but he seemed *very* young.

"Didn't they give you one? That's how you're supposed to identify yourself in the dark. It's just one of those little cricket things, like you get with a box of Cracker Jack."

"I don't know anything about that. That must only be for the 101st. They just told us to say 'flash' and 'lightning.'"

"Not lightning. Thunder."

"Oh. Okay." But Cooper swore again. "This could be a mess out here, Sergeant. If we're all mixed up with each other and some are clicking and some are giving passwords, we could start shooting each other."

"Our division knows either signal. We'll manage." He got up on his feet but stayed in a low crouch. "Let's go," he said.

"Wait a minute. Let me get ready." Cooper finally undid his parachute harness and got rid of it. "All right," he said.

Alex ran along the edge of the hedgerow, under the cover of the shadows. He kept watching, but he could see nothing in the corner where the machine gun had fired. At the end of the hedge, he and Cooper found a road that was several feet lower than the field. As they walked along the road, the hedges on both sides created a cavernous darkness, as though they were walking through a tunnel. They were moving north, Alex believed, and if he was near his DZ, he should be able to find a crossing road that would take them east toward the landing beaches. On the other hand, if Cooper was near *his* drop zone, Alex might have to join up, at least for the present, with the 82nd Division.

What Alex wanted, desperately, was to find his own men. He wondered what was happening to them. He could hear lots of noise from AA fire, and airplanes were still roaring overhead.

He thought he heard some small arms fire, too, but nothing close by.

Alex and Cooper had walked for maybe five minutes when they heard voices—whispers. Both dropped on their chests alongside the road. Someone was ahead, coming toward them. Alex could make out vague silhouettes, but he couldn't tell whether the men were Germans or Americans. He listened closely and heard a muffled voice. He reached in his pocket, got out his cricket, then hesitated. If the men were Germans, maybe the click would only give his position away.

But there was nowhere to go except to fall back, and the soldiers were getting close. So he clicked once and waited. All sound stopped. And then: Click, clack. Click, clack.

Alex got up and moved forward, and he clicked again. Two clicks came back again. He didn't want to make any more noise than that until he got closer. But as he neared, he heard a voice whisper, "Thomas, is that you?"

"Cox?"

"Yeah."

"Who else is there?"

"These guys are from the 82nd Division."

"What about *our* squad?"

"I don't know. Everything is a mess. These men are about ten kilometers off their drop zone, and I think we're three or four off ours."

"How do you know?"

One of the men from the 82nd said, "See that light?"

Alex had noticed it before—a glow in the distant sky, as though something were on fire. "Yeah."

"That's St. Mere Eglise. We saw a road sign. There's a barn—or something—on fire, and a lot of Krauts around. We decided to get away from all that. But we're supposed to be way to the west of here, on the other side of town. We thought we'd head south and work our way around to where we should be."

"There's no use traveling ten kilometers by foot," Alex said. "You might as well stay in this zone. Now that I know where St. Mere Eglise is, I know where to go."

"Where are you headed?"

"East. To the causeways. We assemble at a point just outside Ste. Marie-du-Mont."

The men stood in the dark for a moment. Alex could see little more than the relative size of each of the men. He knew that the four men from the 82nd wanted to get back to their own people, but it didn't make sense to break up. The men needed to create a big enough unit to handle a firefight if they ran into a German patrol.

"Okay," one of the men finally said. "You seem to know where you're going. What rank are you anyway?"

"Sergeant. But I'm just a squad leader. If anyone—"

"Hey, you got us outranked. Colby is a corporal, but the rest of us are just privates."

"Okay. I'll take over for now—until we find an officer. Tell me your names."

The names came out of the dark: Colby, Healy, Eschler, Wilson. "All right. How are you men fixed for ammunition? My leg bag broke off, and I lost my ammo, grenades—everything."

Lester Cox swore. "I lost mine, too," he said.

But one of the men said, "We've got enough M-1 ammo for now. Do you want some clips?"

"Yeah. Give me a couple until I can get some more somewhere." One of the men fished in a pocket and then handed him over two of his clips. Alex wished he could see the men better and get a clearer picture of who was who. He knew he needed to show some leadership and pull these strangers together into something of a squad. "Let's head north until we find a road going east. Who's Colby?"

"Me."

"Okay. You walk the point. Let's walk in a file along the side of the road. If we hear anything, get down next to the hedge. Colby, take my clicker, and use it if you need to."

Actually, Alex was not nearly so confident as he sounded, and as the men set out, it was unnerving to look into the dark and have no idea what might be out there. By now German patrols had to be moving about, and he knew machine-gun emplacements had to be scattered about the area. He did, however, take solace in the knowledge that thousands of Americans were being dropped into the peninsula. Somehow, he was bound to start finding some of them. But he found a crossing road and then marched the men at least a mile to the east before he heard a click.

Everyone got down, automatically. Colby gave a double click and then waited. Two dark forms, a hundred feet or so ahead, got up from the grass by the side of the road.

"We're glad to find you guys," one of the men whispered as they walked forward. He sounded scared.

"What unit are you guys from?"

"D Company. Five-oh-two."

At least they were 101st people. "What rank?" he asked.

"Just a couple of dog faces," the same man said, hardly loud enough to be heard.

"What are your names."

"Nunez."

"Lloyd."

"Do you have plenty of ammunition?"

"Hey, we got more weapons and ammo than we know what to do with," Nunez said. "A bunch of our boys, up here in this field, dropped right in front of a machine-gun nest. They all got wiped out before they could get their harnesses off."

"What happened to the Germans? Are they still up there?"

"No. We got 'em," Lloyd said. "Six of us went in after them—and you see who's left."

Alex nodded. He wasn't sure what to tell them, and so he only said, "Show me where those weapons are."

"We pulled them into this hedge," Nunez said. "There's some M-1s and a carbine. And a Thompson."

"Ammo for the Thompson?"

"Yeah."

"Good. I want that. What about grenades?"

"Plenty," Lloyd said, his voice sounding stronger now. "There were some leg bags full of all kinds of stuff. We even found a bazooka."

"Okay. Good," Alex said. "We're well equipped. Let's get what we can carry without weighing ourselves down too much. Are you guys anywhere close to where you're supposed to be?"

"We don't know where we are," Nunez said.

"Okay. We know where we're going—more or less. Let's get what we need and then move out."

Alex walked to the cache of weapons and sorted through until he got what he wanted. When everyone else had had his chance, they came back to the road and Alex was about to get them going. But then he heard a sound in the distance. "Be quiet," he whispered. "Is that a truck?"

Everyone stopped and listened. The sound of airplanes was gone now, and the big truck engine was unmistakable. It was coming from the west. "That's gotta be Germans. We don't have any trucks in here yet. Who knows how to shoot that bazooka?"

"I trained on one," one of the men from the 82nd said.

"Keep your voice down—but tell me your name again."

"Healy."

"Okay. Get set up with that bazooka right here. The rest of you, push yourselves into the hedgerows on both sides of the road. Healy, you wait until the truck is right on top of you, and then fire a shot directly into the engine. If it's a troop truck, and men come flying out of the back, we have to get them as they jump off or we'll be outnumbered."

"How do we know it's just one truck?" Healy asked.

"We don't. But if we knock the first one out, we block the road."

Alex knew what Healy was saying. If more trucks were coming, Alex could be setting these men up to die. But in training he had heard the same thing over and over: "Don't let any troops get to the causeways. If you can't stop them, delay them for as long as possible." And that truck was clearly moving toward them, the sound getting louder.

"Get out of sight and don't show yourselves until that bazooka fires," Alex told the men as they moved toward their positions. Then he walked a few yards down the road, climbed the embankment, and worked himself, backward, into the trees and brush that formed the hedge. He got his Thompson loaded and ready to fire. He just hoped that Healy knew what he was doing with that bazooka.

Sounds were obviously carrying well; the truck was not as close as Alex had thought. When it did come into sight, it was moving slowly with its headlights off. For a moment Alex wondered whether it could be a French milk truck or some such thing, but he could see the outline, the canvas cover on the back, and clearly it was a German troop truck.

He waited. The truck kept grinding up the road, closer and closer. For at least a minute Alex held his breath and hoped that Healy wouldn't shoot too soon, and then he began to wonder whether he would ever shoot—or whether something was wrong with the bazooka.

Suddenly—boom!—the big shell came like a lightning flash and tore through the front of the truck. The hood flew up, and the truck lurched to a stop, but nothing blew up. Alex thought he saw the driver hunch forward, but he trained his eyes on the back of the truck, and suddenly a man leaped from the back. Alex saw the shape of the helmet, knew it was the target he had been trained to shoot at, and he pulled his trigger at the same time everyone else did. The German was thrown under the truck.

But more were coming now, like a waterfall, and the roar of the fire was constant. Germans kept landing, shooting their weapons wildly, and going down immediately. At least a dozen dropped, and more were still coming, and then, suddenly, there were no more. Germans were strewn about at the back of the truck, some of them stacked on top of each other. For a time, the Americans kept pumping bullets into the heap.

But the fire slowly stopped, and then all was stillness.

"*Nicht Schiessen!*" someone shouted from the back of the truck. And then in English, "No shoot!"

"Throw out your weapons," Alex shouted in German. Two rifles came flying out, almost immediately. They crashed onto the pile of men, thudded onto the bodies, and then clattered onto the ground. Alex watched with curiosity, hardly able to imagine that all this was really happening. "Come out. Show your hands," he yelled, still in German. Two men appeared at the back of the truck, their hands in the air. "It is good. Jump down," Alex yelled at them.

The men, each in turn, jumped to the side, on the ground, avoiding their fallen comrades. They continued to hold their hands in the air.

"Cooper. Cox. A couple of you other men. Take them. Search them."

But all of the Americans seemed to rush into the road at the same time, and they hammered the Germans to the ground. "I got me a Lüger already," one of them yelled.

Alex came out of the hedge and climbed down to the road. "Someone look up front. Check on the driver. Be careful."

One of the men from the 82nd walked to the cab of the truck, threw the door open, and fired his M-1.

"What are you doing?" Alex shouted.

"Just making sure. I think he was still alive."

Alex was suddenly unnerved. He had been operating on automatic, but he needed to keep control of these men. They didn't need to be shooting men who were already wounded and down.

"What are we going to do with these Krauts?" one of the men asked. He stepped to Alex and lowered his voice. "We can't take those guys along with us. We'd better shoot 'em. The general said, 'No prisoners.'"

"Listen to me." Alex stopped. "Which one are you?"

"Wilson."

"Okay, Wilson, until someone with higher rank comes along—I'm making the decisions. And I'm not shooting them." Then, searching for a justification, he added, "I might be able to get information from them. I speak German."

"You sure do." The words sounded like an accusation.

"Everyone take a breather," Alex said. "Let me talk to these men."

The two were sitting on the ground now, and three Americans were pointing guns at them. Alex walked over. "Did you get all their weapons—knives, everything?" he asked his men.

"Sure."

"Okay. You don't need to point your rifles at them. Just stay alert." Alex looked down at the Germans. He couldn't see their faces very well, but they looked up toward him as though they were not terribly frightened. Maybe they were feeling some relief that they were still alive. One of them seemed young, maybe twenty or so, from what Alex could see, but the other was at least forty. "Where were you going?" Alex asked in German.

The older man said, "They didn't tell us. We were only told that parachute soldiers had landed in the area."

Alex realized immediately that he had nothing to learn from these men. "Are other trucks coming?" he thought to ask.

"We don't know."

"Where is your *Kaserne?* Where did you come from?"

"Near Les Forges. We are foot soldiers. We know very little."

Alex looked at the younger man. He seemed a little more nervous than the older one. Alex felt a need to put him at ease. "Do what I say, and you can stay alive," he said.

And then he looked around. "All this noise could bring more Germans this way. We'd better move out. Colby, you take the point again, but let's watch these prisoners. Wilson, Cooper, walk behind them. Keep a rifle on them."

Colby led out again, and the men walked for a long time without any incident. Alex guessed they had covered maybe three miles. By then the first light was appearing on the eastern horizon. Alex was still hoping he would meet a larger unit and an officer could take over. Eventually Lloyd came up alongside Alex. "I could sure use a little grub," he said softly. "I puked everything up last night before the drop."

Alex moved up along the line. He told the men to stay spread out a little but to stop and eat something, quickly. He took the Germans forward and had them sit down, and then he rummaged in his pack for some K rations. He opened up a can of meat. He had thought he was hungry, but the smell of the meat killed his appetite.

"Are you hungry?" he asked the Germans.

"Yes. Surely," the older man said.

Alex handed him the can of meat, and then he looked in his pack for another one, which he gave to the boy. "Thank you," the soldier said. "You speak good German."

"I lived in Germany at one time," Alex said, but he realized immediately that he shouldn't get into that sort of conversation.

"Where?"

"Frankfurt. Heidelberg," Alex said. "A number of places. Just eat your food. We'll turn you over to be held when we get the chance."

"I'm from Mannheim, not far from Heidelberg," the young

man said. "I always hoped to attend the university in Heidelberg—but I ended up in the army instead."

Alex looked away, didn't say anything else, but he wondered what the boy was up to. Maybe he wanted to be sure that all was well, that this American wouldn't chat with him, like a friend, and then shoot him. Or maybe he wanted Alex to get careless and make a mistake. Either way, Alex was uneasy—not only with the young man but with himself.

Alex ate a fruit bar and some chocolate from his K rations. He tried a dry biscuit but hated the taste and chucked it away. He was lifting his canteen to his mouth when bullets began to fly. He heard the pop, the pounding in the dirt over his head.

Alex grabbed his Tommy gun and dove forward onto his face. "It's coming from those trees, up the hill," he whispered to his men. Then he scrambled across the road, where the bank on that side afforded some protection. He worked his way along the bank, closer to the shooter, got a grenade loose from his belt, pulled the pin, and then lofted it up the hillside, into the trees.

Two other grenades hit in quick succession, and all his men began firing their weapons. Nothing was coming back, but Alex didn't know whether a sniper was up there or a whole patrol. Maybe the grenades had taken them out.

"Cox, come with me," Alex called, but in that instant, as he turned, he caught a glimpse of movement across the road. He spun around in time to see that the young German prisoner was reaching for a rifle, which was lying on the ground next to an American, who was down on his face. Alex swung his machine gun around and fired a quick burst at the boy. Bullets caught him in the chest, and his body slumped, and then he jerked as several more rounds pumped into him.

At the same time, Alex saw the older man begin to raise his arms. But someone else fired, and the man caught a bullet in the forehead. Blood flew, and the man fell back. Alex dropped down to one knee and watched for any movement, but both Germans lay still. "What's going on up in those trees?" he said, still trying to keep his voice down.

Cox had already scrambled up the bank. He called back, "They're down. We got them." But a second later he moaned, "Oh, no," and then he cursed.

"What?"

"They're Americans. And they're both dead."

Alex felt a surge of nausea, but he took a long breath, and he made a choice. "All right. It's over. They made a mistake. We had to return fire. But now we need to get out of here. What about this man over here? Is he dead?"

Nunez was kneeling next to the boy who had been hit by the machine gun fire. The light had increased enough that Alex could see it was Lloyd who was down, and he was hit in the chest. As Alex walked closer, he could hear gurgling as Lloyd fought to breathe. Nunez was cursing, fighting through his pockets, trying to find something—maybe a bandage. But Lloyd took a last, sputtering pull of air and then stopped.

Nunez swore, bitterly, and slammed his fist against his thigh.

"That's enough," Alex said. "We've got to move before we *all* get shot up. Let's go. This fire could draw a crowd."

"I can't just leave him out here like this," Nunez said.

"We don't have any choice. Come on."

Alex led out this time. But as he walked away, he looked at the German soldier he had killed. The boy was lying on his side, curled up, his head on his arm, like a child asleep. Alex was taking long, steady breaths and commanding himself not to think about what had just happened.

Cox stepped up next to him. "That German kid made his own choice," he said.

"Yeah, I know," was all Alex said. In the distance, he could hear that the navy and air force bombardment had begun—the softening up before the soldiers hit the beaches. A constant, thundering roar was rolling across the countryside. It sounded as though hell had broken wide open. And it felt that way in his chest, too.

2 8

By 0700 Alex had finally made contact with his battalion—or at least some of his officers and a group of about one hundred men, many of them not actually members of the unit. Alex had kept moving toward his assembly point, and he and his makeshift squad had eventually found a group about the size of a platoon, made up mostly of men from D Company. The troops had continued together until they reached a crossroads, where the 2nd Battalion of the 506th was setting up a head-quarters about three kilometers from Ste. Marie-du-Mont. "We're sorting things out as best we can," Captain Giles, from Headquarters Company, told Alex. "We've got a few other men here from your company, but I don't know where Captain Morehead is, or any of the rest of your officers. Major Higginson has an order for E Company to handle, and I'm afraid that means you."

"What about Summers, our platoon leader? Where's he?"

"Thomas, you're it. We've got men scattered all over this peninsula, and no one knows when they'll get here. We've got four big jobs that absolutely have to be taken care of, and we don't have enough men to make up a company, let alone a battalion. We'll put together a squad for you and send in reinforcements as soon as we can. If an officer gets here, I'll send him down to take over."

"Yes, sir."

Captain Giles looked tired. His uniform was covered with dirt, and he had a deep scratch across his face. "There are four big guns a few hundred meters off that way," he said. He pointed down a slope to the northeast. "They're big, 105 millimeter cannon, and they're zeroed in on Utah Beach. The Germans must have a forward observer, on a telephone, calling the shots, because the guns are raising havoc with the 4th Infantry that's trying to get on shore."

"Are those the guns I can hear?"

"Yes. Our intelligence maps don't show the emplacements, so we must have missed them. We sent out scouts, and they tell us the guns are dug into a hedgerow and are connected by a network of trenches. The gun crews have a pretty good-sized force of men protecting them—maybe a platoon."

"How many men do I get?"

"How many came in with you?"

"Eight, counting me. But only two of us are from the 506th."

"That doesn't matter. For right now, we're keeping anyone who's here. I've also got six other guys from E Company. They're just up the road; I'll send them down to you."

Alex took a breath. He nodded. And then he tried not to sound as though he were complaining when he said, "Fourteen of us against a platoon?"

"I'm sorry, but you've got to do what you can. We're spread out trying to guard against attacks from four directions. Everyone is crying for more men."

"All right. What about weapons? Can we get a couple of machine guns?"

"Yes. We already talked about that. I'll have those brought over. But as soon as your men get here, move out."

Alex saluted. The captain tossed off a quick salute and

began to walk away, but then he turned back. "Thomas, we've got a lot of troops trying to get across that beach. If we can't knock those guns out right away, we at least have to disrupt their fire. It's absolutely *urgent*."

"Yes, sir."

Alex tried to act calm, but he was having a hard time getting his breath. He told his men to rest for a few minutes—and to eat something again—but he decided to wait for the other men to arrive before he explained the order. He used the time to think how he could attack a much larger force, already dug in, but he felt like an actor who had just stepped on stage and forgotten his lines. Nothing was coming to him. His spirits took a huge leap, however, when he saw Duncan and Rizzardi walking down the road, with Campbell and Bentley behind them. Duncan was carrying a machine gun, and Rizzardi had bandoliers of ammunition thrown over his shoulders. Behind the men from his squad were two others, also packing a machine gun and ammo. They were from another platoon, but Alex knew them both: a private named Handley and a corporal named Petersen.

"Hey, Deacon," Duncan said as he approached, "they told us we have a little job to do." He laughed.

The men were dusty, and the paint on Duncan's face was smeared, but none of them looked like they had seen any real action. Cox got up and greeted them. "Man, it's good to see you guys," he kept saying.

Alex was too nervous to laugh or make small talk, but he felt good to have some men he knew he could depend on. "What happened to the rest of our squad?" he asked.

"We don't know," Duncan answered. "The four of us all landed in the same big field, but we never saw anyone else. It's lucky we ran into Handley and Petersen. They figured out how to get over here. Me and Rizzardi had our own plan. We were going to grab a taxi and see if we could get to Paris." He laughed again, in his enormous voice.

"No one saw McCoy?" Alex asked.

"No," Curtis said. "And we spent some time looking for the other guys."

"McCoy got hit before he ever jumped," Alex said. "His leg was bleeding pretty bad."

Rizzardi cursed. "Him and Huff always stick together. Maybe Huff took care of him."

"If they found each other." Alex stepped back a little and pointed to the other men. "These guys are assigned to us for right now," he said. "They're from the 82nd. Did the captain tell you about the guns?"

"He said there might be fifty Germans down there," Campbell said.

"Something like that. Let's talk here for a minute, and then we'll go take a look before we decide exactly how we're going to handle the situation."

Alex filled in a few more details for everyone, and then he said, "We've got to hurry. You can hear those big 105s. They're pounding the heck out of our boys on the beach. I don't want to sound like a high school coach, but we've *got* to stop them. Take your weapons and all your ammo, and any grenades you have. Leave everything else here. Fill the pockets on your jump jackets, but don't take any packs. You need to move fast."

As the men began to shed their extra gear, Alex realized that he needed demolition kits. Some of the men were carrying them, so he had Nunez throw four of them in a musette bag and take it along.

Alex looked at his watch. It was 0830. He split the squad into two patrols, and then he said, "Let's go. Let's get to that rock fence down at the bottom of this field, and from there we'll cover for each other as we alternate our moves."

Duncan laughed. "Listen to the Deacon," he said. "He thinks he's a soldier. He wants to give those Krauts 'heck.'"

Alex didn't respond. He was already striding out, and he was studying the countryside, trying to get a sense of the land in front of them. There was no problem locating the guns, with the tremendous noise they were making, but Alex wasn't sure how to make the approach. He knew he had to take one gun at a time and hope to catch the Germans by surprise on the first one, but he wasn't sure he could get his men close enough to knock out the gun without getting everyone shot up.

After Alex and his men crossed the rock fence, they moved ahead in quick, leapfrogging surges, but they picked up no enemy contact, so Alex led the men around the big field in front of the guns, and then he followed a hedgerow until he found an opening that gave him a view of the emplacements. He lay on his stomach and surveyed the area. He could see helmets moving along the trenches on both sides of the nearest cannon—the one farthest to the south. Men were probably carrying ammunition to the guns.

The field in front of the gun was anything but rectangular, with several different angles, and all of it was bordered with big hedges. The first gun was at the top of the field, near the corner. It was dug in under the long hedge that formed the western edge—the top—of the field, and it was maybe forty meters from the hedge that formed the south end. A little ravine extended from the bottom of the field, like a finger, and pointed at the trench that ran between the first and second guns. The ravine was full of trees and low growth.

Alex crawled away from the opening and got behind the hedge with the other men. "Okay," he said. "Duncan and Rizzardi, I want you to move up along this southside hedge, on the outside. Find a place where you can work your way into the hedge and aim your gun at that nearest cannon. Don't give your position away until you start shooting, but once you start, you've got to keep laying down cover fire so some of us can move in closer."

"Gotcha," Duncan said. He was looking serious now. And Rizzardi was gripping his ammo belts as though he needed something to hang onto. Each time one of the big guns fired, the ground vibrated under them. The sound was terrifying.

"Petersen, Handley, get into that little valley and work your way up through the trees toward the guns until you find a position where you can fire at that same cannon. You can move pretty fast through those trees without being seen, but once you get close, be careful. Don't let the Germans see you."

Petersen and Handley both nodded, but neither one had any color in his face. They had to know what Alex knew: firing on a whole platoon was like hitting a hornet's nest with a stick.

"Cox, Nunez, and Campbell, head up the outside of this south hedge with Duncan and Rizzardi. Go on past them and find a spot where you can get through. Once the cover fire starts, I want you to crawl toward the trench, south of the gun. When you get close enough, throw in some grenades, and then rush the trench. If you can get in, keep throwing grenades down the trench, and charge the gun."

"Won't we be in the cross fire when we're out there in the field?" Nunez asked.

"Not if you stay above the machine gun, to the west. Stay down, but try to move in as fast as you can. If the Germans are trying to deal with those machine guns, they won't see you."

Alex was not sure about that, actually, but it was the only approach that made sense to him. "One thing that will help you," he said, "is that we're going to draw the Germans' attention in all directions—make them think we have more people than we do. Colby and Eschler, I want you to move all the way up the south hedge and around the west side, so you're behind the gun. When the shooting starts, lay down a barrage of small-arms fire through the hedge. Wilson, Healy, and Cooper, you work your way up through that ravine with Handley and Petersen. Get to a spot where you can see, and fire your rifles. Bentley and I are going to break through the hedge on the south and make a run to the middle of the field. I'm going to put down some fire with my Thompson while Cox and Nunez and Campbell move in. As soon as they throw some grenades in the trench, Curtis and I will bust up the middle. We'll try to throw some grenades directly into that emplacement."

"How do we know when to start firing?" Duncan asked.

"You men with the machine guns will take the longest to get ready. But you'll be able to see each other. When you're ready, signal to each other, and then both of you open up. The rest of us will go into action at the same time. Once we get that first gun, we'll be able to use the trenches to get to the others. At that point, I want Duncan and Rizzardi to pull out of the hedge and swing around behind the second gun, with Colby and Eschler. Petersen and Handley, cross that little ravine and fire from the north side of it at the second gun. The same with Wilson, Healy, and Cooper. The rest of us will make a run down the trench."

"How do we know when to start firing at the second gun?" Petersen asked.

"We'll give you time to get in place. But then wait until we toss a grenade down the trench. Keep some steady bursts of fire going, but don't shoot up all your ammo. If we get the second gun, move to the north if you have to, or just fire from where you are, but we need cover fire for each gun."

Alex sounded confident, and the men seemed to accept the plan, but nothing was more clear than that they needed four times as many men to pull this off. Alex felt a shaky kind of apprehension more than fear, and he could see the same tension in everyone else. "Look, men," Alex said, "don't take chances. Don't get yourselves killed. Just play it smart, and we can run these troops off. They're going to think a whole battalion is after them."

"Let's do it," Duncan said.

And so the men deployed to their positions. Alex and Curtis were able to find a spot where they could crawl into the hedge. But they didn't move all the way through. They lay on their chests and waited.

"It's a good plan," Curtis whispered. "It's the same thing Summers would have come up with."

Alex had nothing to say about that. He didn't know. Instead, he said, "I'm going to run hard and get down. Follow me, but stay back some. We don't want to give them a single target to shoot at. If one of us takes a hit, the other one still needs to get to that emplacement with some grenades. Everything hinges on that."

"All right. Good luck."

"God bless you, Curtis."

"Yeah. That's what I meant too."

And then, finally, the MG fire began popping from both sides of the field. Alex crawled through the hedge and then jumped up and ran hard. He hit the ground in the field, in front of the gun in deep grass, and he started firing toward the emplacement. Bullets were flying, but he heard nothing coming his way. The machine guns still had the Germans' attention.

Alex could hear Curtis, not far off, firing his M-1, and he glanced to see his three men crawling toward the trench, exactly as he had told them to do.

Everything happened fast. In only a few seconds, grenades began to explode in the trench, and suddenly Alex was up and running, firing his Thompson. Just as he dropped on his chest, a hail of bullets pelted into the ground in front of him. He fired another burst with his machine gun, then rolled onto his side, grabbed a grenade from his belt, and pulled the pin. He looked up then and tossed the grenade into the gun position. Two, then three grenades went off almost together, and then another followed. Alex knew that Curtis had gotten one in, and so had the men who were in the trench.

Then everything fell quiet. All the big 105s had stopped. Alex waited a few seconds, and then he jumped up and charged—but nothing was happening. He ran to the dug-out area around the gun and stopped at the edge.

Two German soldiers were down on their faces. At that moment Cox charged past them, stopped, and like a baseball catcher, tossed a grenade down the trench toward the second gun. At the same moment, Alex saw three Germans take off across the field. They had apparently been in foxholes out on the surface. Alex spun and fired with his Tommy gun. Two of the men went down immediately. Curtis shot the other one in the back with his M-1.

Cox and Nunez were still charging down the trench, throwing grenades. Campbell stopped to check the Germans. Alex jumped down by the big gun, next to Campbell. Just then Curtis grunted, and Alex looked up as he tumbled into the emplacement. He stared up at Alex, looking shocked. "I'm sorry. I'm sorry," he said.

"Where are you hit?"

"In the butt."

Alex rolled him over and ripped his pants open with his knife. "Who's got sulfa powder?" he shouted.

"I do," Campbell said.

"Get some on that wound, and get the bleeding stopped. We've got to move into position to take this next gun."

Alex looked out from the trench to see whether Handley and Petersen had moved to their next position. But when he raised his head, a bullet flew past him and ricocheted off the barrel of the big gun.

"Cox, Nunez," Alex barked, "let's give those guys with the machine guns about two minutes to get into place. Get your weapons loaded and your grenades ready. Campbell, give me your grenades. You stay here and take care of Bentley."

Alex was still trying to catch his breath, but his chest seemed locked. He took another look at his watch, waited, looked again, and could hardly stand the delay. "All right, let's go," he finally said.

The trench ahead was not a straight shot to the next gun. It had been dug in a zigzagging line. Alex charged to the first turn, leaned his back against the trench wall, pulled the pin on a grenade, and tossed the weapon underhand around the corner. He listened for the explosion and then waited a second or two before he jumped around the corner and fired a burst of rounds. Two Germans were well down the trench, beyond the force of the grenade. They were on their knees setting up a machine gun. Alex kept firing. One of the Germans took three or four hits in the chest. The other tried to spin away but caught a bullet in the side of the head.

Alex charged them, with his two partners right behind. He checked to make sure the Germans were down for good, and then he ran to the next bend in the trench and took a quick glance around it. No one was there, so he ran hard to the next turn. He knew he must be close to the second gun now. He stopped and let the other men catch up with him. "Get your grenades ready," he said. He got another one out, pulled the pin, and then hurled it around the corner. When he jumped around the turn this time, he could see three German soldiers down in the trench, knocked out by the grenade. Two more soldiers were farther back, close to the gun. They had hit the dirt when the grenade had gone off, but now they were getting up, raising their weapons. Alex fired, and then Cox broke past Alex in the trench, tossed his grenade, and dropped to the ground.

Debris flew in all directions, but as soon as the cloud of dirt settled, Cox charged forward with Alex and Nunez behind. One of the Germans in the trench moved, and Cox shot him. The two by the gun were dead, but the crew and any others who had been there had retreated down the trench toward the third gun.

"All right. Hold up a second," Alex said. "We've got to take this next one while we've got them on the run, but we need to let the machine guns move again. A lot of Germans have fallen back. They might be getting ready to take us on this time."

Alex and Cox and Nunez were hunched near the gun, keeping their heads down, but then Cox turned and stood up straight, apparently to look across the field. Just as his head raised up, a burst of bullets from a machine gun struck him in the face. His head seemed to explode, and he was thrown backward. He landed across one of the Germans, on the ground. Alex knelt down next to him, but Cox's face was gone.

Alex spun away and leaned against the gun. He took a long breath and tried to get control. Just then he heard a shout from the trench. "No make dead!"

Alex stepped under the gun barrel and brought his Thompson up. Six Germans were coming toward the gun with their arms up.

"What are we going to do with them?" Nunez said.

Alex was thinking the same thing, but he was also thinking that the third gun might not be so hard to take after all. The Germans must be thinking they were about to be overrun. If they had any idea how few men he had—just twelve now—they would be charging, not giving up.

Alex told the Germans, "Come forward." And then in German, "Drop any weapons you have. Knives. Grenades."

"We have nussing," one of them said.

Alex was thinking he couldn't guard them without giving up another soldier, and he needed everyone. "Nunez," he said, "run and get Campbell. He should be able to leave Bentley now."

Nunez hustled away, crouching as he ran down the trench. Alex aimed his machine gun at the soldiers, who were all staring at him. He wondered whether they were surprised that they were facing only one man. But he didn't speak to them. He wasn't going to do that again.

In just a few seconds Nunez was back. "Hey, we've got reinforcements," he said.

"How many?"

"Four."

"All right. Send them to me."

"They're coming."

"Good. But we've got to disable the two guns we've taken before we get a counterattack and lose them. Where are those demolition kits?"

"Back at the hedge, where I started."

"All right. Let's do this. Take these prisoners back to the first gun. Let Campbell and one of the reinforcements guard them. Then go get those demolition kits."

Nunez nodded, and then he pointed his M-1 at the Germans and gestured for them to move on down the trench. He followed behind them. Alex thought of Cox again, and he took another look at him. The horror registered in his mind, but he refused to let it sink into his emotions this time. He knelt and pulled his friend off the dead German and stretched him out next to the gun.

The new guys soon showed up, walking toward Alex in the trench, single file. "Are you Sergeant Thomas?" the first man asked. He was an innocent-looking kid, just a private, hardly appearing old enough to be in on something like this.

"Yeah. Keep your heads down. Listen, we've taken two guns, but we've got two to go. Are you men ready to make a charge at this next one?"

The private nodded. "Sure. That's what we came for."

"All right. We've got to wait for Nunez to get back here so we can disable the guns we've taken. But when we move again, I'll lead out. We've got some of our men outside, and they'll be firing into the emplacement, but we've got to get down that trench and fill the gun position with grenades."

"All right," one of the men said. But they all looked clean. Alex knew they hadn't seen any action. He saw the young private look at Cox on the ground. When the boy looked back at Alex, his eyes were wide open, fixed.

When Nunez got back, he and Alex dropped a demolition kit into the second gun, got back, and then set it off with a German "potato masher" grenade. The breech of the gun blew out like a half peeled banana.

"Go back and take care of the other one," he told Nunez. "This new group is going with me to take number three."

Nunez nodded.

"How's Bentley?"

"Okay, I think. He's just worried that he let us down."

The thought crossed Alex's mind that Curtis was lucky; he would be getting out of here alive.

"Here we go," Alex told the new men. Once again he charged down the trench, checked two turns without seeing anyone, and then stopped at the third one and thrust a grenade around the corner. He waited about three seconds and then said, "Okay. Let's go." As he came around the corner, he saw movement. He fired his machine gun as he dropped onto his knees and then his elbows. Out of the dust, down the trench, he saw muzzle fire from several weapons. Alex grabbed for another grenade, pulled the pin, and threw it, but just before it went off, one of the soldiers behind him gasped and then dropped onto Alex's back. A series of three blasts went off as more grenades dropped into the emplacement. The dust was thick in the trench, but as soon as debris stopped flying, Alex rolled the man off his back and leaped up. He ran to the gun and this time found three Germans down. The others had retreated again.

Alex turned and looked back up the trench. "How bad is he hit?" he called.

But the men didn't answer. Alex walked back and saw that the young private was lying on his back, with his neck and chest ripped open. He was gagging, and the man next to him was trying to get his first-aid kit free from his belt, in back. But in a few more seconds the boy choked hard and then stopped breathing.

Alex felt responsible. He didn't say it, didn't let himself think it long, but he was sure it was his fault, somehow. The kid on his knees looked up at Alex; he was blinking, scared, sick.

"What was his name?" Alex asked.

"Gollnick."

Alex nodded. "Hold this position," he said. "We need reinforcements before we can take number four. I'm afraid all the Germans we've run down these trenches are clinging to that last one. Be ready for a counterattack. I'll get another demolition kit for this gun."

Alex trotted back to the second gun. "Nunez," he called ahead, "can you make a run back to headquarters?"

"Sure."

"Ask for another squad. We need some help to take this last gun." Nunez turned to leave, but Alex said, "Where are those demolition kits?"

"In that musette bag," Nunez said. He pointed to the ground. "Did you lose anyone down there?"

"Yeah. That first kid who walked in here. The young one. He's dead."

Nunez swore.

The two men looked at each other for maybe one full second, and Alex felt a stab of guilt again. Maybe there was a safer way to do this. He didn't want to lose anyone else.

Nunez scrambled out of the trench and took off.

Alex walked back to the first gun. "We're going to try to get some more men," he told Campbell. "Then maybe we can get Bentley out of here. How's he doing?" He glanced to see the German prisoners sitting in a line along the side of the gun. Some of them were smoking. Alex had the impression they were relieved the war was over for them.

"I gave him some morphine," Campbell said. "I don't think he knows what's going on."

Alex knelt and looked at him. Curtis's eyes looked glazed. "How are you doing, buddy?" Alex asked.

"I'm sorry," Curtis said.

"Nothing to be sorry about," Alex said.

Campbell called to Alex, "When you prayed, you should have mentioned that we didn't want to get shot in the butt." He laughed.

Alex looked around at Campbell. He saw nothing to laugh about. "Cox is dead," he said.

"I know. Nunez told me."

Campbell seemed to know what Alex meant—about the prayer. "We knew it had to happen to some of us," Campbell said.

Alex patted Curtis on the shoulder, and he stood up and looked at his watch. It was 1034, and the idea astounded him. Somehow it seemed as though this operation had lasted days, not a mere two hours.

Alex walked back to the third gun and used the demolition kit to blow out the breech. And then he waited for a long time, which was the hardest thing he'd had to do all morning. He had time to think about this last charge, and now the adrenaline was gone, the sense of urgency. He just wanted to keep everyone else alive.

Half an hour went by slowly, and Alex was thinking he would have to go after the last gun with the men he had, but then Nunez showed up with a sergeant and four other men. "Headquarters sent us," the sergeant said. "They said you needed some help."

"Are you five the only ones coming?"

"As far as I know, we are."

"What's your name?"

"Brown. Skip Brown. I'm with the 502nd. I don't know how we got tied up with a no-account bunch like you."

Alex hardly let the comment register. He was still in no mood to make jokes. "We've taken three guns," he said. "This

last one might be the hardest. We have two machine guns covering for us, but I'm not sure how they're fixed for ammo. Did
you bring any?"

"Yeah."

One of the men stepped forward and slapped the bandoliers around his shoulders. Alex had two of the new recruits
crawl out to the machine guns with the belts. The whole time
he waited for them to get back, he feared the worst, but he
heard no gunfire.

When the men returned, one of them said, "The big guy
out there took a round in the leg. They got the bleeding
stopped, but he ought to get some aid pretty soon."

So Duncan had been hit, too. Alex wanted this over.

"Do you want to take over?" Alex asked the sergeant.

"No. You call the shots. You know what's going on."

"Okay. We need to have one team swing around and come
from the flank, out on the ground, just so we keep the Germans
thinking there are a lot of us out here. You take two of your
men and make the charge down the trench. Get some grenades
into the emplacement. I'll take two men and charge from outside, and we'll try to fill up that hole with grenades. If the
Germans break out of the trench, we have some men out in the
field who can put down some fire. Does that make sense to
you?"

"Yeah. It sounds good. Do you have any idea how many
Jerries are holding that gun?"

"No. We've killed or taken something like twenty or
twenty-five. But there could be that many more holding the
last gun."

"All right."

Reality was setting in for Sergeant Brown. Alex saw a grim
sort of acceptance appear in his face. Alex led the men to the
third gun and then farther on down the trench, checking each
turn as he went. By then he had heard some fire and hoped that
his machine-gun crews were all right. When he reached what

he figured had to be the last turn, he whispered, "Okay, you men going with me, come on. Sergeant, give us a few seconds to get in place, and then I'll start firing. That will start our cover fire. Allow another few seconds, and then throw some grenades around that corner and make your charge."

"Right. We're ready."

Alex climbed out, ran a short distance, and dropped. When he heard the two men drop down behind him, he fired a burst with his Thompson, and he heard his machine guns begin to pop. He jumped up and ran at the emplacement. Halfway there, he dropped down and tossed his grenade. But it hit in front of the hole and bounced the wrong direction. As soon as it went off, he charged again. But by then grenades were going off—three, four, five of them. And then ten or twelve Germans jumped from the trench beyond the gun and took off across the field. Alex watched, and he let them go. But the men next to him were firing with their M-1s, and Handley was firing at them with his machine gun.

Some of the Germans fell. Some kept going. Alex watched as though it were a movie—a newsreel. He could hardly believe it was over. He got up and walked to the last gun emplacement. He held his gun ready, but he didn't expect anything.

"Everything all right, Sergeant?" he called to Brown.

"My two men are down, and I'm hit," Brown called back, "but we've got the gun. There weren't quite as many Krauts as we thought. Six down in here, and you saw the rest take off."

Handley came walking up. "A bunch of them—ten or so— took off before we even started this last attack. We didn't fire at them. We had to save our ammo."

Alex nodded. "That's fine," he said. And then he yelled, "Get a demolition kit, Nunez. Blow this gun up, and then let's get out of here. We have nothing to hold once the guns are gone, but we could draw a counterattack."

Alex jumped down into the emplacement. Brown had

taken a bullet that had gone through his left hand and nicked his side, along his ribs.

"When we broke around that corner, all hell broke loose," Brown told Alex.

"I'm sorry I got you into that. I thought the run outside might be the worst." Alex got out his first-aid kit, and then he yelled, "Handley, check on those two boys in the trench."

"I already did," Brown said. "They're all ripped up. Both dead."

Alex felt the words like a hammer blow. He wanted out of this place.

Nunez took charge of blowing the breech out of the last gun, and then the men cleared out. They carried Curtis with them, and they hiked back across the fields to the spot where headquarters was set up. Duncan and Brown walked on their own. Duncan told Alex, "The bullet just gouged a little chunk out of my leg, but it ain't bad. I've got to stick around and keep covering for you."

Alex was exhausted. He glanced at Duncan, but he didn't say anything. He had a lot of emotions struggling to get hold of him, but one thing he didn't feel was any sense of victory.

When the men got back to their battalion, Alex told them to get some help for the wounded and then to rest and eat. He knelt down next to Curtis and gave him a pat on the shoulder. "Better in your butt than your head," he said. "You'll be getting out of this."

"Everyone will think I was running away," Curtis said. He still sounded groggy.

"No. You and I know the truth. I'll see you again, Curtis. Probably back in England."

"All right. I'll be praying for all you guys."

"Thanks." Alex got up and walked to the headquarters—just a tent with a radio setup out front. The major was talking to a group of officers when Alex approached. For a time no one bothered to look at him, but finally Captain Giles looked over and said, "Thomas, what are you doing here?"

"We got them, sir."

"You got what?"

"We took those guns. We blew out the breeches. They're finished."

"You took them with a *squad?*"

"That's what you told me to do, sir."

"Yeah. But I never thought you could do it."

Alex was stunned. He stared at the man.

"We thought you would start something and maybe keep those gunners busy for a while. Then later we'd get a platoon down there and take care of things. How many casualties did you take?"

"Six. Four dead. Two wounded."

Major Higginson was listening now. "You took out four 105s with a squad?" he said.

"I sent him down there with thirteen men," Giles said.

"A few more came down and helped us," Alex said.

"How many?"

"Four the first time, and then five more."

"All you men are going to get medals," the major said. "Do you have any idea how many lives you saved—down on that beach?"

Alex didn't know. But he didn't answer. The truth was, he was choked up, and it wasn't with joy. He was beginning to shake.

"Get some rest," the major said. "We're starting to get more guys from the 506th in here. We'll try to get you back with your unit."

"Yes, sir." Alex saluted, and then he walked back to the men he had been fighting with. For the first time he noticed how filthy they were, how undone. Some of them were smoking, some sleeping, but Duncan was the only one eating.

"What'd they tell you up there?" Duncan asked.

"He said we deserve medals." To Alex, this was ironic. No hero could be as scared as he had been all morning.

"Shoot, Deacon," Duncan said, "you're the one who left a path of destruction. You didn't give me a chance."

Rizzardi was grinning. He was grimy from head to foot, and dirt was mixed in with his face paint, which was smudged with sweat. "I never expected you to be like that, Thomas," he said.

But Alex couldn't smile. "I wish we hadn't lost Cox," he said. "And those other guys."

"I know," Duncan said, and his smile faded.

Rizzardi looked down at the ground.

Alex sat down next to them. He wasn't sure what had changed inside him, but he knew he was not the same person who had flown out of England about twelve hours before. He looked at his hands, and he was strangely surprised to see they weren't covered with blood.

Duncan tried to laugh. "I'm not sure it was God fighting with you out there, Deacon. I'd swear it was the devil."

That was exactly what Alex was thinking.

2 9

Bobbi read every newspaper she could get her hands on, and she listened to the radio. The reports from Normandy sounded encouraging, but time and again she heard that the airborne units had taken heavy casualties. If something happened to Alex, she didn't know how long she would have to wait to get word, but more than anything, she dreaded that a telegram would come. In recent weeks two nurses she knew had received wires, and, as usual, the news had been bad. One girl had lost a brother, another her fiancé. But there was nothing Bobbi could do except wait—and pray. She had fallen into the habit of saying little prayers every few minutes, asking almost incessantly that Alex would be kept safe.

And then one morning she saw Gene walking down the hallway at the hospital. "Why didn't you tell me you were going to be here?" she complained, but she was thrilled to see him. She hadn't heard from him for a week, and she had begun to wonder whether he had shipped out.

"I didn't know we were coming over here," Gene said. "The ship put in this morning, and we're taking on fuel and supplies, but then we're leaving again—some say in the morning. I talked my CO into letting me off the ship for a few minutes— just because you were here so close."

"A few *minutes?*"

"Yeah." Gene looked at his watch. "I have to be back by 1200—you know, noon—and it's almost eleven now. You probably couldn't leave the hospital anyway, could you?"

Bobbi let out a little sigh. "No. Probably not. But I can take a break. Let's walk outside."

She took Gene by the arm, and then she turned to a nurse at a nearby station. "I'm going to spend a few minutes with my brother," she said. "I'm going to be out in back." Then she took Gene toward the back doors and out into a little garden area. They sat on a bench where they could see the harbor in the distance. "Do you know where you're going?" Bobbi asked.

"No. A lot of people think it's going to be the Mariana Islands, and some think it will be Biak, down by New Guinea, but that's just where some fighting has been going on. I don't think anyone really knows."

"But you'll be going into battle?"

"Well . . . no one even knows that for sure. But we've been practicing amphibious landings the whole time we've been in Maui. So I figure we'll be making a beach landing somewhere."

"Maybe you'll only have to occupy some island that's already been taken."

"I doubt that. There are a lot of guys out there who've earned a rest. We're fresh troops."

"Oh, Gene." She took his arm. "I don't know why this all has to happen at once. All I've been thinking about lately is Alex. Now I have to add you to my worries—and I won't even know where you are."

"I'll be digging the deepest foxhole in the Pacific some-where—that's where I'll be."

Bobbi turned more toward him. "Don't joke about that. Do be careful. Don't try to be a hero—okay?"

"This sergeant I know told me the first landing is always the most dangerous—because it takes a while to get scared enough to really look out for yourself. So I figure I'm just going to do whatever my squad leader tells me to do."

This all sounded rather casual, but Bobbi heard something underneath the words. When Gene had been here before, the war had been theoretical. Now, he was talking about his life.

"Gene, it all scares me so much."

He laughed. "Hey, I know all about that. But I tell myself that what's supposed to happen *will* happen."

"I'm going to be praying for you all the time—and so will the whole family."

"I know." Gene looked off toward the harbor, and Bobbi knew she had said the wrong thing. Gene had always been so attached to the family, and right now he must be homesick. Maybe that's why he changed the subject. "So what's happened to your officer friend? Do you hear from him?"

"Sometimes I do. I got some letters about two weeks ago. But he didn't tell me anything. He can't say where he is or what he's doing."

"He can tell you how much he *aches* for you," Gene said, and he slapped his hand over his heart.

"Not Richard. He doesn't talk that way."

"He's in love with you though. Right?"

"I think he still is. But he doesn't say so." She laughed. "He's like you. He doesn't like the idea of making commitments until the war is over. Have you been hearing from Millie?"

"Yup. She writes almost every day. The guys in my squad just about kill me when they see how many letters I get. Besides Millie, you and Mom and LaRue and Beverly all write, and so do Grandma Thomas and Grandma Snow. I even got a letter from Dad the other day."

"Did he recommend that you live a righteous life?"

Gene leaned his head back and laughed, with that familiar chugging sound of his. "I believe he did say something of that sort. You know Dad." Then he added, "But I'm starting to understand why he preached to us so much. I can't believe how corrupt most of the soldiers are."

"I know. I see it here. Mom and Dad seem to be getting smarter all the time, don't they? I wish I could go home for a while this summer. Just so I could spend some time with Mom and Dad—and see the girls."

Gene leaned forward and put his elbows on his knees. "That's what I think about all the time," he said. "I'd like to be there for the 24th of July. I keep thinking about the wiener roasts we used to have, up in Big Cottonwood Canyon. Me and Wally wading in the creek and hiking into the hills—all the stuff we used to do. Remember that time Dad put that watermelon in the creek to get it cold, and it got away from him?"

"I didn't actually see it happen, but I've heard the story a hundred times."

"That thing started rolling and bouncing over the rocks, and Dad ran down the bank to get ahead of it. Then—bang!— it hit a big rock, and the water turned pink. Then swish, it was *gone*."

"I remember you putting up a big howl about it."

"Hey, I was only about nine." Gene sat up straight, and he looked at Bobbi. "Dad told me something that day that I didn't understand until this year."

"What?"

"He said, 'Gene, if we had eaten that watermelon, we would have forgotten it. But we'll laugh about this one as long as we live. A good memory is better than a watermelon any day.'"

"I doubt he sold you on that concept."

"Not at the time. But I sure believe it now."

Bobbi tightened her grip on Gene's arm. She wished, with him, that they could get some of those days back. She hadn't known how lovely life had been back then.

"No one back home knows what it's like out here," Gene said. "They all write and tell me what a big hero I am."

"You sound like you don't believe it."

"Well . . . let's just say that nothing is quite like I expected. I hear about all the brave young men going off to win the war. It sounds pretty glorious. But I look around, and all I see is a bunch of guys like me, willing to go but hoping, more than anything, that we can come back alive. Marines are about as gung-ho as anybody, but everyone is getting serious now that we're heading into the real thing."

"I see the glories of war every day, Gene. Kids, all torn up and burned and mutilated."

Gene nodded.

"I'm sorry. I shouldn't—"

"No. That's all right. I know exactly what you're saying. Sometimes it just seems like President Roosevelt ought to sit down with Tojo, or whoever is in charge over there, and say, 'Come on. This is stupid. Let's call it off and go home.'"

"I know. But we do have to win, Gene. And you guys *are* heroes. Every one of you."

Gene didn't respond to that. He stood up and picked a hibiscus from a nearby bush, and he handed it to Bobbi. "Here, I brought you a present, all the way from Hawaii." She took it and tucked it behind her ear. Gene grinned, and when he did, he looked very young, that same little boy Bobbi had baby-sat when she was twelve and he was six. "What I'm looking forward to," he said, "is the day when Wally and Alex and you and I all get home, and we can all be together with Mom and Dad and the girls. I'd give anything in the world if we could be home for Christmas."

Gene had tears in his eyes, and that was more than Bobbi could handle. He sat down again, and she rested her head against his shoulder. "If not this year, maybe next," she said. And then they sat for a long time that way, saying nothing, Bobbi crying and Gene trying not to.

Before Gene left, Bobbi held hands with him and said a prayer, asking that he might be kept safe. And when he was gone, she took the hibiscus blossom back with her into the hospital. That night she pressed it in her Bible, and then she got down on her knees and pleaded with the Lord one more time that Gene's wish might be granted, that they could all be together again, if not this year or the next then someday.

* * *

On D day, plus four, the 506th Regiment got its order to march toward Carentan. The regiment was to swing around to the southwest of the town, while the 327th Glider Infantry Regiment attacked from the north, and the 501st Airborne from the northeast. Alex's regiment moved out that evening, and just like the old days back at Toccoa, the men marched all night.

Alex was relieved that he was no longer in command of E Company. Lieutenant Summers, his platoon leader, had arrived at the assembly point on the afternoon of D day, and he had become the temporary company commander. Captain Morehead was still missing. On June 7, the company, by then at about half its strength, had battled through some counterattacks—but the action was nothing of the sort Alex had dealt with that first morning. After that, Summers had received orders to guard the regimental headquarters. For three days the men of Company E had had the chance to rest and recover.

But those days had not been good for Alex. Duncan's main activity had been to search out wine cellars and bring back all the alcohol he could carry. Most of the men in Alex's squad—along with the other men in the company—were drinking way too much. Alex was sickened, too, by the rampant souvenir hunting. The troops went about the countryside searching for dead Germans, and they collected Lügers, binoculars, watches, knives, insignias. Jim Gourley, who had now caught up with the company, even cut the finger off a corpse to get a ring. And then he bragged about it. Alex knew that these kids were using alcohol and big talk to avoid the fear and disgust they were actually feeling, but that didn't change how he felt about the way they were acting. He chewed them out, tried to keep them level-headed, but time and again the wine would show up again.

A few of the men from the company had been killed or wounded, and some were missing, but most had finally made it to the assembly point. No one knew anything about Tom McCoy or Dale Huff. Alex feared the worst for them, but Lester Cox was the only man from his squad that he knew to be dead.

One relief was that in spite of all the difficulties the airborne units had experienced, most of the initial missions had been completed. The causeways had been secured, and the infantry units that had landed on Utah Beach had moved in. The men on Omaha Beach, however, had faced a nightmare. Word was getting through to the paratroopers that a terrible slaughter had happened there. All the same, enough men had gotten ashore to establish a beachhead and push inland a little. The job for the airborne now was to help the units from Utah and Omaha link up so that a secure perimeter could be established. After that, a breakout could be attempted. No one was saying anything now about the airborne troops getting out in three days. The 101st and the 82nd were apparently in to stay, at least for the foreseeable future.

The Germans were proving very hard to move. They kept their tanks and troops lurking behind the hedgerows. Every time the Allies fought their way past one hedge, and took heavy losses in the process, the Germans fell back to the next. There was no way for the ground troops to get rolling across the countryside. The Allies needed desperately to get control of the roads and crucial intersections. Carentan was a town where some of the main roads and a railroad converged, and so it was a key site. The 101st got the assignment to take and hold it.

So now the days of ease were over. "Easy" Company was going back into battle with its regiment, and Alex thought that was just as well. After the exhausting night march, the troops were in place to attack Carentan on the morning of June 11, but the Germans had placed a platoon at a T-intersection on a country road leading into the town. E company got the order to make a direct assault on the position. F Company would attack from the left flank, and D Company would be held in reserve. The regiment had the numbers over the Germans, but the Germans were dug in and much better armed. The Germans had an MG42, a high-powered machine gun, in place and ready. They would surely be firing mortars, too. The attack was going to be tough.

Alex was leading Summers' platoon for now. In the dark, they had sneaked along the road and hid in a dry ditch on the left side. The second platoon was on the right, and the third was waiting in reserve. Alex would move out first and take his men straight up the road suddenly and quickly, to catch the Germans unready. Alex's goal was to get to the machine-gun position and overrun it, if he could. If he couldn't get there, he at least had to draw the attention of the Germans while the flanking company moved in.

At exactly 0600, Summers got up and said, "Move out!"

Alex yelled, "Let's go," jumped up, and bolted down the road. But the Germans were only fifty meters away, and they were waiting. The moment Alex stood up, the big machine gun began to fire. Six men, all from Alex's squad, had gotten up with Alex, but the fire stopped the rest. Alex charged ahead with tracer bullets flying all around him, but then he glanced back and realized that only a few of his men were with him. He ducked down on the side of the road, fired a few more rounds, and then screamed, "Come on, men!"

But the rattle of gunfire was tremendous, and no one was getting up. Alex was in no-man's land. Someone was down on his face, in the road, and the other men who had started the charge with him had jumped back into the ditch. Alex was kneeling, still shouting to his men, but nothing was happening.

And then Summers ran down the middle of the road. "Come on. Let's go!" he was shouting. He ran to the spot where Alex's men were still in the ditch. Alex looked back to see bullets making puffs of dust as they snapped into the road around Summers. Alex jumped to his feet again, and he shouted, "Move out! Move out! Let's go."

Bullets were filling the air, and Alex was sure that at any second he was going to catch one. He ran back toward his men. And then Summers, soft-spoken Summers, bellowed, "Get out of that ditch. Come on!" He swore at a man and kicked him on the backside.

One man jumped up, then two, and then they were all moving—almost thirty of them. Summers took off in front of them. A couple of men went down, and Alex ran past them. He was catching up with Summers when a mortar exploded in front of him and he realized he was falling. For a moment he thought he had tripped. He hit the road hard, on his chest, but as he tried to clamber to his feet and go again, pain shot through his leg, and he dropped. He struggled to his feet once again, made it up this time, and hobbled forward, but the men of his platoon had run ahead of him and were moving quickly away.

Alex saw another mortar explode on the side of the road, and dirt and dust flew. At the same time, he heard an explosion up ahead, and then two more. Second Platoon had moved in, apparently, and they had gotten some grenades in on top of the emplacement. Suddenly the blasting of the machine gun stopped. Small-arms fire continued for a minute or so, and then everything was silent.

It was all over in just a few minutes, but Alex was lying on the road, and the pain was taking him away from any focus on the action. He looked down to see that a lot of blood was pumping from his thigh. He wondered whether he could bandage it and keep going.

A medic got to him in a couple of minutes. He tore Alex's

pants open and filled the wound with sulfa powder. Then he got a compress on it. Alex got enough of a glimpse to see that he didn't just have a hole in his leg. His thigh muscle was torn wide open.

"I believe you earned yourself a ticket out of this mess," the medic said. "A lot of guys would trade you right now."

Alex didn't want to get out this easily, not when his squad had to go on fighting. And yet another side of him was saying, "It's over for me." And he did feel relief in that.

Lieutenant Summers walked back after a few minutes. "Come on, Thomas," he said, "that's just a scratch. You're not going to leave us, are you?" He was grinning.

"You're a maniac," Alex said. "Why didn't you get hit?"

"You've got me. I should be dead right now."

Alex felt the shame. "I'm sorry about my men," he said.

"Hey, they're really my men. And you got up and led them. I can't believe we ever doubted you. You're the best man I've got, and I can tell you, I hate to see you go."

"Maybe I can stay," Alex said. "If—"

"No," the medic said. "You'll get patched up somewhere and then come back. But I suspect they'll ship you to England for now."

"That's right," Summers said. "But I'll do what I can to get you back to our unit."

"I'm going to give you a shot of morphine," the medic said. "The pain will go away, and you might go to sleep. Just let us worry about everything now. You're going to be okay."

"Thanks," Alex said. "But I don't think I need all that. I can probably walk."

The medic only laughed. And then he gave Alex the shot.

"Was anyone killed?" Alex asked.

"Rizzardi went down next to you, out there on the road. He's alive, but he's in bad shape. A couple of guys from First Platoon are dead. And quite a few are wounded."

Alex was already feeling the effects of the morphine, but

he felt this new stab—Rizzardi—deep in his chest. And then he saw Duncan's big moon of a face, looking down at him.

"They got Alberto," Duncan said, and he cursed. "He's hit really bad." But he didn't look angry, didn't look like the hulk of a man he was. He looked lost, his eyes full of panic, like a kid in a crowd trying desperately to spot his big brother.

* * *

Four days later, on June 15, Gene climbed off the side of his ship and onto an LVT—Landing Vehicle, Tracked. Ten minutes later, he was seasick. He never quite got to the point of vomiting, but he came close a couple of times, and strangely, what kept coming back to him was the thought of a trip to Yellowstone Park he had made with his family when he was little—maybe seven or eight years old. He had gotten carsick, and he had had to stop along the side of the road to vomit. His mom had held him and cupped the palm of her hand over his forehead. He had felt better after that, and Dad had told him to sit in the front seat, where he sat between his parents the rest of the way. And once inside the park, Dad had offered a reward of a nickel to the first person in the car to see a bear.

Gene had been the one to spot the first bear—a mother with two cubs, begging for food along the road. Dad had paid off with that nickel, and Gene had been thrilled. Years later his family had admitted that everyone had seen the bear before he had—but they had kept still so he could win his nickel.

Flashes of that trip kept coming back to him as he held on to the pitching, rolling landing craft. Those had been depression years, and times had been fairly hard for the family, but Dad had made sure they all took a vacation as often as possible. A little vision of the cabin where they had stayed, near Old Faithful, passed through Gene's mind, with the whole family crowded into that one little log room.

The craft took a huge lurch as it struck a wave on an angle and got thrown sideways. At almost the same moment, an artillery shell hit very close, and water exploded over the top of the craft. The island was still well off. Gene wanted more than anything to reach the beach so he could do something—not just sit there and wait.

The island was Saipan, in the Marianas. Gene had never heard of it until the day before, but the word was that it was part of the Japanese empire and was held by more than thirty thousand troops. It was an important strategic site—with a port and an airfield—and the Japanese were not going to give it up easily.

Gene was going in with the second wave—which wasn't supposed to be so bad—but the sound of the artillery was constant, the thuds coming in surges but never really ceasing. Great plumes of water kept shooting into the air as the artillery shells struck, and Gene had seen one landing craft, right alongside his own, take a hit and go down. He had seen men in the water, but only in glimpses, and he had no idea how many of them might have died.

The craft kept pounding up and down and then slipping and vaulting this way and that. Gene was fighting just to stay in his seat. Ahead of him, on the beach, when he got a quick look, he could see damaged landing vehicles at the shoreline. Tracer bullets were flashing across the beach, and Gene could see men down, maybe dug in, maybe dead.

It was obvious that things weren't going well, that the invasion was in trouble. Gene held on as an artillery shell crashed just in front of them. He was thrown back and then forward as the craft slammed into the water and seemed to lose power. But then it rose with a wave, and the tracks caught water again and drove the boat ahead.

The waves finally smoothed in shallower waters, and the speed of the craft picked up, but now Gene could see better what was ahead of him, and the shore was absolutely riddled with the carcasses of exploded landing vehicles. He had wondered how anyone could be left alive on the island after three solid days of navy bombardment, but clearly the big guns on the island had survived, and so had plenty of Japanese soldiers to fire them.

As the LVT neared the beach, Gene heard the whistle of another big shell. He ducked as it struck very close and a gush of water washed over him. The vehicle was amphibious, and the hope was that it would come out of the water on its tracks and carry the Marines straight into the jungle without anyone having to make an unprotected charge across the beach.

The big craft did lumber out of the water, and Gene looked up to see that the driver had found himself a good open stretch of sand. He hunkered down and hoped for the best, but then he felt a terrific impact, and he saw the men at the front of the vehicle erupt out of their seats. The craft lurched forward a few more yards and then ground to a halt.

"Go over the sides," Sergeant Lucas shouted. "Get to the jungle as fast as you can."

Gene, with his rifle in one hand, sprang over the side of the vehicle, stumbled, and fell onto his knees in the sand. Then he jumped up and took off up the beach. He slammed into the back of one of his friends, a guy named Howard Slesser, who for some reason had stopped in his tracks. But Howard slipped down, dropped on his face, and Gene caught a glance of the red spot that had formed on the back of his uniform.

Gene stepped around him and ran forward, but he heard the constant rattle of machine guns, saw the tracer bullets, thick as fireflies, everywhere. Other men were dropping into the sand, and Gene dove down too. He began scratching, almost wildly, trying to get into the sand. The machine-gun fire kept sweeping over him, and he kept clawing, but he heard his sergeant shout, "Don't dig in. We gotta get off this beach. Let's go."

Gene saw the squad leader leap up and run forward, saw other guys doing the same, so he came up out of the sand and ran hard. He felt a bullet hit his helmet, and then another one hit him in the shoulder, and he went down. He felt the terrific burn, but he still flailed at the sand and tried to get himself dug in. He told himself that he was all right, not seriously hit, but out of the corner of his eye, he could see the red of his own blood spreading down the front of his shoulder.

The squad leader had disappeared. Maybe he was dead. But Gene could think of nothing but getting himself as deep into the sand as possible. No training, nothing he had learned or heard seemed to be coming back to him. He only knew he wanted to stay out of that machine-gun fire.

But then he heard Sergeant Lucas again, well up ahead of him. "Boys, you gotta get off the beach. We've got to make the jungle. You'll die out here. Come on. Get up and go."

Gene didn't think of disobeying. He came up out of the sand again. At the same moment he felt a thump in the center of his chest, as though someone had hit him with a rock. And he felt a strange, sudden weakness. He was on his face before he knew it. He thought of trying to dig again, but he couldn't move.

"Corpsman," he said. He had tried to yell, but not much more than a whisper had come out of him. And he didn't really understand. A terrible pain had begun to swell in his chest, and yet he was still not sure it was a bullet that had hit him. All he had felt was that strange thump.

Time went by. A lot of time. And his head was full of buzzing, his chest raging with pain. Then someone had him by the legs, was pulling him down the beach. Gene didn't like the pain, the confusion, but he told himself this was good. Someone was going to save him, make the pain go away.

He may have blacked out for a time, because suddenly he found himself looking up, and he was on his back. A man's face was over his own. "Can you hear me?" the corpsman was shouting, and he was ripping away at Gene's shirt.

"Yeah," Gene managed to say.

"All right. Listen to me. You've taken a bad hit. You gotta hang on. I'm going to give you some morphine, and I'm going to get the bleeding stopped. We'll get you evacuated when we can. But it might take awhile. We're in bad trouble out there."

Gene couldn't think. There was nothing to say, no response he could come up with. But he understood. He could see what this all meant; it was in the corpsman's eyes.

"Letter," he said.

"What?"

"Pocket."

"Don't worry about that for right now. We'll get you to a ship, and we'll take care of you."

"Send it."

"Okay. Which pocket? Up here?" He slapped at Gene's vest, and then he reached inside and found the letter. "Is this it?"

"Yes."

"All right. Don't worry. I'll make sure it gets sent."

And Gene, even in the deep confusion that was running through his mind, understood what the corpsman meant.

3 0

Bobbi was at the hospital when the telegram came. Beulah, the receptionist who brought it to her, said, "I'm sorry, honey, but there's a wire for you."

Bobbi stared at her for a moment. She wanted to think it was a mistake. But Bobbi took the telegram and whispered, "Thank you." Then she walked to the nurse's lounge, which fortunately was empty. She sat on the couch, but she didn't stop to think what she feared the most; she feared everything. She tore open the envelope and read:

SORRY TO TELL YOU GENE KILLED IN ACTION STOP SERVICE ON JUNE 22 STOP HOPE YOU CAN COME STOP

And the world seemed to stop. Bobbi didn't cry immediately. She tried to think. How could this be true? How could there be a world with no Gene in it?

When she did start to cry, she couldn't quit. After a time Afton showed up, but Bobbi didn't want to talk, didn't want understanding and attention. She wanted to be alone. So she hurried from the hospital as all the nurses watched her, and she walked across and around the base. She thought of her family, wondered how everyone would deal with this, but every time she thought of Gene, she forced the image away. It simply hurt too much to see him, hear him. She kept telling herself she would meet him again, that life was eternal, but at the moment that didn't seem enough. Nothing would ever be the same in this life; her family would never know that homecoming after the war that Gene had talked about.

Bobbi got her composure before long, and she walked back to the hospital. She spoke with Lieutenant Kallas and made arrangements for a two-week leave. She didn't cry then, didn't cry when she accepted the condolences of her friends. She walked to the base headquarters building, where she was able to arrange to take a military flight to San Francisco the next morning. Then she took a bus into town, where she sent a telegram to her parents. She was trying to stay busy, trying not to think, but once she had sent the telegram, she only needed to pack, and that wouldn't take long. She didn't want to be in her room the rest of the day, but when she thought of going to see Ishi she knew that meant talking, and she didn't want to do that either.

Bobbi walked to the beach, but that hurt too much because it reminded her of Gene's visit with her there, and so she strolled through Honolulu, and she got away from downtown, where so many young sailors and marines were on the streets. When she finally took the bus back to the base, she packed before Afton finished her shift, and then she went for another walk, on base. She thought about everything in the future, tried to make resolutions, but she didn't let herself remember. When she came back to the room, she thought to put her Bible in her suitcase, mainly because of the hibiscus pressed inside. But she didn't open the pages, didn't look at it.

Bobbi slept fitfully that night, and she woke up angry. All she could think was that the stupid war had robbed her, had stolen a vital piece of her life—and it was still after her, ready to take more. Alex and Wally were just as vulnerable as Gene had been, and now she knew for sure that in spite of all her prayers, God was not going to spare the Thomases—not any more than he was sparing other families. Richard was not hers either. He belonged to this terrible time; the war could do with him as it chose.

But she got up and got dressed, and she finished the last of her packing. She did finally talk to Afton a little, but she said what was expected of her and didn't admit her anger. "Call Ishi, will you?" she asked at the end. "Tell her what happened. And tell her I'm sorry I couldn't talk to her. I'll talk to both of you when I get back—but I just don't feel like it right now."

"I understand," Afton said. She was crying more than Bobbi was. Bobbi finally hugged her. She knew what Afton was feeling. She had brothers in the service too.

By late that morning, after a typical delay, Bobbi was on a long flight across the Pacific. It was the first airplane flight of her life, but she didn't think much about it. By then, a kind of numbness had set in. She had attempted to find consolations—explored them, exhausted them, felt no better at all, and now she was tired and deeply discouraged.

But she finally let herself remember those last two visits she had had with Gene. The memories were almost too tender to touch upon, but she had been the last in the family to see him, and she knew that everyone would want to know about those few minutes she had spent with him. As she thought about the things Gene had said, she began to come back to herself. He had been so wise for a young boy. He had tried so hard to be fair to Millie, and he had known very clearly that he might be going off to die. She remembered what he had told her on that day they had walked to the beach: "I believe in heaven. So everything will be all right—no matter what happens.'"

Gene was okay now. Bobbi knew that. But poor Wally; what a pain it would be when he found out about Gene. And Alex, off in France somewhere. When would the word catch up to him? Those were sad thoughts, but Bobbi was beginning to feel the first glimmer of strength.

After the flight from Hawaii, she was not able to get a flight out of San Francisco, and so she sat up all night on a train. The ride seemed endless. Sometimes she found herself doing pretty well, assuring herself that she was going to handle this, but certain thoughts would strike her, and she would go to pieces all over again. She thought of LaRue and Beverly, of how much they loved Gene. And she kept thinking of Millie, who was surely devastated.

As the night wore on, Bobbi finally stopped resisting her memories. She had a picture in her mind of little Gene, maybe seven, coming down the stairs on Christmas morning. Bobbi, who had been thirteen or so, had gotten to the Christmas tree ahead of him, and she was looking at her gifts. Bobbi had looked up just as Gene had spotted his Schwinn. She had known that the bike was secondhand, repainted and fixed up, but to Gene it had clearly been the finest bicycle in the world. He had stopped where he was and stared, as though he knew in that moment this was something to savor, to approach slowly.

He had always been like that, never very excitable, sometimes subdued, but he had cared about things of worth.

Bobbi and everyone else had gone outside on that cold Christmas day, and Gene had gotten on the bike and ridden without difficulty. He had learned by practicing on his friends' bikes, and he had been patient in waiting for his own. Bobbi could still remember how, after the ride, he had put the bike away in the garage out back. He had used a clean rag to wipe it down, so as not to leave any slush from the streets on it. And then, when his cousins had arrived, he had taken them all out to see it.

The memories kept coming once she let them: the trip to Yellowstone Park; the day he was baptized, so gleaming in his white clothes; the day he had broken his arm, falling out of the apple tree out back, and how hard he had tried not to cry. And, of course, the watermelon. By the time Bobbi reached Salt Lake City, she had savored enough good memories that she was

feeling blessed to have spent the night with her little brother.
But when she looked at her parents, and at LaRue and Beverly,
all the pain returned. Everyone looked so crushed.

She hugged each of them, and they all cried together, and
then Dad said, "Bobbi, we have some other news. I hate to tell
you this right now, but you need to know."

Bobbi's body tensed.

"Alex has been wounded. We don't know how serious it is.
We got a telegram last night that he's in a hospital in England,
so we assume he will live, but we don't know that for sure."

"They didn't tell you *anything* about his wounds?"

"No."

Mom looked overwhelmed, her face white, and seemingly
ten years older than when Bobbi had seen her last. LaRue and
Beverly appeared so grown up, and yet childlike with their reddened eyes and flushed cheeks. Dad was holding on, obviously
trying to show some strength but, behind it all, looking
deflated and weary and not at all himself.

"I'm sure Alex is all right," Bobbi whispered, without believing her words. It seemed entirely possible that Alex, too, would
be taken from them.

"We'll be okay" was all Mom said as she took Bobbi in her
arms again. "It means so much to me that you could be here."

* * *

Alex was in southern England, not all that far from
Aldbourne, where he had lived the winter before. The bone in
his thigh had not been struck, but the muscle had been ripped
open by the shrapnel. A surgeon had cut away a lot of dead
flesh, leaving a deep slice in the side of Alex's thigh, but he had
assured Alex all would "come right" with the leg and he would
be back in the thick of things before long.

In Alex's hospital ward, he was being hailed as a hero.
Word had filtered back through some other wounded men in
his company that Alex had led a patched-together squad that
had knocked out four German 105s. A lot of soldiers wanted

to hear the story, but Alex gave only the barest of details, and he was embarrassed by the attention.

What Alex knew was that once he had gotten into battle, something had happened that he had no way of explaining. He had performed the way he had in war games. He had been trained to handle certain situations, and when those situations had come up, he had seen what he had to do. But there was also a kind of inherent competitiveness in Alex. He had never done anything without setting out to do it well. The battle, in its own strange way, had seemed like a football game; he had simply set out to win and had found a way. At the time, the Germans he had fought in those gun emplacements had had nothing to do with the Germans he had known during his missionary years. They were like extensions of their rifles and machine guns. They were men who were trying to destroy him, and he had needed to destroy them first.

Now—away from the action—it was hard to realize that all that had even happened. He didn't want to be complimented for what he had done, and he had to fight against the memories, to tell himself he was all right, that the things he had done had been necessary. The images persisted, however—all the chaos and violence, and the bodies—and sometimes Alex lay in his bed and stared at the ceiling, wondering who he was now.

With so many wounded men being processed back into England, then sorted out into temporary hospitals, and finally transported to various parts of the country, more than a week had passed before Alex received assurance that his parents had been notified. He had sent a letter as soon as he could get his head clear enough to write, but he didn't know how long it would take for it to get to Utah. So he was actually pleased when a nurse brought a telegram to him. It meant that his parents had received notice and knew where he was, and he could stop worrying about that. The first part of the wire was what he expected: "SORRY TO LEARN OF WOUND STOP LET

US KNOW HOW YOU ARE STOP." But then Alex stared at the next line: "SORRY TO TELL YOU GENE KILLED IN ACTION STOP."

Alex was too stunned to react for the first few seconds. He looked at the nurse, who was still standing by his bed. She obviously saw his alarm. "Are you all right?" she asked.

"My little brother," he said, but he couldn't get anything more out. He didn't want to believe it. His mind kept racing, looking for some way out of this. But he was still staring at the words: "KILLED IN ACTION."

He realized that the nurse had hold of his hand, and he looked at her, through his tears. "This stinking war," she said, with her British intonation. "Boys shouldn't have to die this way. Or get their bodies shot up."

Alex hardly knew what she was saying.

"You're such a lovely boy. So good. I'm sure your brother was too."

And then Alex said something that took him by surprise, something he didn't even know was on his mind. "I'm not good. I killed a German boy. Just a kid—like my little brother." Alex shut his eyes and tried to keep control, but he began to sob.

"You can't help that," the nurse said. "Other people thought up this war, and then they passed it along to you boys."

Alex couldn't say any more, but a thought returned that had slipped in and out of his consciousness many times in the past week. He pictured a family in Mannheim getting the word that their son had been killed in France. His thoughts were still racing, and in the jumble he saw his own family receiving word of the German boy's death.

The nurse continued to hold Alex's hand, to pat it. "We need more boys like you," she said. "I hear too many soldiers bragging about the men they've killed."

"They don't mean it. They just . . ." But Alex didn't know how to explain anything right now.

"Listen to me," the nurse said. Alex looked up at her plump

face, her red cheeks. "My son was killed in this war—in Africa. My nephew was shot down over Germany. He's still missing in action. My neighbor's parents were killed in the blitz. I knew a whole family that was killed when a bomb hit their house. Death is everywhere right now. But you can't lose track of one thing: Hitler thought this all up. We didn't. And Hitler has to be stopped. So do the Japs. Your brother died for something good. He's a hero. And you're a hero, not a killer."

Alex was trying not to cry, trying to accept what she said, trying to think how he could deal with all this. He knew he couldn't let himself go to pieces.

"Listen, love, this is too much for you—so many things all at once. You need to sleep. Won't you let me give you a little something to help?"

"No. I want to think."

"That's the last thing you need to do. I'm going to leave you for just a bit. But I'll be back. My name is Margaret, and if you don't mind, I'd like to be your mum while you're here. I'm still missing my boy." And now the tears came to her own eyes. "You're better looking than he was. I'd rather be twenty-five again and fall in love with you. But all things considered, I'll settle for the mothering." She tried to laugh.

But Alex couldn't respond, couldn't even think what to say.

She patted his hand again, and then she left.

Alex felt the silence in the big room. He didn't want to look at anyone. Pictures were blinking into his mind. He thought of Gene falling in battle, but what he saw was the German boy—curled up, his head on his arm. It was as though Alex had gone off to war and killed his little brother. He knew he would have to fight that idea off, in time, but at the moment he wanted the guilt; it was easier to accept the disappointment he felt with himself than it was to struggle against it. And wasn't it right? Didn't *all* the killers share in the responsibility for *all* the deaths?

Alex wished he could be with his family, to share the grief

with them. But he couldn't get rid of the idea that if they saw him now, they would see through him, know he had blood on his hands.

"Are you okay?"

Alex looked over. The guy in the bed next to him had been shot through the abdomen at Omaha beach. His intestines were all ripped up. He had already gone through two operations and was scheduled for another. He slept most of the time, and Alex had gotten used to his silence. "Yeah. I'm all right."

"Your brother was killed?"

"Yes. In the Pacific."

"I'm sorry."

"Thanks." But the words struck Alex with a force he wasn't ready for. Alex was so sorry too—for everything.

* * *

All day, all evening, neighbors and friends and family came to the door at the Thomas home. They entered quietly, usually carrying covered dishes, loaves of warm bread, desserts, hot rolls. They hugged all the Thomases, cried with them, said all the things a person says at such times, especially: "I don't know what we'd do if we didn't have the gospel." Bobbi believed that too—but she grew weary of having to respond over and over, having to talk so much. She felt enveloped in love, and she appreciated the kindness; she was merely tired of all the words.

Lorraine Gardner came late in the day, and she brought a picture she thought the Thomases would want. It was a little snapshot she had taken of Gene and Wally. Gene was wearing an argyle sweater with a bow tie, and he was grinning, reaching behind Wally and holding two fingers up, to make horns. Wally was smiling, posing for the camera, but apparently unaware what his brother was doing. "I took this after church one day, when I was over here," Lorraine told Bobbi.

"Wouldn't you like to keep it?" Bobbi asked.

"I have some others of Wally, but I thought your family would like to have this one."

Bobbi took it, studied it for a time, and then hugged Lorraine. "I thought you were in Seattle," she said.

"I've been home on vacation, but I'm heading back tomorrow. That's why I came tonight. I won't be able to make it to the memorial service. My train leaves early."

"Let's walk outside for a minute," Bobbi said. "I need to get out of this house for a little while."

Lorraine agreed, but she said she needed to talk with President and Sister Thomas first, and so Bobbi walked out to the front porch and waited. It was a pretty evening. The sun was finally setting over the Oquirrh mountains. A long streak of thin clouds was turning pink, shading to gold. All day Bobbi had been aware of how wilted and brown Utah seemed, compared to Hawaii, but she liked the feelings this porch brought back. The dry air felt good. Crickets were chirping, and the sunset was like a favorite line from a poem—familiar, fitting.

Bobbi stood and watched as the color gradually faded. When Lorraine slipped quietly out to the porch, Bobbi asked softly, "Do you miss Utah?"

"Sure. Seattle is beautiful. But this is home."

"When I hear people's voices, I think, 'Oh, yeah, that's what home sounds like.'"

"I know," Lorraine said. "I always feel like I'm being careful in Seattle. People think Mormons are strange, so I worry about the impression I'm making. Here, I remember what it's like to be myself."

Bobbi tucked her hands into her skirt pockets and continued to look across the valley. "When I talk to the nurses I work with, I run out of things to say after a few minutes. I used to get tired of the way Mormons all think alike, but when I'm away from this valley, that's exactly what I miss—the way we understand each other."

"That's right," Lorraine said. "We all start with the same notions about what life means."

"Things are starting to change here, though," Bobbi said.

"And those of us who have gone away, we're changing too. Especially the soldiers. I don't think the boys can come back and just pick up where they left off. They're going to be different people."

"What do you think two years in a prison camp has done to Wally?"

The color in the clouds was almost gone now, but a glow was turning the Oquirrhs into a curving black line. Bobbi walked over and sat down on the love seat. Lorraine leaned back against the railing of the porch. Bobbi thought how beautiful she was, as slender as ever but more completed now—fully a woman.

"I don't know what Wally will be like when he comes home, Lorraine. I can't imagine him changing very much—but who knows what something like that might do to a person?" She paused and then asked, "Do you still think a lot about him?"

"Sure. Every day. Almost every hour."

"But you're not waiting for him, are you?"

"No."

"Are you dating anyone in Seattle?"

"Yes. I met a Mormon guy up there. A navy officer. We've only been going out a couple of months, but he's talking marriage."

Bobbi laughed. "I was about to say we're in the same situation. I've met a navy officer, too. But my guy never talks marriage."

"I wish that's what Neal would do."

"Why?"

Lorraine walked over and sat down next to Bobbi. She crossed her arms and leaned back in the love seat, but it was a long time before she answered. "I don't know," she finally said. "He could be transferred at any time—or shipped out to sea. Everything is so uncertain. And then . . . it's hard to commit to someone when I still have Wally on my mind so much. There's nothing to say that Wally would even be interested in me when he comes home. But he's still the person I've felt the very most for in my life."

"Lorraine, I don't like to say this, but he might not come home."

"I know."

Neither spoke for a long time after that. A little breeze had picked up, and it was making gentle rustling noises in the lilac bushes by the porch. It wasn't like the sound of palm fronds; it was a sound of home she had never even thought about.

"It seems like every girl I know is waiting," Bobbi said. "If not for *someone,* at least for the war to end."

"So life can start again."

"That's right. That's exactly how it feels. The whole world is waiting."

"So here I am with a chance to get married, and I'm holding off," Lorraine said. "The dumb thing is, as much as anything, I don't want to give up my job. I never thought I would have such important responsibilities or have to make so many decisions. I'm actually in charge of a lot of people—even some men. It's pretty exciting, to tell the truth. If I got married, and Neal got transferred . . . but that's silly to make that one of my considerations."

"I don't know if it is. One thing the war has done is give girls some new choices—and I don't think we're going to give them up all that easily."

"Maybe we should. I don't know. But I like being taken seriously. I don't think my mom ever experienced that. To my dad, she's just always been his 'sweet little wife' and nothing more. My mother has no problem with that, but I will—and the problem is, I think Neal wants someone more like my mom."

"Lorraine, I never realized how much alike we are. We've got to keep in touch from now on."

"What do you mean? How are we alike?"

"I've just always wanted to *do* some things with my life.

Make some of my own choices. And not let my husband's life dictate everything I do."

"Neal doesn't want me to work. I think it bothers him when I talk about my day on the job—like it's just as important as what he's doing."

"He sounds like Phil Clark."

Lorraine laughed. "And I know what you did with him."

Bobbi laughed too, but then she said, "I won't make any specific recommendations. But I would suggest that you be careful."

"That's what I'm being, Bobbi, and my parents think I'm crazy."

"I know all about that, too."

"So tell me what to do."

Bobbi laughed again, quietly. And then she said, "I'm too selfish to judge, Lorraine. I've always hoped you would be my sister-in-law someday."

"Thanks," Lorraine said, and she took hold of Bobbi's hand. "I wish I could take some share of your pain right now—and carry it for you. I loved Gene so much." But then, as a car pulled up to the curb out in front, she said, "I'd better go. You're getting more company."

"It's just my grandparents."

"You'll want to talk to them, though, and I've got to get packed." And so Lorraine got up, and the girls hugged again.

"Are you going to be all right?" Lorraine asked.

"I guess so. It doesn't feel like I'll ever be happy again, right now, but I know I will."

"All I've been able to think, since I heard, is how much Wally and Gene loved each other—and how much Wally is going to hurt when he finds out."

"Oh dear. Let's not start that. I can't stand to think about it."

They hugged one last time, and Lorraine left. At the same time, Grandpa and Grandma Thomas were coming up the walk. When they reached the porch, they realized who was sitting in the love seat, and they stopped. Bobbi had talked with them a little that morning, but a lot of company had been around, and since then she hadn't seen them. Bobbi stood up and hugged her grandpa. He patted her back, mumbled softly that he hoped she was doing all right, and then walked on into the house. Grandma took Bobbi's hand, pulled her back to the love seat, and then sat down next to her with her arm around her shoulders. "How are you doing, honey?" she asked. "I mean, really?"

"I don't know, Grandma. Mostly I feel numb right now. It's been a long day."

"You need to go to bed soon."

"I will. But tell me something first. It's been on my mind all day. Was Gene just about the sweetest boy who ever lived, or am I only making that up?"

"Well, I'll tell you. I hate what we do to people at funerals. We take real human beings and turn them into angels—pretend they were perfect when they were much more interesting than that. I just hate funerals for that reason. But I do have to say, I can't think of anything bad about Gene. Can you?"

Bobbi thought for a while. "When he was about ten," she said, "he sneaked into my room and read my diary. For about a week after, he kept teasing me about things I'd written. I wanted to throttle the little guy."

"I'm glad to know that. The boy was a criminal after all." Grandma laughed, deep and rough, the way she had begun to do in recent years.

Bobbi slipped her head under the wide brim of her grandmother's straw hat and rested it against her shoulder. "The only problem is, somewhere along the line he realized that he really was embarrassing me—and he came up to my room and told me he was sorry. I can still see him standing there, his head down, so remorseful. I couldn't even be mad at him."

"That was Gene," Grandma said, her voice thick with emotion. "I've had a notion for a long time that some people are too good for this earth—and God lets them come back to him sooner so they don't have to suffer a long mortality."

"I've thought of that too."

"I'm sure you know about my little girl, Rose—your dad's little sister. She got pneumonia and died when she wasn't quite two. She was like Gene. Her disposition was always just so loving and gentle."

"Grandma, how long did it take before you could think about her without feeling a lot of pain?"

Grandma laughed again, almost silently, and she wiped her white-gloved fingers over her cheeks. "It never goes away, Bobbi."

"Oh, thanks. That's just what I needed to hear."

"But honey, the pain evolves into a delicate sort of joy. Rose has always stayed who she was—that wonderful little girl. I can hold her whenever I need to and know that she's still mine. Most children grow up and decide you're stupid. But Rose is mine, and as I get older, the best compensation I have is to know that when I die . . ." She stopped and laughed. "And that could happen any day now. But when I do, I'll have my little Rose to finish raising. That time used to seem very far off, but life passes much faster than any of us ever think it will."

It was the same thing everyone had been saying all day, but now it seemed real. Bobbi felt the hope: Gene really would be waiting for the rest of the family. "Thanks, Grandma," Bobbi said. "But don't die right away. I need you here."

Grandma gave Bobbi a hard squeeze. "The difference is, you won't have any sweetness to think about when I'm gone. Everyone will get up at my funeral and say, 'Now that was the crankiest old lady I ever knew.'"

"You try hard to sound cranky, Grandma, but it's an act. You're a sweetheart, and we all know it."

Grandma laughed again and wiped at her cheeks. "Oh, Bobbi, I have to admit, you've always been my favorite. You're a spunky girl, and there's nothing I like better. I think we were cast from the same mold."

They both laughed, and both continued to cry. Then Grandma pulled Bobbi even closer. For a long time after, they sat on the porch, saying nothing, listening to the crickets. Bobbi felt wrapped in goodness. She was so glad that at least she had this place, this family, to come home to.

3 1

Bobbi brought Millie into the Relief Society room for the family prayer. Gene's body had not been shipped home and probably wouldn't be. Everyone agreed it was time to hold the memorial service and try to bring things to a conclusion, but not having his body, not seeing him one last time, left everything feeling abstract and unfinished.

President Thomas said the family prayer, and Millie shook with sobs as Bobbi clung to her. And then everyone walked into the stake house chapel, which was packed. Elder Joseph Fielding Smith was sitting on the stand. President Thomas had asked him to speak, but along with him was President David O. McKay, who had apparently come to represent the First Presidency. When President Thomas walked to the stand, President McKay, a tall man with a full head of thick white hair, stood and embraced him.

The building was full of flowers—gladiolas and carnations, mostly. So many people in the Salt Lake Valley knew the Thomases, and almost everyone in the stake had chosen this as a way to thank President and Sister Thomas for all they did. But people knew Gene, too, had known him since he was a little boy, and knew him for his sports heroics. So many young women were in the congregation—all the girls from East High, it seemed. The young men, on the other hand, were noticeably absent, most of them serving in the military themselves.

Bishop Evans conducted the meeting, and it all seemed a little much for him. He was a shy man, certainly aware of the large crowd and the presence of General Authorities. He spoke softly and sounded nervous, but he welcomed the people, and then he read the obituary from the *Deseret News.* To that he added, "Gene was my good friend. He was . . ." But he couldn't continue, so he didn't. He cleared his throat and wiped his forehead with his handkerchief, and then he lifted his glasses and wiped his eyes. His balding head was glowing white, his face deeply tanned, and his brown suit hung too loose on him. He stood for quite some time before he announced the opening hymn and prayer. Then he sat down.

President Thomas was the first speaker. Mom had tried to talk him out of doing that, but Dad had felt he needed to say some things. As he stepped to the pulpit, however, Bobbi could see he was struggling. "I'm moved," he began, "by this large turnout. I'm sorry the building is so warm."

Bobbi was aware of all the fluttering movement in the congregation, with so many fans in motion.

"I appreciate your special effort to come today. I . . ." But then President Thomas did something Bobbi had never thought he would do in public. He broke down, tears running down his cheeks. He pulled a handkerchief from his pocket and wiped his eyes and nose, and he held on until he could say, "I'm sorry. I don't mean to do this. I'm just very touched by your goodness. You have all been so kind. I know that a good many of you have already lost your own loved ones in this war. We all understand each other's sorrows these days."

Bobbi took hold of her mother's hand. Mom had been doing pretty well until Dad had begun to cry. Bobbi was also still holding onto Millie, who was on the other side of her.

"My Great-grandfather Thomas crossed the plains with the early pioneers," President Thomas began. "He and his family were driven out of Nauvoo in 1846. They crossed on a ferry, before the river froze over, and then, as spring came on, they set out across Iowa. Along the way, my great-grandfather buried his oldest child, a son named Alexander. I was named after that little boy."

President Thomas stopped and took a long breath. Bobbi could see his big chest rise and fall. "My great-grandparents couldn't delay the wagon train. They buried little Alexander, and then they moved on, even though Grandma Thomas was expecting another child and was not well herself. That evening the company reached a river where a bridge was washed out. It would have to be rebuilt before the wagons could cross. So the next day my great-grandparents rested. Grandpa wrote in his journal, 'Took care of personal matters today. Felt little desire to do much else. Both Mary and me feel nothing but despair."

President Thomas hesitated, tucked his hand in his pocket, and looked down. "You have to understand, Grandpa had lost his first wife, Elizabeth, along with a daughter, back in Missouri when the Saints were driven out of Far West. Grandpa was a leader, so he was being chased by a Missouri sheriff. That left Elizabeth on her own. Her baby was sick when she started out, with some other Saints, to flee the state. Exposed to the elements, the baby didn't last long, and then Elizabeth, broken by the loss, got a fever herself. She made it to Illinois, but she died soon after. So my great-grandpa had lost his family, but he had started over, married again, and prospered in Nauvoo. Now he was watching the same thing happen to his second family.

"Early in the trek across Iowa, he had buried a little baby boy, and now he had buried his only other child, his firstborn son. So he took that one day off, and that's when he wrote that he felt such great despair. But here's the point I want to make. The following day, he wrote just one sentence in his journal: 'Worked on the bridge today.'"

President Thomas had been building some strength, some

power in his voice. But these words stopped him. He had to wait and breathe again. And he wiped his eyes. "Brothers and Sisters, I've told this story to my family so many times they start to moan when I get anywhere near it. But I want this story to sink deep into the hearts of my children, and their children, and every generation after them. Because that is who we are. My grandparents grieved for a day, and then they went back to work. And things didn't get any easier. Great-grandma Thomas almost died in childbirth in Winter Quarters, but she survived and made it West, and she bore eight more children after that, one of whom was my grandfather."

President Thomas's voice was back. "Brothers and Sisters, the Thomases are not the only family with a great heritage. You have your family stories. Most of you had grandparents who crossed the plains, or who joined the church in Europe and made the hard voyage across the ocean. And they passed on to you not only their stories but also the strength to live through times of great difficulty. We are in one of those times now, and we can sit down and despair, or we can build the bridge that needs to be built. Today is my day to mourn; tomorrow, I must be about my Father's business. And so it is with all of us.

"Gene gave his life to protect us from evil, from men who would rob us of our freedom. What I feel more than anything else today is that I must—and you must—be certain that such deaths are not in vain. We must recommit ourselves to goodness, to the struggle against Satan. Victory on land and sea is not enough; we must win a victory in the hearts of all mankind. Guns will never carry the day; only the gospel of Jesus Christ can save the people of this world.

"As you know, our son Walter is in a prison camp in the Philippines. Another of my sons, Alex, is wounded and lying in a hospital in England. We finally received word that he is recovering, but he's certainly gone through a great deal of pain."

Bobbi heard a stir in the congregation. This was something many people obviously didn't know.

"I also have a daughter here today who will soon return to the Hawaiian islands, where she serves as a navy nurse. What I feel today is that one sacrifice is enough. I don't want to give any more. But the war is far from over, and I have no idea what more might be asked of me and my family—and you have no idea what will be asked of you. The great question is, are we equal to the test? This is our chance to show that we are as strong as the pioneers, that we can carry on, that we will never turn away from our God—our fathers' God—no matter what the challenge."

Bobbi was moved. She really wanted to find this strength in herself. But she didn't feel it right now. She was so tired.

President Thomas's voice softened. "Gene was a boy without guile. He was not suited to be a warrior. He would have been a better missionary. As it turned out, his war was over quickly, and I believe he is now serving where he is best suited.

"Sister Thomas and I—all our family—will miss Gene throughout the balance of our mortal existence. There will never be a way to have back what is gone—not in this life. But we accept God's will and put our trust in the Almighty. We will work unceasingly to build his kingdom here in Zion and to carry truth to the world. That's our commitment to you."

But at that point President Thomas seemed to go away from his planned text. He added, in a hushed voice, "We keep saying it would be a little easier if we had him here and we could see him one last time. But maybe not. Maybe it's better to remember him as he always was—smiling and full of fun."

Bobbi was sure her father had intended to end with power and promise, but he had lost all that now. And so he let himself cry for a few seconds, and then he said, "Thank you all, again, for coming," and then he bore his testimony quietly and sat down.

President Thomas had asked Jesse Evans Smith, a trained

opera singer and wife of Elder Joseph Fielding Smith, to sing. She stood now, and in a voice that filled the big chapel, she sang "Come, Come, Ye Saints."

Bobbi was moved by her wonderful voice, but especially by the obvious sincerity of her feelings. Bobbi could feel her tenderness when she sang the final verse: "And should we die, before our journey's through, happy day, all is well." It was a hymn every Mormon knew by heart, but the lyrics seemed new today. Bobbi was understanding them for the first time. "We then are free from toil and sorrow too." Bobbi told herself to remember that. Gene really was better off where he was.

When Sister Smith sat down, Elder Smith got up slowly and walked to the pulpit. "I shouldn't say anything right now," he said. "I should say amen to that great hymn, that beautiful rendition by my wife, and we should all go home." He hesitated. "That's what I *should* do. But you all know me well enough to know I won't do it."

A little ripple of laughter ran through the congregation.

"We all know what we believe about death. Not one of us here believes that death is a tragedy. We know that this family—President Thomas and his children—are sealed together for all eternity. We know that this life is just a speck of time in that eternity, and we know that the Thomases will be together forever once this brief time ends. I don't have to preach a sermon about all that, because we know it."

He looked down at the pulpit, but he had no notes to look at. "President Thomas has said what needs to be said today. He's given himself this day to mourn, and then he has promised you that he will be back on the job as your stake president. And now my wife has sung with great power a hymn that is an anthem to all the Saints who have gone before, as well as a call to faith for those who will come after. So what else is there to say?"

There was silence in the chapel. Elder Smith was known as a man with as deep a grasp of the gospel as anyone in the

Church, and clearly everyone was waiting to hear what he might add.

"I'm going to tell you something I've said many times. So it won't come as a surprise. But it's not enough to know a thing. We need to live what we know."

Again he waited.

"Brothers and Sisters, we got into this war because we weren't righteous enough as a people, as a nation, to avoid it. The Lord might have withheld all this misery, all this pain, but we didn't deserve that blessing. And so we are paying dearly. But have we learned yet? Are we changing our lives?"

He looked around at the congregation, took a long time to let the people think. "Well, I'm not sure. I see some folks living better, appreciating more, gathering their families around them, and committing themselves to righteousness. But I also visit our boys in their camps, and I'm not always happy with what I see. Some of the boys are preaching the word of God to their comrades in arms; they're resisting sin and setting an example of proper living. But others are letting this war—the atmosphere of the military—carry them right down into the sewer."

Again he hesitated, his eyes darting back and forth across the congregation. He was a slender man, white-haired, with round, wire-rim glasses, and he had a hawklike way of fastening his eyes on one individual after another.

"Far too many of our boys have taken up smoking and drinking. And I hesitate to tell you the stories I've heard of corruption and immorality. I hear the language used by soldiers, and I wonder whether our boys will ever be able to keep their thoughts clean, let alone their mouths. But what worries me even more is the breakdown I see here in this valley. We are changing, brothers and sisters. Some of it comes from outsiders who are coming here to work in our defense plants. But far too much of it is homegrown. I see women walking about in skirts that would embarrass their pioneer parents. Some young people, soon to be separated, conclude that morality is old-fashioned in such an age. I see men justifying every manner of behavior, forgetting that we are a society of Saints, not voracious sharpies who take financial advantage of our neighbors.

"In many ways, as Winston Churchill said, this is our finest hour. Some people are deepening their commitment and serving church and country as never before. But this, my friends, is also our refiner's fire, and I fear that far too many of us will be burned."

He laughed quietly. "I know what you're thinking. Brother Smith is at it again. Singing the same old song. But ask yourselves whether you are better off than you were in the depths of the Depression. This war has brought hardship, but it has also brought financial prosperity. And with that has come pride. Ask yourselves, are you using your prosperity to bless your neighbors and the Church, or are you filling your head with all sorts of so-called modern ideas?"

Elder Smith's hands had slipped up to his lapels on his dark, double-breasted suit, but now he let them fall back to the pulpit. "Now what about this young man?" he said. "Gene Thomas. A nice-looking boy. Tall and straight. True to the gospel in every way. I watched him play football and basketball, and what a beautiful thing it was to see him play. He went into the service because he felt it was his duty. He came back from basic training without bad habits. He came home as good and kind as he ever was. So, good for him. He met the test. He kept his second estate. He's moved on to a better world. We should be very happy for him today. He's just the kind of boy this Church is supposed to produce.

"What about his family? Do they have a right to ache, to miss him, to feel his absence? Of course they do. And therefore we should all ask ourselves what we can do for them. We must rally around them, support them, and love them, just as they have done for you so many times when you have suffered. We must get through this together, brothers and sisters, just as the Saints have always done. We do that by living the gospel, keeping our vision clear, and not giving ourselves over to the money-grubbing materialism that is growing in our society. We must pull each other's wagons when they get stuck in the mud, and call upon the Spirit to give us collective strength. As President Thomas has told us, our boys are going off to die, and we must not let them die in vain. We must win our own private battles—the ones raging in our hearts and souls."

He stopped and ducked his head for a moment. "Well, I've said enough. Too much. Let's all go home. The Thomases need some time together." He suddenly closed in the name of Jesus Christ. Then he turned to President McKay. "President, did you wish to add anything?" he asked.

President McKay hesitated, and then he rose and stepped to the podium. Elder Smith slipped around him and sat down. President McKay smiled. "Elder Smith tells us he has already said too much, and then he asks me whether I want to add some more."

The congregation laughed. President Thomas looked up and smiled.

"I don't mean to sound light-minded," President McKay said. "But it's not in our tradition to be too solemn on such occasions. Let me just say, first, that President Grant wanted very much to be here today. He loves President Thomas and his family and asked me to convey his sympathy and best wishes. As you know, however, even though his health has improved, he's not able to do all the things he would like to do."

President McKay paused and seemed to think for a moment. "As Elder Smith has said, this is, in many ways, a day of celebration. We should all be happy for young Gene Thomas, who met the challenges of this life so well."

President McKay looked down at Sister Thomas, along with Bobbi and Millie, LaRue and Beverly. "And yet . . . I've been sitting here thinking about these women and girls here on the front row: Gene's mother and sisters and, as I'm told, his sweetheart. I know that all their hearts are breaking. How could it be otherwise?"

President McKay's eyes filled with tears. "I'm reminded of another of our brothers whose life was also taken at an early age. And I'm reminded of the women who wept for him outside the sepulchre. Christ chose to visit these women first after he arose from the dead. It was they he chose to comfort and then to send forth to spread the good news that he had risen."

President McKay looked slowly back and forth along the row, making eye contact with each. "Sisters, Christ is with you now. He wants to comfort you. Don't wrestle too much with the realities just yet, but open your hearts and give Christ the chance to heal your pain. Most of us here today have known the heartbreak that comes with the loss of a loved one. *Everyone* eventually will. Only Christ offers the balm that can ease your suffering. I'm not talking about theology now; I'm talking about peace. I'm talking about a spirit that soothes our hearts, gives strength when all other strength is gone. I'm talking about an inner reassurance that lies beyond words, even beyond hope. There are simply times when we must give our hands to the Savior and let him lead us through the dark."

President McKay was a handsome man, with a warm, good smile. He smiled at Bobbi and the others now, but tears were on his cheeks. "I'm not telling you this is easy. But I bear my testimony that when the darkest hours come to us, God doesn't step aside and let us go it on our own. Don't think any more than you have to for a little while. Just turn to him and take things one day at a time."

He bore his testimony of the gospel then, closed in the name of Christ, and sat down.

In closing, the congregation sang, "God Be With You 'Til We Meet Again," the hymn Mom had chosen but which Bobbi had wished not to sing. It seemed to crack her heart in half just when she had started to feel a little better.

After, the Thomases stood at the front of the chapel.

President McKay and Elder Smith came to them first, talked quietly for a few minutes, and then left. President and Sister Thomas, along with the girls, shook hands with many people who wished to offer their condolences and hadn't had the chance to do so before the meeting. Millie waited, still sitting up front. Some people stopped to talk with her, too.

Then the family gathered in the gymnasium, and the Relief Society served a big dinner. After that, many of the family members went back to the Thomases' home. The atmosphere there was strangely like Christmas, with so much family around, and the mood not really so different. Bobbi heard laughter in the house, and friendly greetings, and she took comfort in that Mormon style of consoling each other.

But Bobbi was worried about Millie, and so she took her upstairs to her old room, which was LaRue's now. Millie lay on the bed and cried for a time, with Bobbi next to her, gently patting her back.

"Bobbi," Millie said after a time, "I don't see how I can do this. I have my whole life to live, and it feels like I can't do it without him. I know President McKay is right, but . . . everything just seems so pointless to me right now."

"You've had a crush on Gene since you were about thirteen, haven't you?"

Millie rolled onto her side and looked at Bobbi. Her blonde curls were falling apart and her eyes were red, but she looked pretty, so delicate. "Bobbi, I was crazy about him when I was just a little girl in grade school. As far back as I can remember. He was so shy and so sweet, and I loved him long before he ever took any interest in girls. He's the only boy I've ever wanted. And now, just when he finally started to feel the same way about me, I have to give him up."

"When he came to Hawaii, he talked about you, Millie. He told me he hadn't wanted to make any promises to you, because the future was so hard to know. But I could tell how much he loved you."

"I know. He told me—finally—that last time he was home." She put her head back into the pillow and let herself sob.

"This will be made right somehow," Bobbi said. "It has to."

"How?" Millie raised her head again. "Do I marry someone else in the temple—and lose Gene? I promised him I would wait forever, so do I do that and never have a chance to have a family in this life?"

But Bobbi had no answer for that. She only said, "Millie, I might be in the same position before this war is over, so I've thought a lot about it. I don't know what I'll do either."

"So tell me how it can work out right."

"I don't know. I just believe it will."

Bobbi realized she had nothing to say that would help right now. So she let Millie cry. And she thought of Richard. For Bobbi, the problem was even more complicated. She didn't know Richard very well. How could she reach a sensible conclusion if she ended up having to make the same choice?

After a time Mom came upstairs. "How are you two doing?" she asked as she stepped into the room.

"Not very well, to tell the truth," Bobbi said.

Mom walked over and sat on the bed. "I'm not sure how I'm doing, but I know I've heard enough people tell me that I have to be strong. Right now, I just want my son back—and I don't want any more *kindness*."

Bobbi laughed. "Thanks, Mom," she said. "You always tell the truth."

Sister Thomas reached over and rubbed Millie's back. "I'll tell you this much—the women will have to be the strong ones. Men give good sermons, but they're not half so good at carrying on after the funeral is over. It's all about keeping the clothes washed and the floors swept, when it gets right down to it. Now come on, I need your help. Come downstairs and help me put the house back together. Most everyone is gone."

And so they went downstairs, all three of them, and they washed the dishes left over from that morning—and from the fruit juice Mom had served to the family. They carried chairs back to their places, and Bobbi vacuumed the living room. It was surprising how much good it did her just to do that. LaRue and Beverly helped, too, and after, they all sat down at the kitchen table, and Sister Thomas got all the girls talking about the new styles. "I surely agree with Brother Smith about one thing," Sister Thomas said. "I can't find a skirt long enough to cover me up. I have to make everything for myself, and then I can't get material."

"Dad about threw a fit when he saw my new church dress," LaRue said. "But that's the only thing the stores sell now. I bought it at ZCMI, for heaven's sake." She laughed. "The lady at the store said the skirts are shorter because the dress companies are on rations for material. I told Dad I was just being patriotic."

"You're doing your part, aren't you?" Bobbi said.

LaRue's pretty smile flashed, and she lowered her voice. "To tell the truth, I love the styles. But then, I have the legs for them."

Everyone laughed, and Mom said, "Well, I don't. And it's almost impossible to buy a pair of nylon stockings anymore."

"Get some of that makeup, Mom," LaRue said. "That's what everyone is using. It looks *exactly* like you're wearing nylons."

"You have to be careful with the stuff," Bobbi said, and she started to laugh. "Some of our nurses tried it in Hawaii, and in all that humidity it got sticky. They got makeup all over their white dresses, and Lieutenant Kallas about threw a fit."

"I don't want to use it," Millie said. "It's too much bother."

Bobbi watched Beverly, who was almost thirteen now and clearly eager to be part of this. "LaRue tried it," she said. "She had me draw a line up the back of her leg, for a seam, and I got it all crooked. It was a mess."

Beverly was giggling, but Mom said, "LaRue, you don't need to be thinking about nylons."

This set off a good-natured little debate, but as the conversation quieted, Millie said, "Sister Thomas, my mom told me that J. C. Penney's got in some material—mostly cottons. I thought I'd go down and take a look tomorrow. You might want to take a peek while they still have something. We could go together, if you want."

These were important words, coming from Millie. Bobbi heard her saying, "There's something I plan to do. Tomorrow."

Dad had spent some time in his office, and now, when he walked into the kitchen, he seemed a little surprised to see the five females gathered around the kitchen table. "Did you want any supper?" Sister Thomas asked.

"No. I ate enough over at the church."

"I know. But I need to cook. How about if I splurge and use up my sugar? I could bake something."

"Sounds good," Bobbi said.

"I was thinking we might have a family prayer," Dad said.

"Yes. We'll do that," Sister Thomas said. "But not right now. We don't need to start crying again. LaRue and Beverly, why don't you run over to Piggly-Wiggly's and get us some eggs, and Millie and Bobbi can help me think what to bake. Al, you read the newspapers. You've got four of them stacked up in the magazine rack."

President Thomas nodded. "I do want to do that," he said. And then he added, "Thanks, Bea."

"Thanks for what?"

"Just . . . you know. The bridge."

"Okay. But don't talk about it. We'll all just get up in the morning, and we'll start building."

"That's good. That's right."

But Millie said, softly, "I need a bridge of some kind myself. I don't know what to do with myself right now."

"Don't worry," Sister Thomas said. "We can help with that. In this family, we always find plenty of bridges. And you're part of the family. Do you understand that?"

Millie was losing control again, and Bobbi took her in her

arms. But Sister Thomas walked to the cupboard and said, "Girls, now come on. I need help figuring out what I'm going to . . ."

But she couldn't do it. She broke down.

President Thomas walked to her and took her in his arms. "It's okay," he said. "Grandpa took one day. Let's have a family prayer now. We need to pray for the other boys."

Bobbi was happy to do that, and the prayer helped. She felt some of the comfort President McKay had spoken of, and, as he had advised, she tried not to think too much. She knew she had to let the Spirit touch her heart and heal it, a little at a time.

* * *

Alex's leg was healing very well. The first two weeks, when he couldn't get out of bed, had been bad. He had had way too much time to think. But he was walking every day now, and he was working hard to control what he told himself about the war. He wasn't sure what it might be like to go into battle the way the Book of Mormon prophets had—to feel spiritual and warlike at the same time. Maybe he could never manage something like that. But Margaret had told him she was glad he hadn't liked the killing, and he tried to find some comfort in that. Over and over he asked himself, did he believe in this war or not? The answer was that he did. He had done what he had to do, and he couldn't go through life blaming himself.

But that didn't stop the dreams. Almost every night he awoke, sweating and in a panic, his mind full of bloody pictures. And in the daytime, little flashes of memory would suddenly take his breath away. What he felt ran much deeper than what he was telling himself, and he knew it, but he also knew that he would be going back, and so he had to be under control.

He finally got a letter from his parents, and they seemed to be holding up all right—also doing their best to keep their emotions from defeating them—but he wished he could go home, at least for a while. It was where he should be, and yet, one more thing he had no control over. He wrote a long letter to his family, assured them that he was all right, and he said a lot of brave things about accepting Gene's loss. But even as he wrote the words, he wasn't sure what was from his heart and what was only to satisfy expectations.

And so he walked as much as he could, sat up and read to keep his mind busy, and he dreaded the nights. He agreed to take pain medication, mainly so he could sleep, but that only lasted so long each night, and then he usually waited, wide awake, for morning. He thought a lot about Gene. A great hole had been cut into his heart, gouged out like the slice in his leg, and both scars would always be there. He felt cheated, as much as anything, because he and Gene had never gotten to know each other as adults. The two had been separated just as Gene was coming into his own as a young man.

Alex was lying in bed one afternoon in early July. More men were arriving from the front all the time, and the hospital was filling up. Two extra beds had been crowded into his ward, but he still felt distant from the others. The new man next to Alex now was in bad shape. He had been hit by mortar shrapnel, and his body had been torn to shreds. He was medicated heavily and slept most of the time. Margaret had told Alex that the man was likely to survive, but she didn't think he would ever walk.

Around the room, with ten beds crowded together, there was usually quite a bit of talk, but Alex was at the far west end of the room, and he said very little. At the moment, he was enjoying the afternoon sun. The weather was overcast so much of the time, and so he was happy for the brightness today. He was looking toward the window, seeing the tops of a row of trees—huge, spreading oaks, like the live oaks he had seen in Georgia—and beyond, a little green hill. He thought of going outside, but he had already walked enough that day, and his leg was hurting.

When Margaret came into the ward, Alex paid little attention until she walked to his bed. "Alex, my boy, I have a surprise for you. I know it's a bit too good to be true, so I thought I might warn you just a little. It's *that* wonderful."

Alex tried to think what she was talking about. "I can deal with it," he said, smiling.

"Look toward the door," Margaret said.

Alex saw a young woman walking toward him, and then his body jerked as he realized whom he was seeing. "Anna," he whispered, but he still didn't believe it. Any second he was sure his vision would clear, and it would only be some pretty English girl Margaret had brought to visit him.

But it was Anna, and now she was hurrying to him.

She stopped at the foot of his bed, and the two simply stared at each other. Alex hardly knew what to do, but his first thought was that she was twice as lovely as he had remembered. She was older now, a woman. She was crying, and her huge blue eyes were magnified by the tears.

"How . . . ?" Alex could only think to say.

But she answered in German. "We escaped into Switzerland," she said. "And then to France."

He hardly heard her, could still not comprehend that this could be true. He reached his hand out to her, and she came around the bed and took hold of it. They continued to look at each other, but it was like trying to look into the sun, almost too much for Alex.

"Are you doing all right?" she asked.

"I'm fine," Alex said, and then he remembered to speak in German. "I'm almost healed."

He was pulling her closer now, unsure of himself but needing so much to hold her. He kept looking into her eyes, and now her face was directly over his. She bent a little more, and their lips were almost touching. He had never kissed her, never been this close to her, but he wrapped his arms around her and pulled her to him, and he felt the wonderful softness of her lips.

Then he held her next to him, and he tried to believe that anything this exquisite could actually be real.

He finally realized that the men in the room were cheering and clapping, and he was suddenly embarrassed.

"Hey, Thomas," someone yelled. "How about sharing the goodies?"

Alex didn't answer, but Margaret said, "You boys be careful what you say. This is his betrothed."

Alex let Anna go, and she stood up straight, but she took hold of his hand again. "I know about your brother," she said. "I wrote to your parents to find out where you were. They wrote to me and told me what happened."

"Where are your parents?"

"In London."

"Are they all right?"

"Yes. But something terrible happened. We got split up, and Peter didn't make it across. We don't know what happened to him. People in the French Resistance have gone into Switzerland, but they can't find him. Papa thought it was safest to get us all to London. But Papa wants to go back to Switzerland as soon as he can, so he can search."

"How can your father get there?"

"It's not so difficult to travel across southern France now. The German military has its hands full trying to fight the Allies."

"Are your parents holding up all right?"

"Not really. They're very worried. But we thought people here in England might hate us, and they have been very kind. Once they find out we had to flee the Gestapo, they consider us their friends."

Alex needed to talk to her about so many things. He hardly knew where to start, but that kiss was still lingering on his lips, and he wanted more than anything to hold her again. She seemed to know that, and she bent over him. He took her in his arms.

"I didn't know whether I could ever be happy again," he said.

He felt her body shake as she began to sob, and he felt the warmth of her tears on his neck. "I know," she said. "It's what I thought so many times."

3 2

Wally had been through a lot lately. All during his imprison-
ment, he had watched men die of dysentery, but he had
worked hard to keep himself and his utensils clean, and he was
pleased that except for his time in the jungles of Tayabas, he
had remained relatively free of illness. But in the spring of 1944
he had fallen ill, and the Japanese had sent him to the sick barracks, a place very few men ever returned from.

Wally had come close to dying, but Chuck and Art, along
with Don Cluff, had stuck with him, sneaked extra rice in,
encouraged him to hang on. His friends never admitted it, but
Wally knew they were giving up some of their own food
rations, no matter how little they received themselves. "I'm getting a few vegetables in me—out in the garden," Chuck told
Wally. "I'm healthy as a horse. You need to eat this."

Wally's friends fed him at times when he was too sick to lift
his head, and Wally gradually got enough strength back to
return to his own barracks. He was disheartened to find that
someone had taken advantage of his illness and stolen his
boots, but when he discovered one of the healthy American
cooks wearing them, he was too weak to do anything about it.
"Prove they're yours, skinny," the man had told him, and Wally
had had to turn and walk away.

But Wally gradually began to work again, and he got a turnip or a leek to eat once in a while. The vitamins seemed to help. He was starting to feel fairly strong again when rumors began to circulate that some of the men were going to be shipped to Japan. Most prisoners believed that conditions would be better there. Speculation also had it that the Japanese were losing the war and that the prison camp would soon be liberated, but that was actually a frightening prospect. It could possibly mean freedom, but on the other hand, the guards had often threatened to kill all the prisoners if the camp were attacked, and everyone believed they might actually do it.

Wally wondered whether he should volunteer to join the group going to Japan, and he and Chuck spent hours talking about it, but in the end, it hadn't mattered. The Japanese were taking five hundred men, and anyone who was moderately healthy was chosen. No one knew exactly what life would be like there, but it was a change, both frightening and promising, and Wally liked the idea that the next year wouldn't be another one exactly like the last two.

The trip to board the ship was like others that Wally had taken. He was marched with the rest of the men into the town of Cabanatuaan, where they were jammed into boxcars, and then, in the miserable heat, with no water or sanitation, they were hauled to Manila. There, they were marched through the streets to Bilibid prison, a place Wally remembered all too well. He saw living-dead prisoners, who were supposedly being cared for but most of whom would surely die. What he learned was that the medical personnel had been shipped out, and prisoners in Bilibid were being starved to death.

That night, in the prison, Wally asked around to see whether anyone knew anything about his friend Alan. No one there knew the name, but some told him that not many men had survived the work detail Alan had been with. Wally felt that if anyone had, it would have been Alan. He hoped maybe he would see him again in Japan, or at least after the war. But in truth he feared the worst, and anger boiled up in him as he thought how Alan must have been treated.

The next day a group of another five hundred men arrived from a prison camp on the island of Mindanao. Wally recognized some of the men who were from his old squadron, and he took some pleasure swapping stories about the days before the war. But he also learned, to his sadness, that many of his old friends were now dead. Lieutenant Dark, for one, had gone out on a work detail and never come back. And Harvey Opdyke—big old Harvey—had dwindled down to a skeleton before he had died of malnutrition and disease.

After a few days, all one thousand of the men were marched from Bilibid and through the streets of Manila. A lot of Filipinos lined up to watch the "parade," and some of them laughed and made fun of the grimy prisoners. But others signaled their support. At the pier, the prisoners waited for hours, without food, before being loaded on an old relic of a coal-burning ship. Word was that it was a Canadian vessel, captured and taken over by the Japanese.

Once on board, the men were divided into two equal groups and sent down into the two holds of the ship. There was simply not room for everyone, and the men were crowded close together without enough space for everyone to sit down. Then the guards threw a tarp over the hold, and that only held in the heat and cut off the air. The men were smashed together in the dark, and within a short time the hold was stifling, the smell disgusting, the air so stagnant it was hard to breathe. There were no sanitation facilities until the guards threw down a few five-gallon cans, but with so many men these were almost impossible to get to. All this time, the men received nothing to eat or drink.

The first night was hellish, but finally, toward morning, the vibration of the engines started, and the ship began to move. At least they were underway—or so the men thought. They soon learned they had only been moved out into the bay, where the ship had anchored. All day the prisoners suffered with the heat and the crowding. Wally found himself breaking out with a burning rash. But when the men screamed for air, the guards told them to be quiet or they would receive no food.

The prisoners did get a little rice to eat that day, but when night came the ship was still anchored in the bay. Wally had seen so much in his years of captivity that he thought nothing could test him any further, but conditions had seemed almost human at times at Cabanatuaan, and he had gotten used to that. He had been hopeful that a change might bring something better, but now he knew that this trip, however long it might take, would certainly be the end for many of these men. Another few days like this, and the weaker ones would begin to die.

That night the engines started again, and the ship actually seemed to be heading out of the bay, but in the morning the prisoners learned that the ship had turned around and come back. No one knew why. At least the guards pulled the canvas back and allowed some air into the hold. In fact, groups of prisoners were allowed to go out on the deck, a few at a time, and have a smoke or at least breathe the sea air.

But now a routine set in. Every night the ship would start out, sail out of the bay, then turn back and anchor near Corregidor. Occasionally the guards would throw the tarp back, but most of the time the men were covered over and had to live with the stench and unbearable heat. Fleas and body lice thrived in this atmosphere, and Wally and the others were bitten all over. Two weeks passed that way, and still the ship was in Manila Bay. Some of the men believed that American ships were patrolling the area and the Japanese kept turning back to avoid them, but no one knew that for certain.

Wally stayed with Chuck and Art and Don. They stood up much of the time, to rest their backs and relieve the crowding a little. They talked part of the time, when their energy was up, and tried to distract themselves from all the agony. They told and retold stories of high school days in Salt Lake, and Don related more of his own background. He had grown up in a small town in southern Illinois where his wife and two daughters still lived. He had farmed, as a boy, and the service, as much as anything, had been his escape from that life. Now, he thought it wouldn't be so bad. "Every day I tell myself I've gotta get back to my wife and my little girls," he told his friends. "That's what keeps me going."

"For me," Wally said, "it's the hope I can *have* a wife and kids."

"So what do you think has happened to Lorraine Gardner by now?" Chuck asked.

"I'm sure she's married," Wally said. He looked away.

"What happened between you two?" Art asked him.

"She got tired of me, and I don't blame her. I wasn't doing anything with my life. I was flunking out at the U." Wally was leaning against a bulkhead. His legs were aching from all the standing. His only clothes were a threadbare pair of shorts and a tattered khaki shirt. He was barefoot and he was hungry, as always, but it was such a normal feeling that he didn't think much about it.

"I always thought you were pretty smart," Chuck said. "How come you didn't do any better in school?"

It was all so far back—so little a part of who he was now. "I don't know, Chuck. Things seemed important then that don't matter to me now. I always felt like my father was pressuring me, so I thought I had to show my independence—or something like that. The truth is, I was lazy, more than anything."

"What are you going to do when you get home?"

"I'll go back to college, I'm sure. I'll do better this time. If nothing else, the Japs have taught me some discipline."

"It's good to know we have something to thank them for," Chuck said, and he laughed. "But don't you hope Lorraine's not married?"

"Sure. And I think she'd really go for a good-looking guy like me. I'm slender, have good bones—that you can see—and a heck of a nice beard." Wally rubbed his hand over his face. He hadn't shaved since leaving Cabanatuaan, almost three weeks before. "This haircut is nice too." He ran his fingers through his stringy hair.

But Wally found himself pushed toward a favorite fantasy. When all this was over, he would get a chance to eat all the food he wanted. He would eat meals of roast beef, potatoes and gravy, big glasses of milk, and all the pie he wanted. And then he would be shipped home, and he would learn that Lorraine had been waiting for him all along. She would look *exactly* the same. In fact, on the day he would finally see her, he would walk toward her front door, and she would be standing on her porch wearing that light blue dress with the polka-dots, the one she had been wearing the day he had told her good-bye. She would stand there in the sunset, looking the same as she had then, but when she recognized Wally, she would race down the sidewalk and throw her arms around him.

Wally looked out across the hold of the ship, in the dim light. He saw the dark lumps out there, the broken men, trying somehow to hold on to life one more time. Every one of them was clinging to memories and to fantasies, but the truth was, nothing was going to be the same when they got back. What he also knew was that he could—and would—settle for much less. He would never again need to indulge himself. He just wanted to have three meals a day and a nice bed to sleep in. All his talk about getting rich meant nothing to him now. He had no illusions about having Lorraine, but what he did want was to find a really nice girl, and he wanted to get married and have a family. He wanted to be a good dad, not all that different from his own father, however strict Wally had found him before.

In the third week, men began to die. Wally hated to think

how many wouldn't make it if things continued this way. But he told himself he had to survive one more time.

The guards seemed to be as tired of the situation as the men were. They were gradually becoming more disagreeable, even abusive. They communicated most of their demands through an army general who was on board, and this had become increasingly annoying to the prisoners. The general seemed entirely too willing to please the guards, and the prisoners questioned what he was getting out of it. One morning the general stood before the men and began his announcement, as usual, by saying, "Men, the Imperial Japanese Forces have directed me to instruct you that—"

Someone shouted a foul curse at the general and then called him "your Imperial Majesty." The general surely knew he was without power in this group, but he might have kept his dignity. Instead, he cursed the man in the same language, and suddenly shouts broke out all across the hold, most of the cursing directed at the general.

Wally was sitting with his friends, and they were close to some men they knew from Cabanatuaan. Some of those men joined in the shouting. "Hey, come on, you guys," Wally told them. "Don't start that."

A guy named Eddy Nash turned and said, "I'm sick of that guy."

"I know. We all are," Wally said. "But what are we turning into? We're supposed to be soldiers—all on the same side. The Japs must love hearing us turn on each other down here."

The guards shouted for the men to be quiet, threatened them again with no ration of rice that day, and the prisoners quieted. The general's announcement turned out to be a warning that men would no longer be able to go out on the deck for smoking breaks unless they showed more respect for the guards. The soldiers listened, grumbled a little, but didn't dare complain so loudly that they would jeopardize their food ration.

After the general sat down, Don said, "Wally's right. We've got to watch out or this place could get out of control. Everyone is on the edge—and it wouldn't take much for people to start killing each other over a few grains of rice."

"Yeah, I know," Eddy said, and that seemed the end of it.

But Ray Vernon, a lieutenant like Don, turned to Wally and said, "I don't know how you do it, Wally. You have more self-control than anyone else I've come across."

Wally was taken by surprise. He knew he had changed in some ways, but all his life he had thought of himself as the weak one in his family. It was hard to imagine that anyone would think of him as self-controlled.

"Chuck and Art are the same way. They're all Mormons," Don said, as though that were explanation enough.

Wally, of course, remembered the prayer he and Don had shared long ago, but Don had also known Wally in the days when he was drinking beer with the men and showing little evidence of his Mormon background. It seemed strange that Don could dismiss all that.

Ray looked at Chuck. "Is that it? Is that what keeps you guys going?"

"We all keep going," Chuck said. "Everyone who's still alive has found strength from somewhere."

"I know. But the guys who were on that work detail in Tayabas all say Wally was the one who got them through."

"I don't think that's true," Wally said. "A lot of guys—"

"So what do you guys believe?"

It was a startling question. In all his years in the military, no one had ever asked Wally something like that. Some had said, "So what do Mormons believe?" but Ray was asking, "What do you believe that makes you what you are?"

"We're Christians, the same as most of you guys," Art said. "But we believe a lot of doctrines got lost from the early church—from back at the time of Christ—and a prophet had to bring back the full truth."

That was a nice little summary, but Wally knew that wasn't exactly what Ray was asking. "Our people were hated," Wally said. "Back a hundred years ago, we got driven out of Ohio and Missouri and Illinois before we ended up in Utah. My dad always said that the weak people fell by the wayside, but the ones who stuck with the Church got stronger. My whole life I've listened to him tell me that I have this great heritage to live up to. The truth is, I haven't been very good at doing that. I'm just trying to do better now."

"Your old man would be proud of you now," Ray said.

"Not really. A real Christian doesn't carry around as much hatred as I've got inside me. I try to think the best of these Jap guards, but I have a hard time. Art does a lot better at that than I do."

"If a guy has to give up hating Japs to be a Mormon, I could never get in," Ray said, and he laughed.

But Wally looked away. He had become rather satisfied with his progress at times lately, but Ray had a point. Maybe Wally didn't deserve to be "in" either. Here was a chance to teach some men the gospel, but Wally knew he still couldn't hold himself up as a great example.

Two nights later the ship sailed out of the port in a terrific storm, and this time it didn't turn around. Maybe the storm had provided the cover to sail away without being stopped by American ships. The men all wondered if their ship were spotted at sea, would the Americans sink it? Was there any way for them to know who was on board?

As it turned out, the storm raged for eight days, during the entire crossing to Formosa. The men in the hold were tossed about and were almost constantly seasick. Vomiting was the worst thing for already malnourished men—and many of them died. At least the prisoners were allowed to crowd onto deck where they could breathe the air, even if they were often out there in driving rainstorms. On deck, Wally watched the daily burials at sea. It seemed so tragic to have lasted more than two years, passed through all this misery, only to die so needlessly.

Wally watched the men eat their rice, one kernel at a time, just to savor it and make it last longer, and he watched them catch rainwater any way they could so they would have enough to drink. He knew of several times when men had kept bodies hidden for a day or two just so others could draw the extra ration of rice. That was ghoulish, in a way, but Wally understood how desperately everyone was trying to stay alive.

Eddy Nash could not stop vomiting, and Wally saw that he was sinking fast, so he stuck with him. He and the other men helped him get out to the air every day, and they shared some of their ration of rice with him. When the ship reached Formosa, the tarp was put back in place, and Eddy almost died that evening, but Wally kept finding water for him and got him through the night. The next day the men were allowed to get off the ship and wash themselves with fresh water. Wally and Chuck helped Eddy down off the ship. They undressed and washed themselves, and then they helped Eddy do the same. Formosans gathered around to see the naked Americans, but Wally didn't care. When he signaled to one of the Formosans that he needed food and pointed to Eddy, the man slipped away quickly and came back with a piece of bread and a bit of fish. Wally took a big chance, but he reached out and took the food, and then he fed it to his friend. By that night, Eddy was already showing some increased strength.

Later, back on the ship, Wally could smell the fish on his hands. He licked at it and tasted the oil. He longed to have had some of it himself, but that night as he listened to Eddy breathe, less labored than the night before, he felt good about what he had done.

For two weeks the ship sat at the dock in Formosa. The hold of the ship was being loaded with coarse salt, so the men were allowed to spend their time out on the deck, but the sun baked them, and the humid heat was overpowering.

Finally the ship steamed from the harbor, and the men began their last leg to Japan. Wally had no idea what he would do there, how long he might have to stay, or whether he could keep surviving. The men spent most of their time on deck now, and the weather wasn't so severe. Wally spent long hours talking to his friends. Time and again the talk turned to religion, and Wally, along with Chuck and Art, continued to explain the teachings of the Church.

During the tedious hours when Wally was left to his own thoughts, he always tried to imagine what was happening at home. When the year had begun, he had thought the war might end before the next Christmas, but that seemed unlikely now. He wished, somehow, he could get a letter from his family. At least that would tell him what everyone was doing. Alex and Gene were probably fighting somewhere. If only he could know where they were and that they were all right—or if he could just know that the day would come when all of them would be together—then he thought he could stand anything.

33

Alex had been "in hospital," as the British called it, for six weeks, and for the past two Anna had come to see him every day. Her branch president in London had known a member of the Church in the area, a widow, who had been willing to let Anna stay with her. Anna spent as much of the day with Alex as she could, and the two spent their time catching up on all that had happened to them since they had last seen each other. In many ways, they were getting to know each other for the first time. They talked about their childhood experiences, their opinions, their likes and dislikes, everything. Nothing was more delicious to Alex than to share his thoughts and explore Anna's—unless, of course, it was to look at her while they talked.

They spoke German much of the time, but Anna was trying to improve her English. During the time she had spent in the cellar, she had worked to increase what she already knew, and now, since coming to England, she had devoted herself to the project. She was expanding her vocabulary and doing fairly well, but she understood the language much better than she spoke it. What she couldn't do yet was carry out a long and intense conversation of the kind she and Alex were constantly engaged in.

Alex promised to show Anna all the letters he had written her over the years. That would help him remember what he was thinking at the time. But what he finally admitted to her one day was that he wasn't the same man who had written those letters. "Anna," he said, "I have some things going on in me. I'm not quite sure who I am now—after what happened to me in France. I need to get some things under control. I'm still having bad dreams—and thoughts that scare me."

He expected her to ask for more details, but Anna said softly, "We both have things to forget, or to overcome." She took hold of his hand, and then she told him about her experience with Kellerman—about the attempted rape and the way she had cut his face.

Alex couldn't help thinking that he had set off a chain of events in Germany that had brought terrible grief to Anna and her family. What was even worse was that a suspicion lurked in his brain that he was more like Kellerman than like Anna—not the victim but the attacker. He didn't tell her that, didn't even fully admit it to himself, but sometimes, in subtle ways, he felt he was hiding some of himself from her. And yet she seemed to know that, and she kept reassuring him. It was the best help he could have received, the constant knowledge that she loved him.

The other men in the ward had shown some hesitancy when they had found out she was German, but when the word spread that she had fought the Nazis, and that she had barely escaped with her life, they began to think of her as a heroine. Or maybe they were only too happy to accept her. Anyone that pretty, who walked through the ward each day—greeting them all by name—was awfully easy to like.

Margaret made certain Anna got lunch if she were there in the middle of the day. It was breaking all sorts of rules to have a visitor in the hospital so long—especially a nonrelative—but Margaret also took care of that. Clearly, she loved Anna too.

But gradually reality was setting in. The fact was, Alex

would soon be returning to his battalion. Early in July the 101st Division had been pulled out of the fight in Normandy, and the 506th Regiment had returned to Aldbourne, arriving on July 13. Alex found out that the men all received two new uniforms, back pay for the time they had been gone, and seven-day passes. Most of the men from E Company headed straight for London, where they got drunk and stayed that way. Curtis had been released from the hospital by then and was back in camp. He spent a few days in London, sober of course, and then returned to camp. A couple of days later he decided to visit Alex.

When Curtis walked into Alex's ward, limping a little, he glanced at Alex, but then he looked at Anna and walked straight to her. "Aren't you Anna?" he asked.

"Yes," she said, smiling. "How did you know?"

"From your picture. How did you get here?"

Alex rehearsed the story, or at least a short version of it, and all the while Curtis hardly looked at Alex. His eyes were on Anna. "I'm so happy for you," he told her.

"Are you all right?" Alex asked him.

"Sure. But let's not say too much about the whereabouts of my wound."

"Hey, I won't bring it up," Alex said, grinning. "But I'll bet you're the butt of a lot of jokes."

Curtis rolled his eyes and smiled. Anna had missed the play on words, and neither man said anything to explain.

"What happened to the guys after I left?" Alex asked.

Curtis was still standing near the foot of the bed. He glanced at the floor, and his smile faded. "From what everyone says, you saw some of the worst of it, Alex. But they got into a few more nasty situations, mostly during the next couple of days after you were shipped out."

"Did we lose any more of our men?"

"Yeah. Quite a few. The 506th took about fifty percent casualties. Fourteen E Company men were killed. Morehead's airplane crashed, and he was killed without ever seeing action. You know about Cox. But McCoy didn't make it either. Or Huff."

"I was afraid of that."

"They were together, from what the men heard, and everyone thinks Huff was trying to help McCoy with his wound. I guess a German patrol found them; no one knows exactly."

Alex was having a hard time with this. "So Huff and McCoy are dead," he whispered. "What about Rizzardi?"

"He lived, but he's in bad shape. His gut was all torn up. He'll be going home when he can, but he'll never be the same."

"How many wounded, besides you and me and Rizzardi?"

"Well . . . Duncan took that minor wound you know about, but he kept going, and something sort of strange happened to him. Our platoon had to fight through those hedgerows, and the Krauts were . . ." He stopped and looked at Anna. "I'm sorry," he said.

"It's okay," she said.

Curtis looked back at Alex. "You know how the Germans had tanks set up behind the hedges?"

Alex nodded.

"Well, our men had to get past each hedge, one at a time. Our platoon got in a bad fight, up there by Carentan, after you got shot. The guys in our squad came out all right, but then, for a couple of weeks, they were dug in, in a defensive position. It was supposed to be easy—just hang on to what they had. But artillery was coming in all the time, night and day, and our big guns were going all the time. It was real bad, from what everyone says. One of those days, when they were getting incoming stuff all day long, Huish got hit with some shrapnel. It wasn't too serious, but he went sort of crazy. Duncan ran over to help him, and Huish jumped up and stabbed Duncan with his bayonet, thinking he was a German soldier, I guess."

"How bad is Duncan?"

"Not too bad. Huish caught him in the chest, but Duncan

grabbed his arm in time. The bayonet didn't go in deep—and it didn't hit anything vital. Right now, Duncan's in London, and I'm sure he's got plenty of painkiller running through his veins. No one knows where Huish is. Some think he's in a psychiatric ward somewhere."

Alex was still stunned. So many of the men were gone already. How could anyone expect to make it through the rest of the war if that many had gone down in the first action?

"The first couple of days after the men got back, they talked about everything that happened over there," Curtis said. "They hardly talked about anything else. But now they've all shut up about it."

"Why?"

"I asked Campbell about that. He said that after a few days on the front, he got so death didn't mean a thing to him. He saw too much of it. He figured he would probably get hit, and he didn't worry about it. When he heard about McCoy and Huff, he said he didn't even feel anything. But now, after getting out of all that, he can't stand the idea of going back. I guess you get away from the battle and you start to think like a civilian again—and you get scared."

"So what's going to happen next?"

"We're picking up replacements already. A lot of guys think we'll be back in the action right away." Curtis smiled. "If I were you, I wouldn't heal too fast."

"Are you okay, Curtis?"

"Yeah. I was pretty lucky. I got hit in a good spot." He smiled again.

"I know. But how are you feeling about everything?"

"Well . . . I don't know. I think I was lucky that I got wounded early and got out of there. I saw just enough to understand what it's all about." Curtis glanced at Anna and then back at Alex. "The men who were over there the whole time seem different to me. They were only in the fight for about a month, but they just don't seem like the same guys. Duncan's not bragging and talking about whipping the Germans. He talks about Rizzardi all the time. Seeing his buddy get messed up like that was awfully tough on him. But no one is making any big claims anymore. The only guys who can't wait to get to the battle are these new gung-ho replacements we're getting in."

"We're just getting started, Curtis."

"Yeah, I know."

Alex and Curtis took a long look at each other, but they said nothing more until Alex said, "Curtis, my little brother got killed."

"Oh, man. I'm sorry to hear that, Alex."

"He was in that bloody battle in Saipan. He got killed on his first day of action."

"His name was Gene, wasn't it?"

Alex nodded.

"So I guess that's a lot worse than the wound in your leg."

"Yeah. Much worse."

Curtis tucked his hands into his pockets and looked at the floor. "I guess there's no chance you can go home for a while?"

"No. I'll be back at Aldbourne before too much longer. I won't be able to jump out of an airplane for a while, but I'd rather be back with our guys than sent off with some other company."

"Well . . . at least you'll be back with me, and I really need someone who—you know—looks at things the way I do. And all the guys say you're the one to follow. You can't believe how the men talk about you now." Curtis looked at Anna. "Did you know that Alex is going to get a medal?"

"No. He didn't tell me. He tells me nothing about the war."

"Well, he's a hero. Major Higginson put Alex in for the Medal of Honor. It's the highest honor a man can get in our military. From what I hear, only one Medal of Honor was allowed to each division, and someone else in the 101st is getting it. But as soon as the paperwork goes through, Alex is

getting a Distinguished Service Medal. I don't know if I'm supposed to mention that, but everyone knows."

"What about the other men? All I did was—"

"Everyone who went in there with you is getting either the
Silver Star or the Bronze Star. Even me. Major Higginson said
we saved hundreds of lives down on Utah beach." Curtis
laughed. "All the guys in the squad say the major is going to
pin my medal on my back pocket."

By now Anna was catching on, and she laughed.

But Alex said, "We didn't just save lives, Curtis; we took
lives." And he was thinking, "German lives. Anna's country-
men."

"I know. But it doesn't do any good to think about that,
Alex. It's just the way things are in a war."

"You can't help it," Anna said. "That's what you told me
about the things that happened to me." She had told him about
the young guard Crow had killed at the border.

"Maybe not," Alex said. "But I don't want any medals." He
looked past Anna, out to the countryside. It had been raining
off and on, and the sky seemed to be clearing.

"So what kinds of plans do you two have?" Curtis asked.

Alex glanced at Anna and saw her turn red. The two had
an understanding, unspoken, that lay behind everything they
talked about. They sometimes spoke of the distant future, and
when they did, that time always included both of them,
together. But they had said nothing of the days immediately
ahead of them.

"First, I have to get out of here," Alex said. "Do you have
any idea how soon we're going to be sent back out?"

"Just rumors. Most of the men think they'll drop us in
behind the lines somewhere. The infantry needs to break out
and drive for Paris—and then on to Berlin. There was all this
talk, there for a while, that we'd be in Berlin by Christmas, but
the progress in Normandy has been slow. So I don't know. It

would make sense to bring us in behind the German defense so we could help the infantry bust out."

Alex nodded. It sounded right. If another drop was coming soon, he would miss it. But even if he did, he would be in on the next one—and it was a long way to Berlin. It hurt to have Anna here now and then to think of leaving her behind one more time.

After Curtis left, Alex decided that he did have to talk to Anna about their plans. "Anna, you heard what Curtis said," he said carefully, in German. "We're probably heading back into France before long. After our next drop, I doubt the army will pull us back here. We'll be based on the continent, I would think."

"I understand this," she said.

"Has your family decided what to do? Are you going to stay in England?"

"My father doesn't know. He can think only of Peter right now. He used to speak of going to Salt Lake City to live, but I told him I wouldn't leave as long as you were here, and he understands that. As soon as he can, he wants to go back and look for Peter in Switzerland."

"If I get shipped out, what would you do?"

"Alex, I . . ."

"What?"

"I don't want to lose you again."

"But I can't help it," Alex said. "The doctor says I'll be able to go back."

"That's not what I mean."

Alex was confused. "Just tell me what you're thinking."

Anna leaned forward and took hold of Alex's hand. "I can't tell you. You've never . . . asked me. Not exactly."

"To marry me?"

"Yes."

Alex had hesitated because he hardly knew what to expect in the future, but now he suddenly realized that she needed to know for sure what he intended. Margaret wasn't on duty at the moment, but Alex called for another nurse. When the woman came to his bed, Alex said, "I'm going to walk outside for a little while. Anna can help me."

"It might be a bit damp out there," the nurse said. "And slippery."

"The sun is shining right now," Anna said. Alex looked, and it was true. Some rays of sun had broken through the clouds.

"Well, all right. But don't be prancing about. You don't want to fall and hurt yourself. Don't try to slip off into the woods either. We'll all be watching you." She laughed and slapped Alex on the foot. "If you start showing too much vim and vigor, we'll send you back to your camp, and you won't be able to dally about with this lovely girl all day. Think about that."

"I have thought about that," Alex said, laughing.

Anna handed him his robe. He had walked a good deal lately and was starting to feel much stronger. He was even walking without his cane. Outside, the grass was glistening with the fresh rain, and a rather wild-looking "English garden" that hadn't been looked after lately was producing a host of colors. The setting was perfect, except that the two of them were in full view of the men in the ward. So Alex continued walking beyond the garden and down a path past the row of oaks he had looked at so many times. Once he knew he and Anna were out of sight, he stopped and turned toward her. He kissed her, held her for a moment, and then stepped back to look at her.

"Anna," he said, "the first time I looked at you, I thought you were the most beautiful girl I had ever seen. But I fell in love with you on the day you came back from that terrible fever. Since that day I've never thought of marrying anyone but you. I'll admit that sometimes I wondered whether we would really like each other so much, once we had some time together, but these days have been perfect, and now I have no doubt in my mind."

Her eyes had filled with tears—those bright blue eyes.

"I wish I could kneel down," Alex said. "But I'm not too good at that yet."

"You're fine as you are," she said, smiling at him.

"Will you marry me, Anna?"

"Yes. Yes." Tears spilled onto those perfect, sculptured cheeks of hers.

Alex took her in his arms again and kissed her—more fervently than before. He had never had a chance to hold her this way, standing up, and it was almost too much for him. He held her for a long time.

"But let's not wait," she said.

"What?" He took hold of her shoulders and moved her back from him so he could look into her face.

"I want this time together. We don't know what time we might have after that."

"But if something happens to me, you would—"

"If something happens, I would be married to you forever, and I would have you in the next life."

"But there's no temple here. We can't be sealed."

"I could do that later. I have learned all about that. If we were married, then I could have you sealed to me."

"You want to get married right away?"

She nodded.

It was all a new way of thinking for Alex. He had thought of it at times, but the idea that he could be with her for such a short time and then have to go back to the war was too much contrast to imagine. How could he go from a honeymoon to a battlefield?

"I don't know, Anna."

"Let's accept what we have. We'll worry about the rest later. All I've thought about for three years is you, Alex. I can't let you go away from me without knowing we'll have each other forever."

Alex nodded. "All right. My doctor said he needs to get me

out of here soon—because he needs the room. But he doesn't want me to go back to my unit until I'm healed a little better. He talked about getting me a seven-day pass. We could go to London. But this wound is still . . . not exactly what I would want on a honeymoon."

"It doesn't matter."

Alex smiled.

"My branch president in London said he could perform the marriage, but you have to get a license from the army. Your chaplain can make arrangements."

"You really have been thinking about this, haven't you?"

"I thought you would never ask me," she said. "I worried that maybe you—"

But now he pulled her to him again. "I was only worried that it wasn't fair to you."

"The other way is the most unfair, Alex."

Alex thought he understood that. He had received a long letter from Bobbi, who wanted her officer back and was worried she would never see him again. Bobbi had told him about Millie, too, who was so lost without Gene. Maybe this was better, however awful it would be for Anna if he didn't get back.

Alex got out of the hospital on July 24. Only he, of course, had any idea that the date had any significance. But like those early pioneers who had arrived in Utah on that date, Alex had done a lot of walking lately—at least for a man with a wound in his leg. He wanted to get back in shape, knew he needed to, but he also didn't want to be limping about like an invalid on his honeymoon.

The Stoltzes had come out to visit him on two occasions, and on the day of his release, they came and accompanied him and Anna on the train back to London. The Stoltzes wanted to help Alex constantly, but Alex had no trouble getting about now, even climbing up the steps into the train. By then, he had made the arrangements for his marriage license. His chaplain had made a trip to the hospital, from Aldbourne. A doctor at the hospital had also done the necessary blood tests. Margaret had seen to that.

So Alex and Anna, with the Stoltzes, headed straight to the branch president's house. It was late afternoon when they arrived. President Wakefield had a congratulatory telegram from the Thomases. With it, the family had also wired some money, and so Alex had plenty for the honeymoon. He had already made reservations at a nice hotel, and so the added money would make it possible to eat good meals, and perhaps do some sightseeing. What Anna didn't know was that Alex had managed to talk the doctor into a ten-day leave, and he had made reservations in a cottage in England's lake district, in Windermere, near the area where William Wordsworth had lived.

President Wakefield was a little man, bald, with round glasses that magnified his green eyes. He was a gentle man, too, and thoughtful; he had some important things to tell Alex and Anna. He shook his stubby finger at Alex and told him, "You have a treasure here, young man. You must always treat her with honor and respect."

Alex nodded his agreement.

"I think you will," President Wakefield said, and he smiled, but then he added, more carefully, seriously, "You two are entering this covenant at a difficult time. Your lives are not your own. The war, at very least, will separate you, and it may cause you unthinkable challenges. Above all, you must be willing to accept whatever comes, to stand by each other in every test you may face."

The words were no more ominous than the reality Alex had already envisioned, but they crystallized his concerns. He glanced at Anna, who was breathtaking in her simple white dress. He wished he could cling to her and hide from all that lay ahead.

"My only advice is that you trust the Lord absolutely. Accept his will in your lives. The wounds in Alex's leg will heal, but deeper wounds always come from war. Both of you know that already. When peace finally comes to your lives, turn to the Lord for healing, and love each other without reservation. I promise you that you'll be all right if you do that."

Alex needed to hear that. He was still holding so much in his heart that he knew he would have to expunge somehow.

When Alex and Anna had made their promises, had been pronounced married, had kissed and exchanged gold bands, Sister Stoltz came to them first, held them both in her arms at the same time. She had aged a great deal in the past five years, but she was a beautiful woman, a promise of what Anna would always be. She cried, and Alex understood the complexity of her emotions, of everyone's feelings. But she told them, "I'm so happy for you. I know God brought us here so that you two could be together."

Brother Stoltz stepped closer. "I know that, too," he said, and the words were enormous to Alex. This was that stout, strong man with the rigorous, tough mind—the man who had doubted everything Alex had taught him at one time—and yet he had come this far. Alex felt his own faith leap, and he told himself that if God had brought them all this far, surely he would take them through the rest of the way.

The moment felt right. So many miracles had happened for it to occur. Alex took Brother Stoltz in his arms and gripped him tight. "I'll always be good to Anna," he said. "I promise you that."

"I have no doubt of that," Brother Stoltz said. "What I ask, now, is for the Lord to bless you. If I can see you happy together, and if I can bring our Peter back, I will never again complain about anything."

Alex nodded. Somehow, it seemed, those things simply had to happen. But he thought of Gene, and he knew there were no guarantees.

3 4

The Thomases were building their bridges, but not with great pleasure or enthusiasm. Life for the present was a tedious task, and their greatest hope was that things would gradually get easier, more satisfying. Millie was working at the plant for the summer, and all the Thomases loved her, but seeing her was a constant reminder of Gene's absence.

About two weeks after the memorial service, Millie had received a letter from Gene. For a moment, she had let herself believe that a miracle had happened, that the report of his death had been a terrible mistake. But she knew better, and when she opened the envelope, what she found was a letter that began, "In the morning I'm going into battle for the first time. If I don't come out of it all right, there are some things I wanted to tell you."

He told her that if he didn't make it back, he had to believe that that was what God intended for him—and for her. What he wanted her to do was to go on with life and not miss the chance to marry and have a family. Millie loved and hated the letter. She felt the kindness, the affection, and yet it seemed a proclamation of divorce. Why didn't he fight for her, plead with her to meet him in the next world?

She and President Thomas had a long talk, however, and

he assured her that Gene was right: she shouldn't give up her chance to marry, if the chance came. Millie leaned back in her chair and said, "President Thomas, maybe so. After a while maybe I can accept that, but I don't have the heart to think about it right now. I just want to get through each day and not give in to self-pity; a lot of people are going through as much or more than I am."

President Thomas was touched by her attitude, her nobility, and when she left his office, he thought how much he regretted the loss of the grandchildren she and Gene might have given him. At the same time, he knew he couldn't wallow in self-pity himself. She was right about all the pain that was being borne by so many.

President Thomas also had worries about the added challenges that might lie ahead. The liberation of the Philippines seemed to be looming in the near future, perhaps before the end of the year, but now the terrible word had come that several Japanese ships had been sunk in the Pacific—ships that had been carrying American prisoners of war from the Philippines. Wally might still be on Luzon, or he might be in Japan by now. If he was, who knew how long he would be there and what might happen to him when Allied forces finally got there? But a worse possibility now existed: Wally might be at the bottom of the sea.

Alex was also saying he would be returning to action before too much longer. And then he would be in mortal danger all over again. What would that mean to poor Anna, the daughter-in-law he had never met?

President Thomas told himself every morning that he had to keep going, the same as his great-grandfather had done, but that had sounded so much better, easier, when he had described it in his sermon.

Millie had felt strong on the day she and President Thomas had talked, and she had left his office feeling good about herself. But every time she thought she was on top of things, all the sadness would return again. One morning she was feeling quite good, so she turned on the radio. But what she heard was Jo Stafford singing "I'll Be Seeing You." She could have turned it off, but she listened, and she let herself sink into the deepest sorrow she had felt since the first day. She was fighting to hold back her tears when she arrived at work. Sister Thomas seemed to see that. She walked to Millie and said, "Have you tried swearing?"

"What?"

"I've noticed that some of these women who work for us are learning how to swear. When something goes wrong with the machines, they curse like a man. It seems to make them feel better, too. Do you want to try it?"

Millie smiled, but she didn't say anything.

"Go ahead. You go first," Sister Thomas said.

"I don't know any bad words," Millie told her, and she smiled. "You'll have to teach them to me."

"How would I know?"

"Maybe you could ask President Thomas."

The two grinned at each other. "Certainly *he* wouldn't know," Sister Thomas said.

"Just between you and me," Millie said, "I've *thought* some bad words lately."

Sister Thomas laughed. "Me too," she said. "And sometimes I think about breaking things. Maybe we could try that."

"I thought about breaking my radio the other day when Lowell Thomas started talking about all the great young men who are willing to give their lives for freedom. It was all just a pitch to sell bonds." Millie could have told about the song she had listened to that morning, but she rather preferred the resentment she was finally expressing.

"I know. I'm sick of these men who are too old to fight— and spend all their time waving the flag in our faces." She smiled, slyly. "To *heck* with them," she said.

"*Darn* them all," Millie said.

"Could I tell you my little secret?" Sister Thomas asked.

"Sure."

"Sometimes, when Al brings up our great family heritage, I want to scream. I'm having a hard enough time without piling a whole wagonload of perfect great-grandparents on my shoulders. Just between you and me, I'll bet those Thomases and Snows complained and cried at times, probably even kicked their dogs. They couldn't have been so stoic and spiritual *all* the time."

"*Darn* the pioneers, too," Millie said, and she laughed, her dimples showing for the first time in such a long time.

"Well, we're on the slippery road to eternal damnation now," Sister Thomas said. "I hate to think what we might be saying by tomorrow."

"Maybe 'goll darn it anyway.'"

"No, we wouldn't go that far."

Millie finally laughed, and then Sister Thomas gave her a hug. For no good reason, Millie actually did feel a little better, too.

* * *

Toward the end of Wally's voyage, his suffering from heat turned to suffering from cold, but after sixty-two days the vessel that the men had come to call the "hell ship" docked at Port Moji on the northern end of the island of Kyushu, Japan. The decimated prisoners hobbled off the ship, many with swollen legs and feet, all of them nothing more than skin and bones. They were filthy and smelly and covered with sores; their hair and beards were tangled, full of sweat and dirt; and they were infested with lice and fleas and bedbugs. As they walked down the gangplank, the Japanese sprayed them with disinfectant.

Wally told himself that the worst must be over, that he had now passed so many hard tests that surely nothing more would be asked of him. Maybe the food would be better. The rumor was that the men would be mining coal, which didn't sound very appealing to Wally, but surely if the prisoners were working hard, the Japanese would have to feed them well. Wally could handle that—hard work and good food.

Something in him kept saying, "No matter what's coming, I'll deal with it. I haven't come this far only to be defeated." And the conviction ran far deeper than the words themselves. This was who he was now. He might die here—he knew that—but not because he had given up.

* * *

Alex's ten days with Anna were like a gift from heaven, too lovely to be real, and, unfortunately, made more valuable because he and Anna knew every second that all this would end very soon. In Windermere, they sat by the lake and looked at the dark blue water while they talked about anything but the war, or they stayed in on rainy afternoons, discovering and loving each other.

It was all like a fantasy, a little too good to be trusted, and Alex had to tell himself every minute not to think about the future. But the war was always there, waiting for him, and a clock was running in his head. His honeymoon soon had to end. Still, not once did he regret the decision to get married. These days with Anna had been the loveliest of his life. Whatever else life gave him from this point on, he had experienced this joy here by this beautiful lake, and it was something to be thankful for forever.

* * *

Bobbi and Afton were at Ishi's house on a Sunday afternoon. The kids were taking a nap before it was time to return to the church for sacrament meeting. On the radio, soft Hawaiian music was playing, and the three women, in the living room, were leaning back, Bobbi and Afton on the couch and Ishi across from them in a big upholstered chair.

"I always ruin my Sundays," Afton said. "I love getting away from the hospital so much that the entire time I keep saying to myself, 'This day is going too fast.'"

"I know what you mean," Bobbi said. "I'm tired of the hospital too. Once the war is over, I plan to take a hot bath that lasts about a month and then sleep for six months."

"There's one big flaw in your plan," Afton said. She stretched her legs out in front of her and slumped down lower on the couch. She was wearing no shoes, and her feet were bare. She had long since run out of hose, and there were none to be had on the island, either in nylon or rayon. Fortunately, Hawaiians didn't worry so much about those things, but it still seemed awfully strange to her to go to church with bare legs.

"What's the flaw?" Bobbi asked.

"The war will never end. It's going to go on forever. We're going to be sitting here every Sunday afternoon for the rest of our lives, talking about the great day when the war is over."

"It seems that way, doesn't it?" Ishi said.

And of course, as Bobbi knew, the thought had painful implications for Ishi. Her husband was fighting in Italy now. His unit had been attached to the 442nd Regiment, which was all Japanese American except for most of the officers. Daniel had entered the battle late in March, although Ishi hadn't known it for some time. His battalion had fought at the Anzio beachhead, and every day after, American newspapers had reported the unit's remarkable progress as the men marched steadily northward, winning battles. But recently all Allied forces had bogged down at the "Arno Line," a column of fortifications that was being treated by the Germans as a last bastion. Italy had already surrendered, but Germany was not about to let the Allies stream into southern Germany. The line was holding, and men were dying, and many of the casualties were with the "four-four-two." Letters seemed to take forever, and any word Ishi received from Daniel was always very old. What she feared every day, like everyone else with a loved one in battle, was that a telegram would come.

"I'm jealous of you two," Afton said.

"Jealous? Why?" Ishi asked.

"I know it's awful for you to worry about your men. But at least you have someone coming home when it's over. I'd rather take my chances, and worry about that, than to have absolutely nothing to look forward to."

"You'll have your choice of men, Afton," Bobbi said. "When all the Johnnys come marching home, you can grab yourself the best-looking one in the parade."

"Oh, sure. And ten other girls will grab him at the same time. We'll rip the poor guy to pieces. You think the war is ugly, just wait until all the girls start fighting over what's left of the boys."

Bobbi and Ishi looked at each other and laughed, but not for long. There was a little too much truth to what Afton was saying. The war was certainly going to bring a shortage of men and lots of girls wishing they could find a husband.

"Afton," Bobbi said, "Actually, I think you're right. I'm glad I do have Richard to wait for. It's the worst thing in my life, but it's also, by far, the best. It keeps me going right now."

"Well, thanks. I'm glad we can agree that I'm the one everybody should feel sorry for." She smiled her wide smile and then laughed, in a burst.

"No. Let's all feel sorry for each other—and wallow in our grief," Bobbi said.

Ishi nodded and laughed. "We can stand in a circle and all cry on each other's shoulders."

But Afton said, "Bobbi, I'm proud of you. You're handling things. I don't think I'd do as well if I had to deal with everything you've been through lately—losing Gene and waiting for Richard."

"We'd better form that circle," Bobbi said. She didn't want to talk about this.

"No, I'm serious."

"Afton, the only reason I feel bad about Gene is that I'm selfish. I wanted to keep him."

"I know. But who wouldn't? My brothers are still in safe

places, but I don't know how much longer I'll be able to say that. I couldn't deal with it if anything happened to them."

"That's what I used to say. But what else can I do but deal with it?"

There was no answering that, and everyone fell silent.

"I've got an idea," Bobbi finally said. "I don't think our circle is big enough. Let's recruit every girl in the world who is sad right now, and let's all form one big circle and bawl for each other."

"If we're going to do that we might as well get the moms and dads and brothers and sisters," Afton said.

And Ishi added, "We might as well invite all the soldiers, too."

"That's right," Bobbi said. "And once we all get together, there won't be anyone left to fight the war."

"Good idea," Ishi said. And everyone smiled. But it actually seemed to Bobbi a perfectly good plan.

* * *

When Sister Thomas walked up to tuck the girls in, she found them both on their knees, next to their beds, saying their prayers. Sister Thomas waited until LaRue finished, and then she and LaRue remained silent until Beverly got up. LaRue would soon be sixteen, and she was beautiful and confident. It was Beverly who worried Sister Thomas. She was going to be thirteen in a few days, but she still seemed so very young. She was pretty, in her own way, but not so that people noticed her much, especially with LaRue around. Beverly also seemed to be struggling more than anyone since Gene's death. Yet she said the least about it.

Sister Thomas kissed LaRue and gave her a little hug, and she pulled the light summer blanket up around her shoulders. She turned then and sat on Beverly's bed, and she bent and kissed her, too. "Are you all right, Bev?" she asked.

"I don't know."

"What's bothering you, honey? You don't say much these days."

"I miss everyone," she said. "I wish Bobbi hadn't gone back to Hawaii."

"I know. We all wish that. Just remember how important her work is, though."

"For the war. Right?"

"Yes."

"That's what we say about everything."

"Are you getting tired of it?"

Beverly was saying more than usual, and Sister Thomas thought it had to be good for her to get some of her feelings out in the open. But Beverly didn't answer the question. She said, "Mom, I pray for Wally every night, but I can't remember him anymore."

"Oh, honey. I know. It's hard for all of us." She bent and hugged her.

"Maybe he won't come back. Like Gene. And I won't ever remember him."

Sister Thomas wanted to promise her that Wally would come home, that Alex would make it, and that they would all meet Anna. She also wanted to promise that the war would end before long and that everything would be all right again. But she couldn't say any of those things, and she didn't know what to say.

Beverly was gulping, obviously trying not to cry, but she said, "I prayed every night for Gene and he still got killed."

"I know. I know," Mom said. "But don't stop praying. The war will end. And everything will be all right one day."

LaRue said, "We'll see Gene again, in heaven."

"I don't want to wait that long." Beverly let go and began to cry.

Sister Thomas was thinking the same thing, and now she couldn't hold back her own tears.

A deep voice said, "But we'll do it, won't we?" This, of

course, was President Thomas, who had come to the door. Sister Thomas sat up and looked at him.

"Oh, Al," she said, "we're just crying for a minute. We can't be strong *all* the time."

President Thomas nodded. "I know," he said, and tears filled his own eyes. He walked to the bed, got down on his knees, leaned over, and kissed Beverly on the cheek. "But, Bev, listen to me," he said. "We're all closer together now—no matter how spread out our family is. And that's a good thing. Do you understand that?"

Beverly didn't answer for quite some time. She was still crying. But when she caught her breath a little, she said, "It doesn't feel that way to me."

"I know. But you'll see. When we're together again, it will be better than ever. And Gene will be with us. You'll feel that too. Can you trust me on that?"

"Do you trust him, Mom?" Beverly asked, and now she was getting control, even trying to smile.

Sister Thomas laughed. "I do, Bev," she said. "He tests my limits sometimes, but he seems to know what he's talking about—most of the time."

LaRue said, "He told me if I waited to date until I was sixteen, I'd be proud of myself. And I'm not."

"You aren't sixteen yet," Dad said, and he laughed.

"You told me I'd like that Spam stuff," Beverly said, "and I hate it."

Everyone laughed. "Well, I may not be a great expert on Spam," he said. "But I know our family, and we're going to be all right. That's an absolute promise."

Beverly nodded. "Okay," she said, "I'll believe you."

For the past few years I have steeped myself in the history of the World War II years. I didn't think of the research as a quest to find my roots, but that, in part, is what it turned out to be. I was born during the war, and acquiring a feel for that time has helped me understand my parents and the atmosphere that existed when I was a child. I feel that I've caught a glimpse of the time and place I came from. I'm not alone, either. A great deal changed in the forties, and we all inherited an altered world. World War II was a testing time, and there's something for us to learn by looking at a family (even if it's a fictional one) that found the faith to pass the test.

Since I published the first volume of the series *Rumors of War*, people have asked me about my sources of information. The characters and the story, of course, come mostly from my imagination. What is historical in these books is the setting: the war itself, the effects on home front life, the changes in society, the influence on the LDS Church, and so on. When I provide that kind of information, I try to be strictly accurate. I do not "fictionalize" the history itself. For example, during the D day invasion, the particular experiences of Alex Thomas are my creation: his reactions, thoughts, words. All the background, however, is factual. The paratroopers really were scattered over the Cotentin Peninsula, and very few actually landed in their assigned drop zones. Because I didn't fight in Normandy myself, I am careful not to push my imagination too far. When I describe a battle, for instance, I base it on actual battles that I have studied in history books or in personal memoirs.

For those who would like to learn more about the war and the time, let me suggest some of the books that have been most helpful to me. An expansive general history is probably the best way to begin. William L. Shirer's classic work, *The Rise and Fall of the Third Reich* (Simon and Schuster, 1960), is very important, but there are more recent histories that benefit from newly available sources and that study all the war fronts. Perhaps the best of these is *A World at Arms: A Global History of World War II* (Cambridge University Press, 1994), by Gerhard L. Weinberg. A good almanac of the war is also useful for a chronology of events and a broad scope of factual information. I used *The World Almanac of World War II* (revised), edited by Brigadier Peter Young (Bison Books, 1986). There are also several illustrated histories of the war, which add another dimension to one's feel for the time. The one I found helpful was *The World at Arms: The Reader's Digest Illustrated History of World War II* (Reader's Digest, 1989).

There are many books about D day, but by far the best is Stephen E. Ambrose's *D-Day, June 6, 1944: The Climactic Battle of World War II* (Simon and Schuster, 1994). In describing Alex's experiences, I followed the history of Company E, 506th Parachute Infantry Regiment, 101st Airborne Division. The best source for that history is in another Stephen Ambrose book: *Band of Brothers* (Simon and Schuster, 1992). On D day a small group of men from E Company did actually defeat an entire platoon of German soldiers and destroy four 105mm guns, much the way it happens in this book. I learned added details about basic training for airborne troops from *The Making of a Paratrooper* (University Press of Kansas, 1990), a memoir written by Kurt Gabel.

For United States military history, an excellent book is *There's a War to Be Won: The United States Army in World War II* (Ballantine Books, 1991), by Geoffrey Perret. To understand battle methods, I used *Closing with the Enemy* (University Press of Kansas, 1994), by Michael Doubler. To learn about the operation and techniques of the German military, the most thorough book is Matthew Cooper's *The German Army, 1933–1945* (Stein and Day, 1978). I'm also obligated to my friend Richard Jeppesen, a retired marine officer, who read my manuscript and advised me on the accuracy of my military facts.

There are many books that deal with Nazis and the holocaust. The ones I found most useful were *The War against the Jews, 1933–1945* (Holt, 1975), by Lucy S. Dawidowicz; *Hitler's Willing Executioners: Ordinary Germans and the Holocaust* (Knopf, 1996), by Daniel Jonah Goldhagen; and *Gestapo: Instrument of Tyranny* (Da Capo Press, 1994), by Edward Crankshaw.

Saburo Ienega's *The Pacific War, 1931–1945* (Random House, 1978) explains the point of view of the Japanese and their leaders. *War without Mercy: Race and Power in the Pacific War* (Random House, 1986), by John W. Dower, is a disturbing but balanced look at racist attitudes on both sides of the conflict.

For the history of the Bataan Death March and the American prisoners of war in the Philippines, I have relied heavily on an unpublished memoir by Dr. Gene S. Jacobsen, "Who Refused to Die." I have also read other accounts by other survivors, and I have read *Prisoners of the Japanese: POWs of World War II in the Pacific* (Morrow, 1994), by Gavan Daws, and *Prisoners of the Rising Sun* (University of Kansas Press, 1993), by William A. Berry. These books added insight, but Gene Jacobsen's account is the basis for most of Wally Thomas's experiences.

One of the best ways to understand a time is to read oral histories. Individual experiences can often explain much more than statistics and general descriptions. Edwin P. Hoyt's *The GI War: American Soldiers in Europe in World War II* (McGraw-Hill, 1988) is an excellent collection of personal accounts, as is Russell Miller's *Nothing Less than Victory: The Oral History of D day* (Morrow, 1993). For the Pacific war, a first-rate collection is *Semper Fi, Mac: Living Memories of the United States Marines in World War II* (Arbor House, 1982), by Henry Berry. The famous war correspondent Ernie Pyle also collected many moving accounts from the battlefront. His book *Brave Men* (Holt, 1944) is a classic work. For balance, another important work, but one that shows the great variety of attitudes toward the war, including home front experiences, is Studs Terkel's *"The Good War": An Oral History of World War II* (Random House, 1984).

For information about the home front, a book that breaks the stereotypes and is replete with information is *Let the Good Times Roll: Life at Home in America During World War II* (Paragon, 1989), by Paul D Casdorph. There are also a number of pictorial histories of home front life. The one I often refer to is *V for Victory: America's Home Front During World War II* (Pictorial Histories Publishing Co., 1991), by Stan Cohen. An excellent account of life in London during the war is *London at War, 1939–1945* (Knopf, 1995), by Philip Ziegler.

Along with historical information, I seek books that give me a sense of the time. Paul Fussell's *Wartime* (Oxford University Press, 1989), for instance, helped me comprehend the psychology of the individual soldier. Wallace Stegner's *Mormon Country* (University of Nebraska Press, 1942) provides some wonderful glimpses of Mormon life in Utah during the thirties and forties as seen by a brilliant and observant non-LDS transplant. R. Lanier Britsch's *Unto the Islands of the Sea* (Deseret, 1986) helped me understand life among Mormons in Hawaii. Interviews also helped me prepare to write about wartime Hawaii, including one with Lowell H. Christensen, who lived there at the time.

There are many other sources: family histories and stories;

biographies of important generals, political figures, and LDS Church leaders; pictorial guides to uniforms, weapons, armaments, and so on; histories of particular battles; visits to historical sites; and conversations with the many people who remember the time. Yet, after all the research, the ultimate source for understanding another time is the empathy we can call upon as we attempt to place ourselves in another circumstance. However different humans may be in many ways, there is fundamental sameness in our emotions, our needs, our fears. I try to work my way into the time by experiencing what my characters feel. That may seem a circular process—since I made the characters up—but this is the power of empathy: to know someone else's feelings by knowing one's own. That's why we tell stories—to create a life to look at, and then, in response, to reflect upon our own experiences.

I have dedicated this book to Gene Jacobsen. I owe him a great deal for providing me with so much information. But more than that, we all owe him for his sacrifice. He was a prisoner for almost the entire war, and he suffered terribly. He has lived a rich and good life, but his health was compromised forever by the depredations he experienced. And yet, he harbors no bitterness, doesn't look back. He has been a professor, a scholar, a fine citizen, and a positive force for good. He is one of those who helped ensure the freedom and then came home to work at healing the wounds and creating a better world. As I have looked to my own roots, I have come to appreciate a generation that gave up so much to provide what I now enjoy. I hope that in reading these books, others—especially young people—will be moved to feel that same appreciation.